The School
on
Heart's
Content Road

Also by Carolyn Chute

The Beans of Egypt, Maine

Letourneau's Used Auto Parts

Merry Men

Snow Man

The School
on
Heart's
Content Road

Carolyn Chute

Atlantic Monthly Press
New York

Published simultaneously in Canada
Printed in the United States of America

FIRST EDITION

ISBN-10: 0-87113-987-1
ISBN-13: 978-0-87113-987-0

Atlantic Monthly Press
an imprint of Grove/Atlantic, Inc.
841 Broadway
New York, NY 10003

Distributed by Publishers Group West

www.groveatlantic.com

08   09   10   11   12   13   10   9   8   7   6   5   4   3   2   1

Welcome!
to
the
School on Heart's
Content Road

*. . . as told by Mickey Gammon and
Secret Agent Jane and a little of everybody.*

For
Rose and Jane,
Secret Agents

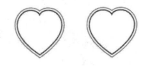

And
in heartbroken-never-forgettem
honor
of Cork Smith
and
Margaret Cannonball Chute
who were lost to us
in 2004

Author's Note

There is a character list for helping with identifying important and semi-important characters. Don't twist your head trying to keep every character straight. Continually referring to the list is not necessary. As you read along, characters who are meant to matter a lot will become obvious. On the other hand, I, myself, love character lists because I like to refresh myself on how characters look. Maybe you do too.

For the character list,
flip to the end of this book.

The
Story
Begins

List of Icons

 Jane Meserve speaks

 Home (the St. Onge Settlement)

 Neighbors

 Out in the world

 The voice of Mammon

 The screen shouts, scolds, grins, cajoles

 The Agency

 The future

 History as it Happens

 History (The Past)

God speaketh

Pluto

 Crow

History
(1900s: The Past)

Once, a great American novelist, Maya Angelou, wrote these words:

> "All we really have to do is die.
> What matters at the end of the day is
> were you sweet, were you kind,
> did the work get done."

Circa
YEAR
2000

Year

2000.

Big things

happened in America.

But you never

heard about some of

them. They were erased.

June

 The screen shouts.

Beeeee afraid! Low types of people are everywhere; in cities, in towns, in your backyard! In other countries. Drugged, crazed, mindless evil is at large!

 Out in the world, Mickey Gammon remembers his last day of school a few weeks ago. Mickey speaks.

Last March, my mother wanted to come back to Maine. My brother Donnie came and got us and he had gotten fat, but I recognized him. (Ha-Ha!) Okay, just a little fat. A gut.

We rode back in the night. To Maine.

The school here in Maine is a joke. Like the other school was a joke. In Mass. You were supposed to keep your locker locked to keep people out, but there was a rule *they* could search your locker on demand. There's two types of teachers wherever you go. The kind with slitted eyes that try to get you to fight. And the ones, mostly women, who talk to you like if they say the right thing, they can change your life, that there is something wrong with your life. I say fuckem, there's nothing wrong with my life. That was the same thing back in Mass. It's like they either want to kick your ass or sniff it.

My brother's wife is sweet*. She has everything: looks, brains, composure. And I especially like her T-shirt with the Persian cat printed on it . . . something about the idea of that cat's face goes with *her* face . . . the big eyes. Meanwhile, she has arms like Wonder Woman, like she could wrastle you down if it got to that. But she's not one of them man-women you see around. Erika is soft like a pillow. My brother Donnie ever lays a finger on her, I'll break his face.

Meanwhile, I was just taking the bus to school, to finish out the year at this school here. I don't mess with their books—you know, frig with them, write shit in them, or vandalize things. That's stupid. But I figured before the last day in June I was going to draw a picture of Mr. Carney sucking a pony's cock on a separate piece of paper. And, you know, *tape* it into the book.

Okay, so my life isn't perfect. You wanna hear this? I got a little nephew . . . Erika and Donnie's kid, name's Jesse. He's got a weird cancer. At first it was slow, but now it's fast. Imagine! A little kid like that. He don't even talk anymore.

So while I was in class one morning drawing some doodles on my paper, listening to them all whine about South American exports and the Incas or some such shit, the door opens and—yes, it's the cops. They have a marijuana-sniffing dog and the teacher who is in on this like some fucking spy says that the dog is here to sniff our lockers, all the student cars, and, yes, us. She says the officer is just going to walk with the dog down between the rows, and unless the dog indicates illegal substances on us, none of us will be searched. "It's just a routine thing," she says. "We're sure that no one here has any illegal substances on them."

Welllll, I was sweating in a cold way all over. I hadn't had any weed on me for weeks, but I had this horror, suddenly, that that sucker was going to take an interest in me because of my *thoughts*.

So the Nazi-Pig comes along and his dog is going along . . . you know, like an ordinary dog . . . and he's cleared two rows without finding what he likes, and as he is coming nearer to me I'm feeling freaked, and this kid Jared behind me, he says, "That dog sniffs my crotch, I'll kick his face in." He said this wicked soft, but Mrs. Linnett, with fucking amplified-radar-electronic ears that could probably hear your faucet dripping in another state, says, "What's that, Jared?"

*Remember! There is a character list at the end of this book.

And so the dog has gone past me and Mrs. Linnett tells Jared to "Go to Mr. Carney's office." And she apologizes to the Nazi and makes a real scene over Jared.

At lunch, we heard that three kids were caught, one with a toothpick-sized joint and two with a smell that meant they'd had the stuff on them recently. Everyone, the teachers and all the obedient Honor pansies and killer sheep were pale in the face, wondering how *our school* has got this terrible *drug problem*. Some were saying they just *know* there must be LSD too, and coke and heroin, crack and crank, OxyContin, and whatever, but dogs can't sniff that yet. The whole cafeteria was in a kind of high squeally furor . . . *loud* . . . like panicked mice. I wasn't hungry. I stabbed my fork into my apple. I said, "Fuck this Alcatraz!!" and I stood up without my tray and walked outta there. And in the hall, Mr. Runnells, one of them that guards the cafeteria doors, says, "And where do you think you're going, Gammon?" And he reaches out like he's going to put his hand on my arm. And for some reason beyond reason, I started to cry—the trembling mouth, the shaky voice, tears in the eyes. It's like they got an electric paddle touching every part of you, making you do things against your will. The place has an ugly power over people.

I stepped away from him and said "Bye now" in a kind of nice way and went past Mr. Carney's office and out the glass doors and out into the sun, and then I started running like hell.

 Screen brays.

These flavorful burgers, these potato-flavored salt strips, these fizzy syrupy brown-flavored drinks in tall cups are waiting just for YOU. Go to it! NOW!

⟨𝒪⟩ Out in the world.

Thousands of little red, gray, white, or blue cars and billowy plastic-bumpered sport trucks and SUVs snap on their directionals and whip into the asphalt passages of the drive-in order windows of any one of thousands of the identical burger stations.

Now, in summer, we see Mickey Gammon at home.

The walls of this old house have a weary cream and green wallpaper. Horses and carriages, men and women. Tall arched elms.

The shades here are drawn, shades yellowed with age. The light of this room is therefore dark but golden.

There's a car chase scene on the TV. Vigorous and bouncy. But Mickey Gammon's mother, Britta,* keeps the sound down because of the child, Jesse.

Jesse, almost age two, is shrinking. A thick-legged, noisy, gray-eyed boy whose favorite word was not *no* but *why*? Now shrinking. Stretched out on the couch. His skeletal legs seem awfully long.

Toys all around. Blue plastic car. Yellow plastic car. And a plastic-haired doll. Plastic: convenient, affordable, but terrible to the touch.

Mickey has just come in. Fifteen and free as a bird. He smells like somewhere different from here. Other homes. Other considerations. He kneels against the couch. His gray, always watchful, almost wolf-like eyes press like a hand over Jesse's baseball print pajamas and the nearest small hand. Mickey speaks something low that his mother, Britta, over in her chair, cannot hear, but Jesse does. Jesse stares steadily through the magnificent pageant of his pain into the soft spoken word.

In this household, there is no money today. No money. No money. No money.

Out there in the world are whole bins of pain pills unreachable as clouds. The key to painlessness is money. Money is everything.

Mickey finds honor.

He is walking the long back road some call the Boundary. He is a light and fast walker, staying to the road's high crown. Light and fast, yes, but also cautious and manly, a gait that is articulated at the knees. Such a fine-boned creature, this Mickey Gammon. Narrow shoulders. Little tufty streaky-blond ponytail. Dirty jeans, and hipless. Fairly androgynous at first glance. At *first* glance.

*Reminder: There is a character list is at the end of the book.

He can hear shots up ahead in the Dunham gravel pit. And then, beyond that, a deeper and darker aggression, a thunderstorm rumbling in from the southwest. When he gets closer to the opening of the pit, the silvery "popple" leaves are already starting to flutter, and upon his hot face the restless air is like a big God hand of airy benediction.

He sees four pickups, a newish little car, a pocked Blazer, and at least eight men, none he recognizes, yet he is under the good and nearly true belief that his brother Donnie knows everyone in Egypt who is near his, Donnie's, own age and, yes, almost anyone might also be a distant relative.

Mickey walks his arrow-straight and light-step walk to where the group is standing with their firearms and thermos cups of coffee, and he sees one man squatted down with a .45 service pistol aimed at a black-and-white police target, a target with the silhouette of a man, only about fifty yards away on a wooden frame. Mickey slows his pace just before reaching this group. Guns? Mickey has no problem with guns. It is having to *talk* that brings him terror.

The man is rock steady in his aim, taking a lot of time. Silence before the pounding crack of a gun is always a momentous thing.

The other men turn and see Mickey. Some nod. Some don't. None speak. One man is sitting on a tailgate, wearing earmuff-style ear protectors, his fingers nudging the double action of a revolver with soft sensuous clicks. The men who have acknowledged Mickey have turned away now to watch the framed target. One guy watches through a spotting scope on a tripod on his truck hood. The breeze rises up and gives everyone's sleeves and hair a flutter. The sand moves a bit. And then there's another rumble coming closer fast from the southwest.

Mickey moves lightly, stepping inside the edgy-feeling perimeter of the group, and sees, there across the tailgate of one truck, a Ruger 10/22, a Springfield M1-A, and several SKSes: three Russian with the star and red-yellow finish, a couple with fold-up vinyl stocks, black, light to carry, easy to hide. And a whole selection of full auto military-issue Colts. Two AR-15s. A Bushmaster. And two AK47s. Some of these are, yuh, the real thing. The thing made for war.

At last the shooter squeezes the trigger, and the deafening crack almost feels good to Mickey's ears.

The guy with his eye to the spotting scope looks grim. "Seven!" he calls.

The shooter, dressed in dark-blue work clothes, no cap, bald but for horsey gray hair on the sides and thorns of gray hair on his tanned and lined neck, dips the .45, then raises it quickly, squeezes off four rapid shots in a row. Echoes among the hills multiply the four shots to a lively staccato. And then the supreme BOOOOMMM!; this the thunder of the storm marching closer.

Mickey spins his studded leather wristband, which is what he always does when he doesn't know what else to do, watching the guy with the spotting scope, who now calls out, "Ten X! Ten! Two sevens!" And the shooter slips the .45 into its holster, which is against his ribs outside his shirt but is the kind you wear under a shirt if you plan to conceal it.

Mickey says croakily, "Anyone got a smoke I could borrow?"

There is a guy standing very close to Mickey who is of medium height, small-waisted, fit, wears a red T-shirt, jeans. Very square-shouldered. Black military boots and a soft olive-drab army cap, a very fancy black-faced watch, looks more like a compass. Maybe it *is* a compass. And sunglasses. Metal frames. Cop glasses. Like the Nazis wear to school when they bring in their drug dogs. But this guy has a mustache, the kind that crawls down along the jaws, a Mexican mustache. Arms are not thickly haired. Nothing hides the impatient pulsing musculature. He says, "What's that you say?"

Mickey can't exactly see this man's eyes because of the sunglasses, but he can tell the guy is looking him up and down.

A hefty white-haired guy with a white sea-captain's beard says, "Right here," in a voice that is high and quavery for such a big guy. He steps toward Mickey with the pack, shakes two into Mickey's hand, and says cheerily, "I'm not starting you on a bad habit, am I?"

Mickey replies without a smile. "I've been smokin' for five years."

"Breakin' the law." This voice is shaly and made for hard reckoning. Mickey doesn't look to see which face owns it. It's *beyond* the sunglasses guy so it is *not* the sunglasses guy.

Another voice, letting go with a small shriek of laughter. But no words. Also *not* the sunglasses guy.

"What? Artie break laws?" This, another voice, as tight as a stricture, and yet it means to be teasy. This voice beyond the first truck.

Many small chortles overlapping and flexing. Earthworms in a can overlap and flex too. Faceless laughter. Mickey keeps his eyes lowered.

Hot breeze blows some more sand around. Then the BOOOMMM! and matching flutter of light in the darkening southwest. Mickey now watches two really young guys, maybe not yet twenty, murmuring to a small, dark-haired, dark-eyed older guy with a mean-looking hunched bearing who is reassembling a black-vinyl-stock SKS. Even his ears have an inflexible, shiny, mean look to them.

A guy with a camouflage-print T-shirt, very thin, bony, urgent-looking guy, clean shave, freckles, almost no eyebrows, reddish hair, and a big smile, asks Mickey, "On foot today, huh?" He selects an SKS from the tailgate, pulling it away quite theatrically with both hands, raises his foot to rest on a plastic ammo case, then places the rifle across his thigh with stiff, animal, almost bewitching-to-see grace. Mickey eyes the flash suppressor on the end of the short carbine barrel, the long, dark, curved, extended magazine, says, "I have a 'sixty-six Mustang in Mass . . . everything but the body is real nice . . . sixty thou' original . . . but needs some stuff . . . tires mostly. Couldn't move it. Not roadworthy."

"Lotta road between here and Mass," declares the hefty sea-captain-beard guy with a cackle. This is the guy called Artie.

Mickey nods. Pokes a cigarette into the corner of his mouth. Snaps a match alive, cupping his hand and hunkering down to give the flame shelter from the wind; takes the first drag hungrily; drops the match into the sand.

"You *walk* from Mass?" another guy softly wonders, great, tall, rugged, clean-shaved guy in full camouflage, heavy-looking BDUs. Long sleeves. Looks hot.

Mickey replies, "No."

The guy with the sunglasses and red T-shirt, thick dark mustache, has turned away, sort of dismissively, but he still hangs back, an ear on what's being said.

The full-camo guy picks up a stapler and fresh target and trudges off toward the open pit area.

The sea-captain beard, hefty, high-voiced Artie, asks Mickey, "Do you shoot?"

Mickey says, "Yuh, some."

The bony, urgent-looking, red-haired guy, not smiling now, advises, "If you keep your aim up, you'll be glad some day."

Mickey says, "I like shootin' all right."

The red T-shirt guy with the sprawling mustache, sunglasses, army cap, and awesome black-faced watch stares after the baldish guy, who is ripping his target from the fifty-yard frame.

Big guy with full camo trudges the long open pit to a frame against the bank at a hundred yards, the wind wrestling earnestly with his target as he staples it to the wood.

The red T-shirt guy now seems to be staring at Mickey, though with the sunglasses one can't be absolutely positively sure.

Mickey smokes his cigarette down. He has pocketed the other. He now leans against a fender, feeling the thunder in the ground, watching the purple-black part of the sky flutter with big jabs of light, splitting open right over Horne Hill, the sweet breeze touching him all over, the tobacco smoke's big satisfying work done inside him, the men trudging around him, and their voices, both grave and playful. Alas now, they speak of the storm and discuss whether to wait it out in their vehicles or leave.

The red T-shirt guy asks Mickey his name. Mickey tells him. He asks Mickey his age. Mickey says sixteen, which he is, almost. He asks him what kind of gun he has. Mickey says a Marlin .22 Magnum.

"Just one?"

Mickey says, "Yep."

The guy asks, "Where do you live?"

"Sanborn Road."

The bony, urgent, eyebrowless guy, overhearing, calls to him, "You live in that new place over there?"

"No, in the big one. I'm Donnie Locke's brother. Been in Mass for a while. I'm livin' here with him now."

The full-camo guy is coming back through the wind and wild sand. Wind getting some real gumption now. Mickey can see through one side of the red T-shirt guy's sunglasses, eyes that never seem to blink.

Now Mickey leans into the open door of the Blazer and casually sorts through shot-up police and circular competition targets. "You guys are good," he says.

"Not really," the red T-shirt guy says, rather quickly. "When your life is at stake, your first four shots are what counts. There's no chances after that. You can't have twenty shots to warm up."

Mickey nods, picks something off the knee of his frazzled filthy jeans: a green bug with crippled wings. He scrunches it. With a murderous CRACK! and the sky dimming blue-black in all directions, light scribbles and splits into veins—and now rain. A few splats.

The red T-shirt guy seems to be looking at Mickey hard.

The tall full-camo guy just stands there looking straight up, eyes fluttering with the beginning rain, his big thick neck looking vulnerable and pale with so much of the rest of him covered. "Is this a break-up for home, Rex? Or should we wait it out in the vehicles?" His voice is soft, but he announces these words deliberately, words of consequence.

The red T-shirt black-mustache guy has pushed his cap forward, as if to hide his eyes, which, because of the sunglasses, never showed in the first place. "These storms aren't usually more than . . . what, twenty minutes?"

And so they wait it out.

Rain comes hard. Smashes down on the truck's cab, where Mickey sits with the red T-shirt guy. The guy has folded up his metal-frame glasses and placed them on the dash. He reminds Mickey of a raccoon, meticulous and wary. His eyes are pale gray-blue in dark lashes, and there's settling and softening around them, which means he's at least forty-five, maybe fifty. Not real friendly eyes. Nor is there rage in those eyes. His eyes simply take in but do not give back. And with the mustache filling in so much of his face, the eyes have significance. But no, his eyes don't show much more of his humanity than his sunglasses did.

He has given Mickey a handful of folded flyers about emergencies and natural disasters and civil defense. There is a bold black-on-white seal on the front of the flyer, showing a mountain lion's form silhouetted inside a crescent of lettering. The guy tells Mickey, "My number is there in case you are ever interested . . . also my address, Vaughan Hill. Come over sometime and bring a friend. You're always welcome." He indicates the truck parked on their left with a dip of his head. It's only a hot grayish-green blur through the rain-streaked windows, but Mickey knows the big quiet full-camo guy is in that truck. "That's John Stratham, my second-in-command. Another officer, not here today, is Del Rogers. He does a lot for us over in Androscoggin County—a unit that's growing, maybe a little too fast. You'll see him if you decide to come to meetings. He's been real important to us in sniffing out some . . . uh, problems we had a few months back. He's dedicated. A real patriot." He places his right hand on the steering wheel, but he doesn't play with the wheel like most would do. He says, "Some people don't give their last names at meetings. That's up to you. This is all in confidence. I *will* need to do a check on anyone who is seeking membership."

Mickey looks down at the flyers in his hands. Mickey is very, very, very quiet. Mickey, whose pale eyes are just as unrevealing and steely as this man's eyes are. The crescent of lettering around the mountain lion reads BORDER MOUNTAIN MILITIA.

On the back fold of the flyer: *Richard York, Captain/Vaughan Hill Road/Box 350, RR2/Egypt, Maine 04047.*

The guy explains that most people call him Rex.

The rain really pummels the hood and cab roof now, and the windshield looks like a thousand dark and silver wrinkles.

Mickey says nothing. His streaky blond ponytail is so thin and silky and without substance, it turns up a little to the right. Sweet. And now his unwashed smell is casually seeping through the humidity of the cab. This guy Rex smells like his T-shirt has had a real dousing of fabric softener. Mickey figures this is because there is a woman in Rex's life. He glances at the hand that's now kind of fisted on the left thigh of Rex's jeans. Yes, a wedding band.

Outside, after the storm, the air is as heavy as a rubber tire. But it smells wonderful. Rex invites Mickey to shoot his own service pistol, which he pulls from behind the truck seat. "Never go anywhere without your Bible and your gun," Rex says, at least three times. The tall soft-voiced second-in-command, John Stratham, gives Mickey some good pointers. For the first time, Mickey notices that John has an embroidered patch on the sleeve of his long-sleeved BDU shirt, the mountain lion and crescent of lettering, black on olive green: BORDER MOUNTAIN MILITIA. Striking to look at.

The target, like most of the others, is of a human shape and is placed at fifty yards for this particular gun. Mickey mostly misses the chest and head. In fact, he mostly misses the black targeted shape. From where they all stand, the spots of his hits show plainly and painfully against the white. He feels this is goofus, but these guys seem impressed. The hefty white-haired sea-captain guy, Artie, says "Good goin'!" and thunks

Mickey's shoulder. The hunched guy with the mean ears growls, "Got 'im runnin'." The big quiet John nods. And Rex, with his sunglasses back on, says nothing, but his chin is up and he is feeling his dark, full, sprawling mustache carefully.

 In a small American city in the Midwest.

A station wagon waits to make a left turn in snarling, fumy, carbon-poofing traffic. It exhibits a bumper sticker that reads MY CHILD IS A PLONTOOKI HIGH SCHOOL HONOR STUDENT.

○   **From frozen Pluto, tiny microscopic Plutonian observatory observers observe the brown daytime spotting and pink nighttime hazing of what we have come to think of as life here on Earth. Tiny microscopic Plutonian officials speak.**

wjox blup sssssooop £G jrigip bot wjp st wjpt xt!*

♡♡ **Six-and-a-half-year-old Jane Meserve speaks from a room at the St. Onge Settlement.**

It is bad for my Mum. Someone help her! Someone with power. Help her! Help me! And my dog Cherish. Gone. Nobody tells me what happened.

 Donnie Locke at home.

This old and loyal house! Belongs to Donnie Locke. No mortgage. Donnie Locke, Mickey Gammon's half brother. It is home for Mickey and Britta too. Britta is the mother the two brothers have in common. Different fathers, same mother. Yes, Britta lives here too since she returned from Massachusetts, because Massachusetts *didn't work out*.

    Donnie Locke watches Mickey hard from his chair at the table. There's a TV here in the kitchen. TV in the living room. Other TVs

---

*Followed by staticky sounds of microscopic concern.

in other parts of the house. Not great TVs, but something to make do with. Both the kitchen TV and the one in the living room as seen through the two open doors of the little entry hall show a one-half-minute musical spectacle of the generic modern woman in the shower with water beading up on the skin of her shoulder, the ecstasy of huge teeth and violent water, America's message, BE CLEAN, BUY DE-TERGENT BARS, and BODY SHAMPOOS, HAIR SHAMPOOS, DEODORANT POWDERS, and ANTIPERSPIRANTS that smell like SEA BREEZES. Cleanliness makes for *opportunities*.

Well, yes, Donnie Locke is clean. Fresh and perma-pressed, nothing to offend. Like obedience to God. Shouldn't this guarantee you something? If not opportunities, at least forgiveness?

Donnie Locke isn't looking at the TV. He watches his unwashed, cigarette-stinking, raggedly-dressed half brother Mickey, the fine yellow-streaked hair tied back into an inessential ponytail, the pale cold eyes that never meet Donnie's eyes. It is easy to watch the boy, to stare ruthlessly at him. He doesn't seem to mind.

Upstairs in this large old house, the younger kids make a racket. Donnie's kids by his first marriage to Julie Nickerson, and then Britta's youngest child, Celia, fathered by what didn't work out in Massachu-setts. And then there's some neighbor kids. A regular shrieking, thump-ing, crashing mob.

Donnie Locke smiles a flicker of a smile, wrenched by a thousand emotions.

Mickey has just come in from being out somewhere doing something, probably messing with cars or snowmobiles with some of his loser bud-dies he met at school this spring. Tinkering. Something to climb into and under. Donnie was never much for that stuff. He made good grades in school, working hard at it, the family's pride and joy. And his BA from Andover Business School. Yeah, he worked very hard at it, and he hated every minute. But what else was there? You *have* to get ahead. Or sink. This is what the guidance counselor said, and . . . well, every-body says it. And what else on this planet besides his "success" could make his mother Britta's heart sing?

The boy Mickey picks open the refrigerator door and gets out the plastic pitcher of red punch and pours a glassful and drinks it. Neither brother has a single remark. No *Hi*. No *Hey*. No *Hot 'nuff for ya?* Donnie is afraid to speak because he knows it will come out resentful. He wants a happy home, like when he was very young. His quiet mother and aunts. His earnest father and Gramp. Hopes and dreams measured by seasons. That's all he wants now. Happy home. Simple life. Hopes and dreams. Yes, that would make *his* heart sing.

This man, Donnie Locke. Mid-thirties. Somewhat bald. But a great big blond, walrus mustache. Short sleeve beige-pinstripes-on-white shirt. Trim trousers. The generic man. The job requires this, his job at the Chain.

Donnie Locke's father, not Mickey's father, "drove truck," made okay money. Was one of the many Lockes and Mayberrys who have owned this house, its various farm buildings, and its land—field, woods, and stream—for a half-dozen hard-headed hard-hearted generations, all those Lockes and Mayberrys gone now, and their crumbling tools and outmoded thinking and outmoded dignity and laughable hopes and dreams, gone now to the Land of Death. More Lockes and Mayberrys there in the Land of Death than here in the Land of Life.

Here in this life in the brand-new century is Donnie Locke, with the pink unused-looking hands and chain-store name tag and after-work pink TV light in his eyes. Still living in the old Locke-Mayberry place, the thing that makes him Donald Locke. Because nothing else in this world makes him be Donald Locke. Yeah, "one of the Lockes." Yes, here he is.

♡ ♡ Nearby, at the St. Onge Settlement, six-and-a-half-year-old Jane Meserve speaks to us.

I am hijack. And kidnapped maybe. I don't even know how to get here. It might be Alaska even. Nothing to eat because they don't let me have food. So I am dying. I miss Mumma and she is very afraid. Mumma my sweet sugar. Help! Help! Hel . . . p!

 ## Erika Locke, awake in the night.

Donnie Locke's wife, Erika, mother of the dying baby Jesse, lies on her side under the thin summer sheet, afraid. Anguished for her baby's pain. Anguished with knowing that a year from now he will no longer exist. But afraid also of *everything* now.

She remembers being told something, *before* Jesse was sick, but it impressed her big-time. Terry, her old friend. Terry, like Erika, young, but *old friend* all the same. Terry with blonde wild-woman hair. Sort of curly, but more like foam and sparks. Terry, who screams. That's her regular voice; just telling you the weather, she screams. On the phone *the voice* cut into Erika's ear, so Erika remembers it was Terry for sure who said this (screamed this): "Hospitals today can grab your house if you can't pay a big bill! And the state eventually grabs your house if you use MaineCare and the hospital forces you to apply for MaineCare if you are eligible. Otherwise the hospital does the grabbing."

Erika told Donnie.

He said that was dumb. "Hospitals can't even charge interest and late fees."

But then another friend, Kelly (Kelly Smelly, Donnie calls her because it rhymes), said, "It was the collection guys at the hospital. They called Matt"—her brother—"and said to pay *bigger* payments on his hernia operation or they'd put a lien on his property—and you ought to see his so-called property, it's just his dinky shit trailer on a wedge of swamp—and they said they would assess his furniture too, and his pickup, because he only needed one vehicle, his beat-ta-shit car. His furniture!!! Television and a beanbag chair! They had him all taken apart for value. Kev"—her husband—"says fuckem, tell 'em to come take the hernia back 'n' stuff it up their asses."

When Erika brought *this* bone home, Donnie said there had to be something lost in the telling here. But then Donnie's cousin Steve was over one Sunday afternoon and told how the DHS had threatened to take his neighbor's kids away if they couldn't afford health insurance. They said, "No health insurance is child abuse . . . puts the kid in danger. You must apply for MaineCare." Donnie said nothing to this. Ever since Jesse has been dying, Donnie is a quiet man who questions nothing.

The screen shrieks.

See the situation comedies that portray Americans who are just like you! They are cheery, bubbly folk with cute, easily-solved problems. And see here! The court trials, not actors, no way! This is reeeeeal court. See the troubles of the victims, their grief and need for revenge, and see those on trial, all these Americans whose troubles are mighty and *ghastly* and *gory* and outrageous and *far* WORSE than *your* troubles. See! Watch close!! Isn't it astonishing!!! Real people on trial. Bad, ghastly, unapologetic people ON TRIAL. Watch close.

Erika Locke at the Egypt town office.

It has come to this. Erika is going to see about some "assistance." She has put this off for a long time, afraid of social workers, the way once you make out that first paper, cash that first check, rip out that first food stamp, the government *eye* is on you. Everything about you, maybe even a print of your DNA, is theirs, quick as a computer key-tap. They, the mighty foot; you, the ant.

Erika is so afraid, she has seen small frisky stars cross her vision all morning ever since she got up.

She has worn her sea-green top with the lacy collar, which fits better since she started her little diet two weeks ago. And a denim skirt. Flip-flops. And socks. Early this morning her hair shined, but now the humidity has claimed it.

Behind the high counter is Harriet Clarke, the town clerk, reciting to someone on the phone all there is to know about purchasing a permit to move heavy equipment. Beyond is a computer with a deep-blue lighted screen with words that run along the bottom, then off the edge, then return from the other side to repeat. BE PATRIOTIC . . . CELEBRATE JULY 4 . . . BE PATRIOTIC . . . CELEBRATE JULY 4 . . . BE PATRIOTIC . . . over and over and over.

And now, repeating across Erika's eyes, her own personal fear-stars. They drift along like something crushed, multiplying into hundreds.

Erika has heard that "social work" nurses will pressure you to let them inside your home to look around, scope the place out. They will interrogate your children. They look at their bodies for marks—bruises, scratches, burns—which all kids have unless you strap them to a chair for the first ten years of their lives. Erika has had three friends lose their kids temporarily, because of two bruises on one kid, a broken finger on another. The third had a burn. Three families. Two families loud and physical; the kids play as hard and rough as lion cubs. One family, quiet and nervous, nasty-neat types; the kids, too, very

nervous, high-strung. None of these families are into heavy-duty pun-
ishment. But all three are poor.

A man saunters in from the hall, yellow, white, and blue motor vehicle
registration papers in one hand. He wears glasses. A shave has given his
pores a chemically scoured look. Wears a floppy madras fishing hat. A
man of the legs-apart, arms-crossed, short, bullish, freckled, fifty-five-
ish, hard-working, old-Yankee-blood, proud, proud, proud iron-fist-
Republican variety.

The clerk finishes with the phone and asks Erika, "How you doin'
today? What d'ya need?"

"Who is it I need to see about some town assistance?"

The clerk has a hard face with lines around the mouth, but a soft
expression. She disappears a moment, squatting down behind the
counter at some floor-level drawer or cubby, then pops back up, paper
in hand. She uses the flapping paper and her other hand to point, shape
out, and underline her words. "Take this. Go over across the hall to the
meetin' room where it's quiet. Pens on the tables there. Make this out
the best you can. Sign it. Then come back and I'll see what I can do,
long's you have everything you need: your last pay slips, W-2 forms, any
proof of pay for the last twelve months. State card if you have it. That
would save us a lotta trouble at this end."

The man behind Erika has been listening in dead silence, moving
his eyes over Erika's breezy little sea-green top and plain brown hair
with its sweet part, her round face and pink spots of emotion, one spot
to each cheek—an ordinary girl, yes, like tens of thousands of sometimes giggling brown-haired American girls who, one overlapping the
other at this hour, would make a vast plain of soft sturdy silhouettes
that threaten no one.

In a voice cracking with anger, the man bellers, as if in a room of deaf
people, "Harriet! When are you people going to do like Representative
Connell's been sayin' an' start fingerprintin' them so they'll stop rippin'
the taxpayer off?!"

The woman behind the counter flushes. "Go on, David. Don't start
on that. I don't need indigestion today." And she laughs.

And Erika walks out. The hall walls are made of skinny vertical
boards painted white. Her flip-flops make an echoey racket. The tall
windows in the meeting room are all open, screened. Little stage at one

end. Bare. The wood worn a warm yellow brown. She finds the can of pens. She takes her time, hoping the man will be gone.

But he's not. When she returns to the hall, he's there, hanging around by the bulletin board. He looks right at her, but he shows no recognition. Light from the doorway just touches his glasses as he turns away. And his face doesn't really look angry anymore. Said his spiel and feels better now? Or is it that, without a gang, posse, or pack, his might is diminished? Here in the hallway, his bald-faced humanity is all he's got.

Now seated in metal chairs between two heaped desks, Erika and the clerk go over what papers and proof of income will be needed. They talk awhile about how town assistance works. Sometimes, Erika's voice seems uncharacteristically little-girlish. The clerk's hair is white. Her blouse and slacks are white and cream. She tells Erika that even though Donnie's part-time thirty-nine-hours-a-week job is not making ends meet, as long as they own two houses they cannot be eligible for assistance. "And all that land too." The clerk sighs. By the guidelines, the Lockes and Gammons are not destitute, and destitute is what they must be. She suggests that Erika and Donnie go to the bank and mortgage one of their houses for a loan to live on for awhile.

Erika begins to smile in a most strange way. And the stars now as thick as TV snow make a cold pressure upon her eyes.

The woman, Harriet, who is on the other side of Erika's silvery wall of stars, is now suggesting they sell the big house and live in the smaller one, or sell both places and keep two and a half acres for a trailer. On the market, they could get quite a sum for their real estate.

Real estate.

Erika speaks now, her voice squeaking with panic. "There's really only one house. The place my mother-in-law lives in is really just a garage and bathroom. No stove or anything. The floor is cement. It's just one room. She's really with us in our house all day."

Harriet smiles. "Can she work?"

Erika frowns. "She's too shy. I mean she's *really* shy."

"Too shy to work?"

"Too shy, yes," Erika murmurs.

"Can't she watch the kids while *you* work?"

Erika blinks. She lowers her eyes and says with shame, "I want to be with my son."

"But can't *she* get a state check? And MaineCare? With her little one, she sounds eligible . . . and the fifteen-year-old. She would probably be eli—"

Erika interrupts. "It would be nice if Donnie could get a raise or something . . . or if they'd give him health insurance. It's not like he's goofing off! He works!" Her voice gets quite babyish. Lilty and brightly amazed.

Harriet laughs. "Well, nowadays they want us *all* working. Nobody stays home." She laughs again. "This gives burglars jobs, too . . . all those empty houses!" And she laughs again.

Erika giggles girlishly, then looks down at her hands with shame. "I really just want to be home with the kids."

Harriet snaps her pen, eyes sliding up and down the fine print of qualification rules. "Perhaps you can get Britta to move out. Turn her place back into a garage. Tear out the toilet and sink. The acreage doesn't actually matter rule-wise, as long as it's all part of your primary residence."

Erika cocks her head, trying to make sense of this. No stars now. Just the clear hard edges of the clerk's desks and the computer screen and map of Maine on the wall and the slight gurgle of realization. Of *it:* the vast order of things, the world's logic, a global thing, even here in this room, especially here in this room, bouncing and leering and hilarious and formidable and growing bigger by the minute.

Erika says sweetly, "I just want a little help with my baby's medicine, that's all. Just his pain pills. Why can't we get just that one thing without . . . all . . . you know . . . all that?"

"Like I said earlier, if you aren't eligible for MaineCare, the hospitals have a program for that!" Harriet says cheerfully. "At least they help with a percent of certain types of medicine. Even doctors, working with the drug companies—they have a way of getting certain drugs free, I heard. There's some paperwork on that. It all depends on income, though. And there are services through various agencies that could help with various areas of need. There's a regional services coordinator who is in here twice a month who can help you make out the right papers to the various agencies. Just bring all your paperwork here and that other stuff you'll need . . . oh, here . . . it looks here like you might be eligible for fuel assistance and winterization next winter . . . oh, and I think maybe . . ." She is running a finger over the small chart. "Family counseling services. You could get that. The services coordinator can—"

Erika interrupts. "I just want pain medicine. Just that."

The clerk goes on studying the charts on her desk, snapping her pen. Her tongue makes a soft deep-thinking sound against her teeth. She sighs. "There *was* a pretty good state program for prescriptions, but the legislature gutted it last term. The waiting list on that one was impossible anyway." She sighs again. "I can see you aren't eligible for MaineCare. The second house will be a problem with them too. And your husband makes a little too much. It's iffy. You could try. It depends on what your expenses are, although they don't give you much leeway for expenses anymore. Maybe if *he* moved out! Your husband." She says this jokingly.

Erika looks down at her hands. "It goes like this. We get his pay. We buy the medicine first. Usually after the medicine and bills, there's just a little bit for groceries. We get the medicine *first* and pay the lights, and gas for the car, and everything like that . . . groceries last. We lost the phone. There's just so much!" Her voice rises, childlike, not a shriek exactly, but a little thrilled thin edge to it. "It's those doctors! And tests! When Jesse was first sick, I couldn't believe how much they ask for those tests. Just the few times we went . . . it'll take us forever to catch up! Then also Elizabeth, my husband's oldest, she has trouble with her feet and legs: special shoes 'n' stuff. Gas for Donnie to get to work is wicked. My mother-in-law's youngest had some infected mosquito bites. Made her sick. That salve and antibiotic was wicked expensive. And this spring all the kids needed sneakers. Except Mickey. He just goes around like a bum. And then the roof leaked! It was only in one little spot, but even that was four hundred dollars to fix! Everything is just so much! Liability insurance is more this year. And my driver's license had to be renewed last month, for the picture and everything . . . and then you know our property taxes; we've stayed right up with those . . . and then propane; we ran out of that but got some last week . . . and toilet paper and wax paper and a new can opener 'cause the other busted and we can't open cans with anything else, and the—"

The clerk has put up her hand. "I'm sorry! The state guidelines determine most of this, even for the towns. At town meetin', we only vote on the total recommended amount for the year. But the guidelines for eligibility are set. It's not up to me. I hear you, Erika, but it's not up to me. I'm sorry."

She has used Erika's name. The warm sound of her name. This woman's voice, the family resemblance of her mouth and eyes to so many others in town. The sweet humid summer air that has oozed in the open windows, mixed with the imposing woody old smell of the building, these things that are permanent and emollient and too beautiful. For the first time since Jesse's cancer, Erika breaks down in front of someone. So unpretty. Her crying is like snorting.

The clerk shoots up out of her own seat and gets Erika a box of tissues, one thing she, as a human being, can do for another human being, a simple gesture, unencumbered, unprohibited, not too costly.

♡♡ **Not far across town (yes, in the town of Egypt), at the St. Onge Settlement, six-and-a-half-year-old Jane Meserve speaks again.**

Somebody pleeeze help! You will not believe this horridable place!

🏠 **Britta at home.**

Her name is Britta Gammon. Her head and face are small. Her lips press together with self-conscious indignation against the toothless, rootless mouth, the dentures never filling out her mouth the way her teeth had. This makes her gray eyes look big and wishful. In Massachusetts, someone had thought her large gray eyes could make him whole. But here she is, back in Egypt, Maine, since Massachusetts "didn't work out."

And now her younger son, Mickey, passes through the living room, coming home from somewhere. Mickey says nothing to his mother, just nods. A nice nod, vaguely friendly.

Britta says nothing to Mickey, but she watches him pass. The TV could hold her attention in the absence of real life, but nothing can win her regard above and beyond her daughter and sons and daughter-in-law and grandchildren and her men who made it all happen.

Shyness. Just how shy is Britta Gammon? Well, she has never been able to look anyone in the eye, not even family. And she's not affectionate. But she's always there. She is right where you'd expect her to be. Like a sturdy little mushroom.

Donnie Locke finds whiskey in the cupboard.

The child Jesse lies soured on layers of sheets in the living room, silent and rigid now, after his last siege of tears, cries that are softer today, for he has no muscle left to belt out his former wildcat yowls.

His father, Donnie, with the pale walrus mustache and chain-store name tag, comes home from work and stands in the doorway, feeling the doorframe over and over and over.

He turns to the kitchen, remembering something. When he reappears, he is gripping by the neck a half-full bottle of bourbon that has been in the corner cupboard for years. But you see it is, of course, still good. He knows, as everyone knows, a good drink sometimes helps. He goes to the couch and kneels. At his back, the TV is giving the world and national news. The child's evaporated monkey-small face turns slowly to the left, toward his father, because he can smell his father, that smell of the great chain store, of its chemically treated fabrics and acres of stock, oceans of stock, with that tidal-wavelike come-and-go rhythm of stock moving, on sale, big sale, big specials, big buys, the universe of all necessity and heart's content there on display.

The father strokes the little one's cool sweaty head, thinking how it is you would interest this child in a drink, in getting drunk, that thing you associate with fun.

Again, Jesse throws out one rigid leg and lets out a sweet, nearly lovely, small trill of agony, and young Erika flies from the back bedroom, where her two stepdaughters await sleep, for she must be a comfort to them too, the healthy ones, can't neglect the healthy ones, whose flourishing you must not resent in the shadow of the other's dying, and Erika is wearing a knee-length lilac nightie, her face so round and pudgy and wifely, but with eyes like a dragon's, red and terrible, eyes that have not slept for weeks.

She slumps to the couch at the end where Jesse's feet are, then sees the ridiculous thing that is in her husband's hand.

He, in the seriousness of the moment, becomes taken with a goofy grin. "Hard stuff."

No money. No groceries. And now and then no medicine. No money. No groceries. No medicine. The hollow precincts of every commoditized need unmet.

He adds quickly, "It'll help him."

Erika hisses something, too much teeth and tongue to be audible. No words, just smoke. A dragon. A bitch. No cooing sweet-natured plump cutie. Not today.

Donnie places one hand behind his son's head, to lift him, get him ready for a swallow, but the young mother leaps up and drives her knee into her husband's shoulder as he is squatted there and he says angrily, "If I were in that kind of pain, I'd want this!!! *I'd* want to be passed out!!"

"*You are nuts!!!!*" Erika shrieks. No fainting fear-stars cross her vision now. Her vision is sharp and actual. Everything in her body and brain is instantly aligned.

Donnie reaches again for the boy's head and shoulders, and Erika shoves Donnie with the palms of both hands, but this also jars Jesse and he is taken by a terrible ghostly lament, both weak and filled with power. And Donnie bellers, "*Maybe it'll kill him!* Yeah, let's *kill* him! Let's make him happy! Die baby boy sweet fuckin' Jesus *die!*" And he grabs the boy's skeletal shoulders. But Erika is, within a split moment, on Donnie's back, so the bottle tips and a stinking bourbon wave spreads over the child's pajama top and face and he goes rigid again with wrinkled brow, wide-open jaws, straight-out legs, arms to his sides, his fair little trill of despair seeming to come from the center of his concave chest, and somehow now Erika has the bottle, running to the kitchen, and Donnie just kneels and covers the rigid, now breathlessly panting, Jesse with himself.

"A gun," Donnie whispers. Then yells it. "A *gun!* For a gun, I would give anything, Erika! *Where is Mickey's rifle?!*"

Erika's voice from the kitchen: "*monster!*"

And then he hollers, "No, you! *You!* You, Erika, are the big bitch monster who says *No, we don't sell the house or mortgage it.* And *Oh my, my, the hospital might take it!! You* are the one who says not to get him his chemo! They *said* they'd save him! *They said they'd save him!!!!*"

In the kitchen, silence.

In the night, into the silence of their wide-awake regrets and into the silence of Jesse's wide-awake dying, Donnie whispers.

"I'm sorry, Erika."

And she whispers, "I couldn't believe you said that."

And he whispers, "It came out."

"We *agreed* about the treatments. We *agreed*."

"It came out."

And now she is off in a free fall of sobs.

And he says, "No no no no no no," so gently, and strokes her soft young wifely neck and wrists and forearms, all the most trusting places. "No no no no no no no . . ."

 The screen shivers.

Be afraid. Poor people are lazy and immoral, and violence is on their fingertips for some reason, who knows the reason, it's just their idea of fun. It's always this way; they steal cars drugs money and gunnnnnz! They are filled with sex and rotten teeth and food stamps and Cadillacs and bad English! The men are bozos and incestuous. Poor women are all victims of poor, domestically violent men. But the big thing to remember is poor men for some reason all want to be armed and want to hurt hurt hurt kill kill kill. Here comes another one out of court, shackled and in an orange suit for shooting three times in the air to scare his girlfriend, who had all the charge cards. Weeee are so lucky to have police and politicians to keep these poor and violent and lazy-for-some-reason guys off of you and your darling Brendan and Olivia and your golden retriever and your *stuff*.

The militia at home.

It is Sunday, early evening.

Two days of rain: warm rain, cold rain, a lotta rain. The culverts hiss and giggle with road runoff from the higher hills.

Mickey moves along the road's crown, light-footed as ever, the rain punching his eyes, punching him all over.

Richard "Rex" York's home welcomes you. When Mickey raps on the door inside the little glassed-in porch, a voice hollers from somewhere, "*In here!*" And beside the door is a varnished plaque shaped like a hand with a pointing finger that reads ENTER.

And so Mickey steps into the kitchen. There is a smell. Something supperish, a supper already eaten. But something else too, something besides meat and potatoes. He thinks it is hot cookies or cake, you know, cookies or cake still baking away. The gray Formica-topped table and the counters are wiped clean. Mickey glances to his right, through an open pantry door that shows a red and green metal Christmas tree stand on top of a small barbecue grill with a laundry basket on top, and other pantry-shedway-type stuff stacked or standing.

This house is an old farm place that rural people yearned to modernize and fulfilled their yearnings with avocado indoor-outdoor carpeting in the pantry and all the walls of the whole house done in cheesy sixteenth-inch paneling that doesn't look at all like wood but just a picture of wood. Funny about fads. Probably in many of these old farmhouses, there is gorgeous golden real knotty pine board paneling completely plastered over with this 1970s plasticky latest-thing-gotta-have-it brown-black plywood sheet paneling.

Also, here at the York residence, those tall, narrow, handsome, many-paned, good-for-the-soul, low-to-the-floor windows, the original ones, have been *ripped out* and replaced with small windows with cranks, set high like rectangular portholes, and, of course, in the living room, a bay picture window covered with glossy fiberglass drapes thick as a fort fence.

In similar homes, you'll find sliding glass doors, always with the accompanying dog-nose prints, splats and smears of ice cream or ordinary baby goo, pollen, woodstove smoke in filmy gray-green streaks with a view of the "deck," where the barbecue and laundry basket and stuffed gray trash bags are kept, and maybe a cat is out there on the rail, licking her paw or eating a live mouse. But here at Rex's home, fad has not gotten that far. The place still feels a *little* farmlike. Coats and jackets hang on hooks on the kitchen side of the thick old cellar door. The old white-painted corner cabinet top is heaped with papers and hats and tools and the innards of a broken lamp.

Again the voice, calling "In here!" from the living room, where Mickey can see feet raised up on the footrest of a La-Z-Boy, feet dressed in black military boots. Mickey heads toward these feet.

Yes, it is *him,* the one Mickey is looking for.

Rex's eyes fall on the rifle Mickey has in his hands, and he nods into Mickey's eyes. Rex seems different. No army cap. No metal-frame sunglasses. No red T-shirt, just a stiff dark-blue work shirt. The shirt makes him seem older, like a father or grandfather, just a regular age-fifty-looking guy. So bare in the face and head, more exposed. His hair is dark brown like the mustache, not much gray. But thinning a bit at the temples. And he doesn't comb his hair funny to hide it.

Mickey speaks an almost inaudible "Hi." Mickey is sopping wet and the rifle is shining.

The man's deep La-Z-Boy is facing the TV, but the TV is blank-faced and silent. The TV remote control is still in his hand.

Mickey says, "Sorry to bother you, but I have something. . . ."

Rex York snorts and leans forward, his booted feet come down with a single thump, and he says, "What *really* bothers me was what was going on before you came in." He aims the remote flicker, makes the TV burst to life, then kills it quick. He narrows his steely eyes. "Six o'clock news." He sneers. "Next they'll be telling us there's a Santa Claus." He tosses the remote onto a pile of newspapers on the floor beside him. "Whatcha got there?"

Mickey says, "This is mine, Marlin Twenty-two Magnum. I wanted to see if you'd be interested in buying it."

"Not interested," says Rex, as he pulls on his nose, eyes on Mickey's face. "I'm not in need of one."

Mickey is frozen in place, standing with legs apart, the rifle loose in his hands, muzzle down, his little wet worm of a ponytail especially pitiful-looking, his small frame especially small. He says, low and soft, "I need to sell it for medicine. It's for a sick baby."

Rex York's eyes are direct, eyes that make you feel as though a permanent picture of you is being taken, the whole picture; your face, body, blood count, shoe size. He moves these eyes over Mickey as if to gauge the truth of this sick baby story. He says, "Whose gun *is* that?"

Mickey replies, "Mine."

Rex says, "I don't know you."

Mickey turns slightly, looks to the heavily draped picture window, beyond which he knows rain is smashing down onto yard and field and winding paved road. "I just thought I'd check."

The man stands, steps over to Mickey, grasps the rifle around the forearm, turns it sideways, jerks back the bolt, checks the breech, then deftly, with one hand, uncocks it, working the trigger and bolt. He feels over all the rain-darkened wood, studies the serial numbers. "You took all-right care of it. But"—his eyes fix again on Mickey's unreadable face—"I got no more use for this thing than a zucchini, 'cept to trade it. But you can leave it with me as collateral, and I'll loan you what you need."

"That would be good, yuh."

And so there's an exchange.

And then a little chitchat, mostly Rex leading the conversation. Talk of the government and the United Nations and the Constitution and the way money is no longer backed by gold and the impending declaration of martial law by the president, of the New World Order and the liberals and the socialists, and then some about jury rights and separation of powers, the Federalist Papers, and on to Waco and Ruby Ridge.

Rex's somewhat young-looking mother appears quietly, from some cool part of the house. There seems to be cool air following her. She gives Mickey cookies, big nice vanilla sugar cookies, her hand cool, the cookies piping hot. She watches Mickey eat them. She stares openly at his hands and mouth, just like his own mother does.

When Mickey stands to leave, Rex pulls keys from his pocket and commands, "Go get in the truck. I'll take you home. You don't love rain *that* much, do you?"

The prince.

Erika lies on the bed that is hers and Donnie's. It is covered with a cheap yellow computerized crazy-quilt-print synthetic-fleece blanket that makes the skin on Erika's bare legs and feet look a bright cheap yellow. The rain has left the air as thick and solid and tinted as green Jell-O. There under the blanket, close to Erika, is her shrinking child. On a small metal and wooden trunk at the foot of the bed is a television turned down very low. Erika's eyes are even more fiercely deep and ringed than yesterday. These eyes are watching filmed excerpts of a trial. The TV has the sound turned nearly off. All the TVs in this house have the sound turned down these days. But no blank TVs. No pressing the OFF button. There is, to so many of us, something frightening about being totally cut off from "society," from our "culture," from the faceless mind that instructs and defines us.

A big bee drones at the screen of the open window, tapping over and over and over, seeming to ask, *Is this it? Is this it? Is this it?*

With the excerpts of the trial over and a blast of jolly commercials, there is now a TV talk show host wheedling a guest, and Erika's eyes watch this dully and she hears footsteps in the hall and knows it's her brother-in-law, Mickey, whose room is on the third floor above her in that uninsulated blistering-hot attic space. She hears him stop. At *this* door. She had left the door cracked open. He hits it with his palm so it flies wide. Erika jumps, pushes herself up off the pillows.

The old part-golden retriever, Boy, raises his head from his paws where he lies on the floor, and his tail thumps to see Mickey. Mickey steps over him. Mickey comes right over to the bed and stands there looking at Erika, stretched out there in her shorts and bare feet and Persian cat T-shirt, which he likes a lot, and she is scooting herself up to sit, then folds one knee up to brace herself for this unexpected moment and she sees that Mickey has a fistful of twenty-dollar bills that he is raising over her. She grabs his wrist. Much strength in her fingers. He laughs.

She works to pry this money out of his fist. His cigarettish and carelessly unwashed smell is enormous. Her eyes are now bright on the money, on the fist, on Mickey's face, on all of him, his thin little, rat-like self, ragged and untended and suddenly now quite princelike.

Out in the world.

Providence, Rhode Island, a rain-drenched evening, the setting sun, a perfect yellow, glitters on chemically velvet lawns and on pavements, glass, and stone, everything green made greener and more urgent. The shopping center parking lot is packed. Most of the empty spaces are on the farthest outer edges. A muted copper-colored two-door car slips into a tight space close to the buildings. Tinted glass hides the occupants, but the bumper speaks loudly: MY CHILD IS A NATHAN BISHOP MIDDLE SCHOOL HONOR STUDENT. (Yes, another one.)

Claire St. Onge speaks.

Gordon has never wanted anything to do with the media. When the call came last night, I was there in his kitchen with a few others. As he held the phone, he listened very hard, with his shoulders, with his neck, with his face. When he hung up and said it was a reporter with the *Record*

Sun, I knew all our lives were crossing a line. What was he doing!!, agreeing to this "little" interview?!

 You, crow, so bright-eyed there on top of the silvery limbless die-back beech, are the only witness when Ivy Morelli, *Record Sun* reporter, shows up for her first interview.

The St. Onge Settlement is hidden in the cleft of the mountain behind the 1800s farmhouse where Gordon St. Onge grew up. He still resides here in the old place, his name on the mailbox and in the phone book, so at first glance things seem ordinary. Your eyes, crow, follow him trudging up the hot flowery sloped field toward a homemade merry-go-round. You fluff your feathers, make yourself momentarily bigger. You turn your head back to the old house. So typical. A Cape Cod. Light gray with white trim. Ell. Long porch. Anyone can see it was once an open porch because of the lathed columns behind the fog of screen and the scrollwork along the top.

Three connected shedways off the ell once protected farmers from icy winds, rain, big snow, as the family made their way to and from the barn, which is now just a stone foundation, lopsided under where the tie-ups would have been. Birch trees are spoking out around one corner.

Bank of solar collectors across the house roof. Big and boxy. Made by kids.

The front "lawn" has nothing to draw year 2000 criticism. No leaning towers of tires or hubcaps. No bundles of used boards. No piles of rusty iron. No farm equipment. No tacky whirligigs. Though some nowadays might frown at the grass itself: sandy, seedy, weedy.

The driveway is rutty and rocky and bunched with plantain. It circles an ash tree the diameter of a small building. The leaves are thin, like the hair of an old man. Its shade is ghosty. A sign nailed to it reads OFFICE. It points at the house.

Fresh paint is in the air.

An old pickup truck is in the driveway. Chains and a gas can are in the bed and wiggly heat lines cover the hood because Gordon St. Onge has just arrived here from somewhere else. The field begins close to the house, immediately rising. A red smog of devil's paintbrushes and the faded purple of vetch, a universe of daisies. Soft greens, tough greens, witch grass, clovers, nettle. And then the woods. And then the mountain, not a Kilimanjaro but it is so near and therefore big in the way a face gets big and hot when it comes to whisper in your ear. To the left and to the right are other mountains, technically foothills, blue in the humidity but intimate enough so you can see the character of the highest treetops.

This is the St. Onge property, nine hundred acres in the wooded hills of Egypt.

You, crow, know every secret of this rocky mean old land. You turn your head for another glimpse of the reporter's red sports car, parked between the ash tree and the truck.

Now back to the action, the reporter and Gordon St. Onge, both having arrived in the shade of the merry-go-round's roof, are not shaking hands. No nice hellos. The reporter wears a stripy dress, bracelets, shoulder bag, camera with strap, the weight of that other world outside this place. That which makes Gordon St. Onge's undigested heavy noon meal freeze.

The merry-go-round is of monsters; wide-mouthed, horned, pop-eyed, some with human heads and spear-ended tails like Satan's. No pretty polka-dot high-stepping horsies. The reporter, Ivy Morelli, is scribbling away on her lined pad after pushing her sunglasses to her head. Her hair is black—no, it's purple, a tint, no doubt, created for urban interiors.

The man is Titan-sized, unlike the reporter, who is small, even for a woman.

In the lacing of one leather work boot, the man, this Gordon St. Onge, has gotten a daisy snagged. His brown hair is not long, not short, not touched up with a comb for this special occasion. Green work shirt. Sleeves rolled up. No visible tattoos. No wristwatch. Which might explain why he was twenty minutes late.

Does the reporter note the belt buckle? You, crow, have noticed that coppery blushy sun. Probably made by kids. It has the face you would expect for the sun, grandfatherly, toothless, eyes closed, too bright even for itself. And the dungarees. New. Oddly fitted. Also made by kids?

Reporter swipes at a deerfly.

Reporter writes across her pad: VIKING.

Then she adds: COULD EAT A WHOLE REINDEER.

Reporter whacks another fly. Bracelets bonk and clank. Her bowl-cut hair slides from side to side in an attractive way.

The man whom you, crow, know very well through many generations of crows—this man is uneasy today.

The woman, who is young, is also nervous. But stalwart. Even wise-ass, almost crowlike.

The two humans are now talking fast, overlapping, arguing.

You tip your head, enjoying.

Now the man steps around the woman, the wild grasses hissing and snapping around his pant legs. Keys on his belt loop jangle once. Squatting in the hot blue shade, he checks the oil and gas of the carousel generator. He yanks the cord hard, then harder. Again, harder. The engine sputters to a ragged hum. Another adjustment. The engine purrs. Now the lever. The circle of monsters creaks into motion. One of the heads is gold, like the domes of some state capitals.

Reflections of monsterific colors brighten and darken upon the reporter's face, her small mouth even more clover-colored now than its formerly honest pink, the eyes in their dark lashes a cold no-feeling blue. Trying to look objective? She cocks her head. Her silky bowl of black but purple hair slides to one side, then back. She has stopped taking notes. Just staring.

She watches Gordon St. Onge's work-smoodged hand on the lever, so familiar in its humanness but in another way new, and now she raises her eyes into and through the traffic of beasts. There is only one that actually rises up and down. It is yellow and black and gleaming as a hornet. It has wings. But not a hornet. It gives off an agonized lowing sound. And it farts. In its eye sockets are red Christmas twinkle lights. One begins to work now, after a long warming. *Twink! Twink! Twink!*

Beyond the slow, hot, miserable trudge of creatures, Gordon St. Onge's face is clear. He has a mad-scientist aspect, one eye squinting, fluttering, blinking, almost in sync with the yellow and black creature's Christmassy eyes. This man is suffocating in burning indecision. His beard is short, darker than his untidy hair. Chin of the beard graying, kingly. Brown-black mustache heavy. His crowded teeth are revealed as he wags his head and gives Ivy Morelli a goofy grin, not goofy and full of sport but goofy as in apology. Doglike.

You, crow, watch all this. You hear the man say, "You have to imagine your own calliope music."

From this perch you, crow, can see over the treetops to the Settlement, its metal-roofed Quonset huts shaped like loaves of bread. Meanwhile, the main building, a massive horseshoe bending around a quadrangle of tall oaks and maples and wooden creatures, one taller than the buildings and painted Popsicle green, and there a silver spaceship, and there a purple cow. Dozens of cottages in both sun and shade, also in stirring colors. Pastures. Shingle mill and sawmills. Gardens, some childly, with too many scarecrows that don't look scary. Some gardens are in effortless rows, the soil dark and loamy, sacred. Mountaintop ledge with windmills paralyzed by the dead heat.

And you can see kids.

But the reporter cannot. She will have to work hard to get that far. You, crow, in whose bony chest beats alert and fretful wisdom, understand the look in Gordon St. Onge's eyes. Fear.

☆ **From a future time, Claire St. Onge speaks.**

It eventually changed everything, his giving in to this reporter. She didn't do the big feature immediately. After she discovered where the Settlement actually was and we were friendly—we were embracing—she settled into a mode of friendship for a few weeks, and Gordon, who can be either a huge downed tree blocking your road or a big puppy wagging and wagging to please, had become honest with her about *everything*. Our Bonny Loo will tell you that this reporter was devious. But I think she was confused. Friend or reporter? How could she choose while flabbergasted by Settlement life and Guillaume—Gordon—St. Onge?

July

 **Tonight Erika is again wearing the Persian cat
T-shirt when he brings her another fifty dollars.**

Sometimes he presents a whole batch of twenties. Once a hundred-dollar
bill. And she says the same thing every time. "Sure you're not dealing
drugs?"

And Mickey sneers at this. "You see too much TV."

He never tells her about the militia, nor about the jobs these guys
arrange for him: mowing lawns, helping vacuum a swimming pool and
"shock it," being a chimneysweep's helper, doing roofing, haying, working in the woods, babysitting, housepainting, feeding rabbits, and then,
over on Promise Lake, crawling under the big summer camp porch of
two out-of-state ladies to get a dead skunk. They were nice ladies. Chatty
and huggy. They gave him root beer and an earful of advice. That's
where he got the hundred-dollar bill. One had a Southern accent. The
other, Boston or something. They had an old well-kept Plymouth
Duster, repainted gold. They were married once to two brothers. There
was a lot of mention of "the Milwaukee days." They wore black bathing suits, the one-piece kind. One suit was white dots on black. They
wanted him to come back one weekend and meet their friend Millie,
another old lady. He hardly talked the whole time, but somehow he
liked them. He keeps wondering if they know that Stan Berry, whom
they also fuss over, the guy who brought Mickey to them, is with a citizens' militia. Even more officially than Mickey.

Now Erika says again, "Sure you aren't dealin' drugs?"

Whatever money he makes goes into Erika's hand, except for buying cigarettes. He has tried to give up cigarettes, but he can't. Where the drive for food is felt in the stomach and the drive for sex is a hot spot between the legs, the drive for a cigarette is felt in every cell. It is a hunger shaped exactly like Mickey inside Mickey, a flaming Mickey shape screaming, *I need! I need!*

And so the summer is passing in this way: Jesse dying, Mickey providing. Erika and Mickey's mother grateful. Everything costing a little more, Mickey's brother Donnie working the Chain for just a little less. Jesse getting smaller, dying. Donnie getting smaller, Mickey getting bigger.

Mickey at home.

And Erika is always right where he knows he'll find her, at home in one room or another, like Britta, his mother. Or in Erika's case, out in the field rounding up the disoriented old retriever, Boy, or hanging out the wet clothes by the dead tree, clothespins in her strong teeth. But mostly these days Erika is curled up on the big bed upstairs, poor Jesse in the cradle of one arm, her eyes on the TV. Britta and Erika, home sweet home. They argue a lot, but gently. Little snippets of despair.

Upstairs, the little girls scheme and pretend to do the things they see on TV. If they bang about too much up there, Britta will take the broom and thonk the ceiling with the handle. Or Erika will if she's downstairs by herself. This makes them quiet down awhile. There are so many children, including the children of neighbors and the daughter of Erika's younger brother, Isabel. These extra children they look after on certain days of the week for no pay, just niceness, just the natural thing people do for one another. And on those days, on the couch, alone but kept within earshot and heart's embrace, is the child Jesse. You never hear his powerful shrieks anymore. The pain medicine money is always just in the nick of time from Donnie or Mickey, the refills hand over fist, the little white pharmacy bags decorate every part of this old house.

Mickey has allowed himself to talk a little bit with Erika about some of his jobs, leaving out the militia connection. His face and arms are sunburned and peeling, sunburns on top of sunburns. A blond brown boy-man.

Sometimes he picks up the pain medicine himself. His bearing is proud as he steps up to the counter at the chain drug.

Today, when Mickey arrives home with another little white bag, Erika, who is putting Donnie's oldest girl's hair into beaded braids, which is the fashion these days (originating from TV), looks not just at Mickey but at his proud bearing and she smiles in a funny way, in the way of women for men, while the girl, Elizabeth, looks at him like she always does, as if there never was and never will be anything different about Mickey or this kitchen or this life, and Mickey's mother's eyes trickle over him, over the fresh white FAMILY FESTIVAL T-shirt he's wearing and then to the bag, and she makes a little cooing sound and he, Mickey, stands straight-backed, spear-straight, the moment supreme. His mother, Britta. He sees in her eyes and the set of her toothless mouth that again he, Mickey, has won something here. Won it over his brother. He is ashamed to think it, but he thinks it.

 In the United States of America, "Land of the Free."

A new prison is being built every week.

 Concerning the aforementioned information, the screen is blank.

Of course.

 The usual rambling, boring academics estimated.

In less than twenty years (even if there are no new prohibitions), more than half of the population of the United States will be in the prison system; if not in an actual cell, in government computers, face shots, eye scans, and compromised rights. And chips. (That's not as in potato chips.)

And what does the screen have to say concerning the aforementioned *urgent* information?

Nothing.

 Well, isn't that the darnedest thing! Who does this guy think he is?

Little dipshit country full of suffering people with absolutely no DE-MOCRACY! Mr. Smarty Pants Dictator who is yelling stuff . . . hear the stuff he's yelling? Well, we'll translate it for you.

Okay, we've had enough of his foolish babble. No DEMOCRACY? No PEACE talks? Here come the bombs. That's us. The good guys. Bomb the bastard. Bomb him again.

KABOOM!

Bomb him again. Wipe out dipshit country like wiping a rear end.

See his face? *Boo, hiss!* We hate him, don't we? He is the enemy of DEMOCRACY!

Bomb him again.

See his face? *Boo, hiss!* We hate him, don't we? We hate him. We hate him. We hate him.

He has tanks and other ugly stuff. He has guns and armies. Maybe even a bomb! Ignore all the people who say the USA gave him all that stuff! Ignore all of them who say USA *put him there!* He got there *all by himself!* Listen to *meeeee.* Bomb him again. *Boo, hiss!* We will bring the gift of democracy to all the people. We, America, the peacemakers. We, America, rich and godly. God bless us. See his face? Bombs away.

Next day, Donnie at home.

Donnie Locke sits at the table in his chain-store clothes. There's a heated (screaming and yelling) soap opera scene on the kitchen TV, but his eyes are on his brother, who has just come in from somewhere, a large paper bag under his arm. And Mickey is happy to feel the heat of his brother's eyes on him, like the kind of heat you have in a house when you come in from the cold: a comfort, even if a little on the scorching side.

Upstairs, the kids are loud.

Donnie says, "What's in the bag?"

Mickey says, in a low-as-possible voice, "Beans and greens."

Donnie says, "Oh," with a haunting smile, just a flicker of his heavy white-blond mustache. He asks, "So how's everything coming along? With your life?"

Mickey likes the way Donnie has said this. The question goes into the muscles at the back of his neck, and the hairs on the back of his neck move, *not* like a chill. It is a man-to-man question, a new thing these days, not the voice Donnie used to have for Mickey.

And so, in a tone unconsciously mimicking Donnie's, Mickey replies, "Good. Considering."

And Donnie says, "Good."

Donnie Locke, like Mickey, is not much of a talker. Now his silence thickens and his eyes drift over to the soap opera, where a woman with earrings that look like chandeliers shrieks, "HE STOLE EVERY-THING! EVEN MY MIND!"

Mickey lowers the bag of beans and greens to the table. Then he moves light-footed to and through the bright little entry hall with the window and two jade plants. The living room is empty. He passes through it, his back straight, everything about him new and wiry and hard.

Upstairs, he passes a closed door, beyond which are the screeches of kids, kids who spend a lot of time in midair jumping off stuff. He hears the tinny wail of the TV, there, somebody messing with the remote, probably stomping it. Maybe it was simply thrown. Celia and Elizabeth, Audrey and Tegan. And probably Jola, one of their friends from down the road. And of course Isabel. They seldom seem part of this household. Always in another room or outdoors. Or down the road at the Hartfords'. A massive girl gang that makes Mickey nervous but which everyone else thinks is cute. Cute? It's nothing but *I win I win I win*. This versus that. Me versus you. No collaboration. No compromise. No sweetness.

Rex's militia seems sweeter.

Mickey takes a second set of stairs, the narrower and steeper stairs that lead up to the small third-floor attic space that is all his. But hot. He likes how Erika has started, these last couple of weeks, to toss a few freshly washed shirts (and his other pair of jeans) in a wrinkled pile on his unmade bed. And she even straightens the top blanket of his bed and changes the pillow case. It used to be he was expected to do his own laundry. But now this, her homage to the new Mickey. Something about his position in this house has changed, something that speaks the word *able*. And Mickey, who resists housework and grooming, is eager to enter in this little secret thing with Erika, to change several times a day into one of the clean wrinkled shirts, more shirts than he had before: yard-sale T-shirts with messages and ads, hand-me-downs, one cowboy shirt, one baseball shirt, and one camo—a nice co-incidence. All clean and sweet from the clothesline. This is the thing a woman does for you when you've made her feel protected. This gift of home, which is also a kind of protection. Protection, yeah, it goes around and around. And thicker and thicker. Like a tornado of love. Mickey smiles.

 What is "the Settlement"? Why is six-and-a-half-year-old Jane Meserve prisoner there? Where is her mother, who is as sweet as sugar?

It is soon told.

The Border Mountain Militia

Mickey knows the way to this house by heart now. He even knows the shortcut through the rest area off the highway, through a narrow stand of planted white pines called "research area" by a paper company, and then another quarter mile across a lumpy, flowery fallow field. He knows Rex has been called Rex all his life. *Rex* means *king,* so of course the guy likes it. Unlike *Mickey,* which Mickey sometimes despairs over, it being the name of a mouse.

With each visit, Mickey knows more about the Border Mountain Militia and other militias across the country. And yet, so much isn't told. Somehow it doesn't seem secret, as in *top secret,* but more or less things Rex can't or won't express, things to do with fear and anger and shame, things to do with the ways evil power can be something else besides a foreign army, something you can't kill.

Rex has told him that the Border Mountain Militia is composed of four hundred members, although Mickey has met only fifteen and heard mention of the names of six or so more. Rex's computer, in the corner of a small bedless bedroom upstairs, glows an agitated bright blue.

Rex has said Mickey can be a full member after he checks him out a little more. This is something above and beyond the already see-and-record-everything gaze of Rex's eyes. Mickey once asked, "You mean *school* records?" and Rex said, without a hitch, "I do not mean school records."

Mickey knows he doesn't mean credit check, and Mickey doubts there's a Michael Daniel Gammon FBI file, and how would Rex have access to it anyway? He keeps trying to figure what Rex could be checking out. Whatever it is, it feels kind of nice.

This meeting has only drawn a few members, which Rex says is due to its being summer. Although today is another dark and steamy downpour. The ceilings are low here, and in the kitchen a coil of flypaper has one fly on it. It is Saturday, so Rex's brother's kids are in and out. Rex's brother Bob lives in a ranch house on the other side of the field. Rex says his brother is *not* into the Patriot Movement. Rex hints that his brother is a weird character, not to be trusted. Over time this summer, it is revealed to Mickey that Rex's brother is, yes, a *schoolteacher*. Mickey feels a bond with Rex in their common disaffection for brother Bob.

At today's meeting, they are talking about the terrain of the White Mountain foothills here as compared with Aroostook and Bangor area highlands and the relatively flat southern Maine coast. Topographical maps are in a loose floppy pile on the foot hassock and much of the rug. Then somebody brings up the subject of radio transmitters, and a guy named Dave goes out to his vehicle for lists of data he keeps on short-wave frequencies and installation and everything one needs to know about shortwave.

There is some mention of Willie Lancaster at this point, a member who was in jail last week for an hour or so. Rex is *grim* about the subject of Willie Lancaster, even though Willie Lancaster has a pretty good shortwave setup and is planning big things with it. So the conversation about Willie Lancaster begins to trickle off under the weight of Rex's steely, pale, disapproving eyes.

Rex's La-Z-Boy is not in its TV-news-watching position. He is sitting on the edge, footrest folded down, his boots flat on the floor, a palm on one thigh, forearm on the other, squinting at the nearest map. He wears a short-sleeved camo shirt with an embroidered patch on the left sleeve that features the snarling mountain lion and around it the crescent of letters, BORDER MOUNTAIN MILITIA. The rest of his uniform is a pair of newish jeans and, of course, his military boots. No cap.

Meanwhile, Rex's daughter. Mickey's only seen her once, except for her graduation picture, which he glances at from time to time. The time he actually saw her, she had been taking a nap and came out the door from the closed attic stairs, her face puffy and blinky. She was wearing a big loose flannel shirt with no pants, maybe short shorts or a bathing suit, but you couldn't really tell. The shirt was just a dumb red and blue and cream plaid. She was hugging herself, acting goose bumpy and looking around at the faces of the gathered militiamen like they were all a little bit funny. She didn't look much at Mickey. But she tossed a scrunched-up Kleenex in the face of a young guy with a soft mustache who was almost asleep on the couch. She didn't turn to look at Rex when she asked, "Dad, where's the phone book?"

And Rex said, "Must be upstairs. In the computer room."

And then she rolled her eyes in exaggerated despair, and tskcd and said, "Jeepers, Bumpa. Nooga putee-way, you bad again, Bumpa." This a special baby language she and her old man share? Mickey doesn't dare look at any of the militiamen's faces now. He looks at his hands. He is thinking how he has heard her name spoken a few times but can never be sure if it's Glory or Gloria. Her hair is long enough to reach the backs of her pretty, nice knees. Auburn. Thick. Ripply. And . . . and . . . awesome. She is frighteningly beautiful, even without makeup, even though her brows and lashes are light and she's freckled thickly. Worse than just beautiful. She's teasy. Mickey supposes that Glory (or Gloria) doesn't lose much sleep over Special Forces, United Nations, and "Socialists in the White House."

No sign of her today.

Whenever Mickey stands up, to get one of Rex's mother's cookies, or to head for the bathroom again to piss out his black coffee, or to smoke on the glassed-in porch, he will see through this or that window two Herefords standing thickset in the downpour, chewing cud, eyes shut. These are the cattle Rex and his brother, Bob, share the raising of and then they share the meat. This leads Mickey to believe that Rex and Bob are at least on speaking terms, if not politically attuned.

Mickey is not the only teenager at this meeting. There's Ben, maybe eighteen or nineteen, the guy Rex's daughter bopped with the balled-up

Kleenex, there in the deep fake-leather couch again, looking sleepy, like he does at every meeting. This time he sits between two big guys. One wears a tank-type muscle shirt and his trucking company advertisement cap; the other wears summer-weight biker regalia, denim sleeveless vest, tattoos, and a small earring. The sleepy boy's mustache is nothing like theirs, just a little red-blond splutter. But he wears a camo shirt with an arm patch just like Rex's.

Also, there's a kid named Thad who is a six-foot-one fourteen-year-old with a massive chest, massive in breadth and frame, and massive in extra flesh. Breasts point against his pearl gray knit shirt as he stands slouched against the kitchen doorway. So studious-looking, with his tortoiseshell glasses and feathered hair. Thad has a relationship with Rex's mother's masterpiece cookie pile. His crunching and chomping demolishes the stack in his hand within the time it takes Dave to unfold another map.

Mickey has a seat, a kitchen chair, set between the fake leather couch and a long blond table with a sewing machine on it. But several guys are squatted or leaning against other doorframes or walls. Not enough chairs. And now a couple of late arrivals, so there's more standing and squatting.

Not many guys here are in their twenties, and not many are geezers. Mostly Vietnam-age guys, late forties, early fifties. One of them is skin and bones and wheezing loudly, seems to be dying. His eyes, with no eyebrows above, are ghosty and deep. Then there is the hefty, high-voiced, cheerful sea-captain-beard guy, Artie, whom Mickey also met that day at the pit. His white hair is in a monkish ring around a bald spot, quite pink. Red suspenders over a white T-shirt. And like the boy Thad, he has breasts.

One guy Mickey can never warm to is Doc, a really hard-assed guy who also wears a camo shirt with an arm patch. Although the word *God* comes up at all meetings in a rather rote fashion, this guy speaks the word *God* like you or I would say the words *club* or *guillotine*. Mickey fears this guy worse than Mr. Carney and his henchmen at the high school. Probably because back last spring Mickey had surmised it was only a matter of time before he'd walk out of that school scene forever. But here, he can't imagine his future without the militia. It is everything.

August

 The inevitably leaky press.

Gordon is working here in the largest Quonset hut with his son Cory. Tall, imperious-looking Cory St. Onge (although he is not in actual spirit imperious). A lament in his black eyes (though he is a fairly contented sort), Cory of the immense shoulders and back (like Gordon), is noticeably Passamaquoddy. Almost fifteen years old. Nothing like his father in the need to blab, no crooked smile, no twitching eye and cheek, no awkward charisma. Just a boy, ordinary as winter.

The rest of the furniture-cabinet-making crew are all and about as well.

In through the hum of lathes, the screech of saws, and drifting sweet light, and sweet dusty air strides a messenger. None of his children call him Dad or Father or Papa or any of that. Like all the rest, she—the messenger—calls him Gordie. She is his child by Claire's cousin Leona, and a sister to Cory. Her name is Andrea St. Onge, the only one who has turned out to look so completely Passamaquoddy, not so much like a Frenchman, an Italian, or a folk of the shamrock (Gordon's side). No, nothing like Gordon—except her stature, long arms, long body, and easy gait. And *some* of her squinty smiles. She is accompanied by two small spotty white dogs who often hang out here and now waste no time in wetting down the legs of the equipment and lower shelves. Three angry men chase the dogs out.

Andrea is not quite seven. Yes, tall. Short china-doll haircut, like her mother's; long Settlement-made skirt of red. Baggy black Settlement-made

51

T-shirt. Settlement-made moccasin sneakers. She is graceful and tiptoe-ish, bringing this "message." Just back from visiting an old Settlement man in the hospital, some doctor appointments, windshield leafleting, and other Settlement-style gang-style missions, all made possible by one van trip out into the world.

Gordon is slipping off his safety glasses, sees in her hands a newspaper folded in a careful odd way. She places it in his hands. She doesn't leave until she's nuzzled into his shirt, found the solidness of his ribs, and patted his back comfortingly. "It's the lady in there who wrote something . . . about us. See the folded part? That's where it is. Okay?"

"Yep."

She leaves, looking neither left nor right, having important business elsewhere.

He walks quickly to the passageway that leads to the other half of the building, a narrow passageway with deep shelves and cardboard boxes and tools and "cultch" and not much light. He squats there under the little dim yellow bulb like a wounded animal, safety glasses still on his head, and reads what Ivy Morelli has written, although she had sworn she would not go ahead with the Settlement story. Quite a spread. Pictures. A lot of pictures. And, yes, a lot of words. He reads each word and the punctuation and the spaces between and the shapes of the columns and the feel of the newsprint against his thumbs.

"Betrayed," he says to himself with a little snort, and holds his face awhile, lids shut, seeing Ivy's blue eyes, the set of her small pointy-lipped clover-color mouth, the stalwart shape of her body, and, of course, her raffish laugh. How is it that when you do right by some it feels wrong to others? What now? What will this media "coverage" bring to his beloved family?

Mickey at Bean's Variety.

He came in for the Eskimo Pie, which is frosty cold in his hand. He is too young by law to buy cigarettes, even though he's low on them. He gets *them* through Matt Ackers, part of the Mr. Carney fan club he met at school here in Maine. Ha-ha. Like Mickey was Mr. Carney's total *biggest fan*. Ha-ha. In Mass there'd been *three* friends who kept him in supply. Now there is only Matt, through Matt's brother, the all-powerful Dom, who is at least thirty. Lots of cracks in the face, like the north side of a house. Fortunately, no chain of people is needed to buy an Eskimo Pie.

The Eskimo Pie is less frosty now due to Mickey being detoured, waiting for a customer who took a *Record Sun* from the rack. And then the Bean behind the counter says to the customer, "See this big spread on the Settlement? Picture of ol' Gordo looking like out of that scene in *Murder at Midnight* with all the carnival stuff." He flaps and crinkles his way through the pages.

The other guy laughs. "That whole place is a carnival."

"Well, this is him"—the Bean is pushing his finger over the colorful picture—"by some sort of a merry-go-round."

The other guy titters almost girlishly. "Like having your desk at Disneyland . . . Morrisseys send their kids up there."

"You ever been up to one of their solstice marches?" Big grin.

The other guy howls. "At four in the morning!?" Shakes head, eyes wide.

Bean sighs pleasantly. "Well, you know they set up a windmill with Whitmarsh and . . . uh . . . what's their names . . . uh. . . ."

"You mean those on the bog?"

"Yeah."

Head shaking. "Can't place their name."

More talk while Mickey waits and waits.

Then, "People been calling Gordo the Prophet."

"Oh, boy. Waco, Texas, in Maine."

More talk. Quieter now.

Of course, Mickey's eyes were riveted on the rack.

Now, on the thick see-through ice-cream-cooler top, he goes through the paper, lifting each page in a heavy way, like a rock, like under it anything could squirm or march out.

Turns out to be the whole first page of a thick inside section. He cannot read very well the words in columns or in lines under the pictures. But he can read the pictures themselves like an old-fashioned Indian on hot deer tracks. He studies the photos. Kids making papier-mâché sculptures, picking cukes.

Then there's one of Gordon St. Onge, aka the Prophet. Yeah, Mickey has seen him in the distances around town, big distances, never this close with the pale eyes looking right into Mickey's own. One of the guy's eyes glows electric. Like a lightbulb with gas inside it, not an eyeball of solid stuff. Probably due to sun on half his face, which also cuts his beard in half, part dark, part sunshiny.

Blurring across, some to the left, some to the right, a bunch of heads, long necks, rears, tails. Some heads are eyeless. A very weird merry-go-round, yes, kind of blurry, while the Prophet's face, shoulders, and one hand are crystal clear.

For two days, *Record Sun* reporter Ivy Morelli tries to reach Gordon on the phone.

Instead, she gets dozens of others: children, women, men, once even a baby that made obscene gasping noises and sucking noises and breathing noises and only one word: "Dah!" Then, finally, Gordon calls her.

She hurriedly tells him that the story went AP. "I'm sorry, Gordon, but they added in *things* . . . like there has been controversy around you . . . which is true. Seems there's been a lot of calls to their offices, not just ours, and AP's been interviewing people right and left, including grandparents and ex-teachers of some of the Settlement kids who have come to the Settlement recently, or recent teachers of kids who left the Settlement a few years ago. AP just says you are *controversial* and mentions *passionate disapproval* by many . . . and then of course some emphasis on kids lacking *education* and *a competitive environment;* these are quotes."

She stops for one small *tsk*.

"Even with all the changes, the AP version is very short. Condensed. Really condensed. It . . . changes the tone of the piece from the way I wrote it. And the picture we never used for *reasons;* they seem to like that one a lot. In all the papers that are using the piece, they rewrite the copy and use *that* photo. One of the ones of you by the merry-go-round. Closer than the one we used. And cropped. You look"—she swallows—"pretty scary."

Claire St. Onge remembers the days following the media stories.

Everything seemed to snap into place. It felt like a thing already existing once, maybe in another life, just needing to be reassembled. We could never go back to what we had before the *Record Sun* feature.

The phone, for one thing; it seemed to burst. Reporters from big out-of-state papers and magazines. A couple of TV producers wanting to do specials or *segments*. Radio talk-show hosts inviting Gordon to go speak about our lives as separatists.

"Aren't they afraid of all the stockpiled AKs and tanks and such?" wondered our Eddie Martin, with one of his happy chortles.

Gordon said no to all the media calls. But then there were calls he was thrilled with. People interested in joining the solar-wind community, or the furniture cooperatives, or the CSAs, or all three, in hopes of restoring interdependence in their economically and socially devastated little towns.

Gordon loved these calls but was now tied to the phone a good part of each evening.

We got a few weird calls, people saying goofy things or making dangerous noises.

The mail increased to six times what it had been before. This included media people, who, finding the phone's busy signal a challenge to their patience, *wrote* to ask for interviews.

Funny, not one educator wrote to speak for or against our philosophy. But the editorial pages of the *Record Sun*, even the editorial pages of other papers, were loaded with letters that decried the fact that our children were not pushed into competitive mode, not aiming for high scores and "excellence." They insisted these children would pay later. They said that not to prepare kids for the highly competitive workplaces of the global economy and institutions of higher learning was irresponsible, even cruel. Some said they weren't against homeschooling *if* it was state-monitored.

A week later, letters were still appearing in the papers. Some called the Settlement a *labor camp* and *brute school*. Several insisted that authorities should "get those children out."

"They don't even have flush toilets!" one letter gasped.

We heard some of the radio talk shows, hashing over whether or not the FBI should be brought in. I remember one talk-show host who was really angry at this suggestion, and, while cutting this caller off in mid-word, said gravely, "Let's keep this conversation out of the realm of the absurd." And right then, a caller got through who ran a small private school up on the coast that worked with principles similar to ours in the

areas of reading and writing. With the deep kindly *patient* voice of reason, she explained that forcing children to read too early will just turn
them off, that before the age of seven they are often still in the motor
stage and need to master any hands-on skills at that time joyfully. She
called the special ed experience a "social crucifixion, especially in the anti-
social competitive atmosphere most schools create."

Then her beautiful strong patient voice was gone, replaced by shrill
ones, all sorts of memorized propaganda about the importance of singling out *special children* and *honor students,* and the word *excellence* was
repeated so often that the hiss of all those *x*'s and *c*'s was starting to give
me a kind of migraine.

On that same show, there came the inevitable. A caller reported that
he had heard things about Gordon, that Gordon was a pedophile. That
there were stockpiled weapons, drugs, pagan worship. The radio host
made no comment except "thanks for your call," and then another caller
said we were Fundamentalist Christians and Jew-haters. The next caller
used the word *Nazis.* The talk show host himself called us *separatists.*
The next caller said, "They are not allowed outside their gates. Only in
chaperoned groups, especially the women . . . *his* women."

There was mention of a possible group suicide and a probable siege
with government agents. The host challenged this statement by asking,
"Are *you* the FBI? How do you come by this knowledge?"

One very low-voiced man, a kind of Boris Karloff sound-alike, spoke
of his "knowledge" that very little girls at "that school" were pregnant.

"Truly amazing," the talk-show host said, in an "oh, wow!" way. His
disgust was gone now. He seemed to be drunkenly resigned to the titil-
lating turn his show had taken.

Days passed. People started coming around to the Settlement in person. Some said they had trouble finding us. But they found us.

One night, I came upon Gordon and his cousin Aurel arguing. Some
of what Gordon snarled out was in French.

But Aurel was *all* French. Valley French. Ah, those Acadian swoop-
ing *R*s! With a few English words like *fuck you!* and *idiot!* and *Ivy
Morelli.* Mostly Aurel raged at Gordon, and Gordon just tried to deflect. He said it would have happened eventually anyway, and he was
sorry. But his sorrys weren't soft, they were yelled. And the two of
them paced around like cats with their backs prickled up.

Meanwhile, as ever, there was so much work to be done here. Gordon and Paul Lessard and Ray Pinette and Eddie Martin and Glennice, all of them who were in the co-op and CSA stuff, they were either in huddles with strangers, answering mail or talking on the phone. Gordon was mostly missing his meals.

One of these mornings, Gordon came late for breakfast to the piazza and slumped down at the head of the two long joined tables, all the seats empty, everyone gone off to their jobs. He was rubbing his face and eyes, a slow self-massage, a self-soothing.

I sat down next to him without pulling my chair in.

You, crow, superintending the new day, shift easily on your roost of the topmost triangular green-Popsicle color plate of Tyrannosaurus rex's mighty wooden head. No Settlement children presently peer out through the teeth (two-by-sixes painted white).

You have a special interest in Claire St. Onge. She leaves dry corn for you just outside the windows of the interestingly small ice-shack-sized sunroom off the east side of her cottage. Everything so cramped, too cozy, stuffed with baskets, notebooks, picture books showing tools and weapons of people gone so long they preside only in the ore layer, lava and ledge, pressed like souvenirs. Or in the tannic-soggy peat pools, where some fell in and drowned and those who loved and missed them fell elsewhere, fell and fell and fell. Some might be in museums alongside stuffed crows.

Also in Claire's sunroom is a tea table carved from basswood in the shape of a table-sized mushroom, which you often admire through the glass.

But nobody is home at the little cottage. Claire is here in the midst of Settlement life. You hear her voice in one of the piazzas of the shops. You love that voice, which calls you Crow but in the old language of the Passamaquoddy. She is not speaking your name now but his, the towering one, Gordon St. Onge, there beyond the checkered shadows of screen. Both are talking of less interesting things than dried corn.

You know the woman loves the man who sits beside her, each in a straight wooden chair. But who would guess? The face of Claire St. Onge is ever so stark of expression, eyes leveled on whoever or whatever it is that turns her head. Reflections of the kettles and dippers, and the many strewn Settlement-made ceramic plates and cups painted a pretty egg-nog yellow, purl and flurry on the glass parts of her specs. A dimple by her mouth once seemed girlish; now, at age fifty, it increases her severity with a look of clenching jaw.

She is short while standing, short while sitting. And fat. Not pudgy. Not chubby. Not stocky. But fat. Her long graying black hair, often worn up and out of the way, sometimes with Swiss-looking embroidered sewing-shop trim or a barrette, is free today. It forks partly over one mighty arm and mighty breast, partly down her back. Her work shirt is pale chambray and tight. Her wedding ring is silver and plain as are the rings of all the St. Onge wives, none etched, knurled, or exclusive.

She raises her chin, staring off flatly into a chaotic memory. With her old steel-rimmed glasses (found in a trunk with ancient tools?) she possesses that sepia dignity of all 1800s people preserved in frames today as they waited then for the photographer's black-powder flashes.

Beside her at the table (empty of other breakfasting Settlementers), the towering one's face lurches through dozens of expressions. In a photo of any era, he would blur or be caught with one or both eyes closed, the illusion of no mouth or two mouths. Claire and Gordon. Such a pair! And truly in years past, they were only a pair, not this branching out, thicker tree of their current lives.

☆ **In a future time, Claire remembers more of that morning.**

Through the nearby doorway into the Cooks' Kitchen there was yipping and yowling like coyotes, the breakfast clean-up crews in true form. Mostly teens long-leggedly galloping by with bins or trays, a few smaller helpers trailing along asking squeaky questions and carrying a real big spoon or towel. I forgot which kid it was who patted me on the head, but it was Heather who kissed me on the head as she passed by with a wet rag in each hand. Heather was twelve. You see, it was their little joke about how I had become much shorter. Actually, *they* had grown too tall for me to kiss or pat *them* on the head anymore.

Glennice pushed a ceramic cup of coffee toward Gordon's hand and offered to take mine and refill it, but I was done.

I looked sideways at Gordon's eyes, swollen, almost purpled from no sleep. "You're damn late," I said.

He took my hand.

I sighed.

He said, "Do you think it'll let up some, all these people? Think they'll lose interest in a while?"

"I don't know. But this is more than we can handle, even the co-op stuff—especially the co-op stuff." I hugged myself. It could have been fall. Cold mountain smells moved foggily with the smells of cold eggs and smoky meat grease.

He released my hand.

I made a teasy face at him. "You don't want to hear that, do you?" I pulled my chair a tad closer, nearer to his warmth.

His chin was up, collars open. He was in a sort of heat.

"Somebody I know is always saying that nobody can save the world. Let me see. . . ." I pretended to search my memory. "He sometimes back-slides. But mostly he's been pretty committed to the idea of doom."

He looked so suddenly into my eyes, it made my insides hop. He grinned.

I was trying not to smile. "Years ago he—this man I know—he said the world of humans was a bucket of maggots." I tried to make my voice deep. "A bucket of maggots."

His grin stretched wider, twisted, overcrowded bottom teeth and straight uppers. Eyes. His whole head. Too merry. He said, "Who is this dude, some crank?"

I could see my young Gordon in the shifting but honest eye of my memory. More colt than stallion. A redneck bookworm in his off hours from the mighty DePaolo construction biz. I liked my history texts sunny-side up. He dove into the cold sea of the total human life story. In those days, I feared he would hang himself. Now, on the big porch, I sighed. "He was young. But his words were not frivolous. Civilizations always end in starvation, tree stumps, washaway soils, madness."

He looked away. He seemed to be admiring the near mountain behind the Quonset huts. I'm sure what he was seeing was free energy for everyone, old and new inventions, spinning, humming, booming, including some of his latest rambling about random jitter, microscopic lightning, electromagnetic energy, zero-point energy—endless energy, enough to purify water—to undo the crisis of the modern age.

I laced my fingers together in my lap primly. In those early days of our marriage I knew that to love him meant I too would dive deeply into that sea of the total story.

Then, in the 1980s he got the Settlement idea and threw himself into its creation like forty men. He never rested. He was tired, loud, and content.

But once we were not an idea but *the Settlement,* and the place was full of kids and our own history unfolding, and food was stored and spring water bubbled and celebrations became traditions, there was time for study again. Time to look outward. Time.

So now, there at the table in the cool leafy morning, sun striking the yellow coffee cup near my hand, I murmured, "I just tend to my chores now. And my little job at the university. Correct papers. Trudge on."

He frowned.

"I can't go back and forth so fluidly as you do, my love," said I.

He rubbed his face some more. Rubbed his hair, his ears. Yawned big.

"But I'm okay. It's okay. Really."

"I'm sorry." His eyes were so pale in those Black Irish Italian French Indian dark lashes. Their violet exhaustion overtook my own.

"Don't be sorry. You know when I left you and went to live with Danny and then came back, I wasn't running *from* Danny. I was running *toward* you. I am not going to say anything mean about Danny except that in this world where we find ourselves struggling to understand, Danny was . . . ah . . . well, he's a plastic light-up Halloween pumpkin and you are Portland Headlight."

Gordon snorted.

In the kitchen a *clang!* and a teen boy voice, "Watch out!" A few shouts of emergency. Then cheering.

"Right now I'm in a place of hope," Gordon said apologetically.

I didn't look into his face but at another memory, one of his other faces. The time our friends from Waterville showed up with a Panamanian whose name we took an hour to learn to pronounce right. It was a winter evening. The man, part Mayan, part African, part European, was dressed like Maine, a knitted red-and-green Pierre cap and huge socks.

He told of how two years before, in order to permanently replace the military of Panama with "North American" military, and to "possess my country," the city where he lived was leveled "in the night, just before Christmas by 'North American planes,'" and his brother, a labor union official, was executed. "Many executed. Professors of the university. Priests. People of the assembly." He had later helped "shovel open" the mass graves "where the North American soldiers dumped the bodies."

He and the others wore masks and bagged the bodies. He said people were wailing "when they recognized a little dress or maybe the watch on the rotted wrist with no hand." He said, "Four thousand people at Christmas mashed by tanks—some as already dead bodies, some wounded and alive—and many executed or bombed. One got melted by some horrible weapon. My friend, he saw. Maybe laser? Whole person turn to blood like hemorrhage of every blood vessel."

Gordon's face had tightened. Then it went ice white.

Later, we walked our guests out to the snowy parking lot. This was around 1991, and we waved good-bye as our friends' newish ballooned-out-looking pickup truck swept away. Gordon stayed out there in the dark as if for a smoke, but he wasn't a smoker. Last I saw him that night, he was leaning against the fender of one of the Settlement rigs, stargazing, arms across the hood.

Yes, sympathy hurts. But rage hurts too, if it can't leap out to strike. More times than countable I saw him face these discoveries, rage, and then back off from what he couldn't do, beat to death the "octopus of U.S. power" or go beyond that into the stratosphere of banks, that "system of faceless unrestrained international mammoneering"—also his words.

That expression of his every time. Bloodless with the agony of restraint, bearded over darkly with his youth, then graying frostily on the chin through the years, and now even grayer.

Yeah, years went on, and here I was looking into the face once again of Mr. Sunshine.

Shouldn't I have been relieved? No, I felt disgust. His face, the farawayness of this aspect, this expression of hope was dazy and—well, it was gooey. Like pie in the sky. Like a man sucked whole into Amway or church. His bucket-of-maggots outlook gave him a grown-up eminence. This is the paradox: Is happiness only for the newborn? the brain dead?

the self-deceiving plastic Halloween pumpkin lighted by a four-watt bulb?

☆   **In a future time. Among the papers sneaked out by
    government agents during one of the Settlement's
    public events is this overly-fondled-by-authorities
    excerpt from a carbon-copied letter written by Gordon
    St. Onge to a friend. It reveals his preoccupation with
    the end of the world.**

*World peace? Sure. When there's nothing left but ultraviolet lint and hot
pond scum and radioactive microspawn, then there will be world peace.*

☆   **Claire recalls the August Sunday, a couple weeks
    following the *Record Sun* feature.**

We always encouraged people of the community to join us for our Sunday meal, to bring a dish if they could, to bring musical instruments, to share stories—a lotta old stories here in Egypt—and yes, we shared gossip. But even with all the Good Neighbor Committee's flyers posted around town and on windshields, we never got more than a dozen Sunday guests, unless it was the summer solstice. Fine. It was sweet. We were content.

But one Sunday after we got famous, something different happened. Long before noon, coming up the Settlement road, we could see unfamiliar cars. They parked. Some of these visitors got out but just stood there. Then more cars, a dozen more, then more. And more. They parked in the lot, along the gravel road, and they parked in the fields where our last crop of hay had been standing, mashing it flat.

Quickly, some of our people had gone out to meet them, redirecting cars out of the hay fields. Mostly, these visitors were not local people. More and more were arriving every minute, but just as many were leaving, driving slowly away. They hadn't come for the meal but just to get a look. "To gawk," as Settlementer Paul Lessard called it.

Gordon was not one of those who went out to the road to welcome the visitors. He sat at a table, off to one side, with his back to a screen, waiting for food to be brought out to the piazzas by the kitchen crew. Some of the men at his table were talking in French. He seemed to be listening, but he offered nothing. Food came; he ate. He chewed everything slowly.

Some of the strangers were coming up onto the porches, invited in by those of our emissaries who had gone out to greet them. A good-sized little mob of strangers, maybe thirty at first, then thirty more, came and found places at the tables, including tables on the adjoining piazzas. We got out every dish and bowl. Our almost-sacred solstice breakfast dishes, yeah, even those, normally reserved for that "soiree." Hand-painted. Mostly on yellow: windmills, smiling suns, animals, flowers, and funny-faced bugs. Only a few of these new people had brought a dessert or casserole. Our usual Sunday guests, attracted by the flyers, almost always brought food. But with this mob, the food we'd prepared wasn't stretching—and there still were *more* people straggling across the Quad. Bonny Loo and her crew were throwing together emergency soup, biscuits, and several pans of yellow cake.

More people came up the road. More people gathered on the Quad, out under the tall high-limbed trees, marveling at the dinosaurs and Martians, asking questions.

And more people left. A lot used camcorders and expensive-looking cameras from a distance, sweeping their lenses around as if taking in the scene of a publicized murder, then driving out fast, raising the blond dust.

As still more folks came up on the porches, most of them quite courteous and friendly, we would find them a place to squeeze in at a table. And they always recognized Gordon, so easy to pick out, a head taller than most of the other Settlement men he was sitting with, and like the AP photo (Ivy's, actually) by the merry-go-round, his devilish dark and gray beard and dark-lashed, pale, dangerous-looking eyes perhaps caused the visitors to feel a little pleasant thrill of fear. He did not rise up out of his seat to go and be gracious, and only a few went near him. This was neither Gordon as we knew him to be on a typical Sunday nor the Gordon of our breakfast talk a few days earlier, gooey and hopeful.

Usually when those few Sunday visitors arrived, he was all over them, pawing, teasing. And he might get a little drunk. Or *too* drunk, loud and foolish. During our sing-alongs, he'd beller all the words off key.

And after our history plays, he'd often do his dove whistle and stomp his feet and be the last to stop clapping. He might lead a group of guests and helpful Settlement kids up to the mountain to see the windmills. Sometimes he would take them up in a caravan of electric buggies and tractors. I remember him once leading the caravan, himself on one of the really small electric buggies, him with his knees up to his chin, a really oversized person on that thing, with a middle-aged visitor, a guy dressed in his best Sundays, clinging to his, Gordon's, waist like a motor-cycle mama.

Gordon loved people. But this? This was not part of his dream. This was media cheap. Now he whispered to me that it was going to get ugly before it got better.

I remember one guy who was with a little group of maybe two couples, two or three, I forget exactly. But I remember his face. He wore glasses and a golf cap of Christmas-tree green, real long narrow visor. He drank from a cup of coffee and watched our Barbara taking away some empty platters and dishes and his eyes slid to the shop doorways, the outside walls of the building shingled and stained dark brown, then the dangling bright mobiles of glass and pottery and wood. And he looked across the row of faces in deep chairs along one wall, old Mo and Helen and Annie B and Chlea, all of them with their mouths hung open, even Chlea, who is only in her thirties, but re-tarded, her lips thick and too bright, her eyes set with the Down's slant. Another woman, Vera, who had a couple of strokes the year before, could barely hold her head up, but on her lap was a sleeping toddler nearly naked, bare feet *very* dirty like little browned doggy paws. We were a mixed people. Not sorted, graded, or scored.

The man's eyes moved on, on to other faces, other surfaces of glass, wood, and screens with dappled sun. And flesh. How those sneering eyes violated my home!

After the crowds were gone, we found our nice leafy-smelling com-post toilets dripping and smeared like restrooms in a bar or roadside tourist stop.

Next morning, a seasonable August deep-bone chill, we didn't have the inside "winter kitchen" tables set for eating and wished we had.

We all munched breads and whatever was left of the eggs and cold chicken. There was no coffee. Everyone was in a kind of mortified hysteria, murmuring about the previous day. Gordon stood and spoke quietly, but we all heard him. We had all stopped whatever it was we were saying when we saw him push back his seat and wave his arm. He said, "No more ads and flyers for Sunday meals."

One of the kids of the Good Neighbor Committee called out, "But it wasn't the flyers that got all those people! It was the newspaper stuff!"

"Doesn't matter," Gordon said thickly, like he'd swallowed his arm or a shoe. "Those flyers give directions."

"Not fair!" called a really small squeaky child. A noble protest.

Gordon looked out into the cold morning, at the impressive wooden Tyrannosaurus rex, purple cow, and spaceship, the really tall high-limbed trees of the Quad, and back at the little kid who had spoken. His face was still expressionless, and unchallengeable. But his voice was kindly. "Let's try it for a while, Fiona. Till things calm down."

☆ Bonny Loo remembers.

A bunch of the older boys were sent down to make a gate, down where the dirt road comes in off the tar road. It was actually just two posts, with a removable pole across and a hand-painted sign: KEEP OUT.

Forty-eight hours later.

The *Record Sun* features a color photo on the back page, which is, of course, as highly visible as the front page. It shows a lovely shady woodsy dirt road with spots of sun and a horizontal sapling pole with a KEEP OUT sign tacked on it. The caption includes the words "separatists" and "barring intruders" and "their leader" and "seems more nervous" and there are words it does not exactly use, words between the lines, words implied, words aquiver, tantalizing, hot and bothered, words that are felt on the skin and beneath the skin of that great big anxious public.

This too goes AP, and within days the written words and the unwritten *felt* words are finding every household of the nation, yeah, this great big anxious nation. The name Gordon St. Onge is not a household word yet, but it has begun to ring a bell with quite a few.

Out of pain medicine again.

Britta Gammon, who is Mickey and Donnie's mother, is not always reliable, you see, because her sadness can sweep her away at any hour. But today she has made eggs, a big batch, and there's more greens, which Mickey has brought from militiaman Artie Mitchell's family's garden, although Britta doesn't know what to do with fresh greens and is right now boiling them to a slime.

She has always been "a lady" and yet too rough with her life and with things, like food and pans and plates. A tender hard person. She was a "Portland girl," she'll tell you proudly, with a *nice education*. "I'm not a kitchen type. Not some hag."

But *nice education* meant high school diploma. How quickly the bar was raised on that, eh? Now you need not just a diploma, but a bunch of degrees to be somebody.

Her dream was Boston, Boston rush, Boston civilization, and to have a kitchen with conveniences, a kitchen that didn't make you old. Yes, she had had good grades in school and the guidance counselor had urged her to take up nursing. How ugly! All that skin and stink and scabbiness and death.

"Be a stewardess!" her friend Maryanne suggested. A stewardess! Her pretty eyes. Her shape, her smile. And good grades, yes, the keys to escape. Her people were good people, but not people of the world. Not people of success. With good grades and pretty eyes, success is yours. The sky is the limit. Goodness is just milk and crackers, vanilla ice cream, flat, no better than death.

But success never comes to those of us who can't look people in the eye. Success goes to the bold and bubbly. The meek inherit only the quiet shelter of family.

This was before the world decided that family was an obstruction, another category of failure. And yeah, she loved hard, her first man (a boy really), Chucky . . . Chucky Locke and the family, the troubles, the excuses, the bills. Nice days too: the new washing machine that had a fluorescent light in it, the refrigerator that had shelves on the door, and the dryer and the dishwasher and everything in avocado or coppertone, and Chucky was a good man, quietly funny, drew a lot of people around for "games," beer and bowling and baseball and sometimes long drives to Boston, which she loved.

But there was the ruin of her teeth and then Chucky died, so there was Mark Gammon and Mark died hard while Mickey was small, and then David took her to Boston—well, very, very close to Boston—and how fast her new little girl babe arrived. The years were like moments, but somehow the days were long, the nights bad, and four different Massachusetts men, none of them dying, just politely packing up, and all along she had that wild hurt-in-the-gut homesickness and sad eyes.

Home. This is it. Finally. To make a meal of eggs and greens, to stare rudely and openly at the faces and profiles of your loved ones, that is the end of the race, home plate, atta go!

So here and now in this kitchen in Egypt, not so far from Portland, where she started out, she carries a plate of eggs and greens to the screen door and stands there and looks out at the yard as she eats and song bugs are creaking in the tall blond grass and the hillside is covered with Queen Anne's lace and goldenrod and something pink, phlox or something, and a car goes by and toots a hello, some old friend of Donnie's, and in the nearly evening sky there are no birds or planes, just a creeping coolness, and her sweater is green, which makes her eyes look almost green, and bustling through the kitchen, past her and out the door, the querulous gang of little girls, and she is thinking how even with this dying and struggle and the horrors of no money, she knows contentment at last. Contentment is never a part of success, is it? Success can only be a big eager smile. Contentment is here in the ashes of her dreams.

Behind her, Donnie and Mickey, the two half brothers, eat at the table.

Round-faced brown-haired Erika sits on the floor on a small gold, red, and green braided rug with her back against a cabinet door, her knees up, with bony two-year-old Jesse in her arms and he is whining oh, so softly, exhausted. He should be dead by now. But he is so young, his heart is as mighty and meaty as a discus thrower's. Little Jesse, center stage in this brightly lighted kitchen, this holy place, room of souls, old trivets on the wall, pastel potholders made by Erika's aunt, and . . . oh, yes, perhaps even more center stage than Jesse, perhaps more demanding than souls and meaty hearts, the tinny electronic voice of the kitchen TV and the other TV in the living room, which you can see through the little sunny hall there.

Where did the money go? you ask. How come they can't stretch their money better? You might demand to see figures in order to make your judgment. You see them there watching TV like the survivors of a bombing watch the glowing console of a radio for word of what they should do next. The TV has to know. It is the guardian of the Dream.

Donnie swallows some egg. He is always, under any circumstances, a solemn and gentlemanly eater. He says to Mickey in a matter-of-fact way, "'Twas hell at the Chain today." This means chain store, not chain gang, but once in a while Britta has heard him singing the *ooh! ah!*s of the fifties and sixties working-on-the-chain-gang song before he leaves for work, when he's knotting his tie, shaving his chin, or inspecting his shiny shoes.

Now he tells Mickey a few details, pressures from his five bosses. That's five bosses and one employee in that department. Employee works, bosses look in the mirror at themselves. But no chitchat. Talking *together* is policy-discouraged.

Travis is in the high chair, he the child of a neighbor who also works at the Chain, and there's no one else to look after him. He spends more and more time here in a kind of sad suspension; he can never be center stage because, unlike Jesse, he's not dying.

There's an explosion in the TV world: sirens.

Britta finishes her eggs and lifts Jesse from Erika's arms, and now Erika stands at the door, looking out at the scheming girl gang by the empty chicken house.

Seems the neighbor's baby, Travis, might be doing something in his diaper. He is jamming eggs with both hands through the nozzle of his covered training cup. He has a huge face, like a woodchuck. Donnie stares dreamily at the eggs in Travis's chubby hands; then he looks at the ceiling, eyes very wide, very blue—all Britta's children have that bright light gaze—and now he says, evenly and deeply, "I mean . . . i'twas *really* hell today at the Chain, Mr. Mickey G.," and he looks at Mickey, and Mickey looks sad and sympathetic, and Donnie leans toward him and touches the rim of Mickey's plate, an urgent gesture, and says, "Like—" But the dying child begins vomiting in Britta's arms, vomiting the few mouthfuls he managed to swallow in the last few hours, and probably Donnie never goes back to his thought.

The next evening, when Mickey comes home.

He senses right away the bad feel of the house, the hard edges of hurt. The first thing he sees is Donnie at the table with a new face. Walrus mustache gone. Face too pink. Face too bare.

The house makes the usual sounds. The TV, first and foremost. The two women talking in the back bedroom (it was a dining room years ago and has a curtain now across the archway), the girl gang shuffling around upstairs, the dog scratching upstairs, the neighbor's child, Travis, in his high chair again, plastic toys on the floor, nothing in his tray but a green and orange ooze. Matches what's on his face. And a cricket somewhere under the sink cabinet. *Creak! Creak! Creak!*

Mickey just stands there.

Donnie says, "Hey, Mr. Prince, what's up?"

Mickey lowers the bag of cukes to the clean counter and pushes it way back.

Donnie's eyes fix hard on the bag.

Mickey feels like Donnie is circling him, his back up, hair raised, circling, circling, sizing him up, sniffing his identity. Or is it Mickey who circles Donnie, circling, sniffing, challenging *him:* Mickey, who has always been so poor in school, whose grades and attitude don't please anyone. It was Donnie who was all *A*s and *B*s, who made their mother proud. *My boy is smart, the older one, Donald.* Seems those schooldays were the peak of Donnie's life, the sharp, clear, thin, beautiful peak. Who has his back up now? Maybe it is really Mickey who has started this.

Donnie speaks in a more friendly way, confiding. "They spoke to me at work. The regional management has a new policy: no facial hair. Clean shave is more *appropriate*. Wisdom from the Chain."

Mickey makes a face. "Buncha shitheads."

"Next comes teeth straightening and plastic surgery. Everyone gets the same face." This is supposed to be a joke.

But Mickey just squints.

Donnie swallows the sheer pain of this. "You know what it's *really* about. It's nothing to do with the customer, who could give a shit about my face."

Mickey nods.

Donnie swallows again. More pain to be put out of sight. Now with a bit of a squeak, he speaks. "It's about breaking us. It's like getting in our pants and squeezing, showing who's boss."

Britta steps from the curtained bedroom, digs in a drawer for a washrag. Runs it under the faucet.

Donnie pushes his empty dish away, reaches down for a plastic dinosaur, sets it on Travis's tray. Travis spanks the dinosaur with both hands, and off goes the dinosaur to the floor again.

Donnie says, "So, Mum, could you toss me coupl'a those cookies from the jar while you're over there?"

Britta ignores this. There are no cookies in the jar. This is just Donnie being sarcastic about the usual food shortage. She steps over to the high chair and slathers the washrag around Travis's chubby cheeks while he is leaning way forward, face down, to the right of his chair, pointing to the dinosaur.

Mickey especially avoids looking at Donnie's naked face. It's as if Donnie has his pants off. Or is caught in a lie.

Donnie asks, "What do you guys do over at those militia meetings anyway?"

Mickey is surprised, not by the fact that Donnie has found out but by the offhand way he's brought it up.

"Mostly just talk."

Donnie snorts happily, leans back in his seat, arms up over his head, thumbs coming together, and he kind of stretches as he looks around and sees how both his mother's face and Travis's face are aimed at the smiling faces on the TV—an ad for insurance—smiling faces, sugary music, and the word *protection* used five times. Donnie says, "Shit. I was hopin' you guys were getting ready to blow the fuckers away."

Mickey Gammon speaks.

It's almost eleven o'clock but she's still up, rocking him. Looks like she's holdin' a new baby, 'cept for his big feet sticking out . . . big skinny feet. She says, "Hey, little brother." And I give her the money and she takes the money and she looks me up and down, my face, my neck, my crotch. Then she looks away. And it's all over. The moment.

The thing she was thinking. Maybe it was the thing I think she was thinking, but just *thinking,* not doing, 'cause she ain't the affair type. Maybe it was just some weird flash, like all women get. Hot flashes.

She says, in a real cute way, "*Sure* you're not dealin' drugs?"

I just make a little spit sound. Like *yeah, right.* Like I would do such a thing. Which I haven't. 'Cause I ain't much of a salesman. You gotta be able to *talk* to deal. At least you got to say, "This stuff's a little seedy and has a lotta lumber, but it's all that's coming in now." Or "You again? I can't front you any more till you've paid up."

She's looking down at Jesse's foot with no expression now. I turn and head up the stairs to bed. I would never touch her. But I can go all night and a week thinking of her hands on me, how it would be. Shit. That's all, just imaginary fucking. Just like dealing reefer or dealing used cars, whatever. With gettin' a woman, you gotta be able to talk to get very far.

Erika at her clothesline.

Her older sister, Patti, and two strange women pull up in a small, newish, copper-color car. Patti's words come out carved and cool, words that can draw you in, gladly, for sales is what she's all about. She resembles Erika across the eyes, but she is neither pudgy nor wifely.

Patti makes the introductions. "This is Nan Bradley and Sass Hilare from church. This is my sister, Erika . . . Erika, we thought we'd stop by and see you . . . and the baby."

The churchwomen say they are very sorry to hear about the baby. Their church is not a fundamentalist damnation kind of church, nor a he-ain't-heavy-he's-my-brother kind of church. But a career-minded, positive-thinking church. Perfect for Patti. But these two women seem different from Patti.

Erika tells each one *hi.* Like her face and shoulders, Erika's voice is soft.

Nan and Sass and Patti are all holding gifts, a covered casserole or dessert and some packages wrapped in lavender tissue with elaborate polka-dot and silver-stripe bows.

The yard is too bright. Just one old oak tree, tall and lacking lower limbs, looking more like an elm. There's a path cut into the tall grass of the field by the barn, and also leading to the clothesline and its mowed rectangle. The clipped grass is stiff and prickly to Erika's bare feet. The lines droop with laundry, including sheets that have cartoon prints. Erika wears shorts. Legs pudgy, shaved, but not tanned. V-neck T-shirt, dark blue. Kids' bikes in the tall grass. A wheelbarrow full of water. Wildflowers. Bees. Erika squints. The visitors squint. Only Patti wears sunglasses, eyes wide and roving.

"How's the baby doing?" she asks cautiously. Patti always asks a lot of questions, which she appears to have no intention of hearing the answers to, but will look around at furnishings and floors as if guessing their value. She has always done this. Long before she was in home and commercial real estate. And there's her nonaccent accent, cultivated since high school. A few years ago, that generic accent made Patti seem peculiar. Now, today, she's among millions.

"Not very well," Erika tells her.

From the open windows there come rustlings and rumblings, a slam, the sound of ice in a glass, *pop pop pop pop pop* . . . a giggle . . . a *whooooosh* and, of course, the multiple TVs' tinny tweedles and little roars. The restless house breathes.

Erika picks a wet sock from the basket, pins it to the line, reaches for another.

The gifts wrapped in such summery paper and the casserole remain unoffered in the visitors' hands, spelling out that these are offerings for passage *into the house*.

Erika glances again at the two strangers, then goes for another sock. All three visitors are dressed like their gifts, pastel and summery. Nan is white-haired, fiftyish. Sass is young.

Patti asks, "Can we see him when you're done with your wash, Erika?"

"Well . . . yes . . . but he won't be friendly. He's not even eating."

Patti glances at the faces of her friends; behind her sunglasses, her eyes are just two meaningful gleams.

"So very sad," says white-haired Nan. "I'm truly sorry."

Erika turns and looks at her, a blinking single nod.

Patti tells on her sister. "They've decided to refuse treatment."

"Yes," says the white-haired woman, which means this has already been discussed prior to their arrival.

Patti says, "They just decided to hope for the best."

Erika feels for a twisted pink pajama top.

Patti says, "They are not Christian Scientists. That's not it. They are just—" She cuts herself off, meaningfully. Her eyes are on her sister's back, the oversized navy T-shirt, pudgy shoulders, the bra line cutting into the extra pudginess of her back. "They have just decided to let him go."

Erika says nothing. She fetches another pastel sock and a handful of washcloths.

"You mentioned before that they don't have insurance," the young Sass offers quickly. The armholes of her dress are cut deep into the shoulders and her arms are tanned and shapely. Not a churchy dress. Her hair is in a blonde Pebbles do. Not churchy hair.

Patti replies, "Well, yes."

Sass says, "With the way things are these days, seems most people don't have insurance."

"It's nothing to be ashamed of," says the white-haired Nan kindly. "My daughter doesn't have health insurance either."

The young Sass nods energetically.

This conversation: third person all the way, like Erika isn't around. But, after all, she is keeping her back to them, isn't she?

Patti looks at the house. Her eyes sweep over to the Lockes' car, parked near the kitchen door. "Where is Donald, not at work?"

Erika says, "Tuesdays he's nights."

Patti's sunglasses turn toward her friends. "The hospital would treat him whether they have insurance or not. They wouldn't turn a child away. I called them myself and they said Erika and Donald only need to apply for a red card and MaineCare."

"It's true," says Sass. "A hospital wouldn't be that mean to turn you guys away."

Erika turns and puts her eyes wide on each of them. "Yeah?" Then goes back to pinning washcloths.

"They'll let you charge it," says Sass eagerly. "Unless you are *real* poor, then the hospital part is free if you aren't eligible for MaineCare. But Jesse himself is probably eligible, even if you aren't. He's under eighteen. Even so, you only have to pay the doctor, maybe. And probably anesthesia if . . . you know . . . if *that* is necessary."

Erika pins the washcloths slowly. She does not want them in her house. She does not want them in her yard. But Erika is a soft person, not one to offend.

"Maybe you could save him!" Sass urges. "Maybe it's not too late."

Patti sneers. "My sister is a conspiracy theorist. There's all this rumor among her friends that the hospitals are grabbing people's houses. Or the state is. Or something."

"Oh, the state wouldn't do *that,*" says Nan.

"We have friends," says Erika without turning, "who the hospital *said* they put a lien on their house. And MaineCare too."

"Probably a bluff," says Patti with a chuckle. "Playing on their *ignorance*."

Sass's voice gets a little thrill to it. "Oh, Erika, why don't you call now? Every minute matters."

"Because," says Patti, "my sister is stubborn and. . . ." She picks fretfully at the yellow bow of her gift. She stares deeply into this bow and says, "This whole discussion is disgusting."

Sass says softly, "They really won't take the house, Erika."

"And so what if they did!" snaps Patti. "It's just a piece of real estate!"

"Maybe she can mortgage the house," Nan suggests. "They don't have to sell it."

Erika hangs another washcloth carefully. There's the rustlings of the children inside the house, those who will still be alive next year. She says, "Jesse would die even *with* treatments."

Patti laughs. "He has a ten-percent chance!"

Erika speaks only to the striped pink and white washcloth and two clothespins. "A five-percent chance of living five more years."

A car passes. The horn toots. Friends of Donnie's.

Patti sighs. "They could discover a miracle in five years."

"They?" Erika asks the dark sock she is now hanging.

Patti's eyes behind her sunglasses are unseen. Her voice comes out like a cheery TV ad. "Erika acts like her own baby is just a piece of furniture. It . . . it is hard for me to understand. Five years of time, Erika! Five precious years! But oh, no, you are not looking at five years as precious. You sit there juggling numbers like your child is just a card game or lottery . . . or something. My God!"

"I do not want him in *this* world," Erika's voice says firmly, into a long stunned silence. She finishes with the last washcloth, turns, and sees Donnie in the doorway in his old sweatpants, blue with white double stripes on the outsides of each leg. And gray T-shirt. She has two fantasies right now. One, that Donnie will keep filling that door, like a brave soldier, and keep *them* out. He will not be his usual wishy-washy self and let people walk over him. He looks so strong from this distance, even without his mustache. The way he stands, the hard fed-up look in his eyes. She imagines he is who she once thought he was.

And she imagines Jesse as he actually was six months ago. Standing in the kitchen. His sly, mischievous, fun little white-baby-teeth grin, cheeks blooming with perfect health, pointing up at his half sister, Elizabeth, who would be fixing his Barney cup with Kool-Aid, and he says, "Mine is reddy," which means either *ready* or *very red*. Even his mistakes seemed so smart. And his delight with everything. His delight: yeah, it was from the same place forgiveness is made. And no one else's forgiveness matters.

Next day, suppertime.

Little girls stand at the table and pick from plates. There's enough chairs, but they don't use them. Elizabeth, the oldest, says "I want one of those" as she watches the parade of products on TV. Donnie says, "Sit down. You're not a cow." He says this only to Elizabeth, his seven-year-old daughter by his first marriage, singling her out. She gives him the finger.

Mickey comes in from somewhere, screen door thwacking, and sees the finger raised and then Donnie standing with his coffee by the refrigerator, tie loosened, top shirt-button unbuttoned, but his light-color hair still neat. And on Donnie's bare, pink, hairless face, a look. Full-blown fury. And Donnie's eyes slide over to Mickey's proud light-stepping walk, the knees, the T-shirt that reads BLAME IT ON EL NIÑO, the slim hips.

Neither Erika nor Britta have seen the finger. And so they don't know of it, and they don't see Donnie's face, nor the brace of his shoulders.

Mickey prances over to Erika and taps her shoulder. She turns from the pan of stewed tomatoes, big spoon in her hand, and into her free hand he presses a wob of money and she breathes, "Thank God."

And Britta. She coos.

So Mickey is standing between Donnie and Erika, and he reaches for a glass from the drainer and Erika pushes the money into the front pocket of her shorts, against that warm place near the hip bone, and Britta is looking up at the side of Mickey's face, at the pale, very soft, very sparse beard appearing there, and the glass slips from Mickey's fingers and smashes into the sink and this gives Donnie's right arm a life of its own. Fist smacks Mickey hard. Mickey's mouth looks instantly thick and bright.

"Donnie!" both women howl, for they are absolutely shocked, this being the first time Donnie Locke has ever struck anyone or anything.

And two of the girls burst into tears, two of the four who live here, while the two neighbor girls slink toward the door.

"Tense! Tense!" Donnie hollers. "Fucking tense, okay?"

Silence from the corner, the pallet of blankets where dying Jesse lies, breathing in an odd way.

Mickey doesn't shout back at his brother, nor does he cry, nor does he cringe, nor does he leave the room, but just goes over to the table and sits, facing the TV, which is showing a pale rerun of a large boisterous family living a lite life.

Breakfast of champions.

Early morning. All the TVs are on, two downstairs, two upstairs. All with the news, three different networks flickering with high-tech efficiency, more efficient than God. Or at least equal to God in its power to bend the knee.

Donnie is in a kitchen chair, T-shirt and jeans, bare feet, legs stretched out, eyes faithful to the screen. Reportage on a trial. Ads. Urban crime. Ads. Welfare "reform." Ads. Tax "reform." Ads. A plane crash with forty-four dead. Ads. A weirdo less-than-human man eats his sexually assaulted boy victims. Ads.

Summer presses on and on at the screened windows and door. Humidity and miles of weedy-smelling flowers, miles of crickets creaking in pauses and crescendos, a rhythm innate and old and creepily genius. And a car passes.

Donnie's day off, so he can let his mustache grow for one day, but its blondness keeps it invisible.

Mickey comes down from his little attic room, wearing a fresh but wrinkled T-shirt. A camo print. The militia look. Jeans. Sneakers with double lacings and his light, proud, catlike walk. And his mouth, still swollen. Bruised berry-blue. A badge. Smacked mouth has given him more arrogance, not less. And his beard shows more now, a bit reddish.

No women. No kids. Only the old deaf dog and Mickey and Donnie.

Donnie keeps his eyes on the TV screen, one bare foot rubbing the dog's back.

Mickey finds one of the brand-new boxes of cold cereal in the cupboard just as that very same brand of cereal explodes full-blown onto the TV screen, golden flakes raining from above into a bowl, then bluish milk and a lot of high-feeling music. Mickey picks open the box, which is glued too well, and it rips.

Back to the news. Music is just as high-feeling as the cereal music.

Mickey pours a bowl of flakes. Fetches the milk—milk he has provided with his own earnings. He settles at the table to eat. Donnie and Mickey both watch an update on the "drug crisis" in America. Drugs. Guns. Victims. A three-year study. Experts speaking from their desks before walls of books. And a spokesman at a microphone telling the whys of the president's "crime bill." Mickey munches. Donnie's jaw twitches.

♡♡ Going to the discount store, six-and-a-half-year-old Jane Meserve speaks.

I wear my new dark pink sunglasses. Dark pink is where you see out through. White is around the edges, which are plastic, shaped like two hearts. And I wear my best earrings, which are like Manda Blake's on the news. Gordic has dark glasses too, but just plain. Not heart shapes. His have metal around them with gray tape stuff to fix where they broke once. But he only wears his for when he is driving into the sunshine.

The discount store is called ROBBINS because it's their garage fixed up, it's in East Egypt and Gordic says this is my last chance. He says, "Tantrums do not turn me on." If I ask for ONE LITTLE THING, he will hate me. And I will not be "allowed" in a store "till the end of time."

You would not believe all the piles of stuff *he* buys. Screws and wires and little metal-shape things. And he is really friendish with all the people at the store. He laughs and they laugh and there's jokes and weird mental talk about "sole electricity" and "passion sole" and some companies everybody hates who send you bills which have made us "too dependent and helpless." All so boring.

I take off my dark glasses. I just go around and look at stuff. This stuff is cheap, called *regulars* and *overloads*. It's good stuff, not just nails. I pick up some sheer lip gloss and feel it. And some Profusion, which there's only one bottle left and has a ripped label. On a big spinning thing are earrings, and there is a two-sided comb that would be so easy for Gordie to buy if he noticed my sad eyes.

Mum has always told me she likes to have a guy with style. Ha! Gordie is definitely out of the picture there. Mum would definitely laugh her head off if Gordie said, "Will you marry me, Lisa?" with his hairy mouth, roundish throat, roundish body, working boots, and junky old truck. *And* gray tape on his sunglasses.

Mum always says my dad named Damon Gorely is very beautiful with a very pretty shirt and a nice car and a million CDs of the best music, and stuff in his apartment, neat stuff like big speakers and wall-to-wall rug and dishwasher and his phone does everything, like it can take five calls at once and *trace*. He is to be famous someday in rap. I like his pictures. He is a gorgeous hunk. You would agree.

Gordie is of the white color like Mum. My dad is of the black color like me. Except I'm more of a middle color. Like a gypsy queen. That's what Mum says. And I know someday I'll be on TV and people will look at me and won't believe their eyes, because I am prettier than other girls and people always stare and stare at me. On TV I'll get to wear long earrings and see-through-ish outfits or outfits that twinkle or outfits made of white fur stuff. And I'll put my tongue over my lips like this and men will die.

♡♡ **Jane Meserve visits her Mum. Jane speaks.**

Claire St. Onge is Gordie's X-wife. Claire is fat. She is as round as a balloon. She was an Indian once. She lived with all the other Indians at a place called an Indian Township. She usually wears boots, like Gordie. She has very straight hair, part gray, which she wears fixed on her head with plain pins or in a clip so her hair is long and swingy. Also she wears glasses that make her eyes wiggle-ish. She is short, like a little kid almost. I am almost taller and I am only six years old!

Claire is a lady of history, knows all the stuff of an olden age. She goes to be a real teacher at a university but only on one day, Wednesday. She says she is an *a-junk*. Probably because she has a special interestedness in historyish clothes and stuff like cruddy old pots and pans and knives and arrows. She has some pictures and she has some real examples. The examples have rust, I think. Yuk. Gordie calls Claire "our history expert."

Claire has two ways she talks. One way is LOUD. The other way is whisperish and she makes her voice very interesting and scary, and the stuff she tells you is secrets. Also she *winks*. All the kids think she's cool and they love to do stuff for her and help her with going on trips to Ivy Leegs and lug boxes and all the kitchen stuff too. She calls them "my slaves."

Today Claire took me to see Mum. And Mum loved my new sunglasses with the pink heart shapes for the parts that go over your eyes. Mum said, "*Where* did you get those great heart glasses?"

I said, "Stuart gave them to me." Stuart is ONE OF THEM.

Mum said, "Jane, you know what those are? Those are secret agent glasses . . . which have special powers of vision!" She seemed especially happy about these glasses. She said SPECIAL POWERS OF VISION.

I said, "I don't think so, because I only see regular through them. But dark. And pink."

She said, "But baby, you will have special viewing powers *at times*. Suddenly, you'll see what no regular eyes can see. So you can be a top-notch secret agent."

The place where we had to sit to visit Mum is where the copguards make you sit. The chairs fold up if you don't sit too still. They are metal and sort of beige. There were kids and people in the other room, which is where all the rest went, but we were in a special room, which was so whisperish you could hear the copguards' clothes being scratchy. Beige chairs look mostly pink through these special glasses. And the really awful orange suit Mum was wearing looked hideous with *and* without my special glasses, but she just laughed when I asked what other colors she could get. Also, people and walls looked pink to me. The whole day was pink. You can't see yellow or white when you have pink glasses. I asked Mum, "What is a secret agent?"

"A spy!" she said cheerishly.

When Claire was gone a minute in the hall, to talk with a copguard who she says *has rank,* Mum explained that I could be a spy at Gordie's place and watch people and then write stuff down in a really small black book, everything they did, what they looked like and stuff and what they said. Then I could report back to Mum and tell her what I have in the black book.

She said, "From now on, don't call me Mum. Call me Headquarters."

One of the copguards sitting at his own table practically beside us heard this, and he frowned.

I told her I would most definitely keep an eye on every one of them, but then I said, in a voice of misery so Mum will know I hate them at Gordie's, I said how I miss her and how when I am in bed at night I think of her and how very pretty she is. But Mum just smiled. And the copguard turned a different way so there was all this scratching sound of his pants and arms. And Claire came back smiling. Everybody very cheerish.

This made me mad.

Mum said, "As of today, Jane Miranda Meserve is hereby sworn in as Official Secret Agent One-one-one."

After a while, I asked if there was a soda machine or one for chips and candy. But Mum said, "Not in this place, Jane. In this place, they consider everything a weapon."

I sort of laughed. I looked at the copguard, but he was turned a little to see people walking by in the hall. He had a gun. I said to Mum, "I like your outfit." It was actually more hideous than a dead vegetable, but you want to always be nice to your mum and never say stuff she wears looks gross.

Mum laughed and looked down at herself, then back at me. I decided not to mention her hair, which is always blonde with extra streaks for beauty. But now she has a plain ponytail like usually just for bed or to be sick. And usually she wears lipstick, red, called Glamourpuss or Scarlett O'Hara. Not now. Behind these glasses all Mum's beautifulish parts look sad and pink.

And I said, "So where is Cherish? Who's babysitting for *her?*"

Mum said, in a funnyish way, "Oh! Cherish ran away to a farm! She really always wanted to live on a farm where she could dig for rats and mice."

I squinched my eyes behind my secret glasses. *She is lying. Something is wrong with Cherish. Something very bad has happened. To Cherish.* But I made my voice sweet and dopey. "Why can't me and her just both stay at Gordie's? There's cows and stuff at Gordie's. *And* guess what! There's another Scottie at Gordie's. Named Cannonball. Kind of mean. Bites. But Cherish won't mind. They could dig rats and be friends."

Mum's voice was still weird. A voice of lies. With secret glasses, lies have a special sound, high and whiny. "I know . . . but Cherish . . . you know how she was! She always made up her own mind and stuck to it. She really *had* to check out the other farm. She wouldn't listen to anybody else's suggestions. Maybe she'll get tired of it and come back. Later."

Through these secret glasses, Mum's face was starting to look wavery. "Mum, when are you coming home?" My neck hurt.

Mum said, "Soon."

"How soon?" I asked.

"I don't know."

"Mum." I didn't scream or run to hug Mum. I almost did. But I had strong willpower so I just sat there cool as a cucumber and said, "How come I can't stay here?"

"You can't."

I take a deep deep DEEP breath and then push breath slowishly out out out out. "Why can't you come out and just visit?"

"I would if I could, but I can't."

I look at her so hard, her beautiful hair and her lips.

"Can't you just come home for one single day?"

"No," said Mum.

♡♡ That night in bed, Secret Agent Jane begins her career. Jane speaks.

I am in my bed at Gordie's house. Gordie says it's okay if I keep the light on all night, even though he wants to NOT WASTE.

NOT WASTE is one of the big rules.

I wear my secret agent glasses even for night because I might need to see something in a special way.

♡♡ Secret Agent Jane finds out *more*. She speaks.

Over the week I got a lot of information which I would never have got without these special glasses. Mostly, I hide behind doors. If the doors are open, I stand off to the edge. Also, I sit real quiet. This is always when they think I'm somewhere else. I have information of both Gordie's house *and* the Settlement, which is plenty of houses called shops, and I've been in them all. I've decided to do mostly pictures in my secret book. Spelling's too hard when you are in a rush.

Gordie is mean and makes me go up there to the Settlement place A LOT. Also, Claire is mean. Bonny Loo is mean. Bev is mean. Barbara is mean. They make me go up there when they KNOW I like it here at Gordie's house better . . . except there's no food here at Gordie's. Just what they bring.

I can tell they are trying to get me to LOVE all those kids at the Settlement and those people, but they are wrong. I'm not falling for it. Guess what. I actually saw somebody's lips actually say, "Oh, Jane. Your school is right here. It's School with a Plus!"

Right. It's so sick. Would you call *this* a school? Babies that suck are everywhere. Chickens that walk with people and peck at your shoes. Old ladies who are nuts. Loud ugly men. One has *no eyes*. One kid has a big bulge on his hand and a broken arm which might smell if I smelled it. The man named Oh-RELL sings loud to himself. One old *wicked*-old lady never talks, just always pats you. The guy Oh-RELL talks in a language. And his singing is awful. He will *never* be famous.

At meals which last for hours—yes, HOURS—kids and people make plays they call skits. For one of the skits we got all fixed up, but I can tell you, it was not beautiful. I wanted to do a sexy dance, but the other kids said that SEX would not fit that kind of play, wait till another one. I wanted to sing "Baby Stands Before Me," but they said it didn't fit.

They all dressed in robes and wigs and masks and head things. At rehearsal, a bunch of them fought over the Thomas Jefferson mask and the mother named Gail said we could make twenty Thomas Jefferson masks later, but for now we had to draw a name and leave it to odds. Some kids were putting lipstick under their eyes. This was blood, they said, for Valley Forge. Some kids just wanted to look terrible and carry guns. These are the boys, of course. And one girl, one big weird girl.

But all the rest are boys. They carry guns or stick spears or sword things or knives or clubs. They said they were "The Hydra mob. The true heroes of the people." But why do the girls try to be ugly too? Like, a teenager named Samantha wore a white yarn wig and pilgrim outfit like a man pilgrim and she had wire made into fake glasses. She was going to be a "Father of the Constitution." She laughed and said, "It was our first NAFTA." The rest of them just wanted to be army or mobs. There was nothing pretty to be.

Samantha told me to be John Adams.

I said, "GROSS!"

She said, "Just say the John Adams stuff, okay? You can dress whatever way you want." She said this sad and sweet like she was talking to an animal. I made my eyes squinty.

So the boys did the war part, dying and screaming and poking each other on the head. Mostly girls were Fathers of the Constitution, and one boy, Evan—who is cute if it weren't for the worst pimples—he said Thomas Paine stuff and dressed in pants that didn't fit him and an actual antique coat. Others wore practically nothing in order to be sailors and slaves. They used purple paint to make whip marks and "scars from the sea." They said their best thing was fire and they said a poem called "Tiger Burning Bright," which is about slaves, and they yelled "Yo mateys!" and "Ahoy!"

Then it was my turn. I was the stupid John Adams. I had put my lipstick on my lips in a beautiful sex way and patted my lips on paper to make them perfect. Yes, lipstick on the LIPS. That is where lipstick is supposed to go.

I put my hair up in a pretty shell squeegie. The shells are varnished and whitish-pink. So pretty. It makes my neck look long and sexy. I didn't wear my secret heart-shapes dark glasses because I wanted my eyes to show. My eyes, everyone has always said, look like Mariah Carey's, which everyone says are "gorgeous, dark, and sultry." Sultry is actually a real word.

And then I wore my sundress which lets a lot show. And I wore my gold ankle bracelet and glitter sandals and my long earrings that look just like Mariah Carey's.

So there I was up on the stage with all these horridable monsters with swords and hunched backs and bandaged feet and green masks and purple scars and white yarn wigs and funny coats and blood and masks made to be faces of the Constitution Fathers, *twelve* Thomas Jeffersons, and one kid had a diaper and shower cap, which everyone thought was cute because he's only age one but was really disgusting, and there was the kid with the busted arm, who was part of the mob, and I was the only pretty person there. You could easily see the difference. My lines went like this:

The Revolution was in the minds and hearts of the people; a change in their religish sintimints, of their duties and of their oblations. This RADICAL change in principals, opinions, sintimints, and affections of THE PEOPLE was the REAL American Revolution!

I spoke all these words with perfect lips and licked these lips with the end of my tongue in a full sex-type lick, like on TV, just the point of my tongue, which is supposed to put thoughts of sex in all men's minds.

After the play, I put my secret glasses back on and mothers said stuff was going on inside the shops and everybody was picking up the tables. I said No thanks to helping pick up messy tables, No thanks to shops.

So then they say, "Jane, maybe you'd like to help with hair in the beauty shop. There's a bunch going over for haircuts right now. Or maybe you'd like to have your hair done, just have Jillian brush your hair and pamper you."

"It would be my pleasure," said Jillian, who has huge teeth. And funny blinky little eyes with hardly any lashes, like an actual monkey's.

"No thanks," I said.

And they said more stuff about how wonderful the shops are. I cried, in a quiet sad way. They said okay, I could go back to Gordie's house with Lee Lynn for a quiet afternoon.

Lee Lynn is one of the mothers. She sort of looks like Thomas Jefferson but no mask. Her hair is so weird. Flies around like it's maybe plugged into the lamp thing. Her face is pretty, but not pretty enough for TV. Sorry.

I hear the mothers whisper (so I don't hear) that I am beautiful, which is something they are not used to.

Boy, do I have a lot of information in my secret book. All their ugly secrets. All their ugly faces. All their noise. All their hideous food. And electric buggies kids ride around in. And weird soap. Oh, God, there's

BARE FEET in the library. And junk everywheres. Would you call that a school? I call it a dump.

☆ Penny St. Onge talks to us from a future time.

Dear heavens! The separation of mother from child with such ease could only happen to civilized humans. A mother bear would rip your head off. A human mother without the clutter of law-and-order would claw out your eyes.

This with Lisa and Jane takes place in the heart of year 2000, the weight of law very heavy.

And yet Jane, six and a half years old, burned through three foster homes in less than three weeks and was delivered to her Granpa Pete's gas station in a state car wearing nothing but a violet bathrobe, her arms crossed over her chest to show who is boss.

Pete Meserve and Gordon, old friends, talked on the phone about the covert transfer of Jane to our home. The Department of Human Services was to keep on believing she was with Pete full-time. And here she landed. How stalwart she seems! This amazing durable little creature, making life hell for us all. Think! Isn't she the bear? The *baby* bear who bites the hand of civilization! Some here say, "No, no, no, Penny, Pete says Jane has *always* been a brat." But leave me to my illusions. Whenever I look at that little person, who comes to Settlement meals so rarely, so straight-shouldered, and a face *too* beautiful, saying no to everything we suggest, I *smile*. Forgive me.

♡♡ More secrets. Secret Agent Jane speaks.

With these powerful secret pink glasses, everything looks so stupid. And people are forced to say the truth before your very eyes. Their thoughts just pour out. And horridable information pours out.

Like right now, this is morning and I am here with these glasses. I'm hiding. It is Claire talking, Gordie's X-wife. She is older than Gordie. She is *eleven* years older than Gordie. This is not the usual way, you know, that people are.

Okay, so she is wearing one of her fat shirts and fat pants. And she wears working boots like Gordie. She does not have pretty legs that show like my teacher at my real school I had last year, Mrs. Varney. Mrs. Varney had sandals that had nice heels and were pink. All the teachers at my real school are beautiful and fixed up and they walk cute like Mum does and anybody normal.

While I am spying on Claire, she is out near the gardens and the garden sheds. People here LOVE gardens and just come and go in the gardens and weed stuff and pick stuff and shovel piles of stuff.

Gardens are dirty and full of bugs.

I am standing by the big farm truck, which has a million crates and a tire. I have already wiped my secret glasses off for a cleaning.

Claire is loading a different truck with two crates of lettuce.

Bonny Loo almost sees me, but she doesn't. Bonny Loo is sort of beautiful, sort of ugly. Sometimes she wears glasses. Other people almost see me, too, but they are off in the distance bent down in the gardens a long ways off. Claire is getting in the little truck so she can go off with the lettuce to where she sells it. Because of these secret-agent heart-shapes glasses, Claire's lips are now forced to tell the truth about my dog, Cherish. ". . . and they left her Scottie in the car with the windows up! You know how hot it was that first day! All cops care about is getting their damn business done. They left the poor little dog alone to die in the sweltering car."

"Those shitheads!" snarls Bonny Loo.

A bug bites my ear. I smoosh it quietly.

Claire says, "Jane was at school . . . or you suppose they'd have left *her* in the car too?"

"Probably," Bonny Loo says in her sexy deep voice.

Claire says, "Meanwhile, they take Lisa off in the cruiser, her yelling and sobbing 'My dog, my little dog!' and begging, trying to convince the cops to turn back and get the dog. They told her not to worry, *it would be taken care of.* Of course nobody did anything. So Lisa was screaming at the jail. They said if she didn't stop, they'd *have to stop her.* And then Lisa's lawyer called that night—Kane—and said the tow guy found the body under one of the front seats." Claire mooshes her hand all over her face and up under her glasses like her face itches, and this makes her face all red and rubbed. She says, "Bonny, that had to've been a bad death."

In my secret agent notebook, I draw my beautiful Cherish black, a better black even than Cannonball, a Scottie who visits here. Cherish so very chubby and stubby, stubby legs, stubby tail. Everything is thick and stubby and strong on a Scottie. I make this picture almost perfect. Even under the circumstances of having to rush, squatted down here behind this big hot smelly truck and hot sweat making my eyes burn wicked. I draw very special details. Little moon places of white around her eyes. That's the way Cherish would always look at you, sideways, like . . . like an old auntie lady would look at you. It was so cute how she did that. My beautiful Cherish.

On the next page I do a special revenge picture of what I wish. Cops. With their heads squashed. I draw arrows in them. And bullets. And needles. And knives. I squash their feet too. Make blood in their eyes. I make their round mouths screaming. Very, very quiet, I tear this page out. I twist my sandal on it till the cops are ripped. Next I will put them in a fire.

The screen purrs.

Oh, yes! Here is the NEWZZZZZ. WOW! Lots of police in special gear . . . thank goodness for FEDERRRRAAAAL funds . . . had to arrest a guy in Nevada today after he ate his mother's ears. Forty-year-old Wesley Fergusson was HEAVILLLLY armed with a twenty-two rifle when police finally captured him this morning after he fled in *blah blah blah blah blah* . . . ads for insurance, investments, banks, loans, a car that seems to fly; a car of squarer shape that shows you are better fancier people; now another car all muddy and funnnn. Insurance. Medicines against aging. Blah blah blah. . . .

Breaking.

After work, Donnie Locke leaves the Chain and stops off at yet another big chain store for groceries, plops toilet paper into the cart, hefts a bag of dry dog chow underneath. He looks along down the seemingly mile-long case of meats, pink and deep red, rising and falling under waves of plastic wrap.

Now, back out in traffic, the late afternoon light gleams off hoods and fenders, Donnie's head hurting.

At a red light, he feels the shape of his head through his cropped hair. He watches the changing set of lights too hard, head cocked, sunglasses giving up thousands of turquoise flambeaus. He sees shoulders and temples of other drivers ooze past on left and right. Bumper stickers and vanity plates and big white campers pushing and pulling away. Metal and tar, world of the cheap. World of progress. World where mistakes are not tolerated, while intentional malevolence is blessed.

He wears a face like a man just fired from his job. But Donald Locke has not been fired. The emotion is the same, hired or fired. The living death, the long thin membrane of a life already lived, his schedule, his soul in the lines between company policy and growth in the next quarter, no day different from the day before in the life that is worth less than the cheapest plastic comb. How can fired be worse?

He wants to die. He wants very badly to die. Though he doesn't envy his dying son. He wants a death that is *fast,* like a hammer striking a nail.

Coming into the dooryard of his home, he feels the dear cloying heaviness of the house, the pull of that back door like centrifugal force when you ride the blue and red buggies of the Tilt-a-Whirl.

But inside the door is Mickey. To Donnie Locke, the boy's narrow face and wolfy eyes look cunning, the arms, the shirtless chest and neck rather skinny a few months ago, more tanned today than yesterday, and more muscular . . . filling this house with threat.

Donnie is breaking. Donnie is dying. There is no shouting this time. Just the *gloink-gloink* of Mickey pouring Kool-Aid or whatever that red stuff is from the pitcher into a cup, and Donnie stepping very close. He takes Mickey one-handed by one bare shoulder. Because of the bag of groceries, he can't use both hands, and he can't think of what to do with the bag. There's no time. There's only seconds to deflect the threat, and it is all so graceful, not like a brawl, because the boy puts up no resistance, is easily shoved along, out through that back screen door, the spring making its thin wiry music, out into the yard with the million crickets in chilling song, sun gone, silver dusk turning to a sweet cold August night.

"Go away," Donnie whispers. "You can't live here anymore. Get out of here. Go!" All in a whisper.

Mickey, no shirt, no shoes, just jeans and his leather wristband, streaky blond hair, untied, hanging all about his narrow face like a little girl in early morning, looks up at one window of the big house fleetingly, then backs away.

 Another night.

Jesse Locke's breathing is ragged, the air stale, these second story rooms holding the heat of many days.

Donnie Locke sits up, reaches for the bedside light. He looks down at Jesse, who lies flat between himself and Erika. The face of his son, dopey with medicine. The enormous bulging veiny head with its ever-soft yellow hair. He runs a finger along the spiny back. Holds his hand there. The child's breathing has great pauses now.

"Erika," Donnie whispers.

"My God," Erika whispers.

Donnie takes his hand away, pushes both hands between his thighs, hangs his head.

Jesse breathes harder and harder, then a great pause, longer than six breaths, then breathing again *hard,* a wizardy larger-than-life concentration inside every one of his elderly limbs. A beautiful thing to see. A *capable* thing.

 Moments later.

When Jesse stops breathing forever, Mickey is somewhere *out there*. No one knows where. Has anyone on this earth seen him since Donnie made him go? It's as if Mickey and Jesse have both masterfully risen out of their insignificant anatomies to start brand-new lives.

 And the screen?

Concerning the aforementioned complexities, the screen remains blank and dumbstruck.

Maybe you, crow, are in the sky. Flapping along (*whump!* pause, *whump!* pause). Below you is the rounded flexing land of Gordon St. Onge, fields and ledge, juniper and dark clotted forest. What is that there below? Something sort of dangling but sort of fixed, quite tiny. You almost missed it. But there it is!

Yes, it's Mickey Gammon's tree house.

 Mickey's secret tree house.

How could this have happened to him? How could he be so cut off? Like a space guy whose capsule gets screwed up.

Nights cold. Days hot. Even the humidity is back. Down through the little gap in the trees that the path makes, he can see how the nearest mountain rises like a steamy green shower-room wall. Hot desolation.

He fears being found, though no one is looking. No search-and-rescue dogs. No Coast Guard helicopters. No bullhorns booming out "MICHAEL GAMMON! ARE YOU ALL RIGHT?!!! WAIT WHERE YOU ARE!!" Donnie would just say he had left pissed off. Maybe Donnie believes that.

But maybe those who built this thing might return. Probably not. It looks as old as the Alamo.

The bugs aren't as bad as even a week ago, there's no feverish swirl of millions through the rubbery air, marching up under his T-shirt sleeves, biting through his "new" T-shirt, even his heavy jeans, sweat running in rivers down his legs. But now there is still something hanging on a string in front of his face, something scuttling up the shadowy wall there . . . the wall of his tree house. And a spider bite on his ankle. And a million ants. A hornet flies in the windowless window and out again.

The woods here this morning look prehistoric, a certain edge to the light, boring down between popples, glossy greenish-gray bark, huge-girthed, sour-smelling. And pines. Like ships' masts. Their carpets are rust-colored and soundless and soft. And all the rest. Miles of waist-deep fern and other bushy stuff. Mostly green, but some edged in yellow. Thousands and thousands of spotted trunks and shaggy trunks and trunks rivuleted with great age, and gold and gray and white birch. All of it pushing and bullying and striving up into the heavy swells of foliage and live needles. This, the violence of trees! Like humans. It is war, yuh, war. Endless, endless war.

Is there nothing in this world that will cradle you?

He feels for his pack of cigarettes. Ah, yes. It takes five matches to light up. Everything damp. Everything stubborn. He almost sobs with impatience. He finally inhales the burning friend. He closes his eyes, exhales slowly.

☆ **In a future time, Claire St. Onge remembers that summer well.**

The outside world's children were coming to us on a painful current of need. I *believed* we were up to this mighty challenge, that we were special people.

♡♡ **Secret Agent Jane visits the county jail again. Jane speaks.**

It's Sunday. Gordie and I get in his truck and go the long way off to see Mum. I walk straight past the copguards with my secret agent glasses, knowing everything about them, knowing *everything*.

Gordie tells me to hold his hand, but I say "no thank you." I feel the power. Cops will die, the giant building will explode, my Mum will be rescued, anything could happen if they make me mad. I stare into Mum's eyes and she is staring into the heart shapes of my eyes and she knows I have the power. She says, "So what do you have to report to Headquarters?" Her voice is secretish and important.

Something tells me I can't report the Cherish part. So I whisper, "Everything they eat is weird. They *love* pepper and green spice. Especially Penny and Stuart and Jacquie. Everything burns hot red and disgusting because of Penny, Stuart, and Jacquie. And Claire. And her slaves. And Bonny Loo. Especially sausages. Mum, they *make* sausages. They use squashed meat in a metal thing. And they love love love fish. Fish with skinnnnnnnn." I point at my pocket down here on my cute sundress. This is to show Mum there's my secret agent notebook and pictures of hot terrible food and fish with skinnnnn and everybody's mouths eating like PIGS, especially Gordie, who is ALWAYS EAT-ING. His pig mouth is the worst.

Mum is smiling at Gordie, smiling into his eyes. "Jane Miranda Meserve is a secret agent. This is Headquarters," she TELLLLS him.

"What are you doing? Don't tell him!" My lips say this but without voice, just lips.

Gordie reaches over to me and runs his finger around inside my ear, inside and around all the curly parts of my ear. I let him.

With Gordie right there it's difficult to tell Mum about all the stuff I found out. Like about THE MOTHERS. And THE TOILETS WITH NO WATER, called COMPOST. And the old man who is dying in a bed. And the GUNS.

So I just kinda pull lint off my sundress and open and close the strap to one of my sandals.

Gordie and Mum talk about the people in Mum's "room." Rooms here are locked. And then Gordie and Mum talk about fedral court and fedral prison and seizures and many many words of fedral kinds, and Mum *whispers* to Gordie something about the house.

I push my foot hard into the leg of Mum's chair. It makes me so mad when Mum and people do that! You know, when they talk outside of me.

Gordie is breaking the copguard rules and reaches for Mum's hand. But then stops. He is always feeling people, especially ears, and he also does a weird-willyish thing to your fingernails. Scratches them, which is just a plain thing to do, you would think, but you almost feel faint. Feels nice. I seen him kiss an old lady *on the lips*. And he blows breath on the man's head with no eyes. And he hugged and danced with Oh-RELL. It was funny.

Gordie is not really Mum's friend. He's Granpa Pete's friend. But I bet Gordie thinks Mum is pretty because she *is*. She is *so* pretty. Pretty hair. Pretty mouth. Pretty mole thing. Eyes very big—blue for a color—like wonderful jewels. Her hair she has fixed, called Light 'n' Streak. It is really blonde with brownish lines. But with these secret agent glasses, it looks to be quite a nice streaked pink.

Mum is not the brown color. That's my father, named Damon Gorely, in California. He is a star. He is famous in rap and has a perfect kitchen, Mum said, which is what he said after the concert. The Civic Center was wicked packed but he picked Mum. When you love someone of the different colors, you get a girl like me, which Mum calls a golden gypsy queen. Queen for sure.

 ## While the child, Jane, appears to be deep in thought, the talk goes on.

Lisa says, "Kane wants me to tell all that I know about Bob Ross and Jeff if—"

"He's trying to get you off," says Gordon. "He's only playing it the way they set it up to be played. Drug laws are now conspiracy laws. You know . . . like you're a threat to the country." He laughs.

"Sure. Rat and run." Lisa frowns.

Gordon touches the child's ear.

Lisa says, "I'd like them to think I have an iron will. That all this about the house, my daughter, prison, and everything won't break me. Not even electric shocks to the bottoms of my feet could make me tell." She smiles. "But I'm no iron will. I just don't know anything. I never even saw any of the stuff. But somehow they're saying there was stuff in the house. *That's made up!* Unless it was some microscopic flake left from that party before Christmas! And Bob Ross . . . I never even *saw* him before. I just knew Carla. I just introduced him to Jeff 'cause Jeff wanted to get some stuff. I'm starting to get the idea that they wouldn't mind a bit if I just made things up! The DA and the MDEA just want to hear stories about Bob Ross. They don't care if the stories are true or not. That's pretty low."

Gordon groans. "So *you* are being framed for a million dollars' worth. It makes perfect sense. *Perfect.*"

Lisa closes her eyes.

♡♡ Jane tells us.

I stare at her mouth. With these glasses, I can read her mind. I can see in her mind that she's really thinking how horridable them at Gordie's are to expect me to eat hot food and fish skin. And also in Mum's brains I see Cherish trapped inside the car watching the cops arresting Mum with *guns* and metal *handcuffs* and driving fast, and Mum can see out the cop car, can see back at Cherish inside our car inside the hot windows, her tongue long and crying and getting very small, for cops go fast and probably had the blue lights and siren noise.

Gordie feels down along both sides of his brown mustache with his fingers, the mustachey part way longer than his beard. One of his eyeballs grows, then it shrinks and blinks and then a way big mess all shivering around.

Mum looks over at the copguard. His outfit is brown and beige if you look at him without pink glasses. He is a huge guy like Gordie, only his middle is HUGE around like a HUGE giant inner tube for floating in the lake is under his shirt. His hair is shaved but for a small place like a little hat, and his mustache is HUGE but no beard thing. He must weigh wicked. He has set back in his chair now and has his arms crossed, and he is staring right at Mum. Mum looks fast back at Gordie, who has his eye very wild-looking.

◎ Time ticks on at the jail.

Though visit time is ordered to the split second, there are moments when a visitor can feel lost in time, even as he or she feels boxed in by the sickly overhead schoolhouse-type lights and the eyes of the untrusting deputies. And you must *never* touch the prisoner.

Gordon St. Onge's fingers move again toward the prisoner's. Not a thrust. Just edging along. It is the fingers of both hands, a giant's hands, one nail purpled from Settlement work or play, that breathing, unbraiding world so far from this unbending place.

Lisa's eyes drop, as though in horror, to the next inching forward of his fingers.

The deputy doesn't see this.

Lisa raises her eyes ("wonderful jewels") to the "madman" (said by so many talk show call-ins), the pale pale eyes of Gordon St. Onge. And here is the secret of his success at drawing so many of his fellow humans to his table, to his hearth, to his embrace. For he is no suave creature. But this, the eyes into eyes, his sorrow, his inability to separate his meaty heart from the wailing hearts of those such as this woman. Her need. There is a tremble to his chin, the widening eye, the narrowing other eye, the horsy twitch. For a moment, he is becoming the caged one.

And Lisa, like so many, is yearning toward that yawning hole of empathy and the face, handsome but for its extreme expressions, particular in its Black Irish and Italian and French and Indian light-dark thick-necked way. Lisa makes a sound in her throat, not a word but a creaking. Like pond lilies against the metal bottom of a small boat. A brushy sound. Her eyes close.

His fingers don't inch any closer, but they don't draw back. His face tightens. He says bitterly, "It isn't just your property they want." His voice louder now. "Besides that." Now louder. "And the kickbacks and a few feathers in their political caps!" He is getting too loud for this place. The walls scowl. "Besides the usual media shilling and all this being a prototype for the whole Fascist scene America is about to experience in more obvious ways just around the bend, besides *that,* what they really want is probably this Bob Ross or someone he knows. You're just a hostage!" He growls the word *hostage*. "Your innocence is neither here nor there. And truth is not the issue, Lisa! Fairness is not the issue! Justice is not the issue!" His voice rises even louder, quite hot.

Lisa looks toward the deputy.

The deputy crosses his arms, seemingly lost in thoughts of an unpleasant personal life.

Lisa says, "My friend Maggie here says that even if I did get off, even if the court says I'm innocent, they won't give me the house back. Everything I own is gone. They seize everything when you're arrested . . . so it's part of the arrest, not part of the conviction. What kind of crazy nuttiness is that?"

Gordon leans a little toward her. "That's why it's called the Drug War. The state of war makes pillaging and hostage-taking okay. *And* the idea that your so-called rights are even worth *less*. That's war. You know . . . like everything's fair in love and war."

Lisa whimpers. "I can't believe this is happening." She sucks her breath in, holds it painfully. Lets it out through her nose slowly like a pot smoker would do, only no smoke.

Gordon squinches his face in matching pain, swallows. "It's a prototype—"

"Yes, you said that. It probably is."

"They're getting us ready for the future."

She leans her right ear against her hand.

He goes on. "They want us Americans to get used to their fucking with our neighbors. One excuse or another. One American at a time!" He leans back and looks down into the shadows of Jane's eyes burning behind the two pink heart-shaped lenses in white plastic frames. He looks around the room, sees that the deputy is watching the hall through the open door. Now in a soft voice, "I wish you hadn't heard about the house. Not good for the spirit."

Lisa laughs. "Fascist prototypes are good for the spirit?"

Gordon bows his head. Doggy expression, full of apology. "Forgive me."

"Dad warned me." She blushes. Her eyes show tears. Small smile. "He said—" She smiles quite crookedly, doesn't go on.

♡♡ Secret Agent Jane's patience wears thin.

This what they are saying has to stop. I sigh loud like wind. *Woooooofsh.* I ask, "Mum, what's the name of the farm Cherish is at?" This is because Mum has *said* Cherish is at a farm when I was here with Claire.

Mum looks at me. Mum looks at Gordie. Mum looks at me. Fast eyes. Back and forth. Back and forth. She says, "That farm doesn't have a name. Real farms don't have those cute names. Only city people who have fixed-up farmhouses give them names. This is just a plain ol' farm with real farmers and real tractors and real mooing cows. You know how Cherish loved to see cows along the road. And you know when she was happy how she made that little mooey noise and that little butting-head thing like she was pretending to be a cow? She really was into cows. A regular cowgirl."

I watch Mum's lips being very thin on this lie she's saying. And her voice. It isn't *her* voice. It's her special new voice for *lies.*

Gordie reaches out and gives my arm a squeeze.

Mum bows her head for one second. Gordie is very quiet. Mum looks up again.

I say, "Mum, when are you coming home?"

She says, "Soon."

"When's that? Soon. What is soon?"

"I don't know, Jane." Her voice is faded and croakish.

I say, "Talk to the man about a visit."

"What man?"

"Kane."

"How did you know his name is Kane?" She looks quickish over to Gordie, then slowish back to my heart-shaped eyes.

I make a face. "You *said* his name was Kane."

"Okay. I'll ask him."

"Ask him now."

"He's not here."

"Call him." I glance over at the door, which is a hallway that goes to the other hallway where the phone for money is. There is always some body using it when we go by.

"I'll call him later."

"Call him now so you can go with us now."

"I can't." She closes her eyes.

"How come?"

"I can't, Jane."

"How come?"

"Stop it, Jane."

"Why? Why can't you come home?" I am almost crying, on the very very edge. I will be crying soon.

"Jane, I can't come home. The government won't let me."

I scream, "The government is MEAN!"

"Yes! Yes it is! It is FUCKING TERRIBLE!!!!" Mum starts screaming, jumps up, and hurries around the table. She holds me and I'm holding her, both screaming, both holding, both hugging and hopping and screaming. And the HUGE copguard with the shaved head and inner-tube middle is standing up so he can do something horridable to Mum and me, his eyes right on us, his mouth moving, but Gordie holds Mum's head back against his shirt and she hugs *him,* and I run out of the room, out into the giant hall screaming and there are cops everywheres with eyes as dead and metal as springs and fenders, more movie-ish than Gordie's scary eye. And they *all* have extra shiny belts. Brown shirts. One gets me by the arm, tells me not to cry, tells me everything is going to be okay. He pretends to be very nice but I can see into his BRAINS that he would cook you or burn you if he wanted to. And he would love to KILL your dog. I stop screaming. I am very polite. I fix my secret glasses straighter 'cause they are tipped and I am very polite. I pretend to be polite. It's all an act.

Here's Gordie coming and he's telling me it's time to go home.

Mum is screaming and sobbish somewhere behind the doors. I run toward her doors, but Gordie grabs me and holds me hard against his middle, his shirt and his buckle, which is a sun face and pokes me a little. He rubs my hair and tells me Mum will feel better in a few minutes.

I see the legs of cops around the edges. But I don't look at them. I pretend I don't know cops are there. I say to Gordie in a plain voice for all cops to hear, "Do they have Cherish's body here?" I look up at Gordie's face and his eyes the one that blinks funny and the other one that is regular . . . both eyeballs look into my heart-shaped glasses. He *knows* I have the power.

Mickey and the militia captain visit the residence of Willie Lancaster.

Fairly new pickup eases along to a stop at the road's edge in front of the dooryard of the Lancasters.

Truck door opens and Rex York steps out, square-shouldered with that military bearing he has always had, long before the militia movement came to give it reason to be, and long before Vietnam.

From the passenger's side, Mickey Gammon drops to the weedy shoulder, sticking a cigarette lighter to a Lucky. He smokes with his head down, scuffing the heel of one work boot in the sand, boring out a shape there, like three bananas. Sand art.

From a dog door, five small, white, flat-faced, curl-tailed, ugly, spotted-in-various-ways dogs with open mouths and lolling dripping tongues hustle out to inspect pant legs, then on to the visitors' truck to do tires and hubcaps. A couple of them bark their reedy small-dog barks, but just for a moment. Mostly they are silent. All business.

Right next to the road is a slumped 1972 Dodge pickup. Paint was red once. Now it is orangey. A mildewy vinyl cap over the bed. All four tires rotted and flat. Stuff in the cab. Stuff stuffed in the inside of the capped bed. Stuff piled on top of the cap and the whole she-bang carpeted with russet pine spills. Hornets go in and out, in and out, through a break in the aluminum and Plexiglas flap. Skinny but hale oak saplings have yearned up through some of the stuff piled behind it. A registered truck parked next to it has a bumper sticker. It says TRY AND TAKE MY GUNS AND I'LL USE THEM ON YOU and shows the barrel of a handgun pointed at the observer. A small oval seal on the window glass reads THIS VEHICLE PROTECTED BY SMITH & WESSON.

Mickey smokes hard, trying to make it quick but complete. Rex has gone on ahead, wanting to get this job done, some of the white dogs hustling along with him, serving as escorts. But now Rex turns and looks back to see how far behind he's left Mickey. Everything Mickey tries to take in looks hazy and blurred. Humidity is blinding. And the smells of pine and someone's barbecue are mated together in each droplet. Mickey is running his fingers over a really new and costly-looking road-going-sized wheeled chipper. Warm to his fingers as a bathtub. Warm as piss. Warm as his mother Britta's hand on his arm would be, if she were the kind of person who would touch you. Warm as Rex's mother's cookies. Warm as Rex's fake leather couch when somebody has sat in it before you. Warm. He leaves his fingers there a good few seconds. The fingers of the other hand poke the Lucky back in his teeth. He sees up ahead, on the walkway where Rex stands, there are two house trailers, one new model and very grand, one a smaller, old-timey, rounded model. These are positioned together so the doors are only a few feet apart, with an elegant latticework archway and flagstone path between. This area is swept and fussed over, nothing stored or heaped here.

As Mickey steps away from the chipper, forcing smoke out through his teeth, he hears a screamed word, "ROAST!!!!!" coming from the larger trailer. It jumps him. But now there is brotherly and pleasant laughter, several men. Mickey almost smiles along. But Rex is not smiling along. Mickey takes a few steps toward Rex. But he needs to finish his smoke. So he is, yes, ass-dragging, as the saying goes.

Now he squintily studies something else, something set off there to the right, a big shingled workshop with a surprisingly fancy window with a fan-shaped thing over the top, something that was part of a courthouse or old customs building or some such fine place. Maybe a judge's house. Or a doctor's. A yellow sign beside the door reads FIRE

THE BOSS. And up above the pine trees, above everything, impressive as hell, an elaborate short-wave radio antenna. As Mickey's eyes rise and then slide back down the tower with its guy wires in six directions, he looks to Rex and Rex is looking at him and Rex's face has absolutely no expression. Just sunglasses. Mustache. Straight closed mouth. Chin up. And the Adam's apple doesn't move. He's like a picture.

As Mickey walks and smokes and looks back at the doorway to the shop, he admires an old American flag on an angled pole. The ornate tip of this pole almost touches the bark of a massive pine. At least a dozen big ol' white pines crowd around here. Straight as man-made pillars. No limbs until you get wayyyy up there, while all the top limbs are raised up like triumphant muscley arms into the white-hot almost fleshy sky above, while below, the Lancasters live shadowy and shady. And hot. Hot is everywhere.

Yeah, except for the short-wave antenna, trees rule here. Everything snug and close. A lot of stuff heaped against the side of the shop. Some would call it junk. But indeedy it is not. It is the stuff of purpose and value and strategy. Mickey smacks a mosquito. Fewer mosquitoes in heat. But nowhere, no time, are there *no* mosquitoes.

The dogs really like Rex, staring up at him in an admiring way. They know Rex. He's no stranger here. But Rex has no squeaky doggy talk for them. No snacks. Not even recognition. He is looking only at Mickey. Trying to hurry Mickey.

Note that there are no doghouses. No ropes or chains for the necks of dogs. Nothing here in the lives of Lancasters is caged. Willie Lancaster's worst fear, they say, is the cage. Makes news of Willie in the Cumberland county jail about three weeks ago most interesting.

Lotta company here today in the shady shadows of the Lancaster residence. A logging rig with its vast high empty bed and clam spread open across the end, chains limp against the stakes, parked at a mean slant inside the road's ferny shoulder, almost touching the stone wall. DICK O'BRIEN / LOGGING & PULP on the doors, Winchester in the rack.

All over the rooty soft parking area beyond the shop are cars and trucks and one low-slung stripped-down Harley. This explains the barbecue aroma perhaps? Lotta Lancasters here in Oxford County. And other related families. Family with a capital F.

Mickey breathes *in* the cookout smell as he breathes *out* the last of his smoke, almost choking, now a few steps closer to Rex and the door of the trailer and the infamous Willie Lancaster, who Mickey suspects is a person he is not likely to feel warm and fuzzy about.

Warm and fuzzy, no. But hot. And hotter.

The barbecue smell is definitely coming from the backyard. Another much deeper trellis arch and flagstone walk is how you find your way to the backyard. And see there, a third fancy trellis walkway, which takes you to the front door of the house of Dee Dee and Louis and Cannonball St. Onge, a few yards behind the shop.

What kind of house is that thing? Tall. Pink. Puts you a little bit to mind of a rocket. Or, yeah, a big prick. Five stories. Yes, *five* stories. On the first floor, a lot of doors. A door on each of the three visible sides. None of the doors match. Why so many doors? Such a narrow house, all these doors must enter the same small first-floor room. And the windows don't match. One is a window of colored glass squares, a proud thing to own. But a sixteen-by-sixteen-foot house of five stories? A lotta ladders and hatches, perhaps. Definitely a code man's nightmare. Has the code man been in the Lancaster vicinity much these days?

Near one of the tall house's side doors, snug between two massive spires of pine, is Louis St. Onge's little beat-ta-shit flatbed Datsun. But Mickey doesn't know Louis (or Lou-EE) St. Onge yet, Louis being a Settlement regular but also son-in-law to Willie Lancaster.

A lot of dog turds around. And heaped against the intersection of trellis archways are several beer bottles and beer cans. Worth five cents each at the redemption. The Lancasters are not drinkers, so these have been brought by guests.

"THAT'S A CROCK!!!!!!" screams the same voice as before. No laughter this time, but much hollering. Sounds like a fight. Now a sound like a stick on hollow wood. And there's TV laughter. Mickey catches up with Rex. Rex is not interested in the barbecue out back. Rex is intent on reaching the source of the screaming and hollering. He turns back again to look into Mickey's face, then jerks a thumb at a glossy one-ton dump truck parked close to the shop. It is the newest rig in the yard, a pretty sight. Printed on the doors: WILLIAM LANCASTER TREE WORK & LANDSCAPING 625-8693.

Rex says gruffly, "Like I say, this guy's a lot more focused than he will *seem* to be. He's smart, and he's a problem."

Mickey has spent his entire life with *quiet* people. He is used to quiet people, the quieter the better.

Now, as they step up on the low stone step, a white flat-faced dog from inside pushes up the dog door, which is rigged in the aluminum combination screen-storm human door. He doesn't bark. He just stands there, panting miserably, the little door resting on his back in its flipped-up position. He gazes past Rex's black military boots toward the other dogs, who are cruising casually around the yard.

Now inside the trailer, a wild thumping and a squeally but hoarse totally sickening laughter. Refrigerator door sucks shut. The little dog jerks backward, letting the flap swing closed.

Mickey looks down directly at his own feet as he crushes the last of his cigarette with his fingers, sees the doorstep is pretty jazzy. Cement with all kinds of stuff set in it. Pieces of flagstone, tiny colored tiles, the sides of old-style painted heavy glass soda bottles that say CASCO and have a ship scene in red and white. Rex pulls off his sunglasses and folds them meticulously, into the pocket. He looks into Mickey's eyes. Anyone might think these two were father and son. Maybe even Mickey has begun to think this.

Saving the republic.

Mickey stoops to pat one of the dogs. He thinks how it is, when a dog is panting like this, it looks like a nice smile.

Rex doesn't knock. He just holds the door wide open for Mickey to step ahead of him.

The place has lost its vinyl new-mobile-home smell. It smells like life.

Kitchen of this trailer is central. Living room on the right is raised with a little wrought-iron rail as a partial partition. Linoleum down in the kitchen is made to look like bricks. Carpet up there in the living room. Yellow-gold. Dirty. Not filthy, just dirty: walked on. A guy stands on this higher level against the wrought-iron rail, nice and high above everyone else down here in the kitchen. He stares in the other direction from the kitchen, however, because he is watching the TV, which shows an old black-and-white movie tinged green. He's a guy in his midsixties, very thin hair, only three or four teeth in front, small head but large thick-lobed ears, red T-shirt faded to splotchy pink, rugged arms, dark work pants splotched with the pine pitch and grease of his life's work. He doesn't look as hot as everyone else. He looks cool. He makes a foolish face at one of the dogs who runs up to him now. Says "*Wuf*" to this dog. This is not Willie Lancaster, this is Dick O'Brien . . . guest.

Two small brown-haired girls, who have just come in behind Rex and Mickey, are now pulling folded-up paper grocery bags from where they've been stuffed behind the refrigerator. They handle the bags in a dainty way, some mission of great honor under way.

"*Three* for you," one tells the other.

Judy Lancaster, Willie's wife, comes in from outside carrying a plastic mustard bottle. She wears a curly frizzy perm. A short, square, firm-looking gal with a T-shirt that reads GIVE ME ALL THE CHOCOLATE I WANT AND NOBODY GETS HURT. She wears polka-dot shorts. Her feet are bare. Her legs are smooth and very white. Her eyes are round, sleepy-looking, and nearly lashless. This might be considered unattractive elsewhere, but in Egypt at least a hundred people have these eyes. The Gallant eyes.

A very young, very tall skinny guy, not even twenty yet, standing with slumped narrow shoulders, arms folded across his narrow chest in a protective manner, steps away from the cupboard Judy needs to get to. His plastic-billed cap reads OXFORD COUNTY POWDER BURNERS. His small face goes perfectly with his small shoulders, the head and shoulders of a little five-foot-two guy with a body stretched to give him the height of six-foot-three. His black hair is parted in the middle and held back in a slim ponytail with a red elastic. He has really nice hair. But all you can see from the trailer doorway is the billed cap, which is enormous and basketlike on top of that small face. His eyes are large and green-gold-brown with dark lashes and dark, perfectly formed eyebrows. Long neck, like actresses all wish they had, but for the Adam's apple, which you can't see because of the long scraggly thin beard that touches the front of his mostly unbuttoned scarlet chamois shirt. His chest is knotty-looking and not much for hair. One dark nipple shows. This, too, is not Willie Lancaster. This is Louis St. Onge, Willie's son-in-law. He is from Aroostook County and lives in the tall pink rocket-shaped house a few yards away. He often wears a cowboy-looking holstered revolver. As you may have guessed, he is a distant cousin of Gordon St. Onge, founding father of the St. Onge Settlement. And he's a Settlement regular, as a few others from around town are, but also a Lancaster regular . . . so, yuh, he stays busy.

Wearing a limp black Harley Davidson T-shirt with sleeves *ripped* off is a stout six-foot-four guy with a clean shave and double chins, jeans and engineer boots. This is Artie Bean, not Artie from the militia; there's a lot of Arties in Egypt. He and a shorter somewhat younger guy drink from returnable cans, one beer, one orange soda. Side by side, they both lean back against the stove and counter. The younger guy is also rather heavyset, with breasts and a plenteous girth, wearing a baby-blue muscle shirt with dark blue piping, red sport shorts with white trim, dirty sneakers, no socks. This short guy is not Willie Lancaster. This is Willie's son, Danny. Danny works with his father in the landscaping and tree-work biz. Danny hates tree work and fixing cute yards, that kinda thing. He loves computers. And movies. And games. And reading. And eating. And people. And fun.

Meanwhile, a medium-built man, small-hipped, with gray eyes, narrow face, and sweaty hair a little long on the back of his neck, a trim, very pointed, Jack-the-Ripper brown beard, a short top lip that causes his lighter-brown mustache to seem insincere, and slightly protruding spaced front teeth—this man stands next to the refrigerator between Louis St. Onge and Artie Bean. He is naked. But he is wearing a handgun in a leather holster strap, like the kind you'd wear under a jacket or shirt if you were wearing a jacket or shirt. And around his neck a long silvery chain. With exaggeratedly narrowed eyes, he is watching Artie Bean tell about yet another law "against the property owner."

"Commies! All of 'em Commies!" the naked man screams, pretending to tear his hair out. Then he covers his head with his forearms and, with uncanny agility, kicks the refrigerator, which woggles from side to side. A few of the remaining folded paper bags behind it slide to the floor. *This* is Willie Lancaster.

Rex glances into Mickey's eyes. Mickey, as usual, is pale and has no expression and won't look directly at anyone except Rex—Rex, a kind of lighthouse in the fog of Mickey's life.

Willie Lancaster makes a short lunge at Mickey for a close-up view of Mickey's face. "Hey!" he screams. "Take your hat off!" Then backs away.

Mickey has no hat.

Most of the men cackle over this.

The TV has some sort of big-music-type drama now, but nobody here cares.

Willie puffs up his chest, something that looks like a dog tag sliding sideways on the silver chain there, toward and away from the holster's shoulder strap.

Rex just stands there looking around at everything except Mickey and Willie Lancaster.

Suddenly Willie is looking intently at Rex. "What's up, Cap'n?"

Rex now looks him in the eye, then shifts to the son, Danny.

Willie asks, "Is this your new member?" He narrows his eyes once again on Mickey. "I heard all about you!" he tells Mickey. "You armed?"

"No," Mickey replies.

"No?" Willie turns his head slowly and stiffly, like Godzilla. Then his gray invasive eyes are back on Mickey. "Never go anywhere without your gun and your Bible. You hear me? That's all you gotta remember!"

Rex says, "There's one more thing. To remember. Never act like a blooming idiot in public with firearms. The jail time, the possibility of a record, the newspapers, the whole mess—it's called bad publicity." Rex doesn't mention the new so-called antiterror law, where all associated people get arrested for one man's crime. No, Rex is not feeling long-winded enough at the moment.

Willie hangs his head. Then, turning away, he slips off the shoulder holster, swings around, and starts to put it on Mickey.

Mickey jerks back: reflex.

And Willie says, "Afraid? Afraid of guns, boy? Be a real man now."

Mickey would say, *No, I'm not afraid of guns,* but his timing is off. He can't keep up with Willie; Willie is already yakking again, and Mickey stands arrow-straight like some virginal human sacrifice while Willie arranges the holster and heavy Ruger over Mickey's billowy orange T-shirt, and Willie says, "Okay, George. If anyone bothers you, you got ten shots all ready to go. You just whip that out and plug hell out of 'em."

A teen girl, dressed in a short terry beach cover-up, with thick but smooth and golden legs, passes by to the refrigerator and says, "Dad, put your clothes on. The neighbors are going to call the constable again."

Almost as quick as the speed of light, Willie runs to the screened front door with the little dog door in the bottom of it and kicks it open. He screams out toward the little sunny and shrubberied ranch house across the road, where two schoolteachers live, "HEY, NEIGHBOR! IT'S FUCKING NINETY-SIX DEGREES, HUMIDITY NINETY-NINNNNNNNE PERCENT!" His body is smooth, not especially hairy. His ass is almost the only part of his body that has a thick dark pattern of hair, and now, strutting back into the kitchen, his whole body shines and wetness drips off the end of his nose.

The kitchen is now cracking with ugly laughter. Six-foot-four Artie Bean mops his face. The aging logger, high on the elevated gold living-room carpet, continues to be the only unsticky-looking person around.

Even Rex and Mickey suffer flushes, a hot rose to each cheekbone.

The young daughter has gotten herself two cold orange sodas. The refrigerator is full of orange sodas. As the girl passes Willie, she pushes one of the cold sodas into his hand.

"Thank you, dear," he says, gripping her hand, to nuzzle her fingertips against his thin mustache. She has rings on every finger. She wrenches her hand back, waves him away dismissively, and pushes out through the screen door. It whooshes shut. Instantly, the dog door flaps open and a very fat, pregnant-looking, pushed-face, curled-tail spotted white dog steps in, looks around with a bored expression, and sashays off down the hallway to one of the small but quiet bedrooms.

From the window over the sink, the barbecue festivities out back are heard—shrill kids, shrill women, the idling but rising and falling engine of a four-wheeler ATV, a batch of firecrackers followed by the remarks of dogs, the scoldings of women, the murmur of men, and chicken parts hissing over the briquettes.

"So," says Willie. "Cap'n Rex is going to have me court-martialed." He grins his slightly buck-toothed grin at Rex. Then looks away, wiping the palm of a hand across his soft mustache. "I already been dehumanized in the treasoners' court of law and their jail. What a buncha monkeys!" He makes a face like something bitter on his tongue. "But I showed 'em the common law is the higher court. They can ignore it all they want; *they're* the criminals, not Willy Nilly." He gives a sprightly little hop which makes his dog tag and plump genitals shake frantically. He holds the soda can up high, glugs hard, then says deeply, secretively, "Portland Police Chief Shitwood knows he don't mess with me now. He's probably got a hundred locks on his door now." He chortles, mostly to himself. "*And*"—he holds up a finger—"the judge, he would've paid dear. Well, his brother would pay. They'd all be wonderin' how the brother's business got shut down. He didn't know—this Judge Bob didn't know I knew about that plumbing and wiring, way back with Jansons, I had it all to myself, the whole layout, and nuthin's changed since. He'd've been sorry he ever messed with the militia. Fortunately, he threw the whole thing out. They didn't have *anything* on ol' Willie. Good thing for the judge's baby brother. The whole works was illegal: plumbing, wiring, and septic. If I had to do what I didn't turn out havin' to do, that little brother would've been stuck with a two hundred thou' fine. It would've been in the works within hours. He didn't know we had people in there."

Rex stands now with his hands crossed loosely in front of him, his dark blue work pants without a wrinkle, his dark T-shirt perfectly fit, the military boots buffed, hair cut razor-straight across the back of his neck: clean, combed with care, eyes like a machine. Eyes on Willie. On the whole of Willie. He says, "We're going to need to talk. You have any time this week?"

Willie says, "It's all the same. Out straight. Jobs all over the place. But if four-fifteen in the morning sounds good to you, I'm handy." He leans back, comfortable now, on one elbow against the corner of the counter, sets his soda can there daintily.

Two women pull open the cheap metal door, step in quietly. Eyes on Willie. Both have loosely curled hair, like perfect hoods of curled-under ocean waves. One has a T-shirt with a picture of a Ferris wheel on it; the other wears a satiny hot-looking gold blouse, too tight across her chest and round back. And a skirt. And dressy shoes with little bows. No time to change clothes between church and the Lancaster cookout, no doubt. Both women have cameras. One of these things is the old cheapie plastic flash-cube type. (Say, where does she find flash cubes these days? Maybe just left over, no picture worth taking all these years . . . until *this one*?) Both women wear very sly expressions. The roundish woman with the gold blouse has an unlit cigarette in her teeth. She bares her teeth into a really devious grin. Good-looking teeth. Cigarette wiggles. She pushes between Rex and Mickey and snaps a picture . . . too close . . . of the naked Willie Lancaster.

Willie jumps away from the counter, eyes wide. He smiles hugely, his protruding teeth seeming to bite at the air. "Me? You want *me*?"

Both cameras begin to blaze. Flash cubes and battery flash are giving the walls and everyone's eyeballs a hectic storm of light.

Even the serene Dick O'Brien, who through the years has seen it all and who is now sitting on the raised step to the living room, patting one of the white dogs, snorts and shakes his head.

Six-foot-four Artie Bean of the de-sleeved Harley T-shirt speaks in his baritone. "Doin' a brown-paper-covered magazine?"

"No," replies the shimmery gold-blouse gal. "This is just for the record."

"Maybe the *Guinness Book of World Records*." The other woman snickers as she jams another cube into her camera.

Willie's gray eyes get even more delighted and huge. He says, "Shucks! My tape measure's out in the shop." Then turns sideways and, with two fingers, takes the loose uncircumcised end of his penis and holds it straight out. Pushes out his pelvis to add to the effect. The flash cubes churn. Big Artie Bean and thick-in-the-middle Danny and tall soft-eyed Louis are almost gagging to death with laughter. The old logger shakes his head. Rex and Mickey remain visibly unaffected.

The women hurry off, their laughs high-pitched, sounding like sirens that fade as they get farther outside in the yard.

Willie looks Rex in the eye, salutes. Says, "Be right back." Then, light as a cat, exits by way of the tinny whooshing door.

Suddenly, behind the trailer, are real emergency-ish screams.

The TV flutters and squiggles, straining to please, but no one looks.

The logger gets up from the carpeted step, ambles over to the refrigerator, and gets himself an orange soda. Tosses a slice of American cheese to the smiling dog who has followed him.

Willie returns, ambles over between Artie and Danny, and spits into the sink. He turns around and leans back against the sink, wiping his mouth on a forearm and eyeing Rex. He says, a little bit breathlessly, "The newspapers got it all screwed up. It didn't happen the way they said. I didn't threaten *anybody*."

"That's what I want to talk about when we talk."

"No need to be all shh shh shh-shhh!" Willie cups his hand beside his mouth to illustrate secret whispers. "Let's talk about it *now*. Nobody here is the enemy."

The teen daughter returns to pull a bowl of potato salad from the refrigerator. Willie's wife, Judy, storms in, flushed and damp, her hair more frizzled than ten minutes ago. "If you had started the briquettes this morning, William, there'd be time for Jim, Donnie, and Joycie to eat. But they have to go in twenty minutes and the chicken is raw."

Willie growls to himself. "I'm gettin' a *gas* grill. Briquettes were used by cave dwellers."

The wife, Judy, places a hand on her hip. "Regardless of that, why didn't you get these briquettes started?"

"You coulda lit 'em as good as I could, m'dear. I'm not the friggin' butler."

The daughter looks inside the plastic lid of the bowl, squeals "Oh, no!" and runs out, leaving the bowl on the round maplelike table.

Wife says in a low voice, "No, but Willie, you was a damn good butler up at Cressey's this morning, and I could hurt you with that." She looks hard and pissed.

He says softly, hoarsely, "You walk the line. Tonight you pay, bitch."

She walks straight at him, grips him by the dog tag, and hisses, "The green machine."

He and she explode with laughter, both shrieking and teary. She gives him a hard poke in the arm. He pokes hers. She kinda squashes his bare toes with her sneaker. He screams, bloodcurdlingly. She walks away straight-faced, her eyes once again sleepy.

"Bitch!" he calls after her. "Tonight you get the crowbar! The whole thing!"

Dee Dee, their pregnant daughter, young wife of Louis, appears, her lavender sleeveless maternity sundress straining across her middle. She pushes a pair of jeans into Willie's hands. "*Dad,*" she says, smiling quirkily, rolling her eyes, then walks away. She carries with her a cool cloud of contentment.

Willie smiles bucktoothishly. "Boss has spoken." He stuffs a foot into each leg of the jeans, zips up. Looks around dazed, as if he had forgotten this unimportant intimate landscape.

The room. Now ten degrees hotter? The air definitely thicker. Odors—of the sink and damp linoleum, dogs, refrigerated crushed ice, mayonnaise and cold potatoes, hot people and pine—are expanding.

Another daughter appears, this the youngest, thirteen or so. Darker-haired than the others, darker-skinned. Naturally golden. And shapely. And she wiggles it. Her bikini is purple with pink lightning bolts. Her breasts are tea-cup-sized but, you know, fatty and full and firm. She smells powerfully of suntan lotion. She and her friends have spent much of this summer stretched out on towels and blankets a few yards behind the two joined mobile homes and between Willie's old junk (but neatly parked) cars, trucks, tractors, skidder, and towers of tires.

She has Willie's gray eyes and narrow face, which Mickey Gammon studies as much as he can in flash-glances, though mostly flash-glances at her body.

She has brought in a dishpan, which she now fills with ice; then, on her way out, she presses one of the small hollow cylinders of ice to the huge Artie Bean's neck. He roars, "Jesus!"

Willie leaps upon the girl, bellering, "You need a spank for that!" Then confers with Artie. "She needs a spank, doesn't she?"

"Yes."

The dog tag on his chain swings out from Willie's chest as he lifts the girl from the floor. Effortlessly.

She cries, "Stop it!" This girl's hair, a tight dark braided blob right on top of her head, is now releasing sweet loose curls over the back of her neck.

Willie carries her bride-fashion to the sink, then lowers her with a flourish. This does not make him out of breath. He says, gravely and deeply, "Ramone, you have gone too far as usual." His face is no longer playful but dark and angry.

"Drown her in the sink," says Artie, then laughs.

Willie ignores Artie. He says with gritted teeth, while looking deeply into his daughter's eyes, "This goes with the school problem, of course . . . which we haven't caught up on yet, dear. I've put it off wa-a-ay too long. Twenty whacks for the school problem. Ten for the ice." His grip on her slim upper arm is not a pretty thing to look at. Her young face seems on the edge of some not unfamiliar grief and shame. Willie reaches into the dish strainer and hauls out a large white spatula. "Turn around," he commands, but he's already forcing her arm, turning her.

She makes an embarrassed profound little sound.

Mickey seems no paler than usual, but his skin indeed feels cadaver cold.

Rex goes to the door and looks out through the silvery screen, paces once, then stands with his hand on the door latch.

"Hands on the sink," Willie orders the girl. She places both hands on the edge of the sink, knuckles whitening, sticks out her bottom with the little straining strip of purple and glossy pink bikini, which covers almost nothing, there the plump browned deep curves of her buttocks show and the smooth hips, not a single scar or blemish. She says something weakly, miserable, which no one but Willie can hear.

Willie turns the spatula around and around, hefting it, delaying the inevitable, such a kind heart, this Willie Lancaster.

Seems nobody in the kitchen is breathing, let alone speaking. Just sweating noiselessly.

The girl, Ramone, hangs her head, and her short fat dark braid flops loose and drops over one shoulder. "Mumma!" she cries out through the little opened window over the sink, but not loud enough. Seems she is choking on a sob. Seems she is resigned to this.

Willie says in a terrible whisper, "Pull the bathing suit down, dear. This has really got to smack the skin to teach a lesson."

Mickey thinks he is going to faint from a nerve-racking clash of fear and horniness. He considers the heavy Ruger against his ribs, the ten shots . . . semiauto . . . *bang bang bang*. He imagines the side of Willie's head missing. Or the girl's head. To put her out of her suffering. Or his own, his own suffering mighty. He also pictures other things. He closes his eyes.

A horrible scream, two screams wavering . . . and, yes, the smack of plastic against bare skin; the screams, one high, one low. It's Willie and the girl laughing. Somehow the big white spatula is in *her* hand and she's whaling Willie over the shoulder with it, his bare shoulder. Now she leaps agilely on his bare sweat-slick back, gripping his rib cage with her thighs and knees, thwonking his head with the spatula. Now she seizes his head, forearms around his eyes. He falls to the floor. "Mumma!" screams Willie.

"*Bad!*" the girl scolds, standing over him. She gives him one hard final stinging swat on his back, then tosses the spatula into Artie Bean's hands. "Make sure he behaves, Beano!" she commands, picks up the tub of ice, and prances past the expressionless icy-eyed Rex York, who steps away from the door to let her out.

Rex says to Willie, "Okay, I'm going. Give me a call tonight." And he pushes out through the door. Mickey slips the shoulder holster and gun off, lays it all on the table with both hands, *with care,* and plows on out after Rex, although Willie has already hopped to his feet and, with raised fist, is yelling after them both—"To the Republic! God save the Republic!"—and the door whooshes shut.

Nighttime in Mickey Gammon's tree house.

He lies on his back, knees up, feet placed flat. He hears night sounds. It is breezy, and so the trees are just as anxious as hunted mice and hungry owls.

He smokes. The taste of the smoke is tired. But its work feels good to his blood. His head is busy, planning his life.

What next?

He is thinking about the people who own this land, the ones with the big leader who everyone talks about since he was in the paper: St. Onge. Gordon, Gordo, the Prophet. Rumor has it that the people worship him, and they are all *very* crazy.

With time on his hands, Mickey strolls.

Going down, down. Down the woodsy mountain. A zigzag path through the trees. Very steep. The sun is straight above. The hot steam is surrounding. The deerflies ride a tornado of their own making. The path is spongy in some places, mossy and mushroomy. But in other places, rooty and rocky. A broad weathered ledge is crossed in one area, wide open. Crusty rock but kinda looks fuzzy in the heat. Mickey's eyeballs are as sticky as jam. The smoke of his cig is hot, too, but dry.

Out here on the ledge, he feels like a stewing carrot. He looks down around his feet at many busy party-faced purple flowers on runners of small thick leaves moving at an unseeable speed around the shady edge of the big opening.

Puff, puff. More smoke. He raises his eyes. Through a triangular swatch of "view" he can see, down there way below, the place called the Settlement where the St. Onge people live or are *kept,* depending on who you talk to.

Big U-shaped building. Like a cowboy town in the old movies. In the yard of the U-shaped building is a grassy square. Tall trees. But also homemade-looking things, made of wood, painted in colors like green and purple and osha yellow. These are gigantic creatures with kids going inside them and on them and underneath. For instance, a dinosaur, a cow, a spaceship.

Some boys about Mickey's age, some younger, go along a brick path, behind them a brown dog. Sort of a shepherd.

But, man, hard not to notice, there are enough little squirts . . . age four, age five, whatever . . . enough to feed the big dinosaur there, all it takes to feed Tyrannosaurus rex . . . tall as a barn. Some of the kids are in the head now, looking out through the tall teeth.

A whole line of women come out of one screen door of the U-shaped building, and most of them have got a chubby-legged baby kid, carried on a hip or neck.

On the part of the square U that looks into the grassy dinosaur area are screened porches and boardwalks with a ton of screen doors. Shadows of people—or, rather, light face or arm shapes—move inside the dark screeny shadows in there.

Some call this a "home school." Mickey wonders which ones of the mean-ass-looking guys over by the Quonset huts—three big Quonset huts—are the teachers. And principal. And vice principal.

People trotting and trudging in and out of the big bay doors, arriving in trucks, and there are two sawmills and a sawdust blower, all quiet but no way abandoned-looking.

A radio tower. Door now opens in the small building. Some people leaving, and people leaving the big sandy parking area. Very busy. Like a town. Like maybe even busier. Also cattle and sheep. Mooing and baaing.

He notices a lot of black chickens, free as the breeze, walking chicken-leggedly along, diving between people, taking dust baths in the parking lot, scratching weeds, poking cow flaps.

Now he sees some girls his own age. *Real* chicks. Not as free as the chickens. They seem weighted by thoughts and thrust forward by missions. Some wiggling at the hips, probably hot for sex. One wears a soft-looking shirt of an April-sky blue. Another a soft creamy orange. Mickey loves soft girls the best. Soft in all ways. He studies the blue and orange one hard. And smokes hard.

Off to the right, up a hill higher than his, some guys on ATVs are pulling small loads. They are cruising as quiet as spaceships at least from this far it seems like that. He studies them hard and again puffs the dry calming smoke.

Now going up a rough dirt road running parallel with rough-looking electric wires are more silent ATVs driven by girls. Three girls. Three ATVs. Three wagons. Wagons with black boxes. Big batteries?

One girl is wearing a bathing suit top of yellow. Very small cups. Too small for her breasts. She is dark. Maybe she is an Indian. He can't really see her face. But the black hair is in a braid as mighty as a ship's rope, thick as her own arm. Something tough about her, the way she handles that ATV, jerking the handlebars around rocks and roots. Not really a soft girl. Mickey decides he is not limited to soft girls, only that soft and sweet are easier to be with. But for purposes of feeling crazy in the jaws, hands, and dick, there are no dividing lines.

This does not seem like a school with rows. And no buzzers and intercoms. This might just be life. *Puff puff puff.*

♡♡ Secret Agent Jane reports from inside.

This is not a school of officialness and for real. NO! NO! NO! NO, it is NOT! No small desks. No giant halls. No bell-buzzing thing to make you stand up or sit down. Nobody here knows the time! No principal to make you scared of talking or not standing or sitting down in the exact right way. No DARE man in a police suit.

Here is just shops with big porches and Quonsets, which are big round-roof things. And sawmills. And a radio house, very small. Everybody is someplace here—inside, outside, either sitting and TALKING or making stuff or reading WEIRD stuff like books of history of a very fat kind, some thin—but NO TESTS. NO REPORT CARDS. So what are these history books for, to hurt your arm?

Crow.

At this hot saggy time of day, you, crow, have so little to report. Trees are filled with your kind, all in pensive attitudes. Perhaps it is prayer. Your prayer might be that you are never as lonely as the boy human, Mickey Gammon, standing on the ledge, his gray wolfy eyes stealing over the sun-bright and shady mysteries of Settlement life.

♡♡ **Secret Agent Jane tells more from inside.**

I am exhausted. Too many people here, as you know. They are all exhausted. Big sizes and little sizes. No time for TV—if you can find a TV. I have looked everywhere. Instead it is just things you DO.

You make boards at the sawmill, screaming noise.

You also make fiddles. Tamya put a color on hers of iodine, a color like out-of-space at night.

Also you make flutes and whistles and kazoos. This is a special shop with a pretty window.

Furniture-making shop is messy and heapy and wood dust goes up your nose. Also it makes screaming noise.

Also some people make *roads!*

Also food, which nobody here buys. They do all these jobs, like seeds, weeds, pick, jars, cellars, cook, just for *one* thing. Ol' food.

Maple syrup starts in pails here.

Also, they do Christmas trees to *sell.*

In real school you do not *sell.*

Back at the tree house, swatting tidal waves of biting bugs, Mickey tells us.

Rex says he'll pick me up on the way to the pit Saturday. So I says I'll meet him down by the transformers. So he thinks I still live over there with *them,* Mr. King Shit Locke and his televisions. Well . . . I *think* Rex thinks I live there. Actually, he said that at Bean's—the Variety—they said a woman called, probably Erika. I can't picture it to be Mum. Erika, I picture. The store guys said I'd been in and told her I looked alive.

So then Rex says to me, "You must have missed supper or something so she was calling around. Someone at the Convenience Cubical said there was a call there too. But they hadn't seen you up that way."

Man, I do not lie to Rex. His eyes read you. Maybe something in his head beeps . . . you know, if you lie or feed him a line. I've seen him look *into* Willie like this when Willie is making up shit, like how he had to shoot an agent once to defend himself. But I knew that was made up and nothing beeped in my head.

So Rex is looking at me, waiting for an answer, truth or lie, pick one. So, me, I just don't say anything. I just stare at the rug we're standing on.

♡♡ More from Secret Agent Jane on the learning situation at the Settlement.

There's actually one of the shops which is a newsroom. For doing news. It's where you collect what's going on so we can make the History as It Happens books. There is a printing press, loud, smelly. Copy machines, but "too many drawbacks," one of the mothers said. Typewriters. Not computers. I say typewriters are too old. And one broke, but they just went and fixed it. I asked why not get computers. A boy named Rawn said, " 'Cuz they're the devil." So the history news books are made with glue and pens and too much work.

People actually talk about history while they eat and walk around, about hydris and commons and slaves and galleys and poppists and robin barons. And they talk about world-wise news which they find out in altrinite news. They have medical education, and natomies studies, kromo zones, and stuff on munny sipal law.

Also fruit flies. And haircuts in the beauty shop. I did one hairdo on Margo. She said thank you very much. Also people learn arki teckture. But not much for sports or any flying balls. And nobody goes home on a bus. They just stay and stay, stuck here like I am, only mostly there are mothers here too, and fathers and grandpeople. In a *real* school you have only kids who are all alike, all one size and clothes-perfect. No mothers or grandpeople allowed.

But in real school at least when you get home your mum is there, but always very tired from helping the dentist with millions of rotten teeth.

Mickey in his tree house, arms around his head to protect his face from the bugs.

I would tell Rex, but then what? Offer me the couch? Then I'd be wicked in the way. Maybe he'd hate me. And her—his mother. They'd hate me, like here's Mickey Gammon in the middle of the living room. Who wants a totally useless guy in the middle of the living room?

And besides, how can I explain what happened? Fuckin' A, what *was* it that happened? *I* don't even know. One minute I was in Donnie's house. The next minute I'm here. Like, *poof!* It's not a thing you can talk about, not like the Constitution, the UN, Mini-14's, and the Federal Reserve Act of 1913.

 Saturday. Mickey, lighting up a "borrowed" cigarette, speaks.

So I'm watching Doc shoot Big John's new Bushmaster at the man's head, the bad-guy shape on the cop targets we're using now.

This is pretty funny. I've got to sit here on Rex's tailgate and pretend I'm not surprised by Willie asking me if his wife should send flowers or something. For Jesse.

Okay. This means Jesse is dead. Right?

How should I know? I'm just out on the moon, the last person to know, right?

But I live there with them, right? I should know if Erika and Donnie want flowers or "something else."

I probably got a look on my face, sorta squinty, like I'm twisting my brains over whether it should be daisies or roses or chicken casserole.

I don't look at Rex. 'Cause he's got the mind-reading thing, remember? I do not look in the captain's eyes.

 Bonny Loo speaks.

My real and legal name is Bonnie Lucretia Sanborn. Sanborn was Danny's name, his family. But Danny is dead. The accident. No drinking. No overtiredness. Just a really big truck and a fluke. Danny the one driving the really big truck.

I won't say things were great before he died. We were having it hard, making ends meet. Even if it hadn't been for the accident, I would like to have had us all move here to the Settlement, Danny too. He would not have wanted to work here with them. He never liked working with a bunch of people. That's why he drove truck. That's just the way it is for some. They don't do their best in a bunch. He was always on the road. If he were to live here, you wouldn't really call him *living* here, just kinda *stopping by*. It would have worked out. But that never happened.

Everything seems pretty good in my life these days. I can't complain. Six years since the accident. I guess it takes that long to get used to your dear one rotting in the grave. But also, all the circumstances, you know, my *financial* situation then. It sucked. You know, everything is affected by the *financial*. Out in the world, outside the Settlement, everything costs. Like Gordon says, "Everything is a commodity. Justice is a commodity. Information is a commodity. Honor is a commodity. Dignity is a commodity. Health is a commodity. Death is a commodity. Land is a commodity. Freedom is a commodity. Air, water, energy, art, song, info, thoughts, peace of mind, your soul—it's all for sale, and if you can't buy it, you will not have it."

Anyway, it was terrible for a while, especially after my mum-in-law Dorothy went to the nursing home and the state grabbed the house. I came *this close* to slitting my wrists. Even with Gabriel depending on me. It didn't matter. My thoughts were not normal; they had gotten gray and small and squeezed. I figured Gabriel was better off dead too. I figured everybody was better off dead. Well, it's true. Life isn't a great gift. It is shit. Just various adaptations by various organisms to various environments of various ages of planet Earth. That's the science view. And me, I've always been a scientist. Don't laugh. *Anyway,* a normal brain says, "A new day is coming! See the fresh morning! Get up and go!" The brain of a human person in a hopeless trap wants only to escape to the comfort of nothingness. It sees everything different. Big things look small. Small things look big. And *everything* is ugly.

My mother says maybe I take after my father, who also fell apart. He flipped. Only he started shooting. And the cops didn't try to talk him out of it. I was right there watching when they all shot him. I was there watching him fall from the top of our cousin's truck, heavy and dead, like a stack of newspapers is dead, like an old sweater is dead, like a book, a lamp, a rag, or a sawdust doll. Where does that aura of vigor go? Weird, huh? One minute you are everything; the next minute you are nothing. Ma says it had an effect on me. Sure it did. But what about the *world,* the real world *here and now?* Trying to get by, you are lost in ice-hot space, the *living* dead.

Until the Settlement people come to save you!

Now when I wake up in my little pale-pink house with my three children nestled around me, or if my new husband is here, I am in his arms and the kids are tucked into their really jazzy carved pine beds, and I think of the day's plans, always so many plans, so many sisters here, and I want to live. My brain is normal. I get the kids in the tub. I sweeten them with kisses. Or a lecture, if they are acting like shits. Then there is the getting-dressed race. And then we head down the path to the shops.

Okay, so everything ain't perfect. The husband situation has a kind of creepy twist. You know, the *P* word, polygamy. Yes, I am one of *the wives.* No, it's nothing like you can imagine. In fact, at the moment I'd rather think about something else. Like cooking!

It's one of my most favorite things. I think of myself as a cooking scientist. Or cooking explorer. I never use receipts or cookbooks. No measuring cups or spoons. Each pot or pan of stuff I rustle up, I wonder why it doesn't explode before I get it to the table. But you know something? Everything I put on those tables, the family says it's the best ever. *The best ever.* And there's seldom a crumb or spoonful left when the tables are cleared. My huge egg-shaped breads they sometimes call "clouds."

I won't report to you now which of my sisters burn food or make food that just doesn't appeal. Mean talk is mean and would quickly turn to heartache among us.

I admit there are nights when I wake with a low moan, and the faces of my sisters here look huge and distorted and leering, and they steal from me or push me and pull a sleeve hard so that I begin to fall . . . off a cliff or something . . . but only in dreams. In real life they are very nice people. Basically.

♡♡ Going to visit Marian St. Onge. Secret Agent Jane speaks.

Gordie takes me in his truck to go visit *his* mum. We bring her peas and radishes and piles of chard in a basket. And orange cow butter shaped like a heart. She lives in Wiscasset near the nuclear thing. This is something Gordie does every week, drives to Wiscasset "to check on my mother."

She is not real friendly. Her house is huge with a white rug and naked angels. When she sees me, she says hello and shows me some of her house so we can look at it like you do in a store, cruisin' the racks. I think she's rich. She has these baby angels with real pee-pees and other statues. Everything is also red . . . like curtains. Or white. Her chairs are white. But it's a pinkish-white when you are me with these special secret agent glasses.

Her TV is in the wall.

Gordie is talking-talking, but his mum is quiet-quiet. Then we go to the kitchen, which is the best kitchen! All the stuff for a kitchen. I bet my dad Damon would love it here. The toaster is more shiny than even normal.

Marian is Gordie's mum's name. She offers me a cookie, which I accept. It is huge. You'll know when you look at a pizza how huge. It is perfect. Big and perfect. With chocolate chips perfectly spaced. She must have paid a bunch of money for cookies like this. Definitely not a cookie made by *hands*.

She puts me at the *breakfast nook,* which is in the wall and has a window to look out and see the *outside* statues. These are also naked boys. And beautiful, with their perfectly curled hair. With pink flowers on bushes. Outdoors is very nice and rich.

She offers me a pretty napkin with cows on it. And milk, but I say no thanks to milk. Even her perfect store kind that doesn't squirt out of cows. I hate milk. Then she goes right into the other room, *another* living room with all-white stuff and a metal God statue of a guy with clothes, and Gordie and her talk very low for a long time.

I eat the cookie real fast, so then all I have for something to do is nothing. I would ask to watch TV, but I guess I won't because it is weird with them. They have stopped talking, and then in a minute she says, "These people are like a disease with you. Like your alcoholism."

Gordie is quiet.

I use the cow napkin to wipe my secret agent glasses clean. If I stand a certain way I can see Gordie's mum through the archway, standing in the middle of the pretty room holding her head. TV is right behind her. If it were on, I could watch it from here.

Now Gordie's mum begs and begs him to use "common sense." She says someday he is going to be in a lot of trouble because of people like Lisa Meserve.

Whoa! My mother is Lisa Meserve!!!!!

Then she says more stuff. "I used to think these friendships you had were teenage rebellion. But you are almost forty now, and it's every hippie and biker and indigent widow and farmer and food-stamp queen and riffraff relative of your father's you can get your hands on. You draw them like flies."

Gordie grabs her and wraps his whole huge arms around her. She is an old lady, old for a mother, a tall old lady, but she is disappeared in Gordie's hugest hug of love. Gordie's mouth says, in a mashed way against her hair, "Mother." He sounds soft and serious and beggish. I adjust my secret glasses, and everything wiggles and bulges out real to me. If I had my crayons and pen with me for my secret agent note-book, which is in my pocket in a secret way, I would draw a picture of Gordie's mum in her pretty purple swirl vest and white blouse, crying. You can't believe what all the people in the world do until you get a chance to listen to them in a secret way and SEE into their brains and hot hearts.

☆ **From a future time, Whitney St. Onge remembers the Parlor Night Salons.**

Bree and I were both fifteen. Everyone thought I was smart. Physics, architecture, anthropology, politics, at least in some humid not-too-academic way, were to me desserts.

But Bree* was ancient. Her face deformed, her brain golden. Day-times she still worked in the woods with her brothers and her father. So we called her Paul Bunyan Woman. After work, she'd sneak one of

*Last reminder: There is a character list is at the back of the book.

their trucks and whiz up here to the Settlement, driver's license–free, sawdust in her cuffs. And sometimes oil paints and ink on her hands, for she was an artist with no boundaries. Our salons began to wheel in high gear around that head of scarlet hair.

One night I especially recall, it was deep summer. She arrived late, her arms loaded with newsletters and hurried notes, her research.

It was damp in the West Parlor. Maybe not the most horrible hot, but that stuffy-clammy that makes the cedar ceiling pour out a prehistoric smell, as my mother called it.

We older girls, the most devoted salonites, were hunched on the rugs digging through a box of Radio Free Maine audio tapes that belonged to our devout leftist, Nathan Knapp who, in his black waleless corduroy jacket and combed-wet dark hair, sat on one of the big couches, his dark-brown eyes level on everything. He was near Gordon's age, late thirties or so.

Our library had a stash of more such tapes, and Bree was sending away for further selections with her logger money. There were enough of these taped lectures to last a lifetime. And some you'd have to play three times or keep backing up so you could unravel all the Chomsky clauses, especially for Samantha and some of the others who would listen with such a toothache-looking squint.

It was Bree's idea to get more beefed up on events in South America, Cuba, Haiti, Africa, the Middle East, Russia, and the old Soviet bloc. We already BB (Before Bree) had researched everything (everything but field trips) on the Open Door policy, the National Security Council document (NSC-68), the International Monetary Fund, the World Bank, the Bank of International Settlements, the Trilateral Commission, the Bilderberg Group, the Council on Foreign Relations, and the Project for the New American Century, adding up to what Gordon and another Settlement man, John Lungren, called the octopus. Those particular study projects, we had guessed, were Gordon's idea of putting a lid on our interest in the outside world—meaning outside the Settlement. Sort of like if you are jolted awake in the night to the smell of smoke, you do not open the bedroom door if it feels burning hot to your palm. You find a window to climb out of. Alternate route!

Or so it seemed. Gordon would lead you down a lot of dark trails for no reason but to observe. He said knowing gave you dignity.

But Bree's idea was to *do* something about the world-sized fire. Yep, there was a lot about Bree that scared Gordon, our father who art on the couch in exhausted sleep at this particular salon.

Bree and Gordon weren't man and wife yet, man and woman, man and hurricane. She was still in that phase where she wouldn't look him in the eye, just giggle and hide behind that explosion of red tendrils. But with everyone else she was not shy. Her face wasn't exactly spine-chillingly ghastly, just nothing like you'd ever seen. It would make your brain hop the first time you saw the distance apart of her eyes and the stretched-out bridge of her nose.

But maybe, to her, *his* face was too much. It seemed to blind her. She saw in his face something nobody else in this world could see. Some of it she was right about. Some of it she was dead wrong about.

That summer night, she came straight to my side, between me and my half sister Michelle. She dropped to a limber squat, our agile logger girl!

The usual salonites were on hand, slouched around on the rockers and love seats, couches, and little needlework-covered stools. My mother was there. Two other mothers, a few brave ten- and eleven-year-olds. Some men, but not many teen boys.

As the daytime shriveled at the big floor-to-ceiling windows, nobody got up to put on brighter lamps. There was just a red stained-glass thing, shaped like a tall can glowing in a spooky way. Robins and wood thrushes were in full chirrup and tweedle beyond the screens. Some cups would clink with turning spoons. We had a few tea sippers.

Yeah, Gordon was a-snooze, face squashed sideways into a palm, slackened shoulder and bicep braced by the puffy arm of the old patched couch. But his legs, straight out on the layers of rugs and crossed at the ankles, were alert-looking. He made gentle-but-lionish *tisk-k-purr* sounds, never a true snorer.

On another couch was the Settlement's head sawyer, Stuart Congdon. He loved the salons: the evening ones, the scattered afternoon ones, and some of the research committees. And what he called "oversight field trips" to the State House, where we all tried very hard to pretend we were docile.

Stuart—who, by the way, stood about five foot, a dwarf, I suppose—got us on to much wow info. Such as how U.S. and British banks and European aristocracy built Nazi Germany and used the craziest guy they could find to terrorize Germans and the world. And they funded the Bolsheviks. Yep, they steered Lenin's car, so to speak. There was tons of documentation on this but not heavily thumbed and pawed through by much of America.

Stuart also got us into the realm of old documents and letters of the 1600s and 1700s written by Englishmen in the days of emptying the Commons. And letters and diaries of colonists. None of these old-time guys could spell any one word one way. Except *slavery*. We went into a research frenzy on sailors and pirates. This stuff is more dazzling and blood-pounding than you think. Jeepers...it...is...who...we...are!

But some work at the Settlement is very hard. Sawmill, for instance. Like Gordon, Stuart would eventually tip sideways, his head pillowed by another salonite's shoulder. He wouldn't snore, but he usually had a growly stomach.

My mother, Penny, was there that night with her Settlement-made skirt and little embroidered vest over a dark jersey, her dark-blonde hair freshened with a hundred brush strokes. She was not much for digging up the socioeconomic-political dirt, old or new. She'd sit through a whole session fully awake but saying nothing. Just a small smile.

On the wall behind her where she sat that evening was an old shredded-looking American flag and a painted plaque. Words of Mark Twain: *I never let my schooling interfere with my education*. Flag and plaque were both on that tongue-and-groove wall before I was born, and I'm the oldest Settlement offspring. My mother, Penny, is so hushed, so invisible sometimes. But she was one of the founders of the Settlement, working away her youth to get the food and energy co-ops rolling. She had been a local girl. Most of the others were from Aroostook or the Passamaquoddy reservation. The big thing for her was *knowledge* and *wisdom for our kids*. And *fearless curiosity*.

My mother's dreams, I believe, have all come true.

☆ **In a future time, once-passionate breathless Bree also recalls that night.**

The West Parlor! It was all simmering in red light, like faces beyond a thickness of plasm, a tissuey many-eyed thing, queerer than my own face must seem to others. And all those rugs, hooked and braided, giving back your voice in a hush. No cold glassy echoes here, no; it was like being tucked into a fold of flesh.

We were running a new tape, taking notes, but also drowning it out with our three-word emergency critiques, our groans. Small kids were there. When they talked, we'd scold. So they'd sit bright-eyed in the breezes of our ardor.

The dim red-glass lamp—leaded glass, Settlement-made—caused a circle of white light on the table below it. But the opening was small, the glass tall, cylindrical . . . many devil reds and one band of a kind of buck-muscle purple.

Stacked on shelves behind it, glowing redly, were fat scrapbooks all labeled HISTORY AS IT HAPPENS in very kiddie-looking print. Yeah, the kiddie thing. You think *kiddie* means *cute*? Here, in the fearsome secret of this mountain-valley world, kids had a different definition.

There were two maternity persons present. Pregnancy, like gravity, the force that holds the planet together, pulling, steaming, seeping. The parlor felt warmer and warmer.

Stuart yawned. Sky-blue eyes, spewing red beard, biker belly, short legs, arms freckled but tanned, folded over his chest. His whole appearance was thick and raw. Unlike Nathan, who was next to him, thin nose and hair so black, so wet. It looked tight. Like it hurt.

Gordon's big, baggy, homemade T-shirt was a blue that I think of as Neptune blue. Almost green. Jeans worn rough. He hadn't given away his sun-face copper belt buckle yet, so it was still there to make its impression on me, its face trying to imitate old calendar suns, but in its eyes an estimation of time passing, which was jolly. Or maybe ridicule. Or just boldness. So positioned above his fly, it stirred me.

After I'd delivered my latest newsletters and tapes to the heap on the rug, two girls on a flowery couch patted the empty space between them. "Come sit here!" one whispered in her cartoony kiddie voice. She was about nine or ten. Maybe a small eleven.

So I did, I sat, feeling the red light and shadows gush all about me, like the vision of a pleasant hell. My heart beat like a tom-tom. Between us through the evening, a lot of words crackled. Rich, the cedar smell and dampness. Rich, the deep huggy feel of the chairs; the way one of the girls wrapped her bare ankles around another's: sisters . . . or like sisters. And everything was sticking together, becoming one thing, commencing in tandem like a slow-motion race or a race backwards. So rich! Even the posters on the walls. Now a child voice speaks—"The Short Life of the Bretton Woods Agreement"—a hand holding a tape aloft through the musty scarlet light . . . a distant screen door slamming . . . our laughter, our ideas, our so-naughty questions, like "What is the real definition of wealth?" Oh, hey, what a coincidence that you should ask.

"This parlor!" I cried out, almost panting.

Richer than gourmet, richer than high art, because it was *complete* . . . or, rather, the rosy tip of the completeness of the entire St. Onge universe. A room. A summer evening. Chapter one. The sweet sugary tip, yeah.

And chapter two? I believed it would be to help save the world. Don't laugh.

☆ Penny St. Onge recalls that night.

I can see blue. A blue shirt. I can see Gordon sleeping on his hand. I can't think now if Stuart, our sawyer, was there or not. He usually was, but it seems some enthusiastic remark of his would have stuck with me.

There was an audio tape playing. Something like water companies moving in on all of India's water or the CIA's installation of the dictator Pinochet in Chile and his recent flight to a European safe harbor. Maybe the tape told of American financiers' roles in the present sadness of Haiti. Those tapes stitched an enormous patchwork of ruin and misery, bank-approved. It would crack your heart but for the lecturers' voices, so collegiate and paper cold.

I would listen with my hands folded in my lap. Some of the others took notes. We would usually have discussions after. I'd mostly listen through those.

By the time we were ready to leave for bed that night, the older girls were making plans to invite real live lecturers from a prodemocracy group that had the lowdown on the history of corporate charters. We often had guests and speakers, so this wasn't a big new turn.

Some mosquitoes had gotten in, and one wanted my neck. My hands came out of my lap.

"They are leftists," said our Michelle matter-of-factly, the dark red light giving her a half-a-face look.

"Yuh. You wouldn't see a capitalist criticizing the capitalist setup," Samantha Butler observed, leaning to get a better look at the flyer. Her Apache-style head rag was school-bus yellow with scarlet diamonds. Her straight pale hair sort of dusted the old box of Nathan's tapes.

One of the girls from the town who was around that night said she thought maybe *some* people with stocks weren't exactly capitalists. "They aren't the ones running the Federal Reserve. Not the ones disappearing Chileans. Maybe they would be for democracy for . . . everybody."

Michelle *tsk*ed. "*These* guys have to be leftists."

Whitney stood up, flyer in hand. "Seems people get into being left or right. Like frogs or toads."

Chuckles and tee-hees.

Bree spoke in her cigarette-softened way that the left was more for people, while capitalism was about accumulation. "Getting more people involved with the left might save the world."

That's when we heard the voice, gravelly and wet. "The octopus is three hundred years old. Its tentacles and suckers are stuck to *ev-er-ree-thing,* left and right." It was Gordon, who we believed was still asleep because his eyes were still closed, even as other folks were stirring to leave.

All the other voices stopped.

The gravelly voice from Gordon's face, dark with beard, and dark with crimson lighting, repeated, "*ev-er-ree-thing*." He opened one eye and it swept the room, lighthouse fashion. "Remember? Remember?" Then he opened the other eye. He fixed his green gaze on Bree. She turned her face away, raggedly red-orange hair tumbling over her work shirt.

"Save the world?" He sat up, blinking. His voice cleared, so it sounded more like himself. "Whoever sees the whole world as their object of fascination will be working toward centralization. Even if you are nice people." He spoke in such a sad way, rubbing his eyes. "You would have to have a second man-eating octopus to fight the first one."

Whitney drew in closer to him, her arms akimbo.

Michelle was holding a photo close to his face of Haitian men in a big cage. "You gave these to us! *You* were the one pounding your fist and slobbering all over everybody about *Mammoneers! Rememberrrr?*

Somebody still on one of the couches, maybe Dee Dee, let all her breath out through her lips, horse style.

Bree was now standing, but outside the circle of girls, which had squeezed around Gordon.

Committed leftist Nathan was leaving, slipping out, like he'd never been there.

Gordon stood, solid and towering, the carnival light thickening his shoulders and head. He said, "Left is only the left legs of the octopus. The New World Order is industrial and centralized . . . and guess what? Debt-based. All tied in with the same bankers and system. And 'open door' imperialist policies. If it's big, they have their suckers on it and—"

"*Weee* know that!" snarled our flashy Samantha. "We want to start a new one. More chopped up. Like . . . anarchism."

"But you were talking global system," another adult voice supported Gordon.

"Weren't you? You said *left*." Another voice.

Bree smiled. "*I* said left."

Samantha was rocking from foot to foot. "What about the Settlement? You guys are *growinnng.* " She said the word *growing* in a sing-song nah-nah way. "The co-ops are all over the state. That's organized."

Gordon said evenly, "*Not* a global system. Not a great net. Not an octopus. And, sadly, we aren't a threat to the octopus, which is the big ugly child of both big communism and big capitalism. Or, rather, all three are tools of the grand accumulators. The world doesn't even know we're here."

"No?" one of the girls said with a squint.

He lowered his eyes.

In most ways, this night doesn't stand out special for me. This was actually a typical night, the back-and-forth of ideas, the way Gordon's squirrelly mind and loud mouth would always derail everyone. You had to get a squirrelly head yourself to defend your premises.

But there was something this night in the eyes of our girls, their eager eyes made scorchy red and deeper by the little parlor lamp. They were not going to go long with the wind knocked out of their sails this time. All over their silhouettes were sparkles.

Samantha leaned toward Bree and, with just tongue tip, teeth, and lips, no voice, said, "No hope." She was smiling.

Michelle now did the same but with the swishiness of a whisper.

Then Dee Dee too, and Whitney, and the others—and now Bree—
a whispered chant of *No hope* . . . pause . . . *No hope* . . . pause. *No hope
no hope no hope,* on and on with fluttering eyes.

 More advice from the screen.

Hi-ho, there! Do not talk among yourselves. Listen to mccccc!

 **History as it happens (as recorded by Rawn,
age seven, and Lani, age eleven, with assistance
from Whitney and Margo and Michelle, who
are right here).**

We listened to a tape of a lecture by Gordie's friend Bob, Bob Monks.
Whitney understood it, Michelle understood it, and Margo understood
it. It was hard but it was good to be there because Margo gave me a neck
rub. I am Lani. Rawn fell asleep but Gordie says Bob is smart as hell.
He talked about the Business Roundtable. Margo said it's the most powerful union in America. Most unions are not powerful but weak due to
laws made by big business. The Business Roundtable is a union of CEOs
of the most giant corporations. So they don't make laws against themselves. Bob Monks is worried about their power, and Gordie said to
notice that, because Bob is not a leftist. He is a corporate lawyer of capitalism. Everyone says this proves that everybody is worried. Where is
everything going? Big question, right?

In a small American city in the Midwest.

Yet another station wagon waiting to make a left turn in light predawn
traffic exhibits *yet* another MY CHILD IS AN HONOR STUDENT
bumper sticker.

**Out in the world in a rattling rocking factory
in China.**

Workers bend to inspect the flow of glossy MY CHILD IS AN
HONOR STUDENT bumper stickers, broken into smaller orders

from varying towns and schools. This batch is green with white English language lettering. Unreadable. Unappreciated.

In thousands of American and other First World schools.

The uniformly practiced fingers of millions tap the keyboards, the uniformly expectant eyes of millions are lit by the yawing radiance of screens. Millions of brains are locked to uniform programs of study in a haze of trust and belief, snatching at the high-speed and uniformly correct answers and theories required for tests, for scores, for honors.

Secret Agent Jane gathers evidence.

There is a person named Gail here at Gordie's house today, one of the mothers, Michelle's mum. Michelle is one of the oldish girls who is always too busy. She goes to the university with Claire on Wednesdays and talks all the time about stuff nobody cares about. This lady, Gail, has a cute body, nice and shape-ish. And her hair is a good long braid, black hair. But her face is line-ish. And she has too much tattoo. If you have a little tattoo on your leg or arm or titty, a little shamrock or butterfly, it is okay. But Gail has HUGE FLOWERS of smoodged colors around her neck—yes, her *neck*. In front of her shirt, over the button; you can always see part of it.

She is making a rug. She didn't bring any books or games. She doesn't even *try* to make me happy.

The cat likes her and sits by her foot or in the next chair. She calls him Duey. But Bev calls him Frank. He is black and scary and lazy. I hate him. Some cats I like. But all cats here are just dumb. Maybe my Mum will call and say she's coming soon. Maybe the lawyer guy Kane has thought of a way. I reach up for the phone a couple of times when it rings. It's the kind on the wall. Turns out it's only people who want people. I let the phone drop and smash the wall right in the middle of their dumb words. Gail doesn't care if I do this. She just keeps working on her dumb rug no matter what I do.

Gordie comes in from a door with sheds and other doors. He has BAGS. Yes, stuff from the store. I squint my eyes and work up the power. The room glows a meanish pink. I fix my glasses better and I know he knows I know where he's been. "What did you bring me?"

He just feels my shoulder in a love way.

I jerk away. "How come you didn't take me to the store?"

"Because you are unhappy when you are at the store." He has more sunburn, more tan, and believe me, he did not go to the beach. The *real* beach. The ocean one where you can buy stuff.

I say, "If you bought me stuff, I'd be happy. You make everything so hard," I tell him. "You are just trying to get me mad. I'm losing patience!"

He looks at Gail and she looks up from her rug right into his eyes, and then he goes over and puts some stuff from his bags into a drawer.

I say, "The reason people go to stores is to BUY stuff. If I go with you, why? Just to go and stand there in useless stupid space? I need STUFFFFFF!" I cross my arms.

He ignores me, goes to look at some messages on the big nail.

With these secret-power glasses, I can see POLICE. They grab Gordie and sit on him with arm cuffs to make his hands behind him and scare him till he knows it was a BIG MISTAKE to make me mad.

He calls somebody on the phone, and his voice is SO NICE, and he talks about *pine furniture* and *medium grade* and *ready market*. This might be in-legal. I will not forget any of this.

Finally, he goes out the shed doors and I scream after him, "STU-PID APE!"

Gail acts like nothing has happened. But the cat is looking at me with evil eyes and twitching his tail in his chair beside hers. The table is covered with Gail's rug stuff. No food. At lunch, we had to eat in our laps, which is okay only if you have a TELEVISION.

She keeps doing her rug. I keep standing around rotting in boredom.

In a nice way, I ask Gail where she got her pretty hair thing made of wood like a turtle, really cute. She says, "Gordon gave it to me."

My eyeballs turn to ice. Everything looks like flames. "How much did it *cost*?"

She pulls it from the end of her braid. She puts it in my hand. It is so perfect, small cuts and lines, green so beautiful, yellow so beautiful. Colors so sweet for your eyes to see. "He made it," she says. Her face is all cracks and lines as she moves her mouth. She smells sweatish, like a guy.

"He made it?" I toss it back inside her hand. "Who cares what he makes? Little kids *make* stuff." I am feeling sick. I sit down on a chair. It has arms. Better than the cat's chair. I watch Gail's hands, the rug getting more designs. Colors of rustish and green. She pokes at it with hooks. Her hands have rings, one a wedding kind.

I say, "Gail, does Gordie have his truck license still X-pired?"

She looks at me. "You mean his registration? Or his driver's license?"

"Whichever."

Her fingers push rust yarn through the rug shape. "I imagine he's kept up on all that. He's very efficient. It amazes me sometimes how much that man accomplishes in a day." She looks me up and down. "Why do you ask?"

I smile a very nice smile and shrug. "Some kids told me he was driving in-legal."

"I don't know. So much goes on here. Maybe one of the farm trucks has a funny sticker. *I* can't keep up with it all."

"It's against the law to do inlegal rej-strations and stickers."

"Mm-hm." She keeps looking at her rug. She always just brings her own stuff to do. Once she brushed my hair. That was nice. But otherwise, she is kind of a jerk. "Is *your* rej-stration paid up?" I ask.

She looks at me again. "I don't have a car anymore. I lost my license. OUI. People here drive me when I need to get anywhere."

"OUI. That's the drunk thing."

She nods.

"Are you drunk now?"

"I'm having one of my dry times," she says, not looking at me. "Ten months now."

"What about the windmills? Aren't they inlegal?"

She keeps her eyes down. "*Ill*-legal. And I did hear that about the windmills: too tall, by a few feet. The code man is Gordon's friend, which helps. And it's not a *crime* exactly. It's some sorta ordinance, not as bad as murder."

"What *about* murder?" I ask. "Or robbed banks? Gordie done those ever?"

She laughs.

I don't laugh. I say, "Well?"

"Of course not, Jane."

Behind my pink-power heart glasses, my eyes squeeze into skinny thin shapes for extraspecial vision. I look around. I stand up and go over to Gordie's desk and feel stuff. I open a drawer. I spin some wheels around, which are these things with people's names wrote backwards on white cards and pink cards. Some cards are empty. There are their name, telephone, address, zip thing, and other words. There are so many cards on each wheel thing. Hundreds. Maybe some are crooks. Killers. Bomb men. Maybe the police would see these wheel things and go, *Uh-huh, this is the evy dents we have been looking for*.

Gail's voice. "Stay out of Gordon's stuff, Jane." She says it nice-ish and jerk-ish.

I look, and the cat is looking up at Gail. Most cats sleep. This one just watches. I say, "What about Bev and Barbara? Are they against the law? Is their rej-stration run out yet?"

Gail laughs, a soft but very long laugh. "You're cute," she says.

♡♡ Secret Agent Jane and the secret side of Gordon St. Onge. Jane speaks.

Claire, who is Gordie's round X-wife, says to me a couple of days ago, "Jane dear, I'm going to sign you up for our trip to Portland to see the quilt show."

Jane dear. I am sick of all this Jane dear business.

I asked very nicely, "Do we get to stop at McDonald's?"

She said, "No."

"I'll just stay here," I told her.

She said, "Most of the mothers and big girls would like to go see the beautiful quilts from all over New England. And the big boys and men are all out straight on work this week, none to spare."

"Well, if you stop at McDonald's, I'll go." I smiled real nice. "Sound like a good deal?" I folded my arms.

She got a wicked mean look. "It isn't going to be much longer, Jane, before you will *have* to do some things around here that take others into consideration."

"So?" I said. I took off my heart-shapes glasses and made my eyes as mean as hers, eyes into eyes.

Later, Bonny Loo came to fix my supper and I said, folding my arms to show I was serious, "Bev and Barbara will do what I say. Tell them they need to stay with me when you guys all go to see stupid quilts."

It was the spatula I don't like that Bonny Loo was using to fix my egg. It mooshes the egg too much. Bonny Loo only makes one egg for me, fried in butter. It usually comes out with too many brown lines. If I give one small look of disgust, she flips the egg to the cat. And she only brings ONE egg and she always says, "Ha-ha, a chicken laid this egg from its CUNT." She is so disgusting she makes my stomach feel vomitish.

So that night while she is poking the egg in the pan and all I see is her back, her voice says in a happy, singing, weird way, "Bev and Barbara are going to the quilt show, ho-ho."

I make my eyes squinty. "Well, who is going to stay here with me since I am NOT going unless we stop at McDonald's . . . or maybe Burger King. I'll go along with Burger King."

Her voice says, "Big Bertha is coming to stay with you."

"Big Bertha?" I ask. Something about the way she says *Big Bertha* makes my neck hurt. And my stomach.

"We hired her. She lifts weights. She's very strong and very big. You will *luvvvv* Big Bertha."

This was a joke. There was no Big Bertha. They were just bluffing me. I was not going to fall for this.

"Oh, goodie," I said.

So the next day is the Quilt Show. That's today. And guess what. There's no Big Bertha. Ha-ha! I knew it. Instead there's *shifts*. All men. And big boys. All sweaty. Some are nice. Some are boring. Some boys showed me tricks, head stands and stuff. I showed them some cheers of cheerleaders. The man Oh-RELL told me about one of his hogs who has a name of Al, who is extra smart. He told me about a horse once that could kiss lips and shut gates. Oh-RELL says he wants to be cremation-ized when he dies and buried with his oxen, which are big cows that pull. Oh-RELL taught me another French thing, how you say "Cummen Sar Vorr!," which means *Hi,* I think. Or actually, *How does it go?* It's very French. Plus I know *ploys,* which are wicked perfect pancakes," he said. After Aurel, a man named Ernest. It was his shift. The boys told me Ernest hates kids and would probably be a grouch. He *was* quiet and didn't tell me stuff or show me stuff, but he brought me an apple.

And he gave me four quarters, which was very nice of him. I said, "Thank you very much."

So guess who comes for the noon shift, carrying a big box? Might as well be Big Bertha. It's big hotshot Gordie. I am sitting at the table with good posture, looking straight ahead at a wall to show Gordie how much I have had to suffer here. I am wearing my heart-shapes glasses perfectly adjusted for special vision.

Gordie walks across my vision and nods.

I wiggle my fingers once to him, like a wave. To be nice. But not to act too excited. If you want POWER you do not act excited to see someone.

He puts the box on the counter. He looks really hot and drippy.

I say, without really looking at him, "I suppose that box is my horridable lunch."

Gordie says, "Right-o." And he goes off to his room, which is actually the living room, and he comes back with a different shirt, still buttoning the top button. He smiles at me.

I smile back. I have already looked in the box. There is nothing good about the box. You can tell Gordie isn't even *trying* to please me. Not even one single maple candy in there. They have hundreds of maple candies here that come in cute shapes, like leaf shapes and cute cows and little smiling fat ladies. They taste like HEAVEN, creamy and sweet. The lady Lee Lynn told me they are kept in a *secret safe* place. That's stupid. I am tired of the way everything here is always secret and safe.

Gordie gets stuff out of the box and he makes me a sandwich with lettuce and tomatoes and beans. Yes, BEANS. Brown, cold, old. He puts the sandwich on a dish on the table next to my crayons and books and stuff.

I say, "No thanks."

He looks at the sandwich a real long time.

"I do not like beans," I say.

So he stuffs half this sandwich in his mouth and says, with his mouth stuffed, "I'll make you one without beans."

I watch his back, his belt, his belt loops. His keys. His knife, which is folded inside the leather thing. His arms with sleeves rolled over and over real high up to show his tan. He is a huge person. Like on TV they wrastle or lift weights. He could probably sit right on you as long as he wanted. With these dark glasses, I can hear squeak sounds in his stomach. I say, "I don't like those tomatoes."

He doesn't turn around, just keeps pawing over the sandwich stuff. His voice says, "You liked tomatoes a few days ago."

"The other ones had sugar on them."

"How about this lettuce?"

"Are you kidding?"

So he brings a plain empty bread sandwich for me to the table and lays it very gently in the little dish in front of me. And there's one with beans and everything for himself.

Some bread in this world is yummy. But this is the beige wheat kind. With these pink heart-shaped glasses, I can see it has very disgusting pink specks. I pull both my hands back and put them in my lap. I say very calmly, "No thanks." Out there beyond these secret agent glasses, his whiskery face is just the funniest weird color.

He goes over to one of his cupboards, and he is very tall so the top shelves are easy. He says, "You like pepper jelly? It has sugar in it." He gets a spoon from the drawer and digs out some stuff from the jar and makes a pile of it on his plate right beside his sandwich. The stuff is black. "Gor-maaaaaay," he says, lapping the spoon and looking wicked love-ish into my eyes.

I look squintish at the black stuff. I say, "What's that?"

He looks at my face. "A spoon," he says. He's playing dumb.

I shrug. With these secret glasses, I can make him hardly there.

"We've got plenty of milk down here today," he says, nodding toward the fridge. Around his eyes sometimes is dark, tiredish and lumpy, which is how his eyes are today. And he is dripping all over his face from hotness.

"I hate milk," I says.

"You need milk."

I shrug "I hate it. Bev and Lee Lynn and Gail and all of them know I hate milk."

He takes a bite of his lettuce, tomatoes, and bean sandwich, a huge bite. And his mouth sucks and chomps and plungers. It makes me sick. I stare at his mouth. The noise gets worser. With these special glasses, actually all these people here eat like pigs.

"You like milk before you came here?"

"You can ask Granpa or my Mum *behind my back* if you want, but they will just say no." I stare into Gordie's eyes. I *know* he and Granpa and my Mum whisper about me on the phone like I'm just a plant. I say, "It hasn't anything to do with your horridable milk here being from Oh-RELL's gross old pewish cows. I don't like milk. You get it?"

His lips and tongue are like a storm, a terrible whirring, everything squishing, juicing, chomping. And this is probably just a snack for him. After this, he'll probably go up to the Settlement and eat a few chickens and sheep and pumpkins and thirty or forty maple candies shaped like cute leaves.

I say, "I would like some sugar on this bread. WHITE sugar."

He leans a little toward me. "No."

Sick monster.

"This is not a restaurant, Jane," he says.

"But I'm hungry."

"Take your pick. Tomato or lettuce or beans or bread and/or milk."

"No thanks."

"Fine," he says. With meanness. And his weirdish whitish blue or green eyes are like knives into my eyes. "I brought you plenty of carrots to snack on through the afternoon. And there's people coming this afternoon, different people, to stay with you, and some are bringing you some afternoon snacks, and you can decide then whether or not you like what they bring."

"But I'm hungry now," I tell him.

"The women—when you first got here—decided to be accommodating. But it is starting to wear thin. Cooking you fourteen different sausages, ten different eggs, ten different cheese sandwiches, seven or eight pans of hot cereal, two dozen not-perfect-enough pancakes is a waste of food. This isn't a restaurant, Jane."

"You already said that."

"Nobody in our family is forced to eat anything they don't like. But most people like *something*. You can wait till snack time and see if the snack pleases you."

I touch the table leg with my foot. With these secret agent glasses, I can imagine it in splinters.

He eats and eats. He smiles a little. He goes to make himself *another* sandwich. I watch his back as he stands over there by the drainboard yanking lettuce apart. He yanks on the lettuce so happily. I hate it when everybody gets so happy just when I'm feeling so mad.

And then what's next? Without even turning around, he says this thing: "Your mother has let you rule. Your mother is a soft and tender woman. A trusting, honest, hard-working, brave, very smart, really generous . . . and very-easily-pushed-around person."

"Shut up," I say. The air is getting hotter and hotter and hotter like real fire.

"I'm not insulting your mum. It's just her personality. But *other* people's personalities take advantage."

"I said to shut up."

"By three o'clock you'll be hungry enough to eat grass clippings."

"I hate you," I say.

He cackles like a witch, walks limply and hunchedly back to the table. "Good," he says. "Wicked evil ugly witches and wizards love it when you hate them. I'm glad you hate me. Hee-hee." He bloms half the new sandwich into his mouth. "Mmmmmmm," he says, around the lettuce that is still pulling itself into his teeth.

I watch him and his eyes are so ice-ish a color and his hair is wet and his mostly brown-black beard is stiff like Cherish, my beautiful Scottie. "I'm HUNGRY!!!" I scream. "I'm HUNGREEEEEEEEEEEEEEEE!!!!" I shake the table, and the big jar of black jelly stuff falls over into a dish, and papers and books and crayons and stuff start a slide. Things go on the floor.

He pats the disgusting beige bread sandwich in my plate, which I do not want.

"Make me some eggs," I say, with just my teeth, and on him I make my expression steady and official. "There are some eggs here in the re-frigerator. There are *seven* eggs. Plenty of eggs."

"You didn't like eggs this morning," he says.

"I did too!"

"No. I was here. Remember, Jane? The scene with the oatmeal? Four pans of oatmeal this time. Then the eggs. And then the toast. How many toasts? Let's see . . . half a loaf? And then the graham snacks Tante Lucienne made special for you. Even the muffins. They were shaped funny or something. You must be pretty hungry by now. And as I recall, you didn't really eat anything of your supper last night . . . or your dinner."

I scream, "EHHHHHHHHHGGGGGs!!!!!" Then I do just a regular no-word scream like a person who is trapped by a robber or a killer.

It is a long scream with little breaths in the middle, kind of painful to my neck, but I make it louder and louder anyway and I don't faint because of the little breaths.

He ignores me for a while, but he has stopped eating. He has finally stopped his pig noises. He is just sitting there, looking out the window.

I feel sleepy and faintish and there are shivers around my head, but my scream is still going good, going on for miles, little breaths in the middles. My head goes flappity floppy. My secret agent glasses fly. Where are they? He is standing up out of his seat. He grabs me. He shoves me, squeezing my arms, and he says, "Nap time, dear!" He drags me to the hall and up the stairs. One of my ankle bones smashes a stair thing. He pulls me into my room. He throws me on my bed. I jump up and run ahead of him, screaming, screaming, everything ripping in my neck, everything popping in my eyes. He runs up behind me, grabs me by one arm this time, JUST ONE ARM, all squeezing on one piece of my arm. He *shoves* me into my room and *slams* the door hard. I try to get it open. Him on the outside. Me on the inside. I scream. I scream. I scream. "MUMMA! MUMMA! MAHHHHH-MAHHHHH! I want MUMMA! Let me out!!" He is *holding* the door. I kick the door. But the door is a horridable rock. I will scream till my throat turns to jelly. Until I am blind. If he gets me the sugar bread, maybe my throat will be too ruined to swallow it. But I will HAVE the sugar bread. And my blood inside me will be happy, not exploding in flames. Mumma isn't ever mean like this. Mumma would give me sugar. Mumma *is* sugar. My sweet Mumma.

☆ Claire recollects.

That year's quilt show was breathtaking. They had the traditional and they had a lot of the new artsy types. Ruth York's star-and-wolf pattern of her own design, done in purples, grays, and oranges, got third place in that category. We all had a grand time.

♡♡ Jane strays (reports to the outside world).

I am at the top of the stairs, where I can hear them talking. The man's voice is not as deepish as Gordie's. But he is as old as Gordie. I am trying to figure a way to plan my escape. I get my secret book and pen marker for my pocket and my secret glasses, which somebody—Gordie, of course—folded on the little table at the top of the stairs. My face is a mess and my hair is a mess and my nose is stuffish from so much suffering. The phone rings. I go down the stairs wicked slow, listen at the door, and Gordie is talking. I open the door. I do not look at Gordie or the other man. I just walk OUT.

Out in the yard there is, yes, bugs. Bugs start to eat me and then more bugs and more. I go out on the tar road and walk fast and more bugs land on me, but I squish them and walk faster and suck some of the snot up my nose, the sad suffering snot. It is pretty hot out. I have had it with Gordie and the horridable people. I am never going back. Somebody has to help me. I see a tiny edge of a house way way way up on the hill after the other hill after this hill. I walk faster. Bugs do not give up. They fly up hills so easy. Right now, trees hang over the road in green pretty shade, but then after that it is bright pure sun. Then in some trees on the next hill is the skinny road that is the way you go to the Settlement if you are in a car. It is a very secret-looking road.

I walk more past that road. Then the next hill. Up, up, up through green shade parts, through sun. I think it has been a mile. I am tired of bugs. My arms are tired of fighting off their blood tongues. Finally, here's the house. Actually, it is two houses, one on one side, one on the other. One is nice and new. The other is an ugly mess, a trailer house and a bunch of trucks and junk, and behind *that* is another house, shaped like a rocket ship. A pink rocket ship. Pink is pretty. I like pink for houses. But I don't think you are supposed to like a house that looks like that even if it is the best pink. Music is coming out of the trailer house. Not rap music. Not R&B. All around the rocket ship and trailer house are big trees with needles.

Over across, at the nice new house, is a tall oldish lady watering giant flowers and grass. No trees. Just round ball-shaped bush things which you are *supposed* to like. Everything is fixed so nice and is cut nice. Her driveway is just like the road, hard nice black tar stuff. The lady looks at me and smiles and I smile back. She has very black hair with bangs. Might be a wig. She is kind of dressed up but wears sneakers. Her legs are real long. I wave to be friendly. She waves. And she brushes a bug off her ear. Bugs like everybody.

I say, "Hi there!"

She says, "Hello."

I look back over at the trailer and the rocket house. Nobody there but a squirrel. I stand there awhile and watch the squirrel, who squiggles around picking things up. Then he jumps and sticks on the side of one of the big trees. He is looking right at me. His eyes are big and shiny.

When I look back at the lady, she *was* looking at me, but she looks away fast, pretending to be busy.

I walk closer to her yard, to the very edge. I scratch my leg and arm, which have twenty puffed bug itches. Also my lip has a big bug itch. And I say, "I like your car."

She says, "Thank you."

I put my foot on her grass. I adjust my secret agent glasses for perfect vision. I say, "Your flowers are big."

"Those are hollyhocks," she says. Her voice is high and loud and tweedly. "We brought them from our other home." She scratches her neck and her arm and her chin.

I step closer.

We look at her flowers awhile and she tells me all about her yard in a science-ish way and how her son had to scrape the house 'cause the first new paint was the wrong color. Her voice is so tweedly and perfect, I think she might be a schoolteacher. A *real* schoolteacher. With these secret agent glasses, you know everything about people even before they say it. Behind the house is a scratching sound. "What's that?"

"That's David. My son. He's having trouble with the weed wacker. Looks like we need a new one."

"Do you like to shop?"

She laughs loud and high and tweedly. "Not for weed wackers."

I look around the corner and there's the man by a cute little red barn-shape thing, lawn mower and stuff by his foot, and he has a very long neck and a popped-out Adam thing. He isn't hairy like Gordie, not on his face. And his hairdo is perfect. He looks so neat and good, almost plastic, which is pretty. His outfit is perfect too. No spots. He is probably a teacher also. I wiggle my secret glasses a little to work up the power.

The lady asks if I live around here.

I say, "Sort of."

"Out for your exercise?"

I giggle. The suffering snot is gone from my nose. But my eyes are kind of sore, achy. And my throat. Screams really wreck your throat. I slap a bug on my hand and when I look he's a squished blood mess. My blood.

The lady finishes with her flowers and turns the nozzler to shut off the water and lays it on the grass. There are drops of water on everything and the hollyhocks drip drip drip.

I say, "I am *really* hungry. And thirsty. And tired."

She looks at her house for a long minute and says, "Oh, well . . . why don't you just come in for a treat?" She walks fast for an old lady. Her legs are so long. Her steps are giant.

"Your man-guy lives here too?" I ask as we go through the breezeway, which is all fixed neat and smells new.

"Yes, my son. David is his name." Inside, she says, "Take your sunglasses off. It's not that bright in here!" She laughs loud and bubbly.

"I need these," I say.

"Oh."

On the fridge is a magnet thing that says BERNICE'S KITCHEN. They have such a pretty house. Full of stuff. Stuff you *buy*. Plants and books and statues and a huge TV . . . you know, the biggest. She has me sit at the kitchen table and pick four kinds of cookies from four cookie jars of different shapes, a lighthouse, an apple with a worm for a handle, a cowgirl, and a cowboy. All cute.

The weed wacker starts buzzing outside and the lady hollers, "Hallelujah!" and this cracks me up. She and I both laugh a minute.

"Is your name *Ber-nice*?" I ask. Like *burr* and *nice*.

"Yes, but you pronounce it *Ber-neece*. And what is *your* name?"

"Jane Miranda Meserve."

"A lovely old-fashioned name. Jane. Feel happy your mommy didn't name you one of those names nobody's ever heard of."

"I've heard of Ber-NEECE before. It's nice," I lied. I never once heard that name, but I am trying to be nice like you are supposed to be.

Her voice is so tweedly and bubbly and loud. "I'll get you some milk, Jane."

"No thank you," I say, very nice. "I don't like milk. Even the good kind."

She says, "Would you like some lemonade?"

"I like Coke."

"We have club soda."

"What's that?"

"Soda without sweetener or flavoring."

I frown. Sounds pretty weird. "Well, I don't really need anything to drink. I'm not thirsty anymore."

"Well, if you change your mind, just say so," she says, so brightish.

I say, "Are you a teacher?"

"Why, yes!" she says. "I retired eight years ago this spring. My goodness, how did you know?"

I shrug. I give my glasses a little wiggle to keep the power.

She sits across from me with a cup of coffee and she says, "Well!"

And I giggle. I look through the archway at her TV, which is not on, just quiet, smooth, grayish. "I like your TV."

"Yes," she says, turning to admire it herself. "David got it. He likes to stay abreast of the news."

"Is he a teacher too?"

"How did you know?!!"

"Oh, I just know stuff."

She says, "You probably know because your parents told you. Where exactly do you live? Are you summering on the lake?"

I look at the backside of a nice butter cookie. "I'm just visiting some people," I say.

"Oh, take off your sunglasses, Jane. I'd like to see your eyes as we chat."

I let her see my eyes just a little, then push the glasses back fast, to keep up the power.

"You have striking eyes," she says. "I don't know why you'd want to hide them."

"I have my father's eyes. You ever hear of Damon Gorely?"

She looks into her thoughts, eyes up. "No, I guess not."

"Well," I tell her, "he's famous in rap. Well, pretty soon famous. He's trying to get publishity . . . pub-*liss*-ity, I mean. He has talent, Mum says. He's in California. Mum met him once in person and has a picture of him which we look at all the time."

She pats my hand.

I nibble a cookie.

She sips her coffee. She says, "Have you been upset? Your eyes are . . ."

I sigh. "I've had a horridable day." I hold my forehead for a moment to show her I mean it.

The buzzing weed thing goes around and around the yard.

I say, "Ber-NEECE. I shouldn't call you that, should I? You shouldn't call teachers stuff like real names. You have to say Mrs."

She giggles. "Here, it's okay, dear." She looks so pleased. She sips her coffee. "So you must be visiting some people on *this* road."

"Yuh. I have to stay with Gordie till my Mum can come home."

"Gordie? *St. Onge?*" Her face gets a wave across it. I can see the thing she is thinking. She does not like Gordie. "You mean" she jerks her thumb in THE direction—"down there, at that . . . *place?*"

"Gordie's house."

"I've *heard* about him," she says, and looks at her coffee.

"He's mean," I say. "He squeezed my arm and threw me on the bed. He is"—I lean forward and make my teeth real plain—"he . . . is . . . big."

She looks up at me. Then she says, even more loud and bubbly, "I want to fix you a treat! I can mix club soda with lemonade and make you a wacky lemon wonder!" She stands over there with her back to me, mixing mixing mixing. It is not too hot here in Ber-NEECE's house. She has all the windows shut. And drapes across the sunshine-side window.

Outside, the weed thing buzzes around. I look out the picture window near the TV, and the awful trailer house across the road has a little dog-sized door and I see it open up and out walks a white horridable dog with dirty fur, a black spot eye, and curled tail. I know that dog! He visits me a lot at Gordie's.

I sniff the air. Ber-NEECE has such a nice house. She gives me the glass of stuff. I don't want to tell her it's gross, so I drink a little. She is so nice. Her eyes are very watery and pinkish-green and her wig hair is so funny and cute. I say, "Do you want to see my secret book?"

She says, "Oooooh. A secret book!"

"I have it on me now." I feel into my sundress pocket. "I am a spy and I watch them at Gordie's all the time," I tell her in a low voice.

Ber-NEECE smiles thin and polite with her lips and she says, in a voice that's different, not as high but kind of cloudish, "How nice."

The buzzing stops outside and in a minute the man comes in and he says, "It died. I'll need to make a trip to town." His voice is thin, buzzy. Like the weed wacker. And boy does his Adam thing jump! Soon as possible, I am going to draw that Adam thing and all of him and his weed thing in my secret book and Ber-NEECE with her funny wig hair.

Ber-NEECE is acting funny. Making expressions at the man.

He comes over and stands by the table. He looks down at my secret book open with Ber-NEECE's fingers there.

"What's wrong?" he asks.

Ber-NEECE says, "David, this is Jane. She's from the school. The *school* down the hill."

He looks at me, my whole face, my whole head, then down again at my secret book under Ber-NEECE's fingers.

Ber-NEECE says, "Dear, tell us true. You are safe here. You can tell us anything and everything. Is anyone hurting you at that place?"

The man is staring at my mouth, waiting for words.

I put both hands in my lap and take a deep breath, and I sigh so deep. "Gordie is very mean. Too horridable to describe. Won't let me have food. All I want is food. But all he has is this *black stuff*! And cold beans. And he squeezed me!" And I burst into tears, real ones . . . which come even worser than before . . . wicked out of control, which is actually a surprise even to me.

   Out in the world.

The people work. The people shop. The people hurry. The people wait at streetlights, grumbling. The people now talk on phones *while driving* —and chewing, swallowing, on their way. Work, shop, drive, talk, chew. Tinted windshields. Flashing mirrors. Automated voices and hidden cameras. The people are on their way. Credit cards. Interest. Faster money. Longer days. Lighter meals. Memories of no past. Catalogs. Packaging that crinkles. Packaging that opens faster.

How the Border Mountain Militia and the St. Onge Settlement come to a rough but workable junction.

Another day. Another evening. Getting dark a little early these days.

Down at the old St. Onge farm place, which sits close to the tar road, Gordon St. Onge and six-and-a-half-year-old Jane Meserve are out on the screened piazza. Each is outdoing the other with fabulous stories, fictions about walking watermelons, and Little Red Riding Hood's wolf friend who rides a Harley and wears a leather jacket, and the girl who goes to California to find fame as a rap singer and meets stars, all of them dripping in jewels and money and secrets. Both Gordon and Jane have a flair for the dramatic and far-fetched. Their stories weave one into the other, the child's giggles and the man's growls punctuating and underlying the most madcap moments, though a tension takes place, each pressing to give his or her values center stage, jewels versus thrift, for instance.

A rare thing for anyone to be alone this long with Gordon, here in the almost darkness, evening time, a place usually so hubbubish with lives. But now, a humid gray night sags around them, their skin is clammy, and all surfaces have an unpleasant dew.

The phone rings.

"Gordie, it's probably Mum calling."

Well, yes, it's too sticky to want somebody on your lap tonight, not a dog, not a kid, not anything with a live temperature, but sometimes you do what needs to be done in spite of the wishes of your skin. Therefore, Jane is curled in Gordon's lap, her long golden arms and legs tucked under her, which makes her seem quite small and beetlebug-shaped. She wears underpants with a pattern of fat purple dinosaurs which, in this dusky evening darkness, are just spots. And she wears one of those little girl undershirts, straps, bitty rayon bow. Her heart-shaped secret agent glasses are in an important tight grip in her hand underneath her, her head is turned to the side, cheek against Gordon's chest, her expression alert. As the phone rings again, her rough velvety voice, the voice more of a young woman than a six-and-a-half-year-old, again speaks. "That is probably Mumma calling."

How many hundreds of calls since this child's arrival here? And how many times has she made this same statement, though it has never once been her mother calling without planning the time?

Gordon says, "That is probably *not* Mumma calling. Probably a goddam TV producer. Probably the *New York Times* or *USA Today* or the goddam FBI or the social worker with all the sharp teeth. Maybe it's *all* of them in a phone booth together sharing a quarter."

Jane laughs deeply. "You're funny."

The phone rings.

All up and down this porch, the silent chimes and mobiles hang while just three rockers away leans a four-foot-tall chunk of basswood tree trunk carved out as a beaked and eared totem-pole face. Painted in anxious colors and ringed all over its flat top like a flaming crown are small handsome leaded-glass candle jars that give off a winking rosy light. The candles inside the glass shapes are grayish-green blobs, which smell like mouthwash. Candles made by Jane. Jane the impatient candlemaker. But such a proud thing! It's as if the rosy light itself is Jane's. Jane's radiance. Jane's willpower. It's no coincidence that Jane's face is directed at that light.

The phone rings again.

"Maybe it's somebody looking for somebody," Jane insists.

Gordon sets his beer down and tightens his moist arms around her. "Everybody who is anybody is here," he says.

She *tsks*. "We are not *everybody*."

The phone rings again and again.

An engine can be heard now, down the hill, working hard in low gear. It shifts down again for the last few yards before the St. Onge dooryard, the steepest part of this mountain. Headlights swipe across the house: a pickup truck turning in. No gate, no KEEP OUT signs here at the old farm place. The notorious gate is at the dirt road entrance to the Settlement, a few yards uphill.

The pickup purrs to an easy stop under the ash tree. A late-model truck, the kind with payments (including interest) totaling what a house cost ten years ago, it has a plastic-looking sheen. Engine and lights die. Door opens. Dark shape steps to the ground. Shuts door nice 'n' easy.

"Who's that?" Jane asks. The approaching figure walks like a cop.

Gordon says, in his momentous storytelling voice, "Looks like Rex."

"Who's Rex?"

"A friend." Softer now.

Jane *tsks*. "Tell him we're busy."

Gordon slaps her softly. "You want to own a person body and soul."

Jane *tsks* and pulls a hand out from under herself with which to slap *him* . . . softly.

Gordon burps hugely and beerily, eyes steady on the approaching visitor. The guy pulls open the screen door. It gives off a squeal, like ecstasy, like it feels so good to that door spring to be strained and stretched.

Gordon says, "Well, well, well."

The guy doesn't speak, just comes to stand before this rocker, which holds the amorphous, dark, Atlas-sized shape of Gordon St. Onge and the child, but the guy is looking in through the doorway of the poorly lit, fluorescently blue kitchen, then down past the fluttering rose candles, down the long porch piazza, with its cluttered gray darkness, and beyond that a darker darkness. He adjusts his soft-visored army cap twice, then, in an offhand way, lets his eyes fall on Gordon and the kid.

Gordon slowly rocks Jane, rubs between her shoulder blades, and teases her ears, and she sighs in that fully absorbed way meant to lock the intruder—new arrival out.

Rex says, "Whose kid? I don't remember that one."

"She's Pete Meserve's daughter's daughter."

Both Jane's arms stretch languidly upward. The hand without the secret agent glasses takes Gordon's lips, pinches them shut. She speaks very quietly in her husky womanish voice. "Shut up. No more."

Gordon nuzzles (with lip farts) Jane's neck, which makes her sigh with tolerance.

Rex studies Jane with grave interest. He wears jeans tonight, which seem pale and foggy, and a brown T-shirt, which looks almost black in this poor light, T-shirt tucked meticulously into the jeans. Belt buckle is a conservative open square, unlike Gordon's blustery sun face. Dark brown hair cut razor-straight across the back of the neck, unlike shaggy Gordon. And, as always, a thick brown mustache to the jaws, brown, no gray yet, though he is soon to be fifty. The beard on the chin painstakingly shaved away. Squared shoulders, a fit, tigerish, efficient manner. He stares into Jane's disdainful black irises with his own, pale as moonlight, his stare that is calm, strategic, direct.

With a rather slow-motion flourish, Jane unfolds her secret agent glasses, not taking her eyes off Rex, slides the glasses on, and continues her stare, which is a look that is calm, strategic, and direct.

Gordon with a big smile. "Well, it's been a long time since we've seen you, Richard."

Rex would rather be called Rex, of course. Remember, it means *king*. He says, "Been busy."

Gordon's eyes twinkle, though in the near dark, twinkles don't show up well. "I believe the last we saw of you was back in the snow. We've seen Glory a couple-three times and asked about you, but she didn't have much to say about the old man. So we've been left to just wonder and wonder, until—"

With narrowed eyes, Rex cuts in. "I work."

Gordon flushes, then smiles goofily. "Yes, yes, of course." Now Gordon's expression changes. It is one of most high regard. And Rex takes one of the lathed porch columns into his left hand, then leans back against it, one knee bent, a boot heel braced against the low porch wall, and closes his eyes a moment, which means he is in a trusted place.

Gordon says, "We been following you in the papers."

Rex snorts dismissively, as this of course refers to bad publicity caused by two members of his militia.

Gordon adds, "Since Mr. Lancaster and what's-his-name raised all that hell in Portland."

Rex runs his tongue around his mouth, feeling the hard edges of his top teeth.

Gordon's eyes twinkle again, twinkles unseen. "We only know you now through newspapers and gossip."

Rex looks at Gordon's mouth, a shaded area in the darker shadow of his short beard. After a long moment, Rex says, "A lotta people only know you through newspapers and gossip too."

Gordon chuckles. "Media subtracts. Gossip adds. Magic happens." Chuckle, chuckle, chuckle.

Rex is deathly silent.

A car passes, toots its horn, then climbs the next hill, probably headed for the Settlement entrance with the gate and KEEP OUT signs. If you belong in the Settlement, you just raise the pole, go on a bit, and replace the pole; then you're in.

But then, the tooting horn could have been one of the Lancasters, or the Emmonses a half mile beyond, or, beyond that, Dick O'Brien's people. It is *not* Bernice, the schoolteacher—unless she bumped the horn by mistake while gawking.

And it was not some media hound come to snoop on the St. Onge Settlement. Unlikely. Snoopers aren't tooters.

Rex's left hand moves to his chest, spreads his fingers open a moment there, high near the shoulder. Gordon sees the wedding band. Still there.

This is *very interesting,* this wedding ring business. What kind of man still wears the ring six years after his wife has filled her little car with clothes and left for Massachusetts with another man, filed for divorce, got the divorce, and remarried? Rex will tell you, *God does not recognize divorce. God does not recognize the laws of the wicked.*

Maybe this is funny. But as Gordon's eyes move quickly, from the shadowy ringed hand to the dark dooryard and unseen field filled with August evening cricket song, his own mouth is, for the moment, set in a tight line of sadness and longing, in sympathy for his friend.

Rex says, "Your name came up a couple weeks ago, and I do not mean the Santa Claus news. I mean the real world. I figured it was time to check in."

"How'd my name come up?"

"In a discussion about shortwave."

Gordon squeezes out one small but necessary beer burp, the kind that just kinda whooshes through the teeth. "Our aspirations here are high, but our outcomes are conservative."

"I say not," Rex says shortly. "You got a lotta stuff here to turn heads."

"The basics of life."

Rex stares hard at Jane a moment, whose white-framed secret agent glasses stare back. Then he looks in the general vicinity of Gordon's throat. "Right."

Gordon says, "As far as the radio thing goes, we haven't fully realized those broadcast possibilities because—"

The phone has started ringing, maybe the hundredth time today, and Jane interrupts the discussion to say, "That really *is* Mum. She might've just got away. Maybe some *good* people made all the copguards die hot in their cars, huh?"

Gordon says, "No, Jane, it's not your mum."

Rex says, "You got a story on that one there, I see."

Gordon says, "The dramas of the new millennium seem right smack out of the Old Testament."

Rex looks at Gordon's hand, now raising the long-necked beer to his mouth: beer, the homemade kind. Rex sort of, but not quite, rolls his eyes and sort of, but not quite, smiles. *A schoolmaster who makes beer brewing part of the curriculum. A school that exists on the edge of every caution, on every pause for thought.* Rex tugs his cap off and slaps his thigh softly with it, like a countdown. His hair is thinning a bit. Though he's—yes—headed for fifty, in most ways he seems younger than Gordon, too young to have a well-built woman-sized nineteen-year-old daughter like Glory York, who gives moaning dreams to every man and boy in her perfumy path. And he seems too young to have seen everything there was to see in Vietnam, and felt *everything,* everything that somehow he now sees and feels in reverse, like a photo negative, everything that some-how tinges all love with regret and gives the past an aura larger than love, and makes him understand that there is no love in paradise, only in struggle. And that life now is getting weird. Weirder than anything he's ever seen before, but lacking the simplicity of war.

Gordon speaks with a thud of silence between each word. "The . . . Border . . . Mountain . . . Militia."

Rex says grimly, "There's no law against it." He sighs hard. "Yet."

"Well, no. Not yet," Gordon agrees, then rearranges Jane in his arms, trying to get himself and her more comfortable. It's a pretty sweaty grip they have on each other right now, especially Jane's grip on Gordon, her suspicions about this coplike guy, her hard study of him interrupted by Gordon's continuous hand gestures. He is saying now to Rex, "I'm just awfully jealous."

Rex bristles, believing he's being teased.

And Gordon says, "It's just good to see *somebody* showing an interest in doing something about . . . about our troubles. Apathy is unforgivable and ugly. I like to think about you guys . . . all your enthusiasm. I like to think about *all* the patriots, all these wonderfully pissed-off people."

Rex leans forward, the skin of his face now shifting, which, together with his dark mustache and pale eyes and the flicker of rosy candlelight, gives him a villainous cast and now most unmistakably shows his age. He straightens his body, slaps his cap back on, and says, "You're mak-ing fun, man."

"I'm not making fun." Bright trickles of sweat cruise down Gordon's temples, disappear into the beard.

Rex exhales nice 'n' easy.

Gordon knows not to bother to offer Rex a beer. Rex is clean in every way. Even sugar. He won't touch it. Even his mother's cookies and fudge. His discipline is evident in the hard planes of his body, unlike the flabby thickness that comes and goes just above Gordon's belt, and that extra chin he sometimes has in winter months. He now raises his beer to Rex for a toast, the bottle gripped in his fist like a torch, and with a howl that causes both Rex and Jane to jump, "TO THE GREAT CHANGE!", then upends the bottle. Jane's head turns so her heart-shaped lenses can sternly behold the spectacle of Gordon's Adam's apple jerking up and down under his beard, her fascination for Adam's apples passionately increased since her discovery of Ber-NEECE's son's, which dances more splendidly than anyone else's. Now Jane's mind flashes to wonderful Ber-NEECE, the schoolteacher up the road, who promises Jane she'll have a tape recorder ready for the next visit. Gordon looks into the hazy spots that are Rex's eyes, his trusted friend.

Moments later.

One of the mobiles turns ever so slightly.

Gordon says, "Here comes the wind," and looks off toward the southwest happily. "National Weather Service says twenty-five miles per hour by midnight. T'would be better to get a steady *ten*."

The candle flames flicker and hop inside their classy leaded-glass holders.

"You still think that is going to do it, don't you?" Rex snorts, stuffing a thumb in his belt.

"With your own hands you helped put her up. Don't bad-mouth her."

Rex says coldly, "It's not enough."

"*One* wind unit is not enough. And one community is not enough, but we are starting to really spread now to—"

"That's not what I mean," Rex butts in. He kind of almost sneers.

Now Gordon also sneers. "*I* know what you mean. But neither are a few hundred small unorganized citizens' armies enough. I don't care if you got a hundred thousand guys running around in the woods learning survival skills and playing army. Shit. The bankers' octopus is just laughing itself silly. Its government, posing as our government, has whole fleets of Apache helicopters. Goddam, *they* got the *bomb*." Pause. "And infiltrators. Bombs away!"

Rex's eyes on Gordon's face don't waver. He says, slowly and carefully and without an inkling of fervor, "It's not just an army. We're getting people into local office and—"

"Nazi school committees. We already got 'em," Gordon snarls.

"The United States Constitution is not Nazi."

Gordon sniffs indignantly. "The Bill of Rights is used for whatever the mega-men want done with it. Man, oh, man, the Bill of Rights feel-good side deal." He snorts. "But the Constitution"—he snorts again—"was American's first NAFTA."

Rex's voice, still careful, clear, fervorless. "Do you believe the United States still has separation of powers?"

Gordon *tsks*. "You are getting sidetracked by details, by the hairs and hooves of the octopus."

"Well, how about this? Who has more power, the judge or the jury?"

Gordon goes silent.

Rex's voice, steady, deliberate, unruffled. "It was intended that a jury of your peers, *the people,* have more power than the judge, that the judge be a kind of referee. But all that's changed. Judges have so much power they can withhold evidence from juries. Did you know that if you are a juror, it is your right, your *obligation,* to force a hung jury by finding the defendant innocent, even if all evidence points to his guilt, if you don't think the law is fair? Like some of these laws they got these days, laws pertaining to the drug war, for instance. And laws on citizens' weapons. As a juror, you are supposed to vote your conscience. It's called jury nullification, see? In this way, the people have power . . . in more ways than just voting at the polls. Also the legislative branch. It has been weakened and Supreme Court judges made into kings."

Now it is Gordon who is silent.

Rex says, "I have some paperwork on this if you are interested. I have quite a bit of material, including copies of the *Federalist Papers* and *Black's Law Dictionary.* If you aren't interested, I won't bother you with it. It's up to you."

"Yes. I thank you. Please. I'd like to see this stuff." Gordon smiles brotherishly, though in the sticky hot darkness his smile is just perhaps seen as a deep wrinkle. "So I see you've been doing a lot more than wiring new additions."

A long flat silence now into which Jane gasps. "I'm bored out of my wits. Is anyone else bored out of their wits?"

Gordon is staring at Rex's dark shadowy form and blue-lighted profile. He says finally, "Meanwhile, back to your army. Your military capabilities. I'm not laughing at you, but some are. An—"

Rex interrupts with, "We know our way around here." He turns his head as the breeze stirs again and the near hills sigh urgently. He looks back at Gordon. "To show you how much the U.S. government knows about Maine, they didn't even have half of the Piscataquis County towns on their maps when they were scheming with the utilities to dump all that nuclear waste on us a few years back. And the military. Any military. It's maps. Not geology maps like the nuke waste outfits, but maps. None of them know Maine like you and I do . . . not these hills. This . . . is . . . home." He swallows, runs a palm over his mustache and mouth, then jerks a thumb toward the road. "Like the Vietcong. How do you suppose the Vietcong did so well?"

Gordon says, "They didn't win, though. The coke dealers won. Both cokes, cocaine and Coke. And heroin, rubber, and tin. And the big banks. World Bank. IMF. Robert McNamara moved from bombing strategies to banking blackmail strategies, after Bretton Woods was dropped. Remember, his next leap was to head the IMF. Or was it the World Bank? Same difference. Even the octopus gets confused. And then there are the CIA types. Oh, I already said drug dealers, didn't I? And the behind-closed-doors chemical makers and behind-closed-doors military jets, bombs, and doodad makers? Hmmm. And the behind-closed-doors manufacturing deals needing Vietnamese wage slaves to work on the island of Samoa making what is called *American made goods,* due to the handy fact that Samoa, with no labor laws, is a possession of the American government—possession? yeah, property—the island and all those quick-fingered Vietnamese girls! Property we speak of. And what else? Hmmm. Who knows what other Mammonish underworld schemes were realized? The truth is lost in a bottle at sea. Boogety boogety shoo."

Rex laughs. "I don't think your mother would let you come to one of our meetings."

Gordon squints one eye, raises the brow of the other. "Probably not." Then he looks down. Jane has pulled part of his soft old chambray shirt from his pants and, still sporting her heart-shaped dark glasses, almost seems to be sucking on the shirt, her arms and legs loose and trusting. Gordon pushes with his knees to make the rocker creak to and fro ever so slowly. "I weep for my country."

Rex says, "Cute."

Gordon says, "You're not as nice as you used to be."

"When was I nice?"

Gordon says, "I understand you guys, I really do. I just wish you were . . . not so charged with self-interest."

"What does *that* mean?"

"I wish you were interested in protecting. This child, for instance."

"She'll be protected."

Gordon raises his eyebrows. "Promise?"

Rex says, "We'll protect anyone who wants to stay on this side of the blockade . . . if it comes to that. We have reason to believe it *is* going to come to that, state by state. She *wants* to be here, she can be here."

Gordon rocks. His face above the beard is beaded up all over, both the heat-wave kind and the nerved-up kind.

Rex plays with his soft cloth cap, a sign that this visit is significant to him.

Gordon says, "Do *you* think the government is up to something? Some *event* . . . so they can declare martial law? Wouldn't *that* actually be a coup d'état? You guys would just bounce off them like mice off a division of sixty-ton tanks."

"I believe they . . . I believe *something* is up."

Gordon says, "Our government, the one we *see,* they are playacting. Obviously, there is another one, the one you never see. It . . . was . . . eventless. A lot of gentlemanly little coups. The transformation is complete." His voice has been mellow. No shouting. But he watches Rex hard in the storybook-blue light of candles and night.

Rex says, "I won't argue with that."

Gordon says, "So the event: it would be to maybe occur. . . ." He pauses. He thinks. "To get the public worked up—" He closes his eyes. "Like the Northwoods project false flag terror—"

"To create chaos," Rex says quickly.

Gordon rocks back and forth. "Okay, so the government to our minds is now an alien government. It sucks; we agree. It ain't we-the-people; it never *was*. It was designed to foster only a limited number of *legal* persons, like ten percent of the population. A master class. The rest of us don't get democracy."

Rex flinches. Turns his face away with a really pained expression. "What?"

"Do not use that word *democracy*."

"Why are you guys so stuck on that? I do not mean direct vote by a majority on every issue, like whether or not people in South Carolina should vote on whether or not people in San Francisco can raise hogs in their backyards." Gordon sighs. "I mean the process of—"

"Whatever. Democracy is not what this is."

"I agree. It is not—"

"Nor do we want a democracy," Rex says gravely.

"Richard, there are many kinds of d—"

"Don't say it."

Gordon snorts. "If you don't listen, you will never learn anything."

"You are not the knower of all things."

Gordon hangs his head, *both* eyes squinched. He imagines for a moment how it would be for all those he loves if, yes indeed, there *was* a direct vote on every issue by everybody in America; if, in fact, they had time for such. He sees legions of schoolteachers, of every school and every grade, marching chin-up to the polls. And school principals. And social workers. Only the most thin-lipped of them all, chin-up agents of the system. The prissy and the puritanical, the hard-assed and the switch-flippers. Those who despise hair. Those who despise free inquiry of the mind. Those who despise untidiness. The *majority,* wielding their whips and their pens, voting away the lives of the Settlement people and—yeah—voting away the patriot types, all the old-fashioned types, leaving them landless and without honor. Like a bad movie that has too many pilots, too many say-so's. Like too many cooks. Too many chiefs. Like a sky of huge hail. And yet the octopus isn't dropping flower petals and May baskets. Gordon covers his face with a hand. Why always does he find himself at a dead end? Why can't he, like everyone else, find a faithful faith-fulfilling hobby horse to ride? He is sickened with envy of Rex.

He looks up at Rex's shadowy face now, his own face tipped, a sheepish smile. "I will try not to use that word, my brother."

Jane says gruffly, "Excuse me, but is this all we are going to do, *this stuff*?" She picks at one of Gordon's shirt buttons proprietarily, but the heart shapes of her all-seeing secret agent glasses are locked on the person of Rex York.

Gordon makes hot whiskery farts-of-the-lips into Jane's neck and she giggles. Then he says, "This is important, Jane . . . very, very important. Remember, patience is a virtue."

Jane says evenly, "Do . . . not . . . say . . . that *virtue* thing. I . . . hate . . . it."

A breeze gives several glass and metal mobiles a shiver, and some large dangling wooden ducks, nearly as big as decoys, spin contentedly. And the candle flames flutter and twist.

 Secret Agent Jane considers.

It is so boring it is hard to keep track. And the number of words is more than a thousand hundreds. I will NEVER remember them all. A black dictionary. Coke dealers . . . or Coke machines, I think. Joories. Even with these power glasses, it just goes on and on. But you cannot imagine how important their talk is. I think it is very important and inlegal and big.

 HEY!

You must stop talking! Look at meeeeeeeee! You ordinary people are children!!!! You need meeee! I am the EXPERT. I am the OFFI-CIAL. Ho, there! Shut up! Trust only MEEEEEE. Quiet down now. Shhhhhhh.

🏠 **In the shadowy night, the voices of two ordinary men continue.**

Gordon says, "Okay, so let's suppose they do it. Create some huge emergency. Bigger than their practice run, the OK City building, like next they do a whole city—Boston, for instance. And everything is shut down. Airports, TVs are all tied up with the event. Soooo then you guys, thousands of you—millions of you, if you got that big—would take over."

Rex's normally steady eyes blink.

Gordon says, "And then those who don't like the militias might *mis*-understand, might think you are not defending but *offending* them."

"Rex says coldly, "Well, that's too bad. If—"

Gordon cuts in. "I, for one, might be a little suspicious, might think you are wanting to take things into your own hands—like executions, all justified in your minds. And you'll be pushing your God on us all.

You will be defending an awful lot of people against their will and, Mister Man, that ain't defense!"

"If they don't like it, they can leave," says Rex, with a hard, level look. "This country has a Constitution. This is all the government we need. We are just upholding the Constitution, state by state. If people are against the Constitution, I am sorry, but this is not the place for them to live. They can leave."

Gordon squints at Rex's unshifting and always dignified figure. "Richard, I beg your pardon, but the Constitution is only a pile of old paper. It was written by followers of the Enlightenment . . . totally out of wack when positioned alongside so-called 'rugged individualism.' Riffraff like us are on our own."

Rex sighs. "The Constitution is for everyone."

Gordon is shaking his head.

"Once you know how it works," Rex adds, after a moment of watching Gordon's shaking head. Then, "You know how it works if you study it. You have to study it. It's up to you . . . or them . . . or whoever."

Gordon growls.

Rex ignores the growl and says, in an ordinary, sane, civilized way, "It's all there."

Gordon howls. "And now all these investor rights agreements, which are above the Constitution! The U.S. one! And the State ones! And bloodsucking foreign policy!"

Rex *tsks*. Rex opens his mouth to offer yet another thought in a sane, quiet way.

But Gordon booms. "The original intent! The Enlightenment has been swallowed up by ambition and the friggin' American dream and complexity and—"

Rex cuts in, "There is nothing complex about the Constitution."

With grim laughter, Jane says, "I don't believe this."

Gordon says, "Oh, yeah, yeah, the Constitution might work if we were a tiny country full of nice people. But then again, not really, because our culture is set up for people who need a bunch of others doing all the shit-work for them. It's not set up for people who expect to empty their own chamber pots and pick their own turnips, it's set up for big commerce. And *growth*. *Cancerous* growth. And . . .

and . . . and . . ."—he stutters now, rushing on, fearing Rex will try to speak—"and even if we did touch the Constitution up a tad, try to make it less about masters and slaves, nothing's going to work 'cause this damn country is full of . . . of humans! Humans are such fuckups!"

Rex stares at Gordon. He's obviously not going to humor Gordon with this kind of foolishness.

But Gordon needs no humoring to work up a spiel. He rocks the chair so hard, Jane grips him to stay on board. He raves for ten minutes.

Rex waits it out.

Militias are BAD! Militias are SCARY!

There are *no* good citizens' militias because citizens should only be working toward excellence and nice scores and diplomas and voting and working at their jobs and shopping and relaxing. Getting entertainment and, *yes, consuming.* And only concerned with being attractive and clean. The rest will fall into place!

Trust us, it will fall into place. We are your strong leaders. We GIVE you defense. We GIVE you security. The Pentagon and CIA and FBI and police and others official enough to do it right; these are good.

Citizens must TRUST their defense providers. TRUST US!

Put your guns down. Guns are bad. Bad boys. Bad! Don't be like those screwball dangerous citizens' militias, which are a bunch of wacko macho racist sexist scary guys who bomb babies!

Fear them. Trust us!

Back on the farmhouse porch, Secret Agent Jane speaks to us.

When I tell the lady up the road, Ber-NEECE, and her guy about this, they will look at me with saaaad eyes. Gordie is very wrong to talk about inlegal stuff. Bernice's guy, who is really her son, says it is very urgent that I keep an eye on things here. They use a very good tape recorder for my words. They are both *real* schoolteachers, not weird like up at the Settlement. Gordie isn't a true crook. He just needs to shape up.

Almost gasping, Gordon continues.

"... and you *are* aware that in 1886, a corporate-pampered Mammon-worshipping courtroom reporter of the California Supreme Court gave constitutional rights to the Pacific Railroad Corporation—a *corporation,* which is a piece of paper? Yes, a courtroom reporter! A little twist of wording and a lotta closed doors after that. The corporate citizen was hatched. It was inevitable. The shit was rising. Nothing can hold the shit down once it soaks a bit! ..." Gordon is in full scream mode now. His right boot blonks the beer bottle he'd recently lowered to the floor. Oops! Over it goes, liquid snaking along the boards.

♡♡　**Again, Secret Agent Jane speaks to us.**

Something about taking over the government. And something about murder. Some words are very real. Some words are like air. Even with these glasses, this job is harder than you think.

The candles flicker.

Quietly, Rex says, "I remember when you used to talk like this. I thought you'd gotten over it. All that commie college crap."

Gordon gives a great hoot. "College! This was not talked about in college. This is—"

"Off the deep end," says Rex.

"But *you* aren't off the deep end?"

"I am for the Constitution."

"You like being defined as a consumer? You miss your old definition? You miss being called a citizen? Though it was an illusion all along, you liked it, huh?"

Rex sniffs to cast aside this vague line of thinking.

Jane swings one leg over the chair arm. The leg twitches and flicks like a really annoyed lion cub might work her long spotted tail.

Gordon grins unhappily. "And because it is inside us all, it has defined us all. We are too childlike to become a resistance."

Rex squints, wiggles his lips around, the big mustache creaturish, his eyes pale and metallic in the near dark. He hears his old friend's voice going incredibly soft, the weird in-and-out tidal waves of his passion.

"It is beyond touch. Humans made it. But it can't be turned by our hand!"

Rex's eyes widen with a gotcha sort of twinkle. "I thought you said it *could*. You are always saying a bunch of your type of people could fix it: windmills, big gardens, cute little villages."

Gordon is profoundly and thunderously silent.

Rex says, "So now you are saying you think it's completely hopeless. You had all the answers a minute ago: democracy and process and whatever. Now you've talked yourself into a hole." He shakes his head, eyes smiling, and turns away. Goes to the screen door, facing out.

Jane's long bare golden-brown leg, dangling over the chair arm, has ceased motion. Gordon closes his hand around it and tucks her into her favorite curled-up sleep position against his chest. She's pretty sleepy, almost gone, even though her secret agent all-seeing glasses remain quite well situated on her face.

Rex turns back to face Gordon.

Gordon has an ugly flash. He sees the lie of his argument to Rex. Not that the words are lies, but talk is cheap, isn't it? In practice, Gordon St. Onge is nothing! Just hiding behind his windmills, solar collectors, and the new gate. He looks up at Rex's face, the thinning hair and heavy to-the-jaws mustache, Rex who has now folded his arms across his chest, looking like he knows Gordon's thoughts. But then he just says, "Democracy is chaos."

Gordon snorts. "Richard, you'd frustrate a fieldstone."

Rex chuckles. "Don't start throwing things. Be nice." His eyes grow almost warm.

Gordon says, "Okay, I don't knock the citizens' armed militias. Your common-law stuff. Your stashing funny foods, guns, whatever. I'm just saying we need something in addition to that, we need—" Again he is stalling out. Again the philosopher has found the bricked-up end of the universe. In the cheery candlelit gloom, he grins. Stupidly.

Meanwhile, all across America, evening descends into the various time zones.

And good American children are studying hard for tests, achieving, succeeding, becoming . . . uh, becoming what?

And then it seems the two old friends are coming to some agreement on something close to the heart.

"My brother, I *understand* how i'tis! All this antigun hysteria pumped up by the media and the foundations. It's fucking scary, man, it *is;* I'll give you that. It's dividing our country like nothing has before, not recently. I am not laughing at you, brother!"

Rex says, "No. You're just talking without cease. Nothing new."

Gordon paws his own face with one hand, drives his fingers through his damp hair.

"I just do not like the Constitution. Not the commerce clause. Not the contracts clause. Not—"

Rex interrupts. "These are God-given rights."

Gordon stares at him for three whole seconds with an exaggerated expression of disbelief.

Rex says, with nearly no intonation to his voice, "Hamilton said in 1775 that these were the sacred rights of mankind and not to be rummaged for among old parchments or musty records. The Constitution is written by the hand of divinity itself and can never be erased or obscured by mortal power."

"And you believe that?"

"I most certainly do."

Gordon says carefully, "Okaaay." He burps. Rearranges the child, whose head now lolls over his arm as limply as death. He lifts her secret agent glasses from her face, folds them with the fingers of that one hand. He looks over and sees one of the glass candle holders has gone dark. "Jesus, Richard, I fear some of this shit."

Rex says, "You just want to come to one of our meetings and argue."

"No, I would not! I promise. I'll be good." He laughs. He leans forward over Jane, resting both arms on her. "I . . . want to get this all straight with you, my old blood brother. You see"—he lowers his voice—"this is a fucking scary time. No time for little-girl-like bickering."

"That's right." Rex's eyes *quite* twinkle. (But the darkness hides the twinkling.)

Gordon leans back, way back. Both the rocker and the floor give low contented creaks. "Have a seat, Richard," he says. He pulls on the arm of the nearest rocker to bring it closer. The smell of pooling spilt beer surges in cold cloudy whiffs.

But Rex, saying "Thanks," just settles on his haunches, elbows on his thighs, fingers laced between his knees. Someone as fit as he is makes this look real comfy.

Gordon says, "I heard you guys did a food drive to help flood victims."

Rex doesn't move anything but his lips, his voice low and grave. "A Dakota Indian reservation. Government wouldn't help them. Nobody helps them."

"Except the militias . . . your big network."

"Right."

Gordon watches as Rex stands slowly but nimbly, no cracking joints, the old porch floor squeaking, sits easy into the chair next to Gordon. His brown T-shirt shows up more plainly against the bluish fluorescent light of the kitchen window; it is spotted blackly with the wetness of both this late-summer heat wave and the exertion of argument.

Jane moans.

Gordon lays a hand on her back. He says, "I've had fantasies about you guys. Like imagining you all pulling up in your trucks with your M-16s and SKSs and so forth just as the cops were draggin' *her* mother out of her little car . . . and you know"—he whispers this on a hot beery breath—"One of those SWAT assholes stood on Lisa's face with his fucking Nazi black boot while they searched her, and they left her little dog to die in the car with the windows rolled up. And they left this child molested, you could say, a molested soul. And robbed; stole her home. Even her little possessions and dresses! The great American civil forfeiture laws. That comes after they frame you or get up a little hearsay. And you're not rich enough to get unframed. The prototype for full fascism, *fullll* fascism coming *soon*. Where were you, Rex? Where were you and the boys? Why . . . didn't . . . you . . . save . . . this . . . child?"

Rex says nothing, just settles more into his rocker, legs stretched out, chin almost touching his chest.

Gordon says, "You see, I can't believe there is presently a conspired date when the president will call for martial law. Because it's already happening."

Rex turns his head away. The porch is for the moment filled with hushy ripples of breeze and a hiss through the treetops, which seem to be coming not from outside this porch but from him, Rex York, weary man.

Gordon snorts in an ugly way.

Rex wiggles one booted foot.

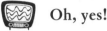 ## Oh, yes!

Oooooh! . . . aren't yooooo just yearning for a brand neeeewww TV . . . one of the big ones like everyone else hazzzz. Yooo could beeee there nowwww in front of it. See my face get bigger and *bigger* and BIGGER!

The two men listen.

Now only the wind is speaking. And the creaking voice of the old New England house. And the homemade mobiles . . . *Clang!* . . . *Chime!* and *Thot! Thot!* And Gordon's chair, rocking slow, deep.

Rex's silence is as significant as a heartfelt pledge. To America? To Gordon? Or to something simpler, just another day's worth of self-control?

Gordon knows for sure now that he and Rex are still really *together* in the same place they have always been.

The wind makes a banshee screech, but no one turns to look, even though a couple of newspaper pages blow out of a chair at the other end of the porch. The sacred wind, part of the St. Onge Settlement's hope. Praise be, the wind.

Gordon's big-guy voice chuckles sadly. "This kid right here—man." He sighs. "There is nothing the great men won't sacrifice to achieve their New World Order." Another sigh. "And here we are, grown men with a lotta talk, doing nothing."

Rex says, "Yeah, it's a mess." He blinks, looking into his hands, palms together, like the game kids play with laced fingers called Here's the Church, Here's the Steeple. He says, "There's a lot to it." He looks sideways at Gordon and Gordon frowns. He says to Gordon, "It's all true . . . it's all real. You and me. We're both right. It's all real."

Gordon thunks a boot heel against the floor. Once. Twice. "What kind of men are we, anyway?" He sniffs. "Baby men."

What sounds like a whole drawer of forks and spoons dumped on the floor at the far end of the porch goes clanging and skidding far and wide, while more wind finds the old house's gables, yipping and sobbing, a whirl of grief.

Rex says, "We're gonna die, either way. It's just a matter of whether or not we die facing front or with our backs turned."

Gordon's rocking chair eases forward: once, then back; once, then back.

Rex says, "However it goes, they are coming. Somehow, they are coming. You know it. I know it. They are going to be standing here and everywhere, bustin' heads. And the militias have various ways of how to deal with that. We're just trying to stay cool for a while longer. Sometime, when you are ready to listen, I can tell you more." He opens his hands again, as if looking in at the people of his finger church. "Nothing my group is doing is really covert, not really. Not yet. I mean nothing serious. But we are careful because we have to be. I'm sure the Feds find us just about as offensive as the real quiet ones. It's all a problem to them. Their Project Megiddo report laid it all out. Just owning guns, you are considered a terrorist. Being a Christian puts you on their list."

"A certain kind of Christian."

"The report states *Christian group*." Rex looks like something is wrong with his face muscles. His eyes grow wide a minute, then blink fiercely, the rest of his face unchanged. "Gordo, you know at some point there will be martial law." He swallows dryly, pushes the tips of all ten fingers against his mustache, then chuckles disgustedly. He wags his eyebrows at Gordon. Teasingly. Like a brother. The point on which they agree *and* disagree.

In a most sincere and embarrassingly tender way, Gordon says, "I weep for my country. I weep for all."

Rex says, "Ayup, maybe it *all* fits."

"So if I come to one of your meetings and bring a couple of young people, will we be refused?"

Rex places a hand on each of his rocking chair arms and sinks even farther back, stretches his legs way out, his plain belt buckle catching a little woeful shimmer of blue kitchen light. He waggles his boots in a really most contented fashion. He *tsks*. Then sternly, "All right. You can. But don't come over and act like King Kong. You have got to remember, *I* am the captain."

And so.

The militia movement grows.

God speaketh.

Near and far. Inside and out. Infinitesimally small, infinitivally large. No right, no wrong. No ugly, no lovely. No conservative, no liberal. Just chemistry. Just spark. Just the hum of it all. I am always satisfied.

Secret Agent Jane tells us.

Next time Gordie makes me mad—like no sugar for "Jane dear" (well, not enough sugar, just stupid amounts I can bearly taste)—I will escape again. It's pretty easy, and I will have so much stuff for Ber-NEECE and David, more than I can remember. My spy books are getting waaay too small. My power glasses are super strength now.

Meanwhile, on the other side of town.

Rex's mother's name is Ruth. Worked the shoe shop off and on till shoes went to Taiwan or Mexico or somewhere. She and her husband, John, Rex's father, did a lot with the American Legion, keeping the hall up, making some really great Saturday night dances happen, and the Memorial Day stuff and the Veterans Day stuff, and the people, terrific people: Doris and Carl, Anne and Joe, John Gregory and Peg, Ray and Joan. It was a long drive to the hall, sometimes twice a day, but the Yorks were sociable, quietly sociable. Steady types. Hardworking. Law-abiding. No trouble to anyone in this world.

John is gone, buried in another county, too far to visit regularly. But "you don't need a grave to grieve," Ruth will tell you.

Ruth is only fifteen years and ten months older than Rex, her first child. She has veiny wrists and hands and a settling neck, and her voice cracks some, but her face is still heart-shaped, her black hair has hardly grayed, her eyesight is almost perfect, and she walks a kind of hip-swingy walk without trying.

She is the possessor of a half dozen T-shirts with Southwest Indian themes: eagles, wolves, and spotted horses. Black T-shirts, black being her favorite. But also one green and one baby-girl pink. Then there are her turquoise earrings, which dangle. A turquoise and silver wristband. Sometimes she braids her hair, just one nice thick dark braid. Two would be going too far, too cute for today's world.

She is sixty-five. She has a boyfriend now from the Legion: a quiet man, a Korean War vet. Was a drinker once, twenty years ago. Was a smoker once, eight years ago. A quiet anxious type but kindly. Takes her places special. A quiet relationship.

Ruth hears Rex's van pull up outside. She pulls plates and forks from the drainer, sets them out. A reflection of late and nearly setting sun on Rex's opening van door plays on the wall.

The clock up over the table has a nice *tick-tock*. There's a rhythm to the life she has, now that Rex is back here living. And Glory, her grand-daughter, Rex's only child. Glory is in and out, mostly out. But Rex (her name for him is Rick or Ricky), he is as the seasons, the tide, the sun, the moon, the swing and sway of the zodiac, heart of the home, the dis-tant, wary, protective heart. He is everything now. He is the son she almost lost. But the soldier came home.

The van. It is pretty new. Not as new as his pickup. More or less paid for. It is charcoal gray with red black-edged lettering that spells out YORK ELECTRIC. And a cartoon lightbulb with legs and a handful of tools, cute face, and a little hat—a lightbulb on the run, heading out to help you with all your electrical needs. Rex York has a reputation in the area. He's good. He's fair. He's quick to get back to you and doesn't seem overex-tended, even though everybody wants him. He's creative and really gets into wiring for the more difficult restoration jobs. And he is polite. He's not what you'd call charming and not a real yakker. His smiles are brief, rare, and never forced or phony. If he smiles at you, you can feel very special.

You might notice that on his key ring is a little American flag. (This is long before the 9/11 media hype.) Or that he wears a wedding ring.

Right now, he is coming up onto the glassed-in front porch that leads to the kitchen in the ell. Handful of mail. Brown bag of groceries. No military cap. No cap at all, not when he does business. And his dark-blue work uniform is just as pressed-looking as when he left this morning. If you look at his feet, you'll see he wears heavy black high-topped military boots, but always with his pant legs over them.

The kitchen smells potatoey and oniony. And of hamburg.

He finds a gift on the table. Wrapping paper made by kids with a design of little clouds and smiling suns. A card. Says REX on it. Inside, the card is signed by a whole bunch of names, some of which he immediately recognizes.

"How'd this get here?" he asks his mother.

She is standing by the whirring microwave with her arms folded across her big red-and-black flannel shirt, worn with the tail out over her jeans. And on her feet, moccasins. And on her heart-shaped face, a funny little charmed smile. "*He* brought it," she answers. *He* meaning Gordon St. Onge.

Rex hefts the package. Feels like a big book.

The microwave bings. His mother moves away, a kind of black-and-red shifting blur in his periphery vision.

He peels off the wrapping paper.

A dictionary. Feathers are inserted as place holders, feathers of a goose, a blue jay, crow, rooster, hawk, thrush. Words are marked in red: *democracy . . . republic . . . socialism . . . capitalism . . . state . . . mammon.* He frowns. Somehow he feels both insulted and deeply touched.

He snorts to show his manly dismissal of this gag. And pushing him aside, his mother is setting her reheated yeast rolls on the table.

He goes to the cool quiet bathroom to wash his hands, comb his thinning hair, and rake a little water through his proud lush mustache, and then to the living room to put his feet up for one or two blessed moments before supper.

Time passes. Somewhere in the woods on St. Onge land, unbeknownst to anyone, Mickey Gammon is in his tree house. Home sweet home.

He can't just wear it around anywhere. Only to Rex's meetings. And here, alone. Not that he fears the FBI. Ha-ha-ha-ha. He imagines the FBI guys all being the spitting image of Mr. Carney or one of the other high priests at the school here. Maybe the principal back in Massachusetts, who actually was the spitting image of Mr. Carney, at least in that tight-jawed, big-nostriled, bug-eyed, striding-the-halls, Mr. Hotshot way.

Or maybe all the FBI guys look like his brother, Donnie: tight-lipped, gray-eyed, and angry. Big eyes, much bigger eyes than Mickey's. Donnie has the Locke eyes. Mickey has the Gammon eyes.

"FBI are just eyes," one of Rex's guys says. "FBI eyes are everywhere." Sort of like in walls? And telephone poles? Maybe even trees? Big fucking deal. Unlike some of Rex's men, Mickey thinks the FBI is the smallest problem in his life.

Anyway, he wears it now, here in the dying light: his new camo BDU jacket with the official patch of the Border Mountain Militia high on the left sleeve. Olive patch with black embroidered lettering around the black outlined mountain lion. He's never seen a mountain lion in Maine, though rare unconfirmed sightings are reported. Kinda like having a Martian on your militia patch. Well, no, not *that* weird.

Mickey twists the clasp of the olive pistol belt into place. Then he leans back against his bags of belongings and rolled-up blanket and lights up a cigarette.

Some nights he lies here lonely. Some nights he lies here feeling worried about how it's going to be here in this tree house when snow flies. And at the moment, only one blanket. Some nights he lies here feeling pissed off at his brother, Donnie: *shithead*. Sometimes he lies here thinking about Erika, Donnie's wife: her softness, her little sexy expressions. Sometimes he lies here thinking about how his nephew, Jesse, is in his grave, only two-fucking-years-old. Sometimes it is cancer he thinks about, how it is like being possessed. You are eaten and digested from the inside out. You can't run from it. Sometimes he mulls over the jobs the militia guys get him: odd jobs, some easy, some hard, some silly. Sometimes he thinks about Rex and how Rex never eats sugar and never gossips. Sometimes Mickey lies here feeling depressed. But tonight he feels tough. Tonight he feels like *somebody*. Mickey Gammon: Border Mountain Militia. Fifteen years old and fucking hard. If it rains tonight, the tree house leaks like a sieve. And he doesn't give a shit.

The screen shivers. The screen warns.

Terrorists are among us and hiding in the hills, loaded to the gills with gunnnnz! *Citizen militias!* Omigod! How can we stop this!? Where will it lead to!!?

 Out in the world.

Today, somewhere in America, more foreclosures. More auctions. Another farmer plots his own death. And another. There is an art to making your death by combine look like an accident.

 Another day.

A farmer is staring at his supper, not eating. How do you say good-bye to your wife and daughter when you are the only one who knows that tonight will be good-bye?

 Across America.

The militia grows.

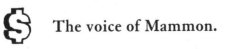 **Concerning all the aforementioned details, the screen seems to be . . .**

Blank.

$ The voice of Mammon.

Thousands upon thousands of pairs of hands trained to the keys, in thousands of sunless weatherless carpeted spaces and perfect room temp, the death stare, the screens of the service industry. *Your opportunity*, it is said. Work, America, work! You are dead but still alive. Thousands and thousands more pairs of hands being trained at this moment, and thousands of others ready for that creak in your wrist tendons or your complaint, if you should complain. But you won't complain, will you?

Across America.

The militia grows.

 The screen screams.

Omigod! The militias! Terror! Terror! Terror! Terrrrooooorrr!

Each night after supper over the next three days.

Gordon's old Chevy truck and one of the Settlement's flatbed trucks is seen parked outside the home of Rex York, captain of the citizens' group called the Border Mountain Militia and Gordon's old pal. Each evening, Gordon has brought seven Settlement men—Paul Lessard, Ray Pinette, Rick Crosman, John Lungren, Chucky Bean, Eddie Martin, and Butch Martin—with him. And Tim Cash has been coming in his own car, having to leave early for this or that errand. No kids have been included, so this is not part of the school experience yet.

Neither has Rex's militia been on hand these evenings. Just Rex. And of course the hot cookies, compliments of Rex's mother, Ruth.

Tonight it is Saturday, a night with a weird cloudy green-looking sky and the first clump of autumn red leaves on the maple that stands by the Yorks' driveway. And tonight Gordon and the usual six Settlement men are accompanied by one youngster, Gordon's oldest son, Cory St. Onge, age fifteen.

And Mickey Gammon is there—wallflower Mickey—but with a difference. Straight-shouldered in his woodland camo BDU jacket and pistol belt. And the green-and-black mountain-lion patch.

All the Settlement guys have brought guns. A rather sooty-looking, old muzzle-loading LG&Y three-band rifle musket with 1863 stamped on the lock. Cap lock. Bayonet. A long gun, dark and dignified and rangy, like an old soldier. And there is a bayonetless cut-down model 1884 Trapdoor. And, yes, an AK-47. Also a Bushmaster, an AR-15 look-alike. An M1-A. And some handguns.

These are the total sum of war weapons owned by the Settlement people, give or take a musket or two. You could hardly call it stockpiling, as some of the call-in radio shows have declared. They are brought tonight to show Rex. Just for a little gun talk, military versus sport. Auto versus semiauto versus pump action versus lever action versus bolt action. Actually, tonight the talk has gone off onto the subject of hunting for a good half of the visit. Talk of hunting Horne Hill and out behind the Towne Farm. How the old Boundary Road is all posted now. New Hampshire laws versus Maine laws, deer versus birds versus moose. And they tell some of the old stories, including the one about the Vandermasts and that Maine Guide scheme John Vandermast's wife's people were involved in some years back.

Then just a little bit about Vietnam: not a story, not a memory, but a joke, convoluted, with deep meaning for insiders.

But before the Settlement men leave—they are all grouped around the door—the talk finds its way back to preparedness, their usual subject. They are at the door and here it goes, the difference between hunting and preparedness, plain on the face, in the posture. One a voice of triumph, the other the voice of brooding anger, a sort of tough whine.

Then, when they are outside, it is this very weird dusk, light reflected off high clouds to the east, so it seems more like morning than evening, and the men stand around the trucks in the driveway, wrapping the guns. They don't have enough cloth or leather carriers, so they use some blankets. The guns all go into the bed of the pickup, except for the M1-A that Cory has pushed into the gun rack in the back of the cab of the flatbed.

And now a car pulls up behind Rex's van. Car door opens quickly. It is a man alone, dressed in a plaid flannel shirt, but he moves like an urban man and has two cameras and a bright and happy-go-lucky look on his face and his eyes are on Gordon. "Mr. St. Onge! How are you tonight?!!"

Gordon backs away, flings the pickup driver's door open violently. He is inside in a quick second and both trucks load down thereafter with others, but for Mickey and Rex, who are still out there, and the stranger is saying now to Rex, "Nice night!!!" and all this time, even as he is so friendly and jolly and calling out, this stranger's cameras are clicking and flashing, first one camera, then the other. And, yes, there had been one moment there when Gordon still had his hand on the truck door, one foot in the truck, one on the ground, before Paul and Raymond and

Chucky and Cory and Rick and Butch and Eddie and John and Rex had all had a chance to stop staring wide-eyed, Butch still handling that yellowy SKS with the thirty-shot extended magazine (which is cheap-made and always sticks, but is, nevertheless, a little bit illegal in many states when it is attached to this particular make of rifle) when both cameras seem to be clicking and flashing at once, one camera in each of the jolly stranger's hands.

Mickey speaks.

So me and Rex are all that's left. He says to come in the house. He takes me upstairs to where his computer is. He says it is asleep. I figured he was going to e-mail the rest of the militia, special bulletin about the weirdness in the yard. But we just sat there in two fat chairs and Rex breathed through his bottom teeth.

We both stared at the door and around. He was thunking his fingers on the bookcase next to his chair. The room smelled like the heat register and also like new blankets.

We sat there some more and then I say, "Where'd that guy come from?"

Rex's eyes move from the sleeping computer screen to my face and he says, "Watching our house."

"Is he the FBI?"

He squints down at the legs of the computer table. "More like Hollywood. That sort of thing. Between Gordo and this militia, there are" —he smiles sickly—"fans."

I don't want to seem dumb so I laugh.

Then he stretches his right arm out along the bookcase, wiggles his fingers, looks at his watch, nods his head like to music. This with the nodding is not his usual thing either.

"So," I say, "it's probably not the FBI."

His head keeps nodding. "Newspapers are read by the FBI."

"And computers too," I add.

And he says, "Without a doubt."

I look at the computer keyboard, so clean you'd think fingers never touched it.

Within hours, the newspapers fill up with independent photographer Cal Alonsky's creep-out-the-public militia photos.

Gordon St. Onge, thirty-nine-year-old leader of the Maine separatist group known as the Settlement, is identified in the photos, although his face is just a profile. His body—one visible leg, dark work shirt, and pale jeans —is blurred, truck door blurred, and there's a most definite fleeing look.

Forty-nine-year-old Richard "Rex" York, captain of the locally notorious Border Mountain Militia, is also named in the caption under the photos, while Butch Martin and Mickey Gammon and the rest are just called *unidentified men* or *unidentified others*.

The SKS in Butch Martin's hand is called an *assault weapon*.

Each newspaper offers a brief article to accompany the photos, just to let you know there is now a St. Onge armed militia connection. Though mostly what you see is a rehash of previous articles, borrowing and lifting, and what you wind up with from so much borrowing and lifting is that in some of the newly hatched articles, Rex is living in *Edgecomb, Maine,* and he's an *electronics engineer,* while Gordon appears in a Buffalo, New York, paper as a twenty-nine-year-old, which is okay because the man identified in the photo as Gordon St. Onge is Butch Martin.

But the pictures themselves don't lie, do they? See there? The expressions on all the men's faces are mighty unfriendly.

Mail pours in. The phone gives the kitchen wall a continuous shaking.

And again the call-in radio shows buzz with the name *Gordon St. Onge* and *the St. Onge situation in Egypt* and now *the militia connection*.

Clippings are sent to the Settlement, one with the caption ANGRY WHITE MEN IN MAINE. One photo shows Rex—yes, always the soldier— facing the camera down, his olive-drab army cap covering his forehead but not his eyes. Dozens of versions of the same article, some photocopied, some the actual clippings, some sent by Gordon's friends, some sent anonymously. Perhaps these are people who *were* friends but who now no longer think of themselves that way.

Federal Building: Special Agent (S.A.) Kashmar thoughtfully reads reports.

Okay, so you Guillaume St. Onge (alias Gordon, Gordo, Gordie, the Prophet) are developing. *You* know. Like a case of spotted-ass purple fever. You'll be seeing new and absolutely improved terrorist laws someday, two or three years down the lane. As soon as the network, rogue or otherwise, can get something big and creepy to sway the public, you know, wackos such as you or wacko Arabs, wacko Cubans, or some stinky mix, the hydra swinging its heads in the wind and having an intimate relationship with the cause of brightly burning booming buildings, jihads, massacred American schoolkids, whatever it takes our network of—ahem—specialists to create a wave of public indignation. You see, it's all about the two Cs, control and consent. *We* control the population, and we let *you* all consent to our doing it.

Gordon St. Onge takes two small boys and three older girls to a meeting of the Border Mountain Militia.

A friend of Rex's, one of his old volunteer fire department and rescue connections, a certified CPR man, comes to start the militia on CPR lessons and other first-aid skills.

Some of the Settlement kids already know this stuff, right at home.

Mickey watches from his straight-backed chair by the sewing machine and TV. His eyes function like a falcon's, on target, recording every smallest move, but his eyes appear to be disinterested, not like the eyes of something that is fainted or dead but just pale temperatureless boredom.

Most of the militiamen get a kick out of the Settlement's smart kids. A couple just seem annoyed, as old tomcats would be in a room full of hell-raising kittens.

Okay, we just said Mickey looks bored, but basically he's paralyzed. Her name is Samantha, blonde as snow, a blonde-white-gold girl with Apache kerchief around her forehead, a print of diamonds and cyclones the color of warm gore. Her breasts (tits to Mickey) are inside a black burlappy top. Her bra makes her breasts look like small warheads. Jeans, not tight but not empty. Work boots, the kind skinheads wear. Would take five business days to lace them up. Mickey's neck feels like an ostrich's with a cantaloupe in it.

There's another girl, about the same age as Samantha, he thinks. About his own age. Her name is Bree. Most of the Settlement kids are part of things, asking questions, blabbing away, please and thank you and all that. Eager, like blue jays. But Bree doesn't talk. *Can* she talk? She is certainly wrecked in looks. An accident? A birth problem? Leprosy, like the Bible? She has red hair, orange and snaky. Kind of great hair, actually. There's a ton of it, long and alive. But her face—man, it is split in half. Or maybe stretched, mostly between the eyes. Her face scares Mickey for a while. Her eyes are brownish yellow. Her lashes yellow. Each eye is kind of sexy, if it were in a human face . . . like Samantha's. But her face is outer space.

Still, she keeps her face straight ahead, hair bunched around the sides, smiling at the little kids, while the big ones she communicates to with ESP or some other animalish vibrations. But she does *not* look at the Prophet. She sits next to the Prophet but she never looks at him. They are squeezed together side by side on Rex's deep fake leather couch. Actually, it's the kind of couch so squishy that you sit *in* it. The third person who sits there varies: sometimes a Settlement kid, sometimes one of Rex's men. Because of the CPR and rescue lessons, people are moving around a lot, nobody falling asleep as they do at most of Rex's meetings.

The Prophet, Gordon St. Onge, whatever, he is like the newspaper. Eyes as light as Rex's but not controlled. Rex has controlled eyes. The Prophet has totally insane eyes. And one cheek jumps. And—what Mickey can never get used to—he's, like, seven feet tall, or almost anyway. *He* talks; his voice is like a big drum. He wears a billed cap on sweaty hair. His neck is as wide as four necks.

The youngest Settlement kid, Max, is chosen to be the heart attack victim.

Ruth York is not home today, but she has left two pans of blond brownies on the table.

There on the couch, Bree (with the red snake hair and stretched face) and Gordon St. Onge are sitting in a way his bicep touches her shoulder and the outside of his left boot and her right come together. Looks like it's not on purpose, but who knows?

Rex and the rescue guy talk about *profuse bleeding*.

Willie Lancaster isn't around today, but Doc is. CPR is not his subject. *Jews* or *fags* or *socialists* or *welfare whores* are his subjects. He looks restless, jiggling his leg and reddening his ears.

Max, the heart attack victim, chirps from his prone position on the rug, "Imagine me squished by a truck!"

Mickey watches the Prophet, who is also distracted. Mickey knows there is not a word he can speak that would get the white-haired Samantha to feel for him, Mickey, what he, Mickey, feels for her: *bothered*.

And now the fire department guy is resuscitating the little kid on the rug.

Doc jiggles his leg faster.

Art, with the sea-captain beard and high voice, breasts, big belly, and mostly nothing like Doc, asks a question about lungs and trachea, which one of the teeniest kids has the correct answer to. And the reddish-haired Bob of Rex's militia, who is dying and gets a disabled vet check every month, laughs like a tree full of monkeys.

Next will be tourniquets. And then contusions. Whatever.

The blood-red chamois shirt the Prophet is wearing draws Mickey's eye. He sees the guy is staring out the window (with its stout fiberglass drapes swept open today) at the Herefords pushing their way through tall weeds across the wet gooshy part of the field.

And Gabriel, one of the Settlement kids, says, "You would look like a pizza. You wouldn't want to be resuscitated." He says this last word slowly but perfectly, as far as Mickey can tell.

Mickey speaks.

So we all say good-bye out in the yard. One kid is so little, the Prophet carries her out on his shoulders. The blonde one, Samantha, yells "Horripilation!" and hugs herself. I guess they like big words. Whatever. The important thing is this time nobody jumps out at us with a buncha cameras.

Between militia meetings, they meet in the gravel pit on the Boundary Road.

The day is hot, but a dry hot. Kind of feels good. Clouds shaped like bunnies and little fishes slide along in the blue-green sky. The tall grasses chorus with every kind of creaking hopping insect. The goldenrod, in full glory, smells wild and weedy. And now, too, the smell of gunpowder.

Gordon St. Onge wears earphone-type hearing protection, stands with feet apart, and squeezes the trigger of the Russian-made SKS, one of Rex's many military weapons.

The impact of this shot gives the target frame a little shiver, but his shoulder doesn't budge. This is his worst hit. One cautious shot at a time, he has been trying to pull his hits back into the cluster of holes around the 10X circle of the silhouette target's chest.

He likes this SKS. He's seen them before, handled one, but never shot one. Some of the others had paratrooper stocks. This one is plain. Yes, the SKS is considered cheesy. But the tabby-cat-like grain on this Russian and its high, rather restless red flush please his eye. And this one has a thirty-shot extended magazine. *Really* cheap-made. But doesn't jam. One of the *few* that doesn't jam. Hard to come by. The Chinese SKS lying across the tailgate is not his friend. He glares at it. Jammed on the eighth or ninth shot every time, pinching a line across the cartridge. Cartridge half in, half out, on top of the gun, inches from his nose. He fingers one of the cartridges, steel of a greenish cast, slender and seductive as a church spire. He loads the magazine of the Russian with only four of these. Then he's ready, raises the rifle, fires.

Rex sits on the tailgate of the truck, one foot on the ground, one foot swinging ever so slightly, watching the target through a spotting scope, eyes glinting behind his dark glasses.

Rex and Gordon have just had a rugged argument about common law. And then about Russia. And although Gordon has done most of the ranting, this time Rex stood up for himself.

Gordon steps away, losing interest in his target, which he knows is bad without asking. Shooting is like art, not carpentry or chemistry.

There are good days, bad days, blocks and rushes. He doesn't watch as Rex walks the hundred yards to the bank, his boots out of hearing now, just the stirring *careeeeek . . . careeeeek* and *innnnnk . . . innnnnnk* of the bugs in the nearby weeds.

When Rex returns and plants his feet apart to take aim at the fresh target, Gordon's eyes jump to his friend's back. By some fluke, they have both worn pale blue chambray work shirts. Cute, Gordon thinks to himself disgustedly. He sees the way Rex unhesitatingly settles the M-16's stock against his shoulder. Like you'd grab a broom and poke its straw ends into a dusty corner. He doesn't dawdle. No squinting or painful concentration and indecision and deep breaths. No shuffling and cocking his head from side to side. None of that. He just does it. *Bang!bang!bang!bang!bang!bang!bang!bang!bang!bang!* This is his favorite rifle. You could call it a sniper's gun. Springfield, thirty-ought-six. Now with a serious scope, mounted just in the last few months. And, yeah, a big hole. Many big holes now in the X of the target man's heart. Hits that are so tight, they make one single shredded two-inch gobbed mess in the paper. Gordon would be able to see better through the spotting scope on the truck, but he doesn't look.

Rex's earphone-type hearing protectors are gray. Gordon stares dead center of Rex's dark head as Rex fires again and again, working the paper heart into oblivion.

Gordon speaks, assuming Rex cannot hear him. "You goddam right-wing fucker."

Rex turns smoothly, kind of a pivot. Rifle loaded with ammunition that costs an arm and a leg, not nice cheap SKS ammunition. Rifle lowered, finger now flipping the safety up, he looks at Gordon's mouth. His pale eyes are wide. "What?" he demands.

Gordon wags his head apologetically. "I called you a right-wing fucker."

Rex raises his chin. His chest fills with a deep carefully taken breath. He says quietly, "I'd call you a name too, but I do not know what you are." He doesn't smile, but his eyes crinkle a bit at the edges. He pulls off the ear protectors and puts a hand through his thinning dark hair. "So I'll just call you a fucker."

Gordon dwells so much lately on the past, that which was between himself and Rex, some memories silky and thin and shredded, others clear.

He came to know Rex in the years after the war. After the *conflict,* that is. Yeah, the *conflict.* Like the difference between a little argument and a punch in the face? No, rather like the difference between a story and a lie. Because it wasn't even a war. It was a barbeque. And the hotdogs were alive. So he has heard.

Rex wasn't married any too quickly after Vietnam. He once put his cold gray-blue eyes on Gordon's face and said, "You don't go from the three-legged sack race to the tea-and-dolls party in the same day." He was talking about something else at the time, not the war. But Rex *never* talked about the war. Vietnam War knowledge wasn't a thing you could just store neatly, like gardening hints or small-engine repair. It was a thing that would blister and pimple and seep from life in general when you least expected it.

So instead of getting a girl, Rex joined the "volunteer fire" and sported a special volunteer license-plate holder and, on the dash of his new truck, a red light to flash when he was on his way to a fire. And during most of his after-work hours (he worked in a lumberyard and box shop before getting his electrician's license), he hung out at Gin-Tom's Lake View, which is now what they call the Cold Spot or Hot Spot, depending on the season. When Gordon was old enough to drink legally, Rex had already been situated awhile in that bar.

So there they were, Gordon eighteen. Rex twenty-eight. Rex drank moderately most of the time. He just liked that dark, crampy, smoky, noisy place, which had, despite its name, no view. No windows, in fact.

Sometimes Rex *did* get drunk. And he was *fun.* A dry weird humor, not noisy, almost on the edge of playfulness. Like if you gave a mountain lion a catnip toy, who would then roll quietly onto his back and chew on his own tail or the bars of his cage. And his eyes would be different.

Across the road from the barroom, throughout the winter months, Promise Lake (then called Swett's Pond) was the hub of the male social wheel of Egypt and other nearby towns. Twenty to forty ice shacks. Snowmobiles. Trucks. Bonfires. And bass and trout the size of small men. This was the years before mercury poisoning. (Or before the public discovered it). Though these fishermen, even now, have never believed in such scares. Rex and Gordon and half a dozen Beans and Sonny Ballanger and Donnie Rowe and Russ Pelter, Tim Cash and any number of Verrills (different ones at different times), and guys from the salvage yard (different ones at different times), and that biker bunch from Brownfield, all fished and laughed and argued and drank and pissed, fished and laughed and argued and drank and pissed. . . .

Over the years since then, even after Gordon settled in with Claire over in Mechanic Falls and Rex married Marsha and their little girl, Glory, was born, all those years, Gordon and Rex would stop in on one another. And keep track. And neither forgets the past, though, like war, it's not really mentioned. Not a lot of this "remember the time" like you hear some people do.

But surely Rex must hear the boot steps of the past following him, as Gordon does. That part of the past following that other past, and preceding the more recent past . . . and now the Gordon and Rex present.

My brother.

How did Gordon start to think this way of Rex? Rex as brother. What was the moment? For there was, indeed, a moment.

Somebody—he thinks he remembers it was Paul Gregs, another vet, dead since then in a paper-mill lab chemical "accident"—Paul and Rex and Gordon all piled into Paul's car . . . maybe there was another guy, he can't remember who.

Paul wanted reefer, so they went to fetch it.

Paul's dealer came to the door and said he was out of stuff, but if they drove to Harrison and went to the bar there, they'd find plenty. Gold. All bud. "Ask for the Fly," the dealer said.

So they got to the bar and people were in the parking lot smoking stuff, and when they asked for the Fly they were told *inside,* and the air outside was all smoky and herbish and nice, right up to the door of the bar, and inside the door they asked for the Fly and a thumb was jerked toward the bar, so they all herded over to the bar and got beers and looked around, and there up on the stool was the Fly, no need to ask.

A woman with short legs. A kind of hefty woman. Dressed in a leather jacket, with Harley wings across her back and a little chain zipper on each pocket. And an aviator cap liner, a soft olive thing that fit her head perfectly, and a dangling strap from this cap. And, yes, goggles, pushed up

on top of the aviator cap. And her face was round and flushy and she wore
a nice big ear-to-ear smile, not to show her teeth, just a big smile of the
lips, like a smiley-face Have a Nice Day button. She wore black pants and
boots, all black. Paul asked her if she was the Fly, and she eased off her
stool and headed out.

All the men followed. Out into the cold parking lot, the deal was
made. But the Fly also sent a free fat lighted joint around the circle,
and they talked about people they all knew in common. And they discussed movies and reloading shotgun shells and rifle cartridges, and
then some relating of disasters around raising turkeys, and the Fly,
Gordon remembers, was so nice . . . so funny . . . so motherly. And
suddenly her very small blue eyes fixed on Gordon's face and then
Rex's face and she said, "You guys are brothers, aren'tcha? You're
Gary Cram's cousins, aren'tcha?"

And they, of course, said they weren't.

But she kept looking at them, from one face to the other, then shook
her head and said, "Shit. I coulda sworn."

After that, Gordon would say it: "My brother." And Rex never dis-
missed it.

Okay, the Fly. That was fun. But there was pain too. And one of those
occasions of pain had to do with the old graveyard over on Seavey Road
and Rex's aunt, who lived over in New Hampshire (which is the next
town, Egypt being on the state line of the western border). There was
something fishy and weird about Rex's behavior that Saturday morning. He just said that if Gordon met him at that cemetery, they had a
job. And Gordon agreed to meet him there, but what the hell was going
on? Rex added that his aunt had made him promise he wouldn't divulge
where she lived, her name, or *anything,* and that he, Rex, would have to
go over to her place *alone;* she would pick him up at his house and he
could get a guy to help him, but the guy had to wait at the graveyard
and not ask any questions.

Gordon knew the graveyard, though it was overgrown and you
couldn't see it real well from the road. There were eleven graves, Mortons
and people married into Mortons. All dead for, if not a century and a half,
the next thing to it.

So that morning while Gordon waited, listening to his radio and
eating potato chips or something, a car came along the road. It was a

great big ark, a Chevy, white, and its ass end about dragging. And it was driven with a foot that would ram the gas, then let up, then ram it again, so it lurched ahead over and over—*rummmmm*-slack, *rummmmm*-slack, *rummmmm*-slack, *rummmmm*-slack—and Gordon could see that Rex was the passenger in this vehicle, straight-shouldered and dignified as ever, and that the driver had a small white head.

The driver got out much faster than Rex and within seconds was at the back of the car. Gordon got out and stood by his own truck, hesitant to approach. He nodded to Rex, as Rex shut the big ol' car door behind him, but Rex would hardly look at him. The driver was a woman, Rex's aunt by marriage. She was skinny and little. She wore dungarees with a plain white very snowy T-shirt tucked in, gold frame glasses with scalding black eyes inside them. And a brown More cigarette pouring smoke. Hair a perfect helmet of white frizz.

"So where is this fucking graveyard! I don't see it!" her scratchy voice demanded.

Rex answered quietly.

Gordon stepped close just as this aunt person popped open the trunk: two full-sized very old elegant slate gravestones inside there. The top one read: *Anna Morton, wife of Charles Morton 1801–1844.*

The woman's scratchy voice commanded, "Okay, now . . . get these damn things out of my sight!"

Gordon and Rex worked to lift the first stone out. It was, after all, a *stone*: heavy. The woman was right at Rex's shoulder, twitching her brown cigarette and commenting on ways to improve the carrying of the stone.

The graveyard was up a short but *steep* hill. Big trees. Dark. Sweet and mossy. A stone wall, wrought-iron gate. Inside, Gordon saw a stone standing which read *Anna Morton, wife of Charles Morton 1801–1844,* which was identical to the writing on the stone they were gaspingly lugging. Gordon pointed this out. Rex looked at him and made a face that said, *Shut up.* But Gordon couldn't help himself. He said it again as they lowered their stone flat in front of the standing stone.

The aunt narrowed her black fiery eyes, not on Gordon, who had spoken, but on Rex, and replied, "I don't give a shit! These stones belong *here*!"

Rex said to Gordon, quietly and with no expression in his voice, "There's nine more of these back at her barn."

Gordon insisted, "But *this* one—"

Rex quietly interrupted. "Yes. It's a double. The others are too." And he made another face at Gordon to *say no more*.

The aunt looked at Rex, not Gordon, and said commandingly, "That stealin' shit. Don't that burn my ass. I hate that fuckin' stealin'!"

Rex quietly and expressionlessly said to Gordon, "These stones have been in her barn . . . *huff-huff*"—like Gordon, he was winded—"for a *long time*."

Gordon raised an eyebrow, looked wildly around. "Ah . . . they musta been stolen—*huff-huff*—a hundred years ago—*huff-huff*—then replaced . . . not long after. They're the same style. Everything's—*huff-huff*—the same."

The aunt's smoke was filling all the outdoors, billowing up through the heavy hemlock limbs. She screeched, "I hate that fuckin' stealin' shit. Nothin' burns my ass more than stealin'!"

"But—"

"These stones belong here, and they shall *be* here!" the aunt fired into Rex's eyes.

And so there were more trips with the Chevy, Rex passenger, the aunt driving—*rummmmm*-slack, *rummmmm*-slack, *rummmmm*-slack —away down around the curvy road while Gordon waited at the graveyard for the stone of Forest Morton and the stone for Lottie Morton Granger, these also dead for more than a hundred years. And this was true of all the rest, each stone gruntingly deposited alongside its replica but out flat, sort of over the dead person's face.

Through all this, young Gordon wore his wildest expression. But Rex was gravely polite, trying to please the aunt, even as she bullied him in ways painful to see. And Gordon knew that back at the aunt's barn, wherever it was, Rex was loading these stones all by himself.

When all eleven stones were finally in their final resting places, the woman did not thank. She only turned as she was leaving and gave them each a sharp look and screeched, "Both you boys go cut them Christly whiskas off. Looks like hell. Deputy oughta have you arrested for exhibitionism and indecent exposure!"

"Okay," said Rex quietly.

And away she went in her big ol' white Chevy—*rummmmm*-slack, *rummmmm*-slack, *rummmmm*-slack—down around the curving grade, and the two young men stood there with their hands hanging at their sides, both feeling emotionally bruised.

That was summer. Then fall, maybe the same year, maybe the year before, maybe after. Memory, like God, likes to play with you. But it was for certain, October. The Fryeburg Fair.

And this also was for certain: Gordon and Rex taking turns ramming their mouths and teeth and wriggling tongues up inside the stripper, who offered herself to each of them at the rail. Rex gripping her by the thighs above her bent knees, Gordon by her hips, each standing back to allow the other to take his turn in a perfect one-two rhythm, and the loudspeaker trickling out stripper music (an old record, it sounded like) so tinny, so weak, seemed it was coming from another attraction farther up the midway, and the face of the young girl looked at neither man, she having her head back, her eyes almost closed, probably forgetting at moments which man was which, though she was clear about when she wanted one to stop and the other to take his turn, while the tent full of three dozen or so quiet men standing around Gordon and Rex got quieter and quieter, and the stripper music crackled thinner and weaker, and the only thing the stripper was wearing, a tiny gold cross on a delicate chain, slipped slower and slower from side to side between her sweaty breasts, while the midway so merrily tweedling beyond the canvas also seemed fainter, nothing mattered more than this: the rather ridiculous babyish-sounding slurping sucking sounds of the two Egypt men, and the swish of the stripper's long hair as she swung her head from side to side in what appeared to be ecstasy, face to the ceiling, back bent like a gymnast, her soft inner thighs gripping the head of first Gordon, then Rex, whichever of the two was leaned up inside the rail there, her feet thumping, first one foot, then the other, not to the music from the speaker but some rhythm *she* orchestrated here, like a slowed-down heart, *thump . . . thump . . . thump . . . thump. . . .*

Why is it that, over the years, Gordon associates this with the graveyard incident?

And then, another time, a summer, no telling which summer, Rex and Gordon and Big Lucien Letourneau (who is small, not big at all) hit Old Orchard Beach. A late hot roaring night. Something had caught on fire, and there were fights, fire trucks, and police cars, and people yelling from car windows, topless bars, and regular take-it-all-off shows, all guarded by cops, unlike the fair, which had no cops. These cops looked like hairless gorillas, and then there were bikers who looked like regular gorillas, and somehow Rex and Gordon and Big Lucien made it alive to the dark beach, whiskey and beer and fried onion rings oozing from every pore. Ah, the beach! The vast dark starless sky and the vast white beach, sand of silk and crisp crunchy seaweed, and these *big shapes* walking toward them: bikers . . . bikers on foot . . . bikers from somewhere else, big twelve-foot-tall bikers from a grim planet . . . bikers all with something in hand—rocks, clubs, brass knuckles, drive shafts, cement blocks—too dark to tell.

They beat the shit out of Gordon and Rex and chased Big Lucien, who somehow stayed on his feet, all the way back to East Grande Avenue (it was later known).

And Gordon lay there in the warmth of his own bleeding, left to die in a big squashy smarting heap and the cold wet feel of the thing that was kissing Gordon's boots and ankles. What *is* that thing kissing, kissing, kissing, kissing, then sliding away, kissing again, each cold kiss getting bigger and more passionate?

The incoming tide, of course.

Where is Rex?

Gordon thinks he remembers dragging Rex to safety. Something like that. Memory is especially funny when framed by whiskey, bulging crusty eyes, and four broken fingers.

He does remember that Rex bled a lot. He was all blood and jelly and white sand. And his clothes were mostly ripped off. Hamburglike elbows, knees, and knuckles. Blood black as used motor oil leaking from the top of his head and teeth. One nipple looked missing. An eye fat and cute and as closed up as a pig's pink twat. Rex's whole self, at least in spirit, seemed flattened out, like you see a cat after he has gone under the tires of a dozen cars. By the time Gordon got Rex back to the truck parked at the top of Old Orchard's steepest hill, Gordon had more of Rex's blood on him than his own, and he realized how savagely Rex had fought for his own life, and how trust between some men—between Rex and himself, for instance—is a state of free fall. A state of perfect grace.

My brother.

Those years were all a hard mix of work and play and new frontiers crammed into a time so bright and small, for Rex an epilogue to war, for Gordon something religious, like God's big hand opening before Gordon's eyes, offering gifts. Or was it a test? One of those God tests, where you are asked to recognize the difference, if not the ironies, of bounty versus tribulation.

And now this. The militia.

My brother.

♡♡ Secret Agent Jane speaks.

This Sunday, Gordie takes me to see Mum. She is very weird and tired-looking. She says, "Gordon, I'm homesick."

I never take my secret glasses off here. Sometimes I stare at the cop-guards. They do not stare back. They look away. Sometimes I stare almost the whole time at one of them and fold my arms to show I mean business.

Willie Lancaster's gift.

The cab of Rex's truck always smells new. And it smells of Rex's various T-shirts' megadoses of fabric softener. And when Mickey is riding around with Rex certain evenings, or a Saturday perhaps, there is the smell of Mickey. Unwashed. And sort of mildewy, like his tree house.

As they ride along the back roads of Egypt, casually swerving around potholes or a dead porcupine, braking gently here and there for a darting chipmunk, there is no radio and not much conversation. If you were a fly on the windshield, you would see just two pairs of pale eyes staring ahead, Rex's steely (behind sunglasses), Mickey's wolfy.

They are going to pick up "a setta points" for the tractor that Rex and his schoolteacher brother share. Mickey had figured this meant auto parts store. But Rex is flipping the directional, which means Heart's Content Road. Oh, shit. Willie Lancaster. Mickey feels a sudden difficulty breathing.

There are *two* guys in the militia that Mickey wishes would move to another state or something. One is Doc, who goes on and on and on and on and on about Jews and fags in a way that makes Mickey feel edgy, even though he is neither Jewish nor gay. Somehow Mickey feels it is his very soul that is in the sights of Doc's scorn. And somehow Mickey feels blurred in with Doc's generalizations, Doc's suggestions for lynching, skinnings alive, and that sickening low laugh. There is a pink sticky dizzying cloud around Doc. Poison for one is poison for all.

Then there's Willie. Willie doesn't go on and on and on about these things. He's too busy acting like something that flies in your face out of the night woods . . . or out of a dark attic.

Rex's pickup climbs the mountain in third gear, downshifting even more as they pass the gray and white St. Onge farmhouse, a thing Mickey is confused about. It's the house where Gordon St. Onge *lives*. But some say he lives at the Settlement.

So then Rex is steering the truck on past the dirt road of the Settlement, the road entrance that is almost hidden, framed by low-hanging hemlock boughs and oak and beech and ferns and moosewood, and also gated off. The newest hand-lettered sign says KEEP OUT. TRY IT AND YOU'LL BE SHOT. Mickey glances toward Rex here, wishing the man's expression would change and give Mickey a clue on this subject of the place some people are starting to call Waco, Maine.

But of course Rex's face doesn't change. The dark crawling-along-the-jaws Civil War–style mustache doesn't flicker.

A half mile more thereabouts and it's the Lancasters', and there is Mr. Willie Lancaster right now, out among his big pine trees looking satisfied with himself.

Mickey's unwashed sweatiness warms up a notch.

Some guys have a pumped-up sort of muscularity. Some have a thick wrestler muscularity. But Willie, standing there in his black T-shirt and jeans, looks built to fly. Powerfully light.

In there among his big-trunked pine trees, he freezes melodramatically, gray eyes squinting at Rex's truck. To get the full picture, this is Willie as usual: No watch. (Time is built into Willie Lancaster.) No compass needed. No speedometers needed. No radar. No yardsticks. Willie needn't memorize much. He is a skewed creature, a twisted chapter of science.

The Lancaster yard is full of vehicles. Everyone must be home, including the older girls, including Dee Dee, who is married to Louis St. Onge and lives in the pink rocket house with Cannonball, a black dog with short legs, huge head, eyebrows, and teeth quite blindingly white.

Before Rex's truck is stopped, several white pug-faced, curl-tailed, homely-beyond-description but nice-guy-type small dogs surround it. They are constantly changing places so you can't count them.

Mickey's door is on the Lancaster side, Rex's door opens onto the pavement. Rex is out. Mickey isn't. Rex doesn't look back so he doesn't see how Mickey is finally out but lighting a cigarette and sort of oozing around to the driver's side of the truck. But Willie Lancaster watches this with interest.

Mickey listens to Rex talking and Willie's hooting and giggling and gagging and hoarse whispers.

Now silence.

Mickey takes another drag, staring, without seeing, at the modern house with hot-top driveway across the road from the Lancasters. Short grass. Hollyhocks. Picture window. No trees. Nobody he knows.

The small white pushed-in-faced dogs sniff Mickey or sit by him as if to guard him from something. One is doing Rex's tires, a few squirts to each.

The sun is a little overwhelming. Having cleared Willie's trees, it stands in the middle of the vast empty sky over the neighbor's ranch house. Mickey smokes, squints, breathes, sweats.

Now there's running feet. And now a *thwump* sound and a scraping *swoosh*—it's Willie, somehow spiderishly landing on the hood of Rex's truck, then leaping off like an evil Superman, landing on both feet in front of Mickey. "HEY, GEORGE!! WHAT'RE YOU DOIN', HIDIN' FROM OL' WILLIE?!!!!!" He is reaching for Mickey. Mickey is ready this time, unlike those other times. He does not shrink away. He does not flinch. He does not even sort of flinch. He is holding his breath and locking his muscles against any sort of cowardly behavior. Yes, Willie is a series of tests. Mickey has now passed the Willie-grabbing-your-shoulder-or-arm-or-shirtfront test.

Willie flicks at Mickey's small, thin, streaky blond ponytail of hair with a forefinger. The test goes on. "You a hippie? A girl? Or a rat?"

Mickey doesn't blink.

Willie snickers, feels his own beard, which has a slight point. His slightly buck teeth add to the effect. Now his eyes widen with *meaning* on Mickey's chest and waist. Mickey's T-shirt depicts four Weimaraners wearing hats.

Rex is coming around the truck now, the white Lancaster dogs sort of smiling up at him, panting, and Mickey sees a little box in his hand. The points. Rex's face has the same expression he wore when passing the gray farmhouse of the infamous Prophet and then passing the blocked-off entrance to Waco and the same expression he had when he left his own dooryard where Mickey had met him an hour ago.

"HEY!" Willie shouts. "Cap'n Rex does not go anywhere without packin'. What kind of little girlie has the great Cap'n been carting around here? This George just runs around naked. Georgie *girl*. Georgie *girl*!"

Willie always has other people's names for Mickey, never "Mickey." George is the one he uses the most.

Willie says cracklingly, "Hold it, boys, I've got to do something to repair this scandalous situation." Then he's gone.

Rex has situated the small box in the cab somewhere. Through the yellow haze of fight-or-flight and too much sun, Mickey can't see Rex's face now, even though Rex is standing in front of him. Mickey leans over the side of the truck bed, *trying* to look casual, sees clearly the red lettering on the doors of the truck parked up there among the trees, close to Willie's workshop: WILLIAM D. LANCASTER, LANDSCAPING & TREE WORK.

Now he sees, coming from one of the two connected mobile homes, Willie with a gun. He turns back around to face the weirdly perfect ranch house where he has heard ordinary schoolteachers live. Probably very thin-lipped Mr. Carney look-alikes. But Mickey sees no sign of life there presently. It *looks* like a safe haven from here.

The sound of Willie's work boots on sand and then tar, coming closer, make color and light against Mickey's closed eyelids as he draws hungrily on his now-short cigarette. He has a sudden desire to chew up the cigarette and swallow it, hot end and all.

Willie's gray eyes are fixed on Mickey's face even before he gets around the truck. "*I thought you were following me, Roger!!!!*" Willie shrieks. "You sure are in love with that truck handle."

Mickey's eyes drop to Willie's right hand. It's a service pistol. A Colt, Mickey observes.

Willie stands squarely, more military than a TV Western, but absolutely over-the-top showmanship. They are eyes into eyes, no words, Willie grinning, sort of, his bucktoothed grin, Mickey straining not to lower his eyes.

Now Willie whispers, "Max, I want to give you this Christmas present."

Mickey's eyes fall now firmly to the pistol.

Willie snickers. "I am giving you this Christmas present"—it is August—"because it bothers me so much that I want to wet myself —bothers the hell outta me—to see a member of my militia going all around out in the open air like you do, all. . . ." Willie wiggles and shudders all over, signifying what, Mickey isn't sure. "I am giving you this Christmas present so you need to put out your hand for it . . . but, Chuck, you gotta promise me that no matter how grateful you are, you will *not* hug me."

Rex is out there somewhere, sane, strong, Godlike Rex, wayyyy out there on the edges of Willie Lancaster's zone of twisted lights and sounds—and now the absence of sound. Here is Mickey, dead to everything except the soundless look of Willie's muscular hand holding out to him, muzzle down, the gun.

 ### Midnight. Tree house residence of Michael Gammon.

He is surrounded now—by the feeling. He falls asleep with it—the feeling. He dreams the feeling. He wakes with the feeling. It is a feeling that is dumb and confusing but it is good. A kind of security, like high walls. Shoulder to shoulder. Brother to brother. The gun? Yeah, but when he dreams it, there's no steel, just that muscular hand and the gray eyes, the voice, the moment.

Spread out on the floor of the clothes-making shop.

It's a full-sized flag. Dark blue. Painstakingly assembled with pieces of almost expertly dyed cotton sheeting to resemble the State of Maine flag, but with an arch of yellow-gold letters across the top that reads THE TRUE MAINE MILITIA. Three teen girls on their knees. "What about the eyeball on this moose?" "It's *way* too big." "Dorky-lookin' moose! We gotta fix it!" Meanwhile, leaning in one corner of the room, a hornbeam pole with an eagle carved on the top. Eagle came out perfect—almost. This will be the flagpole in due time. This will be the True Maine Militia. "Waaaay better than Rex's militia," someone whispers. "Yeah, 'cause we aren't *afraid* to go public. We *love* public." A pleasurable sigh, then another teenage girl voice. "No limited membership. We welcome the *world*!"

September

 **There's been some plans to get Jane settled,
not just daytimes but nights too.**

Maybe with Aurel and Josée, or with the Butlers, or with old Lucienne
in her little shady house at the end of the brick path, closest to the shops
and the quadrangle of trees and mowed grass. That would make a lot
more sense than the present arrangement. Gordon feels uneasy about
the farm place, not gated off in any way. Strangers often stop there, either first or after they find the Settlement road blocked. The phone rings
and rings. Much confusion since Ivy Morelli's feature story went to press.
And then the "angry white men" photos. Everyone suspects it's just a
matter of time before the DHS SWAT teams come through the door of the
farmhouse some night to "rescue" Jane. Tear her out of bed, shove her
into a social worker's car, and off they go. It seems better all the way
around if Jane were settled with one family or person instead of the constant shuffle of nighttime sitters here.

But this dusky September evening, Jane is still a resident of the old
St. Onge house. She has refused to hear a story or play a game, so Bev
and Barbara hang out in the old dining room, looking over some old
photo albums that Marian, Gordon's mother, left when she moved,
almost everything in this room the same as when Marian lived here,
even a bookcase with her "ceramics": dogs, deer, horses, Jesus in the
manger, Bo Peep and a sheep, some cherubs. Marian St. Onge has a

fetish for cherubs. Her cherubs here are painted a blushing pink. Wall-paper is blue. Room cool, usually closed off. Some of Gordon's papers and books, maps and letters are in cardboard boxes stacked in one corner. A braided rug, the factory-made kind, with blues to match the walls. Some phonograph records: Frank Sinatra, Lawrence Welk. Curtains, white with frills. Not Marian's curtains, though. These white frilly things were Claire's touch when she was here as a young wife.

When Gordon comes in, he catches Jane spying on Bev and Barbara: Jane beside the partly open dining room door in the little hall. She is making a picture in one of her small notebooks and wearing her secret all-seeing heart-shaped glasses. *Deep* concentration. Gordon's sudden appearance makes her really jump.

Gordon pretends not to notice that he's caught Jane at something, and Jane pretends that she hasn't been up to something, and the moment passes.

Now, out in the kitchen, Gordon is running a glass of water for a couple of aspirin. He turns and sees she is now sitting at the table, her glasses on the table, folded. She is glaring at him, her round dark eyes filled with mortal contempt.

"What?" he asks.

"You ugly pig."

He blinks. He grins. He snorts, like a pig.

She rises most dramatically. She is dressed in a little pink sweater made by one of the mothers. She has such long-limbed ease, more beau-tiful than any ballet or symphony, that old African grace that swims through tall grass and rolls with hard orange suns. She opens the re-frigerator door and lifts out a long speckled enameled pan . . . *empty.* "What . . . is . . . this?"

He cocks his head, squints. "My mother brought something for me when she was here the other night."

She sniffs the pan. "What . . . was . . . it?"

"Éclairs."

"How . . . many?"

He shrugs. She shoves the empty pan back into the refrigerator and turns, the door closing behind her soundlessly. She sinks gracefully to the floor, wraps her long sweatered arms around the knees of her long knitted matching pants, and buries her face. "I want my Mum," she says, against her knees.

He says, "Jane. I'm sorry. I should have saved you one."

She raises her face, tears wiggling in her huge black eyes, spilling now. Her mouth opens, a large square of real grief. "Mumma," she whispers. Softly, wearily. Turns her head slowly from side to side, tears dripping from her chin. "I can't stand it here," she says into Gordon's eyes. "Because you are so fat and full."

He tries not to smile.

She says quaveringly, "I can punish you." She sniffs. Her voice now bears a hard edge. "I got secrets about you, Gordie. About the milishish. Milishish are wrong. Everyone says they hurt kids. They *bomb* kids. I am going to tell. I know of a DARE man who is nice. I will tell him, and I will tell him to tell the other ones, the ones that's narcs, and you will be very very very very sorry."

Gordon stands frozen, looking at Jane's slim fingers, now picking at the knee of her knitted pants. He is seeing something, something that is not in this room. He is *seeing*.

Barbara, a short, ruddy, square, gray-haired person, is in the door of the kitchen now, and she says firmly, "Jane. People are not pretty when they blackmail."

Gordon steps over toward the refrigerator, to Jane sitting on the floor, her eyes unblinking.

He says, "What DARE man, Jane?"

Jane's eyes drop. "A nice one. He likes me. I bet if I told him to, he'd get the narcs to put you you-know-where."

Barbara is deathly silent. Behind her, Bev, also short, square, ruddy, and gray, is putting a hand on Barbara's upper arm, like steadying herself while walking a narrow board over high water.

Gordon squats down to get his face closer to Jane's. "What DARE man?" he asks again.

Jane squinches her nose. Laughs nervously. "Just joking."

Gordon takes Jane's shoulders, pulls her slowly to her feet. Hugs her head hard, maybe a little too tight. Rubs her hair. He looks into the eyes of the two women in the door. He shakes his head slowly. He says, "We need a lot of time to ponder certain profoundly painful possibilities in Jane's past—and Lisa's *present*—before we react. For now, a moment

of silence, aye? And a nice long quiet night to follow where we don't
react. You know? We're just going to ponder . . . the possibilities."

Word goes around the Settlement.

A serious development. There shall be one appointed person at all times
to make sure that Jane Meserve never steps off the property. No more
little strolls out on the tar road. Never alone with the phone or with
visitors. *Never*. And the profoundly painful possibilities of Jane's part
in her mother's arrest are discussed.

Secret Agent Jane tries to make sense of the recent past, before she came to the Settlement.

I just wanted to scare Mum. It was because she wouldn't buy it for me,
even though my heart was melting into ruins: the leather skirt. It was
the best thing I have ever wanted. But she said, "Later, Jane."

I said, "Now."

She said, "We have to wait till I get the credit cards paid next week."

This credit-card thing she always said. Just an excuse. If it was something *she* wanted, she didn't have excuses. I figured I could scare Mum
just a little, just a little scary thing. Not real bad.

At school, the DARE man, a police guy, said to us all, *You ever see one
of these things in your house?* I said, *Oh, yes*. He was so friendly. He talked
to me special, and we went in the place where teachers sit. I knew he
wouldn't hurt Mum, just scare her, and I could say to Mum, *There! Now
where's my leather skirt?*

So he asked me if I knew what *it* was called.

I said, in a very smart way, *A joint*.

The DARE man said, *That's very good, Jane*.

So I told the DARE man about the other part he wanted to know. *She
knows some people. She was on the phone. She thinks it's big. She thinks it
might be really big. Mum calls the other one Dr. Eric because when you get
a bag to smoke, it makes you feel better. That's funny, isn't it? But Mum
met this other man, I think. It is something with boats. I think Mum is a little
scared.*

The DARE man was very interested and very nice and kept asking me more stuff like where Mum worked—which is for Dr. Grossman, a real dentist, not a man who sells stuff—and I told him about the leather skirt and he said, *I'll see you get that leather skirt, Jane.* He was so nice. He said not to tell Mum about our talk.

Then it was days and days . . . no police yet . . . but I said to Mum, *You are about to be real sorry you didn't get me the leather skirt.* Meanwhile, I was afraid. What if somebody else bought it and it was the LAST ONE, no more in stock? It looked like the last one.

More days and days, and the nice DARE man never showed up. I kept looking out the window for his police car and his real pretty dog that sniffs your marijuana.

More days. Then I guess he forgot.

But somehow a bad thing happened when I was in school. Very mean cops made Mum prisoner, a *real* prisoner. Killed Cherish, my beautiful Scottie dog. Left her hot in the car. It wasn't anything to do with the nice DARE man, you can be sure of that. He didn't even remember my leather skirt. He has a bad memory problem. He promised to get me that skirt. He's, like, *really* spacey. The cops who arrested Mum are a special government kind: narcs, rhymes with *sharks*. The kind that make people cry. If I told Mum about the nice DARE man, she would agree that he probably forgot about Dr. Eric and all that. Who knows, he might show up right here with my leather skirt. It will take him awhile to find out where I am. And when he does, I'll talk to him to see if he can get Mum out. He had a gun and police outfit. They might listen to him. He was so nice.

However, Jane escapes.

Without the smallest detour, no zigzag, no slouch, she hurries up, up, up the paved road, up, up, up that long hill to Headquarters, her new friends who give out cookies and Wacky Lemon Wonder, both schoolteachers, a mother and son, virtuous, yes, not afraid to shop, not afraid to be what everybody is *supposed* to be.

She knocks crisply on their door, curtain of green dots to cover the door window, little wooden girl in bonnet and watering can and the word WELCOME, all so pretty. But nobody is home.

Jane *fumes*.

Moments later, she is stepping across the bristly dried-out grass and sees a familiar person stepping from the door of the Lancasters' scary-looking mobile home across the road, walking on the path between the giant trunks of the giant trees. He walks like a cop. Yes, it's him, Rex, Gordie's milishish friend. Jane calls out "Hi!" and waves.

Rex nods grimly.

Jane steps out onto the crumbly tar just as he too reaches the tar, and she hurries over to him as he is putting a hand on the handle of the cab door of his shiny new red truck, and she speaks in her velvety, Africa-husky voice. "Can I have a ride to Gordie's?"

Nothing of a welcome on the parts of his face that show, but not much of his face shows. Dark coplike glasses. Big mustache crawling to the jaws.

Jane adds charmingly, "I really love your shirt."

Short-sleeved camo shirt with the Border Mountain Militia's embroidered patch on the left shoulder.

He goes around to the passenger door and opens it, Jane right behind him, stepping along long-leggedly, her new handmade knee-length smock of a patchwork of harvest colors swirling around her. Big orange patchwork cloth flower in her upswept, floofy, curly topknot. She scrambles up into the seat. Rex closes the door for her.

Now they are riding along, slowly, down the steep and winding old mountain road, heaped with stone walls on either side, stone walls and ferns and tawny late-afternoon sun and chipmunks and red squirrels who mostly watch and wait.

Rex doesn't talk at all. Just, "Fasten your belt." Meaning seatbelt.

Jane has nothing to say either.

After a few moments of the ride, Rex glances at the kid and it jumps him to notice that though her face was bare when she first boarded the truck, there are now two white plastic heart shapes aimed squarely at him . . . staring. These, her dark tinted glasses for spying and special powers of vision.

Still, he says nothing, just steers one-handed, the hand and wrist with the black-faced compass watch, the sleeve with the militia patch fluttering on the arm that rests on the open window, the black combat boots working the pedals. And fear. Yes, Rex York is just a little bit afraid of Secret Agent Jane.

Time chugs on. Late afternoon of a mid-September day.

In the cold parlor of the St. Onge farmhouse, deep in the old collapsing couch, sort of wrapped in the couch, in its waves of whimpering springs and hills of upholstery of frazzled blue nap, are fifteen-year-old Brianna and Gordon. His thick legs are stretched out, feet on the rug. She has her legs curled under her as she leans toward him and he is looking at her, face-to-face. His face normal, hers stretched by birth defect.

He smells of the hot fields and hot work, perhaps even some chaff in the seams of his faded blue T-shirt. She places her hands on his shoulders; her hands and her body and work shirt and jeans smell of the woods and of hot work too—of a logging operation, specifically, woods-spiced with skidder grease and a smoodge of pink bar-and-chain oil—and she looks steadily into his face and she does not giggle. She is his wife now. She takes herself for granted. She sees his eyes on her face and on her bright ripply hair, which falls over her back and over her shirtfront. These eyes of his are filled with her sweaty, woodsy, ciga-rette sweet opulence . . . his eyes and his being are drawn to her, pulled to her, *stuck*. As in a web, yes.

She says huskily, "We are mind into mind. We are getting mixed up."

He smiles, in a twinkly, restrained way.

She sees his forty-year-old eyes crinkle at the sides, eyes the palest she's ever known, like some great big cat. She almost giggles. They are on the edge of so many sort ofs and almosts as she leans closer, now forehead to forehead. This is painful to him as he is becoming far-sighted, but he doesn't draw back. He accommodates.

She says, "There is only one big soul, but nature stuffs pieces of the soul into all these separate skulls. My dear beautiful male thing, if we mix souls we are breaking the law of nature and it could be hard on us."

He says, "Baby, we are breaking all the laws."

She reaches with her fingers behind his ears and along his neck and sets all the nerves there alive; her stiff logger fingers have the lightest touch. She draws her head back and, still staring into his eyes, she says, "We have our windows open, dear husband." She flutters her strange far-apart eyes. "Our souls are getting out of our skulls!"

He snorts happily over this thought. Ah, Bree!

"They are getting alloyed!" she says urgently.

He folds his hands around her head like holding a squash or some enormous fruit, her hair alive and too red underneath and through his fingers. And her brain, too busy there, under his palms. Her entire universe in his hands.

His breath is coffee, hers cigarettes.

Her eyes focus closer together. "I love your nice big Frenchie nose," she says.

"I'm glad," he says.

From the editorial section of the *Record Sun*'s fat Sunday paper.

A lengthy article that arrived only four days ago on the editor's desk in stunning calligraphy, signed by several persons, many with the last name of St. Onge. The article starts off with:

> Some of you may have the idea you are in danger. Let us be more specific. Some of you can clearly imagine that, in the not-too-far-off future, "they" will come and put you and your family out of your home. All you have grown up and worked for is threatened by some large conspiring force.

The article goes on with many skin-chilling details; then, in bold print:

> YES, OH, YES. SOMEBODY IS GETTING READY TO TAKE EVERYTHING AWAY FROM YOU. EVERYTHING!
>
> We are members of the True Maine Militia, not to be confused with the plain Maine Militia, or the Border Mountain Militia, or the Southern Maine Militia, or the White Mountain Militia. But with those militias, we do have a bit in common.
>
> Like them, we are not ostriches.
>
> We are angry.
>
> And we know the government sucks.
>
> It is not a government of We, the People, but one of Organized Money, of Big Faceless Financiers ruling through their shrewd tool, the

corporation. And money laundering and fraud and other creepy stuff. And the Fed! It is instrumental in making the dollar worthless. It is a centralized debt-based banking system.

Welcome! We welcome EVERYBODY! We are not a right-wing militia. We are not left-wing either. We are NO WING. We are everybody's militia!

Now there is a cartoon of The Abominable Hairy Patriot, lovable but stern-looking Bigfoot with hands on hips standing on a mountaintop. He wears a tricorne hat, camo spot vest, and army boots. (Usually he is barefoot, to show his big hairy feet. And usually he does not wear clothes.) Behind him waves the American flag. (Remember, this is BEFORE September 11, 2001, so the flag isn't tacky yet.)

The article finishes with:

The True Maine Militia already has a lot of members, but not enough. Our goal is a million for starters. Because we are planning the Million-Man-Woman-Kid-Dog March on Augusta, for starters, and we will all be armed. With brooms. We will arrive at the doors, all the State House doors, and begin to very very gently sweep the great floors of this, which is our house . . . yes, the People's House. We will sweep out every corporate lobbyist. Corporations out! We, the People, in!

And if this doesn't work, we'll be back next time with plungers.

If you are interested in joining up, it is totally free. No dues. Just promise you will be angry and you will be nice. Get in touch with us today at militia headquarters, RR2, Heart's Content Road, Egypt, Maine 04047, or call 625-8693, or find us the old-fashioned way. Sundays are best. We'll open the gate for you! We love you! We are your neighbors. Keep your powder dry and your ear to the ground. Let's save the Republic together!

The article is signed.

Militia Secretary: Bree St. Onge
Recruiting Officers: Samantha Butler and Margo St. Onge
Other Officers: Whitney St. Onge, Michelle St. Onge, Dee Dee St. Onge, Carmel St. Onge, Kirk Martin, Tabitha St. Onge, Liddy Soucier,

Desiree Haskell, Scotty St. Onge, Heather Monroe, Erin Pinette, Rusty
Soucier, Chris Butler, Lorrie Pytko, Jaime Crosman, Shanna St. Onge,
Alyson Lessard, Rachel Soucier, Christian Crocker, Buzzy Shaw, Theoden
Tarr, Josh Fogg.

And just in case readers need help making the connections, the *Record
Sun* editors have helpfully added a sidebar with a summarized rehash
of the publicized Homeschool–Settlement–Border Mountain Militia
relationship, as well as a mention of the "thirty-six" terrorized-looking
governors' wives to whom Gordon St. Onge once gave a talk. And there
are two photos. One the rememberable merry-go-round shot, the scary
weirdly-lighted face and upper body of Gordon St. Onge that sensation-
alized all the earlier St. Onge-as-madman articles, and one of the gate
and KEEP OUT signs. This boxed piece reads: GATES OF ST. ONGE SETTLE-
MENT WILL COME DOWN.

☆   **Claire St. Onge in a future time tells us of
the days following the article.**

You could almost feel the ground tremble after that op-ed. The phone
rang. It was answered. It rang again as soon as it was back on the hook.
Working people wanted to do something. They weren't apt to use the
word *revolution* or call themselves radicals, but they were "coming out."
No, these were not just college lefties. These were also regular Mainers. The silent presence, until now. It was sweet. Surprising to me, actually. I never realized how many people were ready, once you put it to
them in a way that touched them personally—which our fifteen-year-
old Bree and the other young people, mostly Bree, had done. *So* young!
Our darling insurgents.

So it was people of all kinds calling, writing, leaving messages down
by the gate. My gosh, some of us even joked that messages might come in
bottles, down the Little Boundary Stream or out of the sky under wee
parachutes. People, people, people. It was a chillingly beautiful thing.

That very first day or two, the call-in talk shows were about
nothing else, just the True Maine Militia. Radio listeners wanted in.
Though some didn't want *in* as much as a chance to talk on the radio
about their fears, and there were plenty who wanted to show off

what they thought they knew about *democracy* and *government* and *corporatism*.

Meanwhile, yeah, there were calls to the shows by those warning of *the mad prophet* and references to his *blatant polygamy* and *child abuse*. And some called the True Maine Militia "crazies running through the woods with hand grenades."

But here it was. People were stirring. Democracy was in the air. Corporatism and globalism were in their sights.

But Gordon, when he found out, hit the roof. He hunted Bree down with the newspaper. When he found her, he was thin-lipped and too quiet. She told us later he was shaking. We all agreed we like it better when he's noisy.

 As recalled by many.

But he got over it. Sort of. After all, whose fault was it that our kids knew the world honestly enough to want to "save" it?

 The Bible.

Time, 4 p.m. He has nowhere else to be but right here. And nobody knows he is here. His tree house. Home sweet home: 1 Wilderness Highway, ha-ha-ha. It's sort of a log house, maybe more of a stick house, one a wolf could blow away, ha-ha-ha, though the wolf would have to climb up this tree first.

There's one little window with a flap. And a big hatch in the floor. Two ways out. Like a rat.

He is squinting in the growing woodsy dark at a Bible. Gift from the captain of his militia, Rex. It has a few glossy color pictures of Bible days. Some people have bare feet, some have sandals. A lot of sun there. Not much for trees. None of them look Jewish. He knows Jewish from school in Massachusetts. These pictures just don't look Jewish. In fact, they don't look human. The kids, that is. They are too chubby, like babies on steroids. Their eyes have expressions like . . . well, not stoned, exactly, more like people do when they are reading dull poetry or Shakespeare aloud in school and they're acting it out in an overdoing way. Bible artists absolutely can't do little kids right. Or Jewish. But

especially kids. He thinks about Jesse, not quite two years old. His
nephew. Dead. He can hear the wet sticky sound of real live Jesse's
mouth slurping down milk or red punch from a cup and the wet sticky
sound of his words and phrases and funny ideas.

Most of the Bible kids have wings, or else they are hanging around
grown-up Jesus, looking up in his face. Here's one with Jesus patting a
little kid on the head. One kid is blond like Jesse was. Mickey thinks, if
it were Jesse, he would be holding up a toy helicopter full of brown leaves
(helicopter found under the porch) or an old toaster (not plugged in).
Jesus would be stuck holding the helicopter while Jesse went off to collect some little army guys or animals to stuff inside. When Jesse got back
with his animals and guys, Jesus would hold the helicopter steady while
Jesse stuffed.

Before Mickey's eyes, the picture of Jesus and Jesse explodes into the
greasy grinding and *ernk!*ing of the schoolbus stopping in front of the
Locke place. His chest squeezes as if from an attacker's arms meaning
to hurt. Yeah, today is the day. SCHOOL IS OPEN. DRIVE SAFELY.

He breathes with relief as the imaginary schoolbus door slams and
the creepy ark drags itself off in the direction of the fenced-in SAD 51.
Yeah, perfect name, huh?

He looks back at one of the dreamy-faced Bible babies, its small feath-
ery wings. Imagine. Wings.

Power.

Hello, crow. You see the sky brightening in eager increments. Some of
the stars are losing their grip. This is *the mountain,* mostly on St. Onge
land. One of two, but this one is closer to the heavens. Some humans
call them *foothills* because they are so old and slouched by time, not the
childly rugged Rockies.

All around you is naked ledge and blueberry and juniper and blis-
ters of lichen, the hard faces of rock with small cupboard-sized cave
openings, which from a distance are the sockets of empty eyes.

Speaking of no eyes, wasn't it just yesterday that one of the damaged
elder humans (whom Gordon St. Onge has welcomed into his world)
visited this summit? The old eyeless man is one whom you, crow, are
especially keen about. How does he get around? A youngster always

steers the way, one of those little tractors they call *buggies,* which strain
and jerk over trails and the rocky summit road. Makes no roar. It hums.

The old blinded man, blinded by some scarring violence such as
working a dragger, or maybe it was war, sits behind and locks his arms
around the driver, the sweet hot evening or fresh morning is forced
across his cheeks and bald skull. He smiles steadily, serenely, though
the rough ride abuses him. This type of love draws your eye, because
endurance of the human flock is more than a spectacle.

But today, as the sky is glowing pearlesque, the only human in sight
is the lonely boy, Mickey Gammon.

For this morning's observatory, you use the structure that looks and
sometimes turns like a big eggbeater.

Down the mountain in the valley of the Settlement, a rooster crows,
setting off four more. You cock your head.

The boy is smoking as always, but this is the first time you've seen
him here at the crown of St. Onge creation, the Wind Project. The bull
mastiff of the wind structures, tallest, heaviest, is designed in the way
of the old countries, you have heard them say. Wooden door to the room
where the windmill crews go in and out, straining with recharged batteries for their buggies and the few cottages that aren't in the open.

The rest of the working wind plants are on modern steel derricks and
wooden poles: two-blade windmills and eggbeater ones and a couple
made with old barrels painted a sharp yellow.

As you study the boy, he is studying the mighty force of forty-seven
chest-high, nonutility, no-purpose-whatsoever, purely artistic windmills, child-made—charming pink, purple, and grasshopper-green
monuments to that struggle of human children of all recorded time to
learn the tricks of their elders' huge and bubbling civilizations.

Mickey Gammon, whom you think of as the Tree Boy, tosses his cigarette butt and gets to his feet from where he has been sitting on the frosty
step of the Old World windmill. He circles around on the edge of the
steep drop-off of ledges that overlook the east. He sees way down there
the narrow end of the pond that the humans have renamed Promise
Lake, the names lining up down through the ages. And there, the village of East Egypt, where obscene spots of orangey commercial electric
light hither and yon pose as *security.*

You, crow, watch him very carefully as he steps to the edge.

Answers.

A couple months ago, he was a fifteen-year-old living with his older brother's family, and he was as free as the breeze. Now he is a different kind of free, though still fifteen.

He stares down into the tops of trees below this ledgy drop-off. He's out of cigarettes now but smoke still comes out of him, the smoke of frozen breath. The way it does outdoors when you work or have fun. And now, when you live outdoors. His gray wild eyes zero in on the hard-looking utility sun picking its way up through the cold and distant red-orange September trees. How prehistoric this silence is, the way nothing makes a sound. Except his lips and the inside walls of his mouth and the frosty smoke ghost-breathing in and out, sailing away in a solid steady clump. He hears his brother's voice in his echoing memory: Go away go away go away . . . you can't live here . . . GO!

That night he was kicked out, Mickey was barefoot and shirtless. Yeah, it was *night*. Like outer space.

No fucking shoes.

Donnie's command just a whisper, like the very last bit of air leaving a flat tire, so slow, not much *whoooosh*: *Go away*. And yet Mickey remembers it in billboard-sized letters: GO AWAY! The words look down at him now from the schoolbus-yellow dawn sky, the big but soundless command.

Mickey hardly ever asks questions. He just waits for answers to bonk down on him like ready coconuts. And that's how he finally heard the full scoop on the Prophet. Real name is Ghee Yome or something. He grew up in that gray farmhouse and still officially lives there. But his wives live up in the valley in the Snow White cottages, which are all colors, and some have little porches. Some are in the fields, some in the woods. Nobody actually lives in the brown-with-green-trim horseshoe building. In the morning, the smell of breakfast in that building reaches his tree house so huge it's like getting a whiff of the Fryeburg Fair.

Yes, wives. Like Waco. Like Arabs. Like weird. Like, imagine it.

Mickey imagines being completely lost inside a solid pile of warm women.

But uphill here, where Mickey is, is where you go when you are in a solid pile of *cold shit*.

Something moves, catches his eye: a crow on one of the windmills. Willie Lancaster says he knew a crow once that talked, one or two words at a time.

Like Mickey.

And also like Mickey, the crow—*this* crow here on the mountain—seems to have no jobs lined up today, nobody to meet.

He sees a finger of fire coming up through the trees beyond East Egypt. Wriggling. Now it leaps, pulls free, ball of fire. The giant old-timey windmill is instantly covered in gold. Except its six walls are painted black. Then there's faces and bodies of spirits and mermaids and woman devils with flying hair. The hair on the mermaids is green. Woman devils have red skin or pink with veins. Eyes dripping. Around to the other side are a couple of guy devils, totally purple, naked, with long peckers shaped like Christmas stockings filled with candy and oranges. One sheep eating grass. Or is it a turtle? Man, oh, man, these are obviously painted by kids on ladders. Some dripping. Some blobs. But some are very artistic. And stirring. Many realistic breasts. Big ones. He nods. He sees the orange wicked eyes of the largest woman devil, eyes of power.

These Settlement people are nothing like he's ever known before. Could you call them students? Mr. Carney would have you in three months of detention if he caught you painting shit like this, for instance on the brick walls of the gym. Mickey chuckles. He kinda likes these St. Onge types. Except mostly he feels like just your regular sick peeping Tom, outside, not inside.

Caw! Caw! Caw! Caw! Crow takes off, flapping toward the stone wall that zigzags down through the woods to Mickey's tree home. Mickey rubs his cold hands together, shoves them deep in the BDU shirt's pockets. Rex said the next meeting might be here at the Settlement, so the men who live here can give Rex's men a tour. A radio studio and tower, not finished but *ambitious.* An *experimental wheat field* and *alternative energy* projects. Nothing wrong with a sneak preview, Mickey whispers to himself, and marches sort-of proudly onward.

For the next few hours, he'll just lie on his back at home and aim the service pistol at the tree-house ceiling, the walls, the window.

Uh-oh!

The temperatures around the world are bouncing: rising, falling, *boing! boing! boing!* The earth is now so sporty. A bowling ball. Maybe a game of pool. Something is melting or leaking. Or spreading. Receding. Autumn leaves forget to fall. Lightning strikes twice. Sheep are going blind. Politicians talk in oily ways, like butter or broken thermometers . . . mercury pooling on the porch . . . a silvery eye. Dither is everywhere.

   Hey!

Pay no attention whatsoever to the sky. What you need to think about is the way thirty-eight-year-old Mindy Curtis of Gitchy, Nevada, left her four kids in her old junky car and pushed it over a cliff. Think about *that*! And think about the death penalty for the deserving!

   Meanwhile, somewhere in a major city in America.

Several thousand mostly collegey professional-type people and a few labor unions march. Raised banners and placards represent numerous discontents and objections, mostly relating to corporate power, government corruption, sicko foreign policy, and questionable law enforcement practices. Huge puppets bow and prance. Buttons, leaflets, flyers, songs: a festive spirit. Dull speeches. City heat. Skin dripping electrolytes. Telephone numbers of legal counsel scribbled on forearms. Civil disobedience, peaceful blockades, singing and drums. Police gas and bash. Many arrests. Charges inflated to felonies for just blocking streets. Young college kids' faces smashed into sidewalks while handcuffed. A few broken teeth. Many broken hearts. "Is this how the system reacts to the sound of the people's voice?" one young man asks.

   The screen sneers.

A tiny but irritating incident today. See the *rioters*! See the bad bad bad people bothering the city, which is trying to conduct itself, and the nice government and cops, who sometimes look like Boy Scouts except when they have to wear their riot gear and padded stuff to protect themselves from these extremist people who just like to start trouble for some reason.

 Back in the city.

Another day of noisy but hopefully peaceful protests heats up, but the police are one step ahead, using battering rams on a warehouse door to get at the collegey kids in there who are making giant puppets. The giant puppets are bad. They will tell of police corruption and government policy that is against people. The police say *Death to puppets* and stuff them into Dumpsters. Puppets away! Seal those big puppet mouths! Young puppet makers are dragged out and stuffed into buses. What are the charges on these terrible puppet makers who make puppets that telllll? Nine felonies for this young girl. Ten for this one. Seven for that one. Puppets could be used in a crime, police say. It's *the intent,* say the police.

 Concerning the aforementioned particular details, the screen

is blank.

 Donnie Locke is late for work again.

He'll be docked. He may be fired, maybe not. Whatever. Since he started *job two* at the sub shop, there's that funny little overlap—not really an overlap, but the time between jobs has a shape and size into which he has tried to fit things that don't fit, like a quick trip home, or stopping to mail back that pair of shoes that didn't fit his oldest girl, Elizabeth. And now, with Erika working at the day care, and their own kids in the other day care and the after-school-care, this car, their only car, needs to run like a rocket, but *chunka chunka chunka.*

He sits in the car now, in the parking lot of the Chain, staring at the busy glassy store entrance and the puddles, dimpled with rain, a lighter rain than a few minutes ago. Headlights on. Windshield wipers whapping. Gauges lit in green, yellow, and blue. He is late and getting later by the minute.

But the pressure inside him is worse than outside him. It's like inside him, pushing at the skin, is a muscled thing the size of a man twice his height: arms, chest, organs, all hurting with hardness. He can't fight anymore. He is just turning into a rock. Soon he will be a petrified man.

He has moments of zest, whenever he has worked himself up to put his plan into action. He has everything ready: vacuum cleaner hose, everything. But like everything else he's tried to do lately, he fails. But he is going to do it. Before the week is out he is going to do it. He doesn't have a bye-bye note. He doesn't need one. Nobody will have to guess why this piece of shit wanted out. 'Cause, man, he's doing *everybody* a favor.

WOW! WOW!

The economy! See it grow! See it GLOW. Wow! Wow! See how lucky we are to have a great economy now, after that recession a few years back, which was so hard on everyone. Wow-eeeeee. Grin. Grin. See all the people in other countries living in cardboard. See how lucky *weeee* are. We. We. We. Grin. Grin.

In a major city in America.

Several thousand professional liberal-type people and a sprinkling of labor-union folks again march and rally to show deep discontent. Again, big banners about government corruption and corporate power (one and the same?). Again, huge puppets bow and prance. Again, streets are blocked with peaceful protestors. Faces are smashed into the sidewalk. Tear gas. Pepper spray. Hundreds of FBI, thousands of cops. Cops beating plainclothes cops, *oops!* FBI and cops trying to arrest each other, *oops!* Warehouse doors bashed down again, as in other protests; the big puppets who talk must be silenced! Silence is a must. Too much noise in America.

The screen moans.

Not again? This small group of extremist troublemaking rioters and violent types bothering police . . . throwing tear gas back at police, tip-ping over Dumpsters. Why do people keep doing this? Haven't they got anything better to do? See here, an interview with a nice man trying to get to work, but traffic was snarled by the silly protesting violent rioters. Something very terrible could happen with all these blocked streets.

 The screen breathes a sigh of relief.

Today, the city is back to normal. Oh, well. Just silliness. The *real* news is that Senator James McVie is proposing another investigation concerning you-know-who in that lust scandal. STAY TUNED!

 Mickey speaks.

Doc wasn't at the meeting today. He doesn't come to many meetings 'cause he works most weekends. I guess God is different for different people. I always pictured God to be this big giant squishy white-cloud guy, kinda like a snowman. No eyes. But he could *see* everything, see how everything was going.

Doc . . . I bet if you asked Doc what God looked like, he'd describe himself. Little shithead with fat red lips and mean-looking ears and black hair with a spot of bald on top—small spot. Hair looks wet. Eyes brown and bulgy. No beard. Just face.

Rex doesn't get tough with Doc. Not like you see him do with Willie. I wish he did. I don't like it that maybe Rex likes Doc. I want him to think Doc's a problem. I can't tell what goes on in Rex's brain. Except for Willie and Rex's brother, the teacher, Rex doesn't talk about people much. He's all business, all militia. That's okay. I don't give a shit. I just wish he'd give a sign that Doc's brain ain't like his brain.

Okay, so I ain't all for queers . . . you know, the queer thing. Men and men. Women and women. But I don't spend a lot of time thinking about it. Who gives a shit? As long as they use their own sheets. And then, with Doc, it's abortions and rock 'n' roll and movies with sex and divorced women and—oh, yes—welfare people. Doc wants all these people crucified. I mean it. He said he wants them *nailed* to crosses in the middle of town so everybody can walk by and learn from this.

He says the Constitution will make this possible. I'm not real good reading the kind of words that are in the Constitution, but this other guy, Art, he's got all the amendments memorized and . . . you know . . . like some people tell jokes, he tells amendments. None so far say anything about crosses.

You won't see me argue with Doc. I don't say anything to him, not even "Hi." Nobody argues with him. In fact, nobody argues at meetings. Sometimes there's quiet spots where I think someone is pissed at somebody. And I know there's talk behind backs, a *lot* of talk behind backs. Rex is probably the only one that don't talk behind backs.

Anyway, so Doc also likes to say God wants the *fags* and *whores* and *liberals* and all people of *false religion,* especially Jews, to die bad, to die slow. And he says, if we don't do God's will, God will be mad at us, that leaving these people to their own sin makes us sinners too. Makes us *cohorts.* So we gotta stop them.

Makes me nervous. I start feeling like . . . like he might think *I'm* a fag, and every time I move I think he's watching me with his bulgy mean eyes to see if I do something faggish. Like I say, I never thought much about those kinda guys before, but now I think about them . . . how I gotta be sure I don't make some impression like I'm a fag supporter. I just don't think God gives a shit about those kind of guys one way or the other. After all, God made them. If God is so perfect, then he doesn't make mistakes, so fags aren't mistakes. They're just . . . you know . . . weird. If God is really just a big cloud man, snowman or somethin', he probably thinks *all* the ways *all* people do sex looks pretty hilarious.

Anyway, Doc wasn't at today's meeting. We are planning a buncha things. Like the food drive, which involves the Maine Militia too, which is upstate. And maybe we're gonna meet with the White Mountain Militia. I ain't met any of those guys in New Hampshire yet. We also've got plans to do a winter survival bivouac after Christmas—a weekend, maybe three days. We went to the preparedness expo in Bangor last weekend, so we had to talk about that.

Finally, when the meeting was fizzing out—two guys were asleep— Rex announces that nine Settlement guys are joining our militia officially, including Gordon and his son Cory, who I met. He looks like an Indian or Japanese, but I'd say Indian.

Rex then said it again that we ought to all go up to the Settlement at some point to see their shortwave setup, which is better than Willie's. When it's ready, they can do a pretty good radio show. I figure it'll be a good opportunity to see the Prophet's wives up close. I wonder if Samantha is one of them. Bree, the one with the stretched face, was acting horny over him, I think. It's going to be like going to a circus. Man.

The screen philosophizes.

Without me, you would be cut off. With events, I am on top. And I am fast. Without me, you'd be lost. Without me, there is shame, a low score for you, so to speak. An F in staying abreast.

Mickey speaks.

Stopped in to see Rex.

His mother says to me, "Sorry to hear about your brother."

I look at her but I don't know what she's talking about.

"I'm really sorry. You tell your people if there's anything we can do, to let us know."

I kinda watch the microwave, which has just beeped, but nobody notices. I say, "Yep." I look at her and nod to be polite. But I think some shit has happened with *them* where I *used* to live. Maybe she means about Jesse, but she's already talked and talked about Jesse, so this is not Jesse. Rex's mum thinks I live back there with *them*. She thinks I know all the shit already, but *those people* might as well be on the moon. I want to forget *those people* and all their shit. Especially Donnie, my brother, the king, who oughta have his crown shoved up his ass.

She says, "Mickey?"

"Yep."

"You okay?"

"Yep."

"I have something for them. Just a pie. I hope your sister-in-law and your mum like peach pie."

"Yep."

"Sure you're okay?"

I smile sort've, so she'll stop asking me if I'm okay.

In his tree house in the woods, Mickey contemplates.

I'm not a talker. I can think, but I can't yak it up. I'm not stupid. Them at school always acted like I was stupid. They said I was a bad boy. Ha-ha. Maybe I *am* bad. Once, I wasn't bad. You know how it is: until you go to school, everything you do is perfect and cute; then you gotta start being something different, *proving* something. Like you are steppin' into one big test. It sucks.

So, okay, I got bad. But bad is better than stupid, right? Bad makes them look up to you. They fear you a little. That's what respect is. Respect is fear. Some teacher with her little tight-assed walk says, "You are late," "You took too long in the library," "You didn't read the whole chapter?" And everybody is looking at you. Are you going to look dippy? Are you going to cry? Are you going to *apologize?* No. You say as loud as you can, "Dry up, cunthead."

Well, I didn't actually say that. But I thought it and she didn't like my expression. She didn't like my *face*.

And she didn't like the smell of cigarettes on me. Or when I had a buzz, she didn't like the look of a buzz.

There were others who were bad, and we hung out together. But they would always try to break you up. Like you made each other bad.

Before I became really and totally *bad,* they talked to me in baby talk. And they have *Special Ed*. This means you are retarded. More baby talk and all the *special* shit. Everyone looking down on you.

When I got really and totally bad, like *sleeping in class* and, my favorite, *leaving the premises without permission* and *putting my feet up on a desk* and *doing deals*—you know, firecrackers, twice, weed, only once—and then this guy Derrick brought his Remington hunting rifle to school to see if I was interested, which I wasn't. You know, it wasn't loaded. But when they caught us, it was like we were death penalty material. If they'd had an electric chair in the office of the Holy Principal, they'd of used it.

Nowadays since the "Million Moms," which Rex says is the CIA, they've gone into total mental mode over people's guns. You trade a gun like that in your school, your life would really be over—no joke. You'd be on TV. You'd be put up for all the twittipated world to despise. Fine.

That's still lots better than stupid. Smart, famous, and despised. Or stupid. Pick one.

Okay, so me, I got elevated to semi-evil status. It was great. No more wet baby talk. I could walk down the hall like a man, not baby goo.

So then instead of baby talk, they squint their eyes and threaten: DETENTION. SUSPENSION. And they scream down the hallway, "GAMMON, WHERE ARE YOUR BOOKS?!!" "GAMMON, WHAT ARE YOU DOING OUT OF CLASS?!!" Big army talk.

They use you as an example of fucking up. "GAMMON, STAND UP! SIT STRAIGHT! WAKE UP. SEE, EVERYONE, YOU'LL BE LIKE GAMMON IF YOU DON'T TAKE THIS SERIOUSLY."

My brother, Don, was always good in school. They loved Don. "Good in school." This means you are smart, they say. This means you are a good person. This means you are a success. My brother Don, they loved. He was even pretty good in sports. He was a fucking suck-up.

And now, guess what? He's dead.

Long night.

Tonight, sleeping on his back in the center of the bed, Rex York is jerked awake by that gasping screech he knows so very well, a screech that boils bright red and electric between lunacy and grief: the sound of his wife when she comes. His *ex*-wife, whose ring he still wears.

Up on one elbow now, eyes swollen by sleep, he knows it was a dream. No pictures in this dream, just the screech. Marsha York. His wife. How many times did she make that sound, hundreds? You don't count a thing like that. She told him once that coming felt just like a contraction while having a baby, a labor pain. *Just* like it. Only instead of pain, it is . . . well, the opposite of pain. And yeah, he knows there's nothing else in life that feels that far over the edge, there is nothing else that takes you a hundred miles from this planet, stars drifting left and right, which is all you can see because you are fainting and falling and turning inside out. Part of you is fire. Part of you is snow.

Sometimes Rex is angry that Marsha left him and, worse, remarried. But sometimes he just feels cut free. Not in the dazzling starry space of coming but the dark bottomed-out space of waking up in starless desolation. Alone.

He gets up and finds the bathroom, then spends the rest of the long night in the back attic room, on the computer, tapping out plans for the three-day survival drill in a wooded hundred acres above Bethel. Lists, directions to and from, and exercises to test the mettle of those who participate.

 Long night continued. Mickey Gammon doesn't pray aloud, but his lips move a little.

Father or God, please don't be mad if I say it wrong. It is kinda cold tonight. I used to like tree houses. Now it's different.

I like to think of you as Big Cloud Man. I hope that isn't insulting, 'cause I mean it as a good thing.

I wonder how Ma and Erika are taking it: Donnie's suicide. I bet Erika is crying her eyes out. You can probably see right into the house now. I'm glad in a way I can't see Erika. But in a way I want to see her more than anything else about that friggin' place.

So Jesse is dead. And Donnie is dead. Okay. All dead. You can see all the dead people, right? And they can see you?

Nobody knows I'm here, I guess. Nobody has come and told me to get out. I heard different things about the people who own this land. They seem kinda nuts. I heard they have orgies and have a time when they are all going to take poison. And all the women fuck the leader, the big guy with the weird eyes, the Prophet. And they are real religious, I think. Maybe, God, you like that part. Rex doesn't say they're nuts. I've seen some of them. Just the other day, someplace near Bangor, we checked out this windmill they made. Also they came to one of our meetings. They seemed okay at the meeting. We did CPR. There was a girl named Samantha I would like to have done CPR with instead of the little kid we used. Then I saw her in Lincoln. Near Bangor. She is an officer for their militia. Ha-ha. They call it a militia, but it's pretty pussy-ish. Kind of like a girl's club.

I try to imagine her at the orgies they're supposed to have. But the poison part is weird. She has real perfect little tits and blonde hair she wore with a kerchief wrapped around her forehead to the meeting. Like a blonde Apache. She wore military boots and camo at the windmill thing. She looks like she might bite and it would feel great.

I hope I'm not saying anything wrong here. I don't have any real prayers memorized, but Rex says it's good to pray. I hope you are real nice to Jesse. He's just a little guy and probably doesn't understand why he's flying around up there with you now. I . . . I still can't believe what happened to him. Cancer is a bitch.

Okay, so I was hoping I could make enough money this past couple weeks to rent something . . . a room or a camp on the pond winter rate . . . or to buy a truck. *Old* truck. I could sleep in a truck and run the heater. There's a way to rig it so you won't get fumes—longer tailpipe. Even if I don't have a license I could at least own the truck. But stuff is expensive. Please, Father or God, get me a place, one to come along soon. I'll pray more often. I'll pray tomorrow night too. Also, my Bible that Rex gave me. I am sorry I have a shitty time reading. I can't keep words straight. They just fuzz over and mix up. I am sorry. But maybe if I just open it and think about you. And Jesus, who used a bullwhip on the money guys. Can that be true? Anyways, the pages feel soft, like skin and flowers. I keep it with my service pistol in the box at night—as you know, of course. When I get a truck and a license, I'll wear the pistol under my jacket and I'll put the Bible on the dash.

Donnie and I . . . it was bad. Probably he was up there with you reading my mind before I knew he was dead, and I was calling him a shithead. When he was dying, was he, like, depressed? How did he feel? I wish I could know. Fuck. Everything's coming down.

♡♡ **Another lesson in government. Secret Agent Jane speaks.**

After supper, Gordie wants to take me for a ride. He says it's a date. It is kind of coldish with cloudishness, so I wear my new jacket, which is black and sexy with a belt and puckered sleeves that I almost made myself except Suzelle made most of it. I have this purse that is all beads. White. And five dollars that Granpa gave me when he was on his visit yesterday. His name is also Granpa Pete.

Where Gordie and I go is to the beach on Promise Lake, which is dull and almost dark. Across the road is Kool Kone. But CLOSED FOR THE SEASON. No place to spend money. But Gordie hugs me and we walk. My shoes are not good for beaches. They are clogs. So I take them off, and my socks, and Gordie carries them for me but still hugs me while we walk and my feet humple along in the cold sand.

When we find a rock to sit on, Gordie holds my hand and kisses both my ears. Then he explains that we can't go see Mum tomorrow after all because she has something to take care of. In Boston. She's in Boston in another jail place.

I stare at him. Without my secret glasses I can still see Gordie's thoughts because when he is thinking fishy thoughts, he looks weird. His eyes squint and blink an *extra* amount.

"So when is Mum coming home?"

He says he doesn't know. He says, "It's hard to explain, Jane, but it's not up to a judge anymore. Not these days. It's not up to a jury. It's all decided. It's a political thing. Laws made by Congress and the guys who control them. It's a very awful thing, and, I have to tell you, Mum might be there a long time."

"*When* is she coming home?"

"We'll go see her next week and find out. Your Granpa Pete will ride down with us. Her trial will be in Boston. It is a *federal* trial now. Not the other kind. It's a very serious thing."

He pulls me really close to his shirt.

"Is Mum coming home for my birthday?" I ask, in a plain cold voice. I can't see his face. He squishes his nose and mouth against the top of my head and hugs me hard enough to hurt. I think he thinks I'm going to cry. But I don't feel *sad*. I feel *mad*. I feel like I want to kick this rock. I feel like picking up this rock, which is as big as a bus, and throwing it. If a government guy walked by right now, he would be sorry. He would be under this rock in about five seconds.

📺 The screen is indignant.

Oh, isn't this just awful! Our country, Number One—yes!—but crawling with these low-income and no-income types who want to get your darling precious perfect Catherine and Joshua hooked on drugs: heroin, crack, ice. Here is one now, wearing orange, right from the Oxford county jail, between two sheriff's deputies, all making their way down those stairs in the wind and rain to a vehicle. Destination: Boston. This one is Lisa Meserve, especially frightening because she was posing as a dental assistant, an ordinary person, right there, hovering around the faces of your Catherine and Joshua!!!! The deal was worth so much!!! This makes it EXTRA CREEPY!!!! SHE might have become RICH while YOU work like a slave at your three dumb jobs making NOTH-ING. The brave Drug Warriors will make your darlings safe. One less sneaky lazy wolf-in-sheep's-clothing monster drug dealer roaming the clean otherwise safe streets and alleys of our red, white, and blue America. God bless!!!!!!!!!!!!!!!!!!

☆   **Glennice St. Onge recalls.**

It was fall, after the Fryeburg Fair, I *think*. It was in and *around* that time. Under the sinks there was a cricket creaking. I remember that. You couldn't find him. He'd get quiet if you put your head in there. I remember how he would start up at funny times, significant times. He gave even crowded mealtimes an edge of loneliness.

After one of my committee nights, I decided to go in and check on things in the kitchens before heading up to my cottage. I had my flash-light in my hand, swiping it around; then I switched it off.

Sure enough, the cricket started up, as if to remind me that I was not alone in the dark, on this dark earth, in this Life so few have reverence for.

But then I understood that the cricket was telling me something else. Yes, something perfect.

I saw a shape in the dark Winter Kitchen side of the room, there on the other side of the half wall of cubbies. I pressed on my flashlight and swiped the beam across Gordon's face. He kept right on sleeping. He was in a rocker, legs out before him, and Jane was curled in his lap, face buried in his old work vest, both of them dressed heavy like they had just arrived or were just about to leave but had been cast a spell upon by a fairy-tale evil queen . . . because they were both so beautiful, my heart ached.

She with her part-African part-Indian parentage and her Frenchie mother, a golden girl with a profile right out of some mythic tale of beauty and tribulation, dragons and evil trees. And Gordon, head flopped to one side—a great big man like that, you'd think he'd radiate protection—but I had a terrible terrible terrible premonition of him being not long for this world. I could hear his heart! It was strong, squeezing blood through its chambers in a most perfect way. There was nothing wrong with his health. No growths, no stuff in his veins clotting or blocking, no failures of any kind. He was strapping and perfect! But, God help us, the enemies of goodness were closing in!

I got down on my knees right then and there and prayed that I was wrong, prayed for help from the Almighty. I prayed aloud. And I even wept. And believe this or not, but neither Gordon nor the poor little child woke up due to my weeping, rustlings, and pleas.

I have prayed ever since that I never forget the image of those two.

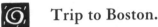 Trip to Boston.

Pete Meserve drives. His car is one of the "midsized" Pontiacs, which means it is small. It is not new, but it is nice. Gordon rides with him, watching the scenery pass. Jane rides in the back. No room for three people in front. But she is not interested in the front seat anyway. To Jane, Granpa Pete is always quiet and icebergish, but he's *very very* quiet now, and his face has gone old.

♡♡ Secret Agent Jane tells us about the Boston jail.

Gordie had to wait outside. You are only allowed *two* people. And they said no to my secret agent glasses!!!! We had to put them behind little doors in the wall. Plus you have to take off your shoes and do X-ray and Granpa said to the copguard, "This is like a Communist country." Gordie would have said a bunch of stuff.

Then we go in a hall with a big line like school, and guess what? We could sit *with* Mum in the other jail place. But here it's a big window and Mum is on the other side sounding like a telephone through a radio speaker thing. But Mum was glad to see us anyways.

Still, she didn't say much. Mostly we just looked at other people in the room cuz it's weird to look through a window for a visit. Mum put her hands on the glass so we put our hands up on the glass to pretend there was no glass. Hands to hands. First me. Then Granpa Pete. Granpa Pete's hands are not as nice from working on too many cars.

Mum said some jails have TV screens, that we are lucky for glass.

I said, "But we were *waaay* better before when we were lucky to have just air."

Granpa Pete said, "In Russia they have salt mines. No visitors."

I made squints at Granpa Pete. I folded my arms and said to him with very careful teeth: "We . . . are . . . here."

Granpa Pete laughed.

I asked Mum if maybe she could just come home for a visit for my birthday so I can turn seven. She said a weird thing. Like this: "The world is not nice. The human race is crafty but not very bright." She said Gordie told her that once. I said, "Figures."

Granpa Pete said everything was okay back home. Everything was all right. Which means he's too busy to take me places and do stuff, which is why I had to go to be at Gordie's. Granpa Pete is busy on so many broken cars, he has a very junky-looking gas station but no gas for sale.

So I say, "Great. My birthday. Right around the corner. Nobody listening. Muuumm. Could you get a day off from this place?"

Granpa Pete laughed and poked me in the arm.

Mum smiled at him, sort of.

Getting mad, I said, "So. On my birthday, I bet I know where I can get your favorite ice cream, Mum. Chunky Monkey."

Mum said, "I can't believe you'll be seven. So fast."

I said, "So you will need to be there. It . . . is . . . important."

Mum said, "It is important."

I crossed my arms again and made so much air *whoosh* into me to be bigger. I said, "Be . . . there."

Granpa Pete laughed again. So loud, guys visiting all around looked over in a eye-wide way.

"Do not laugh," I told Granpa Pete, giving him the hairy eyeball.

He says to the window with Mum there, "You know who she reminds me of?"

Mum looks at me.

"Aunt Bette," he says. "*She* was a ticket too."

Mum smiles, but sickishlike. Probably germs in Boston. I heard there was once. Leprissy. Stomachaches. Pee demics.

I keep my arms folded. No secret glasses, but with only open eyes I can know more than I used to.

♡♡ At night, alone, Secret Agent Jane considers.

Today I worked on the Beauty Crew and cut Dragan's hair and Rawn's hair. One is only age three. One maybe is actually four. You practice that way, then you get real heads. But I was only halfway near Rawn's ears and started to feel sick from Boston germs. I felt very *on edge*. I threw the scissors on the stupid floor. I think I was shivering sort of. A fever about to hit. But Penny said I wasn't hot. She is very pretty. She's Whitney's mum. She said, "Let's walk to the pond." I told her I was sick of beauty. I said I wanted to get a bomb and blow up the government. She looked at me funny and said, "We should all be good to each other." I said, "Who's we?" She said, "Humans." I said, "Sorry . . . But . . . I . . . Am . . . Ready . . . For . . . Bombs."

The pond is little, an ir'gation ditch with big pipes sometimes. But pretty. Penny saw I was collapsing. She sat with me in the grass while I went wicked to pieces, screaming and snot everywheres, not on purpose, but I got empty so then it was quiet, and cold too. And the bugs were cricking all around and the pond was getting pink and dark like the sky and she rubbed my hair backward the whole time. And after it was more pink and more dark out, she said, "The human race is crafty but never very bright."

I covered my ears.

With the assistance of a five-year-old and a four-year-old, Jane Meserve writes a letter, addresses it, and finds the right cubby in Cook's Kitchen to mail it from.

DeaR Govimint—

Let a PeRson name Lisa Marie Meserve coMe HoMe. She is my MOTher. I am heRs name Jane. Jane Miranda Meserve Ejpt Maine Hearts Content Road. Yours last chance Jane.

Out in the world.

The machinery of this vast cracking overripe civilization, which shreds up small concerns, does not reply.

 Long night.

Going on 2 A.M. The school on Heart's Content Road is in session. Well, yes, the True Maine Militia is meeting. But is there a difference? Nine girls in the East Parlor, five more in the print shop. Many pairs of scissors chomping into stacks of blue index cards that have been run through the Settlement copy machine. Four True Maine Militia membership cards from each index card. Some will be mailed. Some will be handed out. Hundreds of finished membership cards are now in the boxes. Fingers quick and strong. Fingers with purpose. Fingers with patriotic ardor! *Chomp! Chomp! Chomp!* Scissors that never tire. Glasses of milk and maple candies going around. A few sandwiches. Musty-flavored wild cranberries picked and dried for cooking by Settlement crews, eaten now by the mouthfuls. Membership cards for the whole planet.

Just a few candles now in the East Parlor. All the windows are covered with blankets, here and in the print shop as well. You never know where Gordon is, and you can't trust him on this. One minute he's *green light* concerning activism. The next minute he could be *red light* again. Best to lie low.

 Next night, up in the woods: cold.

Colder than last night. Frost in the open fields. Not the kind of frost that frizzes gardens and makes a squashy goo of your window-box impatiens, but an open field of granule-sized stars, palest silver, under the snow-white high-powered moon, and all the crickets and singing night bugs are quiet.

On a small mountain in Egypt, Maine, a tree house made of found planks and trash. A young boy is curled up in this, tight as a squirrel. He wears one T-shirt, a sweatshirt, and over that a camo BDU shirt with the patch of his militia. Jeans. No long johns, but some nice new wool socks. New work boots. No pillow. No mattress. He is the new American youth, multiplied by thousands across the land. His hands are fisted against his stomach. His dreams are complicated, his testicles flattened into his shuddering musculature, in fear of the impending. How much worse can it get?

He is now fully formed, the masterpiece of a culture that rends souls with its clean hands. He is what we asked for, fifteen-year-old Mickey Gammon. Will he pull the trigger someday? On us?

 Another evening. Ten-thirty P.M. St. Onge farmhouse on Heart's Content Road.

Gordon thinks the phone is off the hook, though mistakenly it has been hung back. At least right now the thing is quiet. He is sitting at one of his heaped desks under the cold fluorescent light. Alone.

In one heaped box of mail, a fat old tortoiseshell cat is curled. Her nose whistles. She's a very old cat, nearly twenty, having been his mother Marian's cat in the last years of her living here.

Many boxes of mail. Some say INCOMING. One box says OUTGOING. On the edge of one desk, looking like it still might be warm from the copier, a fresh ream of one of the True Maine Militia songs he's taken a special liking to. He sends copies of it out in his letters to friends, yes, with his fat philosophical letters. The songs are such things as "This Land's *Not* Your Land." Dozens of tiny Abominable Hairy Patriots, with open mouths singing, make a busy border around the song sheet's edge.

How clever the Settlement young people are! he is thinking. Though other times, their activism scares the living shit out of him. He does not want to attract the gooey soul-stealing hand of the growing police state of the "outside world" to fondling and frisking his family.

He squats to the floor, to a large diagram of a community-friendly "wind-turbine-solar-combo" regenerator for electric vehicles, with fold lines like a road map. He spreads his hands on this but then stands, distractedly. On the table a buff-colored pamphlet featuring micro-energy. Fuel cells. Frictionless flywheels. They call to him with an urgency louder than voice.

Meanwhile, against the wall, an old shoebox of letters from the superintendent of schools' office, some opened, some not, none answered. Always these superintendent's letters, but never a phone call from the superintendent. *Some things best left unconfronted and undealt with* is perhaps the superintendent's feeling on the St. Onge situation. But, for the record, stern letters do exist. None of these call to him. He almost knocks them over accidentally on his way to his old desk chair.

Now he moves his pen across a postal money order, two money orders totaling $1,500, both going to the same place. He signs each one in careful print: EGYPT ENDOWMENT FOR SMALL LOCALLY OWNED AND OPERATED BUSINESS AND THE SELF-EMPLOYED. Then he writes *Happy Birthday* in one corner of each, a tax write-off trick he learned from the old construction-biz days.

These money orders are both made out to Russ Welch, owner of Welch's Service Center, this, Gordon's little secret for a few years now. Once every three months, all the interest from a certain batch of his inherited stocks, those last few he has not sold off, goes to one or two small locally owned, locally situated businesses or farms or to plumbers or loggers or carpenters, strugglers, diehards, tough old relics.

Egypt's small businesses. He knows their faces. Concerning these, Gordon always has his ear to the ground. If someone is about to go under, he hears it. Those who are fair and never cheat you. *Never cheat you.* Yeah, yeah, without cheating, it's a game you can't win. Yes, yes, honesty is silly. According to the new way, this is especially so. Be honest and down you go! And so Gordon makes out another money order, bearing hard on the pen to make the print perfectly clear.

As he licks the envelope, he sees his mother's disappointed face in his mind's eye. His actions will ruin him in the end. Marian says this. And he knows this. Lately he has had to start selling off the last of the stocks. The rainy-day nest egg breaking down. But doesn't he despise stocks anyway? And besides, the stock market is on borrowed time, no? Everyone says so. *Borrowed*, yes. Well, the nation is. Borrowed, bloated like a heat-ripe corpse, but still lustily hungry. The globe is its apple. *Eeeeeha!* And Marian's voice, "*You invite disaster,*" voice of the human mother, echoes of the other. He is weary of the fuzzy edges to right and wrong, the cruelties of kindness, the rightness of greed.

He hears voices and feet out on the piazza. He tenses. A late-night reporter? An old friend with yet another homeless family? Or Settlement people with emergency needs, that which are the heaviest responsibility of all?

Soon he hopes to get a crew together to fence and gate the yard to this place and—sure—a sign much like the one to the Settlement road: ANYONE TRESPASSES WILL BE SHOT. TRY IT.

He considers the True Maine Militia's *opposite* goals. He sighs.

Piazza screen door slaps shut. He lays the envelope down, stands up quick, burping the taste of homemade hard cider. Reading glasses go into his chest pocket.

Inside door opens. Several young men swagger into the kitchen; Joel Barrington in the lead. Joel, not a Settlement resident, but the next thing to it. It is always good to see Joel, a bright-faced thick-shouldered blond twenty-year-old, sporting the gregarious and sometimes bossy ways of the Soule family, which he is blood to and raised by. And yet also Joel has carried on that mysterious high-minded sneaky thieving look in the eye like his father, Lloyd Barrington, who plagues the rich or unconscionable around town but never sees the inside of a jail.

"Nice night. Clear as a bell," casually remarks Evan Martin, who is the one kid of all the Settlement's kids to get cursed with pimples, pimples of every shade of blue and purple and red and yellow. His cheeks look burned and torn. But his hair, a shock of black, flopping to the left side of his forehead, is lustrous and appealing. He dresses just like a lot of the non-Settlement kids do these days, cut-off sweatpants or ballooning things that look like culottes, cut up sweatshirts, and a blaze-pink-billed cap turned around backward on his dark hair. Fashions of the outside world, no matter how ridiculous, reach in through the gate of the Settlement like a big hand that teases and tickles. In spite of all the busy sewing machines. In spite of everything.

Christian Crocker, whom everyone calls CC, who looks like a born-again Huck Finn, freckles and all, heads through to the attic stairway to find the bathroom.

The little group at first seems to be all Settlement kids, all but Joel, all facing Gordon with that not-used-to-the-light squint (although the light here is dim). But now Gordon sees there is a stranger who keeps drifting over behind Joel, now just a bit of elbow sticking out.

Gordon folds his arms over his chest and scratches his back on the red painted chimney. "You all come all the way down here just to talk about the weather? That *it*?"

Joel says, "We brought you a present." He beams Soule-ishly. He looks around. "Now where'd that ol' present go?" He steps to one side, revealing the boy behind him, a fine-boned androgynous-looking kid, little streaky-blond tuft of a ponytail, a wishful sort of beard on the chin. Shoulders girlishly narrow inside the well-fitted camo BDU shirt. Yeah, a small slim person. But the hands, hands that know the wrench, the pliers, the clamps. Hands with the raised arteries of young manhood and fingernails smashed by fearlessness. And, yes, he has *seen* this kid somewhere.

"Who're you?" Gordon asks, stepping away from the chimney. "You look familiar."

The boy's eyes, a wolfy gray, shift away. No answer, just a nervous smile.

"It's Mickey Gammon," explains Joel. "We just found him in a tree."

Gordon sort of smiles. Eyes looking off to the left, trying especially hard to imagine the kid in a tree and what for? He looks back at the kid's face.

"A tree *house*, actually," says the pimply purply-faced Evan Martin, "up behind the hog pens."

Gordon asks, "How old are you, Mickey?"

The room is cool tonight. Old curled linoleum. Walls and old plaster damp and old-smelling. To Mickey, it smells like home. Home of the Lockes, what's left of them. Mickey stuffs his hands into his jeans pockets with a really thin little smile. He mumbles an answer.

Gordon looks quickly at the thick-studded rebellious-looking leather wristband on the boy's skinny wrist. He is almost remembering where he has seen this Mickey. Quiet Mickey. Wallflower Mickey. Lost even in the tiniest crowd.

Jaime Crosman says, "You're about thirteen, ain'tcha Mickey?"

Mickey frowns. Thirteen is not the right guess. He looks straight into Gordon's eyes. "I said *sixteen*."

Phone rings.

Gordon looks irritably at the phone. "You got any family?" he asks Mickey, turning to lift the receiver and to cup his hand around the mouthpiece, still looking at Mickey, waiting for the answer.

Mickey drops his eyes to the box on the desk with a spotty cat in it. Makes a face to dismiss the family idea.

Gordon speaks into the phone with a high squeaky falsetto. "Hold, please. This is Gordie St. Onge's secretary. Gordie will be with you momentarily." Mashes the phone receiver against his work shirt. Speaks now in his own real voice. "What do you do with your time, Mickey? When you aren't in a tree?"

Mickey raises his chin and says, as clearly and deeply as his crackly teenage voice can go, "I'm with the Border Mountain Militia."

"Ah, yes," says Gordon, and now, with a wild grin, takes a lunging step forward to the end of the phone cord, puts out a hand. Mickey reluctantly pulls a hand from a pocket. Gordon's handshake is crushing. "Good to see you again. Good to have the patriots represented here in my humble kitchen!"

Mickey squints. This guy reminds him of Willie Lancaster, sort of.

Gordon winks at Mickey as he turns, phone to ear, saying deeply, "Gordie here." He listens and talks with the caller a few moments. Once or twice he turns back and, through the frugal low-wattage light, studies Mickey, the boy's surly expression, the big hole in his jeans showing a white skinny knee, the significant green-and-black embroidered mountain lion militia emblem on his sleeve.

When Gordon is done with the phone, he lays the receiver on the desk and sinks into his wheeled desk chair, rubbing his face till his eyes are reddened. Eyes on Mickey. "So the tree-house thing is probably part of the woodsy survival maneuvers you guys are required to do . . . or is it along the lines of the short-on-finances concept?"

Mickey says, "I've got money. I'm workin'."

"Doing what?"

"Different stuff."

Gordon nods over and over slowly, as if Mickey were still talking, long after Mickey isn't talking. Now he stops nodding, and his eyes fall back to Mickey's hands. "You know cars?"

"Yep."

Gordon raises a palm to blow Mickey a kiss, just as the phone receiver bursts out with ear-crippling shrieking advice: *Hang up and dial again!*

Mickey flushes.

The other boys, including CC, who has returned, laugh heartily. Joel Barrington pokes Mickey's shoulder. "See, I told you Gordo would love you."

Gordon is stroking one side of his long mustache and scruffy beard thoughtfully. "Would you be free tomorrow morning?"

"Yep."

"Six-thirty?"

"Don't matter."

"Okay, six-thirty. I have an errand to do, gotta pick up some kids who are staying down to East Egypt tonight. You come along, we get to be alone for a minute, we can shoot the shit, then come back and I'll give you the whole fucking tour, including the European-style windmill, which is fifty feet and which Rex, your worthy captain, helped us design and construct. And you'll see Our Purple Hope. She is sweet. And still"—he lowers his voice—"still a virgin." He licks a finger and wiggles it, then winks. "Sound like a plan?"

"Yep."

"Aren't we killing that hog tomorrow, *early*?" Evan asks with a squint, Evan who has already started out the door onto the piazza but now leans against the frame, drumming his fingers there.

"I don't know," replies Gordon. "I haven't seen Aurel. I was in Portland all day."

Evan groans. "I gotta find out. Man, I hate this being-in-three-places-at-one-time shit."

Gordon stands up wearily. "Only the dead know rest."

📖 History (1900s: the past).

The intelligence it took to bring us to modern society may not be enough to get us out of it.

—Albert Einstein

 Six-thirty A.M. thereabouts. Dark. Not pitch dark but an iron gray, growing silvery by increments. Growing fast.

Mickey shows up. Dressed the same as last night. Big flappy hole in one knee. He doesn't knock on any of the farmhouse doors. He just stands out under the ash tree smoking, his shoulders hunched. Waiting.

Gordon steps down off the piazza. Screen door bangs behind him. With one hand he pulls the ring of keys from his belt. He doesn't look prepared for this appointment. Under one arm, a green-and-black-plaid wool outer shirt, too much of a hurry to put it on.

Mickey drops the short dry butt of his cigarette, crushes it under his heel. He follows Gordon up a long broad path, little bridge, more path, through the dark woods to the Settlement, the big sandy parking lot where Gordon has left his truck. A bit of a trek, going back the same meandering way Mickey just came.

Once they are there, Mickey climbs up into the passenger's side and waits while Gordon jogs across the quadrangle to the horseshoe of Settlement shops and up inside through one of the porches to fetch something. He returns, flumps a satchel and the wool shirt on the seat between them, and starts the engine. Snaps on the parking lights so that the gauges glow. Gordon listens hard to the engine for a minute or two. He looks at Mickey and smiles.

Mickey flushes. In some ways, Gordon St. Onge *is* like Willie Lancaster. Mickey doesn't feel truly safe from nerve-racking surprises.

Gordon pats the satchel. "Breakfast." He drapes both hands over the wheel and squeezes his eyes shut. Yawns. "Don't ever go anywhere without your gun, your Bible, and your breakfast." He chortles happily to himself, eyes watery. He switches on the heater, which sounds awful, sounds like something flapping inside it. Mickey's eyes lightly caress the satchel, while Gordon quickly studies for the hundredth time the olive-and-black mountain lion in the crescent of letters on Mickey's sleeve.

Now he stares off to the shadowy fenced-in acreage of young oaks, where a few spotted tractor-sized hogs stand on a high spot in the growing light, all watching the truck. Then he yawns again. Through watery eyes, he looks at Mickey, big grin. Mickey winces. Not in a way that shows, just his blood and guts and insides; everything goes on temporary hold.

Gordon reaches into the satchel and pulls out muffins and rolls. A lot of bready things. A big glass jar of peeled boiled eggs. Ham sandwiches made with big hunks of smoked pork, mustard, and funny farm cheese. Jars of milk. "Maple milk," he tells Mickey. "Try it."

Mickey asks, "You always eat this much for breakfast?"

Gordon looks serious and intense, hefts one of the weighty pork sandwiches. "Eating," he says quietly. "It's kinda basic."

Mickey unwraps his own sandwich and chomps into it. There's something goaty about the cheese. Like the air smells around a buck goat in the fall. The smoked pork is salty. The bread chewy and fresh.

With a full mouth, Gordon says, "I thought it would be great to eat these down by the beach. Like a picnic. But I'm hungry *now*. I won't make it to the beach." He had growled the word *now*.

The idea of a picnic seems a little fruity to Mickey. He keeps his eyes on his sandwich.

The dawn increases fast. A buttery light has already filled in around the trees of the larger mountain to the southeast.

They eat and talk, the engine running. Something not quite right about the engine. Gordon keeps cocking his head at certain skips. Mickey suggests it's probably just the plugs. With smacks and slurps and swallows of the sandwich, Gordon tells him, "I've abused her lately. She hasn't had the fuss she needs. My obligations elsewhere have accelerated." He stops chewing. He looks like he's about to cry. Instead, he looks out at the yellow haloed mountain and burps.

Mickey finds the maple milk both disgusting and appealing.

Gordon tells a little about Settlement life. He talks about what it's like for teenagers here. Then Gordon explains that everyone, starting at one's sixteenth birthday, gets an equal share of a certain percent of the profits of the sawmills and furniture sales and the Community Supported Agriculture program veggie and meat sales, and the veggie sales to the IGA and farm markets, and the sale of sheep and eggs, the skinning and meat cutting in hunting season, and the wreaths and Christmas trees. "So far, it's worked out pretty good. It gives everyone spending money. Not a lot, but there's been few complaints." He explains how food and most basic things come to a person free here. He confesses that the one thing they're wrestling with right now is health insurance payments. "Evil whoring insurance fuckers have us by the balls. If it were just me, I'd say screw 'em. But . . . it's not just me. Forgive my vocabulary, Mickey. Are you Christian?"

"'S'okay. I don't care if you swear."

The sun is not quite free of the eastern skyline but hovers in a sticky way behind a tall hemlock. Only the tops of the trees to the northwest are painted with the orange light of this new September day.

Mickey is wondering when Gordon is going to really start talking wacko, like about the poison the Settlement people are supposed to be planning to take together or maybe something about the orgies. He doesn't really want to hear any of it. He listens to Gordon stuffing practically a whole muffin into his mouth and then shifting the old truck into gear. Truck starts down the gravelly Settlement road. Along a ridge of sand to one side, possibly pushed there by someone plowing snow last spring, there is what looks like a tiny piece of broken glass or a huge flake of mica, which explodes with light as the sun finally strikes this little valley, and then the sunlight begins to crawl over the blond Settlement fields. Gordon spreads his fingers right in front of Mickey's face, rubs his fingers together in the sunlight. "The sun," he says in a muffled way around his cheekful of muffin. "Nobody owns it yet. Nobody charges us for sunshiny days."

Mickey looks amused. He has finished eating; he just holds his big jar of maple milk between his thighs and studies the passing hillside of busy-looking Settlement gardens with their army of scarecrows, a tipped-over wheelbarrow, one standing shovel, and one fat woodchuck sitting up on a rock watching the truck pass.

"Sh!" warns Gordon with slitted eyes, looking all about suspiciously. "Whatever you do, Mickey, don't tell anyone about *sun tax*. Or sun meters. Sun as a commodity. T'would give 'em ideas. They'll do it, by God. There's nothing they won't steal and sell back to us." He rests one hand on the shift knob but doesn't shift, even though the truck lugs down, shivering a little as the Settlement road levels out. He looks at Mickey. "What's with your family?"

Mickey picks at his leather wristband. "My brother gassed himself in his car."

"Locke?"

"Yeah."

"So you lived there until—"

"He went nuts on me. I had ta get out."

Gordon says softly, "Livin's tough."

Mickey says nothing. Just sips his maple milk.

Gordon says, "Now it's the tree condo."

Mickey says quickly, "I *was* in Mass. We were there awhile. Me and my sister and my mother." He leaves out his mother's boyfriend Ross, whom he misses.

Gate ahead. Heavy maples closing in, almost dark as night again.

Gordon says, "How's the baby? I heard there's a sick baby over there."

Mickey shakes his head, looks away. "Died."

Gordon snorts. "God's been a busy son of a bitch, ain't he?"

Mickey looks at Gordon's closer knee, then quickly away, nods.

"Sorry, I did it again. It pops out."

"S'okay."

Gordon says solemnly, "I thank God when he's good. I cuss him when he's bad." He grins at Mickey. "I'm not afraid to be honest with God."

Mickey blinks.

Gordon downshifts. Brakes easy. Mickey gets out and lifts the pole, admiring the ANYONE TRESPASSES WILL BE SHOT. TRY IT. sign while Gordon takes the truck ahead. Mickey lowers the pole and hurries back to the truck.

Once out on the tar road, Gordon asks softly, "What was the baby's name?"

"Jesse."

"Jesse," Gordon repeats the name and the name in his mouth has a warm loving familiarity.

Not much talk now as they head down the creepily steep Heart's Content Road, then they turn onto the highway that winds down to the lake and beach area: Kool Kone, the Cold Spot (called Hot Spot in winter), and, after that, one bed-and-breakfast with striped awnings called Your Host. Gordon tells Mickey, "We're goin' hot 'n' heavy on a couple photovoltaic cars right now. It's a real bitch. We thought we'd have one of them rolling by now, but there's been one delay after another. . . ."

 You, crow, have studied the old truck as it left the Settlement and chugs along down Heart's Content Road.

You had sent out four warning *caw!*s, so now eddies of the tribe's *caw!*s far and near, as well as the multiplying echoes, are disturbing the peace all around purply September-cold Promise Lake. Through the cloven

backs and shoulders of cruelly logged mountains, over neighboring
fields, dwellings and barns, utility poles, road signs, stone walls, snowmobiles, artesian well covers, bird feeders, and blue-tarp-covered mysteries, black wings thrust onward, this gossip going even farther,
following the worn and many roads of tar.

Crows, all of you know well the old pickup truck painted by kids.

Brush marks and dribbles. Starbursts of extra gloss. The truck body, the
black-green of living hemlocks. The cab done thickly in the white of a
sleet storm. Cab mounts sag. Inspection sticker unthinkably old. Besides
the driver, the vessel includes the tree boy (hurrah! hurrah! you say) as it
lurches forward on its crooked journey around the lake. But the journey
will be short. Of this you are certain, because your many generations know
perfectly well the ways and habits of Gordon St. Onge.

They make their way.

Mickey has never seen anyone drive so slow and talk so fast. He has never
witnessed such excitement coming out of a person's mouth. Especially
about stuff like gas-free cars, solar and wind power, microenergy-using
flywheels. And "zero-point" energy. And plots by international financiers to keep these lifestyles down and "maintain petroleum as king!"
Lots of plots. Lots of "thick closed doors."

Mickey figures this is probably true but can't think of what to say
back. The Prophet keeps turning toward him with his large nose and
wincing scrinching wild eyes, leaving only little-little spaces for Mickey
to talk back. Mickey's once-in-awhile *yep* seems good enough, 'cause the
guy then launches into a speech on the collapse of this civilization, how
it's time has come "anthropology-wise."

Mickey has no doubt this is also true, but shit—there's so much. Where
does it all come from? They don't even have TVs at the Settlement, Joel
Barrington had told him last night, when he and the others walked
down to Gordon's place. Big rule: no TV. It doesn't at first occur to
Mickey that Gordon is a big reader, a hungry reader and big-questions
redneck philosopher. And that the Settlement from time to time has

fascinating worldly guests for Parlor Night Salons. Instead, Mickey suspects that the big noisy guy is probably psychic. The Prophet, right?

So Mickey continues to reply *"yep"* and *"yep"* and *"yep."*

There are too many vibrations coming off this guy. Like Willie Lancaster. Like Willie, the Prophet likes to muckle on to you, mostly the shoulder. But Mickey has gotten to be an expert at staying cool during that sort of thing. Willie musta been rehearsal for this more huge test.

Balancing his maple milk jar on his knee, he tips it back and forth, back and forth.

When they hit bumps, there's swinging and jouncing of a green plastic Godzilla on its string from the rearview. It has mean little hands and rows of teeth for tearing. But it's a toy. How come not a cross? Or a shrunken head? Or something voodoo-ish (whatever that would be)? A toy Godzilla seems kind of silly to Mickey.

Meanwhile, the truck cab smells of the big breakfast but also like tools, transmission fluid, a banana (no banana is in sight), and a trace of cow shit. And damp wool. And dog. Kind of homey.

You, crow, of the East Egypt branch of the tribe, watch the green-and-white truck stop at a yellow house next to a green-door church.

The tree boy doesn't go in the house with the towering one. No, he stands at the back of the truck making baggy puffs of smoke through teeth and nose, being manly. His dirty tiny tail of hair, in an elastic above his collar, is curved up like a sprout.

Back in the cab, the new passengers cram in with twitters and squeals and the smell of butter. Someone in the doorway of the yellow house waves good-bye. The driver of the truck beeps the horn and, finally getting his leg and foot in, slams his door. The truck windows are all aflutter with waving hands, the house person waves again, and the waves go on and on as the old truck rolls back toward the road.

You, crow, flap your way to the top of the utility pole directly over the action.

Even with Gordon St. Onge's foot's light well-meaning touch on the truck pedals, exhaust from the tailpipe blooms far and wide. You sneeze. Yeah, petroleum is king.

The prayer.

Too many people squashed together in the cab of this truck. Gordon, Mickey, a preteen girl named Stacia, and two little kids that look like they might be girls, though they are boy-haired and tough-looking. One has a commercially made baseball jacket but has its arms around a Settlement-made rag doll almost as large as Gordon. The doll has black button eyes and a smile made of white fake pearl buttons, embroidered ears, yellow yarn hair, and a patchwork dress with embroidered pockets. The other small kid has a paper bag on its lap with the top neatly folded over, and this kid sits on the lap of the preteen girl.

Gordon turns up a back road a half mile before Heart's Content Road and stops the truck off on the shoulder. "I need to see a man about a horse," he says, and galumphs off into the trees.

Mickey gets out to smoke and one little kid, the one with the bag, rolls down the window to ask Mickey questions like, "Do you like night?" and "What do you think Gram calls her cat now?" Mickey answers all these questions with a manly nod, or just a hard stream of smoke from his nose and a small smile. The preteen girl keeps glancing at him when she thinks he's not looking. But she has nothing to ask him or to tell him.

When Gordon returns, he invites everyone to go up in the woods for a quick history lesson.

This is the Settlement way. Life rolls out opportunities for lessons. Lessons pop up everywhere!

The kids inside the truck step down, chattering. Mickey crushes the last of his cigarette in the sand. One little kid runs ahead up the ferny trail. The other one starts crying. The preteen girl starts yelling at the running one. The huge yellow-haired doll waits behind, slumped against one door.

Gordon says, "I haven't been up here in a while. It's grown up a lot. Used to be a stone cattle pound here somewhere." He stops and stares at a humpy area around a jungle of sumac. "Every one of those pieces of granite are gone. People steal rocks nowadays, you know." He looks at Mickey, his pale eyes blazing with disgust. "Yuppies take 'em."

Mickey pictures hundreds of yuppies lugging off the big rocks.

Crows are cawing in the near distance. A great dither.

Gordon starts walking again. "I want to show you a neat old grave-yard. It's up here." The crying little kid rushes Gordon and throws itself

at Gordon's legs, and he hoists the child up, makes a loud smooching noise
into its crying mouth. Little kid laughs tearfully. Its short hair is all dark
curls, and though it wears little jeans and little leather boots and a sweater,
its shirt is really just a pajama top left from the night. Mickey now hears
Gordon call this kid Anna. Gordon carries Anna against his shoulder, her
legs clamped around his rib cage. He says, "I just wanna check this little
yard and see if it's still there. Antiquers steal graveyard gates. Everything
is a commodity these days, even our history."

Mickey notes that Gordon's face is different now. Voice instructive
rather than frantic. How many guys *is* Gordon St. Onge? Mickey isn't
creeped out by this, but he is braced.

They find it. It is still all there.

There are ten graves in all, five with fine old slate stones, tall and elegant with weatherworn old script. But there are also five graves with
just plain small rocks for markers. The yard itself is built up on three
sides with high walls of impressive granite stonework. The granite pieces
are long, like coffins. Wrought-iron gate still intact. Young trees have
taken over the graves, forcing some stones to lean, while shifting earth
tips the others. Gordon explains. "Barringtons don't do this one. Only
military veterans get care, orders from the selectmen. And as you see,
there's no veterans here. Let the good doctors, mothers, farmers, and
little dead babies and pocked children sink into the earth's core, devoured by trees! Forget 'em! They were nothing but plain boring glory-
less trashy peace types. Ack!"

Mickey looks down at the plain gray rocks that mark the graves of
babies. All those babies nobody could save. Somehow, in his heart, there
is momentarily the confused image of yuppies lugging rocks, veterans
lugging rocks, everybody stealing the rocks and handsome iron gates of
babies' graveyards, helpless, suffering, shrunken, cancer-killed babies, all
babies with his nephew Jesse Locke's face. He feels a hand. Little kid with
all the questions pats him on his shirtfront. "Are you sad?" he or she asks.

Mickey's answer is a shrug.

Gordon talks and talks. Mickey likes the way Gordon knows so much
about these old graves, the old families of Egypt, farmers mostly, and all
the ways they are tied into the families here in Egypt today. Through some
exhaustingly tangled mess of *then Elizabeth such 'n' such married Abigail
such 'n' such's cousin, James such 'n' such,* Mickey and Gordon realize that

they are both related to people in this yard, and therefore related to each other, through about fifteen such 'n' such's and many marriages. Mickey likes this. So what if it's *distant*? Related is related. If the tribe includes you, you are in it. You are embraced. You will survive.

Gordon starts pitching some dead limbs out of the cemetery. "Honor our past," he says, and everyone thrashes limbs out over the granite edges of the little yard.

Mickey smiles to himself, imagining Mr. Carney and the rest doing shit like this.

"Check this out." Gordon holds his hand out for everyone to look. On his palm, an inchworm is raised up, poking its blind face around, looking a little frantic. Gordon says, "He has wonderful skin. Don't pity him. He knows what none of us know."

Mickey strikes a match for a cigarette, still smiling his ghosty smile.

When they turn back, the once-crying Anna is in better spirits, her baseball jacket flapping as she runs ahead, all the kids gone on ahead, shrieking happily.

Three or four song bugs have begun to creak as the sun warms.

Young noisy crows lead each other from tree to tree in an open bright space off to the right. As Mickey walks, he squints one eye manfully and blows smoke. Gordon is behind now, paused in his tracks, staring backward down the path toward the crows and the golden brightness. Gordon says, "Come here a sec. I'm just curious." Mickey follows him now toward the crows and the alluring golden light.

It is a clearing, S-shaped. Mushy. Wet. Filling it, a sea of late September yellow, the greener parts, splotches of a color that is otherworldly and whisperish, the leaves pointed and alert in a way that makes them seem centuries old, older than rock and water: plants that observe you. And there are clumpy buds the size of children's fists. And a smell. *The* smell. And mixed in between, all the regular Maine-type wet-loving weeds and other green, lesser smells.

Mickey looks at Gordon. Gordon closes his eyes. "My God." A breathy whisper. He opens his eyes and says, "Shit." And then, in another breathy whisper, "Lady Ganja."

Mickey says, "Yep."

Gordon grabs Mickey's thin left arm and pulls him into an emergency-ish trot through the crackling ferns till they are out of the light, back into the dappled world of oaks and birches. "Get on your knees, man," says Gordon.

Mickey's eyes widen. His cheeks flush maroon. He doesn't question this scary guy, who is not the principal at school or any one of those types, not *that* kind of power, but a twisting, turning, pounding force, both sticky and awful but mostly sticky. Mickey gets down on his knees.

Gordon gets down on his knees beside Mickey. Aloud he prays, "Dear God, give us the strength to never ever *ever* speak of this what we have just seen. Is this not the greatest Commandment of them all? *Thou shalt not tell on your neighbor. Thou shalt not bring calamity on your neighbor, nor the evil of SWAT teams and guns and force and smashed children and imprisoned mothers and fathers.* Give me more strength than for anything I have ever needed strength for before, to keep the knowledge of my neighbor's crop to myself and never return here. Amen." He springs up and starts running, keys jangling.

Mickey, his ashless cigarette bent against his palm, runs too. He burps up a goaty cheese-maple taste. He gets an acorn cap wedged in the tread of his boot but just keeps on running.

 Back in the truck.

Mickey has the kid with the baseball jacket on his lap now, one hand holding her steady, but he fixes his gaze on the rearview mirror's toy Godzilla, twirling slowly and heavily from the *poofs* of the slammed doors. His eyes slide to Gordon's profile, which now wears a goofy grin, like a kid when he's being what Erika used to call *devious*. One of the Prophet's many selves that Mickey is beginning to memorize.

Gordon sighs and his face goes into deep-thought mode. He suggests that Mickey may want to live at the Settlement, there's plenty of room. And Mickey says, with great dignity, that he'll think about it.

A jubilation of crows.

You all take notice as the truck sputters to life and putt-putts up the road of many forks and twists, with its name of heart's content, up, up, and away. You love the way things are turning out for the tree boy. So far.

October

◉ **Media magic.**

The papers (mostly in-state), with their letters to the editors and one-column updates, radio call-in programs, and the occasional television moment keep the Egypt matter covered daily, like a granule of sand in the eye or a pebble in a shoe. Some are still fascinated with the sign at the Settlement gate that promises to shoot trespassers. Others speak or write glowingly of how outgoing the St. Onge people are. And Gordon St. Onge seems like such a "loving man." Some rave about the need for solar and wind and vegetable or hemp fuels, in order to save the planet, and speak of the Settlement people as shining examples we should all follow. Others warn that we should fear these separatists, or at least fear *for* the St. Onge followers, "especially the children, especially the girls." "He speaks truth!" one caller exclaims. "He's totally insane," snarls another. Others stutteringly repeat the word *militia*. And *paranoia* and *fringe* and *wacko*. "Dangerous right-wing types," say some. "Refreshingly leftist," applauds another. With a sigh, one caller tells listeners, "It's an embarrassment to our state. People will believe all of us in Maine are like this, losers with a grudge! Even their kids. I don't know what exactly their problem is, but if people stop making so much of them, maybe it'll all die down. It's disgusting!"

Out in the world, in a federal building somewhere, in America, S.A. (Special Agent) Kashmar is browsing through reports.

He looks up as someone passes in the hall, headed out. It's late. He draws his coffee to him and presses it against his shirt, as though giving it shelter from a storm. He flips through more printouts, clippings, pictures, faxes.

Lotta bad eggs out there. Lotta bad boys with guns. Lotta crackpots with intentions, bad intentions. Putting into a lotta other people's heads intentions those people never thought of. Stirring up discontent. Scaring everyone. Meanwhile, all kissy-kissy and talk of brotherhood, talk of God. How's that go? *"Praise the Lord and Pass the Ammunition."* Yeah, but those guns used to be pointed at Germans and Russians and Japs and Vietcong. Commies and Jap crap. *These* guns are pointed at the United States of America.

Okay, Mr. St. Onge, Guillaume—however you pronounce it. Okay, pretty boy, keep it up. You don't get it? We do *not* allow groups, *tight* groups, groups intended to steer away from America. There's only one thing worse than attacking America with guns or voices, and that is *steering away*. You see, buddy? If you become a nation, a new overzealous nation, you take a lot with you that is *ours*. And—well, you are not America. So you are dog shit. And—well, you are an *example*. Either you are an example of us putting down *danger,* or you are an inspiration to others to do what you do.

And *that* example cannot exist in America.

And so, yeah, it is our humble job, our employment, see, to neutralize you. *Neutralizing leadership* of problem organizations and situations doesn't mean pretty please. It's more like an Irish setter gets neutralized at the vet's: *snip-snip.* Maybe even *that's* not enough. You know what they do with rabid dogs? The head is cut off and sent to the state lab in a plastic bag.

Okay, so you, Guillaume St. Onge, alias Gordon, ain't nothin' yet. Just a photo opportunity for the papers and talk-show subject matter. But it's your intentions we don't like. We've kicked down a hell of a lot of doors because of intentions we don't like. At the same time, you could be very very useful to us.

The agent now cocks his head. So much carpeting these days, even in these rat-trap old mausoleum-type buildings. Carpeting and cork ceilings and windows with glass as thick as two-by-fours. With only himself here now in this suite so late at night, it is absolutely and eerily soundless.

The voice of Mammon (today).

Food is money. Money is food. Food is a weapon. No bang, just a whimper. It crosses the sea. It zigzags. Food from here goes there. Food from there goes thataway. Special seeds. Special soils. Special stuff to squirt on everything. And poke it into cows. Do as we say and you can be part of the deal. Look at the pretty food in sky-high piles. It is in the sky, headed somewhere to win this bloodless war.

And—

With rich and artificial hopes, the population grows richly, but in the absence of frontiers.

And—

Corporate power grows.

Meanwhile.

Latest studies show that Americans now have 15 percent more anxiety than two years ago. Twenty percent more mistrust. Experts explain that these trends should level off, as Wall Street and their economists expect the *dazzling economy* to continue and the spectacular profits to continue. Experts explain that Americans were just edgy in that last study, due to the imminence of the new millennium, that the anxiety was just a normal response to that.

 ## The screen croons.

Everything will be all right if you just listen to *meeeee*!

From frozen Pluto's tiny microscopic Plutonian observatory, observers speak.

juto pssssdrip pt truk bxox wjp litopt jlswdn mnrd prtd ncln!*

 Out in the world, *all over* the big round world.

The militias grow. And the resisters, the raised fists, the pamphlets, the huddles, the blocking of streets. Cries for liberty, *libertad,* free will. The hydra coalesces. It is beautiful to its mother.

 God speaketh.

The create-lings are ever busy, following design, *never* unnatural. *Never* "bad." The dynamo of the universe is rosy and warm in the chambers of my "heart." No complaints on my part. (Yes, it's true. Nobody ever understands God.)

 The tromping of feet and the warning caws of a nearby guard-duty crow wake Mickey.

Not that he was truly asleep. Nowadays, as everyone says, mosquitoes stay around until snow flies. He has had three or more on each ear all night. The creaking grass and tree bugs, which he likes, have all gone silent, due to the moose-herd-type tromping on the path. And also a jingling. Takes him only about fourteen seconds to flip himself over the door hole in the floor and drop, landing Superman-style on the scruffed rooty spot below: visitors. He stares them down.

It's the Prophet with a buncha women and kids. A dog in the lead, a golden retriever's head, body of a beagle.

Uh-oh. Mickey has not gone very far to use "the toilet" since he has resided here. A dog is the last thing he needs snooping around. He shuts his eyes very tight for two seconds, a hurried prayer.

---

* Translation: The situation on Earth intensifies: floods, winds that whirl, droughts, erosion; water, even when clear, glows in ways unseen by earthling eyes; heat like the insides of a sick Earth cow's stomachs; dropping food production—the great net of the one whole global civilization frazzles, bigger lies, bitter cold, explosions, fire. A pity.

The Prophet says, "Good morning!" The jingling Mickey heard was the keys on the man's belt.

Mickey nods, rubs one eye. The other eye is on the bushes, where the yellowy-brown tail of the dog is all that shows.

"We brought breakfast!" an Indian-looking girl about seven shouts, running up with a darkly varnished basket.

Behind her, more baskets, more Indians, and a boy as blond as an old man. Three women, not exactly hot babes, as Mickey had liked to imagine, but somehow he knows these are St. Onge wives.

A crow veers in and settles in the tree's tip-top above the rummaging dog. The crow is silent, its feathers rippling and adjusting as easy as pond water.

Kid hands are reaching into the softer baskets; lids of the hard baskets are flipped wide.

The small Indian girl hands Mickey something wrapped in cloth. Feels cold and dead.

Gordon says deeply, "No American home is complete without *stuff*" and hands Mickey a can of paper flowers, spotty with on-purpose-looking raspberry-juice-looking dye. Gordon's eyes widen. "Say you love them." He winks, rolling his eyes sideways toward the kids. A mosquito finds the Prophet's big neck. Big hand mashes it.

Mickey takes the flowers.

"They look real, don't they?" says one of the taller Indian girls, tall enough to be a teenager, but Mickey figures she's not. She has Gordon's doggy smile, one of Gordon's many types of smiles and grimaces.

"Do you think somebody made them?" asks the very blond, very small boy.

Mickey says, "They look real." He looks into the faces of this boy and the little girl, much easier than looking into the gaze of an older person.

Another of the taller girls, as tall as Mickey, hands him a jar sloshing with tan stuff. Looks like maple milk. She says, "We're learning to make paper. You have to press it." Her eyes—light brown and deep as molasses—are on the flowers. Her black hair looks like it has been pulled out in chunks. A fight? A mean older brother?

His eyes sneak to the three women, their profiles, two of them noticing the dog circling in the ferns. Mickey's chest is tight. He feels his private world stabbed through the middle.

One of the wives looks like a witch, her hair gray straw, too stiff to be just human. And her face too young to have gray hair, not full white, but turning. She is stepping toward him with a jar. She is braless. Her dress is the same color as the flowers: raspberry juice or something. Their idea of making stuff pretty? The dress material is thin, and her nipples are as clear as noses. She has a necklace of hardware, big chain links, and one around her ankle. Like a slave. There is something troublingly sexy and disgusting about her, Mickey thinks. She is on the bony side, but she has a way about her, her long arms, the wagging breasts, her voice now, too tiny: "Yarrow is for healing." He jams the flowers under one arm, the cold wrapped thing too. Takes the jar of salve. "It is especially good as an anti-inflammatory for muscles that ache," she goes on. "Notice it's green." She makes him look. Yep, green. She says dreamily, "It's my favorite. You think yarrow, you think white, like little sister to Queen Anne's lace. But no, the salve is green." She reaches for him; her long arms kind of hypno-tize him. Or is it her voice? Her hand melts upon his wrist. "I tend to use it even when not needed, just for its meadowy smell." She prods his wrist doctorishly. No, motherishly—if mothers were that touchy-feely. Her voice is almost grating and yet kind of like singing. "I keep little-little jars to last through winter. If you want more, stop by. My place is one of the solar ones. My roof is brown." She kneads his wrist a little farther up now, nowhere near his nervous pulse. "I have a whole shelf in my medicine room teetering with salves, yarrow and others. Some just for you!"

Other hands push things on Mickey. Other voices explain. Corn bread. Tomato juice. Bowl of warm pork. Mickey thinks the Prophet prob-ably picked out some of this—ahem—breakfast.

The witch continues, telling him her name is Lee Lynn. She shows him a large wire-style canning jar of dried-up leaves. "You can smoke this," she says. "It's mullein."

A big greasy meaty sandwich balances in front of his face.

A whole loaf of bread "for snacking," the girl with patchy hair tells him, and produces a towel-wrapped thing shaped like a giant egg.

There is a goat smell in the air. The meat? Mickey realizes he's squish-ing the cold towel-wrapped thing under his elbow. Seems the smell rises from there.

Big green area is Gordon's work shirt as he hangs out to the far left of the mob, turning to look at the dog, who is now headed into the center of the group, Mickey's eyes are huge, waiting for the smell to turn up too. The dog is grinning *big*.

A woman in a plaid flannel shirt, large-frame glasses with tiny eyes, tiny smiling eyes, standing real close, now says, "Bonny Loo, where's the you-know-what?"

Bonny Loo looks pregnant or something. Maybe not. Maybe just a gut. Glasses. Very dark hair with orange bleachy streaks pulled into a high ponytail. Eyes sexy with makeup but also sexy anyway. And fox color: that is, orangey-brown. Her breasts are melons. Her earrings look store-bought. She barges in up close to Mickey, smelling more kitcheny than the breakfast items themselves. Digs in her pocket.

But another object is straining for his attention, small hands from below. A smoodgy crayon drawing of big fish or whales and dots that might be stars but are green. This is framed in wood but no glass. "For your walls!" the smallest Indian girl announces in a voice that is booming for such a small person.

Lee Lynn, the witch, says, "Do you have any wishes, Mickey?"

Bonny Loo snorts. "She means, do you need anything besides decor?"

Lee Lynn scowls. "I meant more to do with his well-being."

Bonny Loo's big hand with short nails isn't as noticeable as the block of cash in it. "Some of this is Rex's," she says. "He was around last night, and we all gossiped about you."

The dog is sniffing his ankles. There is no smell of shit. Mickey likes this dog, who has managed so far not to totally fuck up Mickey's day. He would pat him, but his hands are full.

Bonny Loo says, "So, according to Rex, your jobs have—were the summer kind."

"It was nice gossip," Lee Lynn says. "Everybody loves you, Mickey."

Bonny Loo makes a face like swooning. Something between her and Lee Lynn. Is it play or war?

Glennice, with the big glasses and small eyes, *very* small mouth, like an eye with eyelids, and flannel shirt over loose jeans, says, "We're making a town run today, a bunch of us. There's a spot for you."

"Tell him about—you know. Remember?" It's the older of the girls, hair sorrowfully mangy, T-shirt orange-sherbet color, her eyes quite green.

Bonny Loo says, "*You* tell him."

"If you go to the sewing shop—it's four doors from the West Parlor; we can show you—they have gloves and blankets, clothes. Piles of stuff all made, or we can make you something special."

Bonny Loo makes another face, which causes her long nose to get longer, her mouth to suck in. "As long as you don't mind wearing things made by beginners. You could wind up with five sleeves."

"Mean! Mean!" sniggers the older girl and falls against Bonny Loo for a wrassly hug.

Glennice smiles at Mickey, eyes into eyes. "You see, Mickey, it might have looked scary for a while, but God provides."

Bonny Loo laughs almost burpingly. "God isn't at those sewing machines."

Lee Lynn's face appears at Bonny Loo's shoulder just as a jar of yellowy fruit floats by on a small upraised hand. "Mickey, we beseech you to join us at our tables at mealtimes."

Bonny Loo reaches for the head of the older girl. "Just do not, Mickey, whatever you do, let the Beauty Crew touch your head."

"Look at Andrea's hair as an example," says a girl between the smallest and the tallest.

The older girl ruffles her own hair. "They do nice hair sometimes. But Jane, the *secret agent*?" She laughs a laugh of flustered admiration. "A mower."

Gordon, standing a little nearer now, is the quietest Mickey has ever known him to be. And Gordon's eyes are on Mickey.

Mickey feels something press around his wrist. Again. It's Lee Lynn, all witchy and breathy and high-pitched. "You are as skinny as a ghost, Mickey," she says.

Now Glennice's hand offers Mickey what looks a lot like church tracts, though he can't read the sentences blazing across the busy thunder-and-lightning sky painted there. And he has no hands for her to put them in.

"What's *that* about?" Bonny Loo demands huskily. Mickey notes a shape in Bonny Loo's shirt pocket. Cigarettes.

Glennice says, "Nothing that will hurt him."

Bonny Loo's eyes flash to where Gordon stands, still just a green work shirt in Mickey's vision.

Lee Lynn lets go of Mickey's wrist, smiling. She doesn't seem too uncomfortable in her neck and leg chains. Her weedy hair and waggly, perfectly visible breasts are more breezy than weighty, and not even one ounce of shame.

The oldest girl, green eyes, patchy hair, says, "Everyone says you might come work on the solar cars."

Mickey nods.

A smaller girl says, "One we call Our Purple Hope. Like a name."

Mickey nods a few times. "I heard about it from *him*." He doesn't look at Gordon. Of all the people here, Gordon's intense, almost vibrating eyes are the last thing Mickey wants to see.

Bonny Loo seems to grow taller and heavier, and even more pregnant, definitely closer. "Don't you want to come down to the Settlement to live? Hot water. Real beds. No bears."

Mickey squints up at her, the sun behind her shoulder now, chewing its way through the trees. "Sometime."

Glennice, the flannel-shirt church one, says, "Dinner is always around noon. And we have skits, poems, announcements, music, and sing-alongs."

Bonny Loo says, "There's a seat. It's all yours." She grips his arm. His bicep. Cuts the blood flow off, sort of.

The older girl says, "Our Purple Hope is important. You should do that."

Lee Lynn says, "Our Purple Hope cries out for you!"

Bonny Loo shakes her head to dismiss these invitations. "First things first. Mickey, you need a ride to town. And maybe to Ames. Car leaves at eleven. Be there."

"Dinner is at noon," says a smaller girl.

Bowl of meat carried in the small blond boy's raised hand glides past between Mickey and the women, dog nose following in the meat's wake.

Glennice says, "Let me pray with you, Mickey, for thanks. This is quite a surprise I'm sure, and—"

Bonny Loo says, "Pu-leeeeez, Glennice!"

The women bully each other awhile. They bully Mickey. The nearness of their bodies makes almost a real squeeze around him.

He sneaks a flash glance at Gordon's face, the big dark mustache, the short beard. One eyebrow raised, on the verge of squint-blinking, a sort of seizure of the face. His hands hang down at his sides, huge, like bear paws. Strong, but weak. Bullied and bossed. Mickey was wrong. Gordon St. Onge isn't really a man with a harem. He's a man with a problem.

 ## Evening, up in the woods.

What looks from a distance like a little bird stuffing a great swatch of batting through the hole of a birdhouse is really Mickey Gammon, stuffing through the hatch doorway of his tree home his brand-new 10 degrees below zero sleeping bag, a necessary item for any serious militiaman of these northern climes, in preparation for the Emergency, which, as we know, comes sooner for some than others. No way, no how, is Mickey ready for a Settlement bed and Settlement women.

 ## Mickey's tree house, next morning.

Another basket. Just one basket. The picnic kind. With a crow on it, trying to pick it open, but who lifts off, hearing the unzipping sound and wooden thumping sound of Mickey waking up.

So somebody had just sneaked quietly up the trail and left breakfast. Mickey, rummaging through, finds two notes. One is a folded note from Bonny Loo reminding him that dinner is at noon. A bit of a command there. But only if Mickey could read it. All he can make out is DEAR MICKEY. Though if *dear* were mixed in with the rest of the writing, he'd probably not know it. It's all guesswork.

In a sealed envelope is a blue membership card to the True Maine Militia, and again he can make out MICKEY and GAMMON, but other words are just alphabets out of order, about as readable as rows of corn. Then a note:

> *DEAR MICKEY,*
> *Please join our militia. We need you! We need your expertise! Let's meet here at your place tonight at 4:30 for quick meeting, updates, and that sort of thing. We have something in the works not to be written in a note. Over and out.*

If Mickey could read, he might be interested in the signatures on his membership card, including *Samantha Butler,* the one with the blonde

Apache-like hair whose image arouses him many nights. But Mickey's eyes are not held long by print and scribbles. He quickly unwraps the goat-smelling cheese sandwich, the small bowl of crispy but cold bacon, tall canning jar of peaches in juice, two canning jars of maple milk, big spoon, folded cloth with print of teacups. No words needed. In this selection of goodies, he once again senses the hand of Gordon St. Onge.

 Later, a secret meeting. It's the True Maine Militia. In the woods, the militia way, which Mickey found out about when everyone showed up.

A single electric buggy's headlights serve as lighting, a frostiness drifting across it.

On a carpet of pine spills under Mickey Gammon's tree house, figures are hunched in their jackets and big Settlement sheep's-wool sweaters. Mickey Gammon wears the camo BDU shirt of his *other* militia. He takes quickie glances at Samantha Butler, Recruiting Officer, whose pale hair is topped tonight with a black felt crusher hat made for a larger head. The end of Mickey's cigarette glows prettily with each hard draw that follows each of his glances in Samantha's direction.

No little kids at these planning sessions. "Little kids have loose lips," Samantha reminds everyone. "And, as we all know, *Loose lips sink ships*."

Dee Dee St. Onge, absolutely pregnant, is part of this. She sits in a grand way on a sheepskin on the ground. She sits Indian-style like Samantha and, like Samantha, wears a crusher, what she has always called "a log driver's hat."

They are going ahead with their new statehouse plan. If Gordon had said *yes,* they wouldn't have to be so secret. But when Bree had asked him for permission to round up all the littler kids for this, he had said, *no*. "Clandestine," says Erin Pinette. "Privy," Samantha adds, in her usual naughty way, and Mickey Gammon's Lucky glows cherry red.

"So this isn't exactly the Million Man Woman Kid Dog March," Dee Dee observes.

Samantha laughs. "That's going to have to be a long way down the road. For now, just this reconnaissance mission. For now just the family. No public announcements for this." She tosses an acorn at Kirky Martin, who tosses it back. Harder.

Whitney explains. "We finally reached Senator Mary, and she is mailing us a map sort of thing with the whole layout of the statehouse and office building. It's got that tunnel we might march through. Mary says these are the exact times the governor will be in his office next week. But we have to call her again the night before we head out."

"Senator Mary gave us her secret cell phone number too," says Sophie, swanlike Sophie, so silvery a person she shines in the night.

"This!" crows Carmel St. Onge, wearing a checked cap with flaps, "is going to be a siege!"

"So we need to bring everything we need for the whole day, two weeks if we have to: dried cranberries, nuts, apples, and we oughta pop vats of corn the night before," Kendra B suggests.

"Lightweight long-lasting rations," says Rachel Soucier, with an ivory-white megasmile.

"They're not going to get us out of there without tanks," declares Kirk Martin with a manly (he thinks) growl.

Dane St. Onge speaks, voice both deep and squeaking in that adolescent way. "They'll need a *lot* of tanks."

"Excellent!" three voices of three preteen girls chime, then fall away into giggles.

Bree, the deformed-faced girl, is there, only fifteen, Mickey's age, yes, but a wife, no shit, of the Prophet.

Bree's eyes sweep over the beautiful faces, unbearably beautiful in the frosty light. Even their red noses are beautiful to her. And that soft scratch of the record keeper, Margo's, pen. Bree's eyes also move over Mickey, the only one standing, leaning, slouching in his beautiful insolence against the tree trunk of his abode. Smoke around his face. No hat. Just that uneven streaky blonde part in the middle of his forehead. And then Whitney, her confidence, her humor, her father Gordon's eyes, Gordon's nose, Gordon's mouth. Hair blond like her mother Penny's.

If Bree stares at these faces long enough, she feels confused. Nicely confused. The warm whirl of St. Onge genes, their somewhat husky voices all merging, the similarity of their body movements, that laugh, that squint-blinking of the eyes. Even those who are *not* Gordon's children have taken on his manner. Maybe even Mickey already has begun to adapt. And Bree?

When the group breaks up, pens are pocketed, everyone stretches. Michelle and Margo are helping the laughing, very pregnant Dee Dee to her feet, and everyone is saluting each other and calling out in militia fashion, "God save the Republic!"

☆   **From a future time, Claire recalls.**

Yeah, Gordon would actually *wed* each wife. Not a license from the state. But a little ceremony. No newspaper announcement, no invitations, no cake or dancing or silver-papered gifts. None of that. But there was this little man, about ninety, maybe a hundred and ninety, Andy Emery, the Reverend Andy Emery, who would show up one evening to talk with Gordon and the about-to-be bride. He had an old car, flat crappy blue with a black top. Big car. Paint dull, but motor quiet and dignified. Seems he had that same car all his life. I don't remember any other. You'd see that blue-and-black car parked down to Gordon's house— usually that's where they'd meet, in the dining room with the door shut—and the news would start flying: *Gordon was taking another wife.*

Then, a day or two later, the wedding. Up to the ancient Hurleytown Church, which had no heat and met only in summer, worship services presided over by another minister, the Reverend William Capp. But anybody could do weddings there. Rent was next to nothing; some small donation was all. It was a sweet church, a poor church. Outside paint, white of course, was peeling like the scales of a long-dead fish. Walls painted on the inside a blazing turquoise, a pump organ that was out of tune. But tall windows filled with yellow and orchid glass, so even a cloudy day looked sunny! But on a really sunny day there in late summer, the harsh sun transformed into a big corral of light, a glowing crown in which you stood gladly subordinate, and you would have "God" really visit you there, almost in the flesh.

As I said, this wedding would be quiet. Nobody there but Gordon, the bride, Reverend Andy Emery, and Beck (Andy's sister-in-law's daughter), a woman in her sixties who was so fat she almost couldn't walk, but she could sing hymn solos quite prettily. Though I don't think she sang for any of these weddings. I know she didn't sing when Gordon and I "married" that second time. She just served as a kind of matron of honor, hovering, telling me how happy she was for us when it was done. And she took some snapshots. She sent me the snapshots a few weeks later. I believe she has sent snapshots to all the brides, at her own expense. These pictures take on significance, and so does this woman's blessing, because everything else about the day seems a little too much like pretend.

But at the same time, it is profound. Those few words Gordon speaks to you and you to him, the kiss, the flowers you wear in your hair—or evergreens if it is winter. The silver ring. The promise. Don't laugh. You could take his promise to love you forever seriously. Gordon was forever.

Yeah, laugh if you want. Sure you shared him, but you would never be deceived. You would never be dumped. He would never fall out of love with you. And from his hands into your hands was transferred the invincibility of the family, diametrically webbed across the whole. Yeah, he was giving you something ancient: a whole. Like the grit-and-ore planet under our feet.

 Dawn of another day.

You tip your head, your hearing troubled by the rain, which punches you all over. You consider Mickey Gammon's tree house, seeming to produce rain from its soggy edges. The uncovered window reveals the inside space still stuffed with tree-boy gear. But no Mickey.

 The whole.

In the west side leg of the Settlement's horseshoe are shops and piazzas—screen ones and open ones—parlors and library, also the kitchens. Built at first as one room, the floor is laid with Settlement-made ceramic tiles painted in designs and images with all colors known to the eye, especially lime and red. Under the tiles, copper tubes flow with sun-warmed water when needed. The floor surface is fiercely attended by cleaning crews to make things right for crawling babies.

This Grange Hall–sized space is divided into two areas by partial walls of cubbies and an archway of sign-up sheets, mailboxes, notices, complaints, photos, and art.

The first kitchen you enter from the piazzas has sinks and stoves. Tall many-paned good-for-the-soul windows frame at this moment a small dawn-dim foggy field, the rain solid and sparkling. Sometimes three deer appear there to graze, churning, fluttering ears and tails giving them away.

Significant thumps and clangs of Settlement life will bring their heads up.

And always there are crows, who can't seem to mind their own business. Even now in the downpour one is out there slumped on the point of a broken-off pine.

The first kitchen is called the Cook's Kitchen. It is hotter than the other, warmed by shouts, orders, jokes, frying smells, and lots of lid, drawer, and door slamming.

People who need to be fed by other people's hands are arranged in thronelike chairs near the radiance of this hubbub, and on days like this a few extra sticks crackle in one cookstove firebox.

The bigger kitchen you get to through the archway. This is called the Winter Kitchen. Only on stuffy days or steamy days are the piazzas fully set up for meals. Today they are not.

See from this inner kitchen the same little field through the tall windows. To the right of the field, close enough to block the summertime view of the southwest sky, are the rain-blackened shaggy trunk and limbs of a hundred-year maple. Its foliage is hot-tempered, more purple than red or orange. Majestic to human eyes.

But most eyes are turned inward. Many dozens of persons this moment, making plans, gobbling hungrily or daintily, testing the steamier stuff, sipping, leaning back—or forward and ready to lunge out into the big day.

Three long tables are made up of smaller ones, and smaller ones are in Ts or alone. Biscuits in piles. Meat and eggs in bowls. Raw milk of the cow and the goat in tall pottery pitchers, and some pitchers of well water, if you prefer. Jam and preserves in jars with missing spoons, some empty. Real butter. Black store-bought pepper and salt. Roughly sliced dark and light breads, warm or cold. Ripped-apart breads. Muffins with bites. Syrup of the maple tree in jars and pools and trickles. Potato cakes. Tomato juice in shapes like the bottoms of somebody's shoes crossing the floor. Someone with a mop is already on the way.

Lights are dimmer in the kitchen of tables than in the kitchen of stoves, but Settlement-made candles hither and yon make a greenish light on faces and throats, the same green as the candles' wicked green and weedy scents.

A catlike sound, a very new baby, stops suddenly.

Groaning laughter at a bad joke trying too hard to be good.

Stories. Always the stories.

Gossip. Always the gossip.

Gordon St. Onge sits with a table of snowy-haired solemn-faced women and men who have eaten before sunrise to get that out of the way. Tea-cups, coffee cups. A dried-out muffin. Each set of hands clasps a fan of playing cards. A spindly hunched-into-contortion woman slides her eyes to Gordon's face and winks. He squeezes both eyes shut. A code? Are they cheating?

Gordon doesn't have cards, just one Zeus-sized arm around a woman who is asleep. Her cards still rest where they were dealt. In a moment or two, her nap is over and she awakes with a smile. Pats Gordon's arm and speaks, part French, part English. All brightness, not at all sleepy.

The cards whir and slap, open and close. A gravelly voice speaks of the rain. Gordon now watches a man wearing a brown dressy sweater and pastel shirt. He dolls up like this for meals and for Settlement meetings (announced on the bulletin side of the kitchen archway). This gentleman's chin lifts slightly, faking a good hand.

Gordon's chair goes back suddenly as he sees a storm of small boys headed his way. *Swamp monster!* they scream.

"Red ants!" Gordon groans, covering his eyes. Cringing. The wob of keys on his belt jangling almost tunefully.

The kids (red ants) cover him, some climbing up both sides, some just muckling onto his legs. Some tug his shirt.

Guitar strumming mixes in with the screams, bad jokes, whirring of cards, oven doors. On a foot-high stage in a corner far from the tall windows, sort of shadowy now, a teen, maybe twenty, wearing a choco-late brown satiny Nehru jacket, gives the breakfasters some early morn-ing chords, heartbreakingly beautiful. Three-dimensional paper fish churn lazily on strings over his head. No kazoos yet. Eventually, a gang will whip out their trusty kazoos for more cheery wake-up music.

Gordon is now effortlessly holding a screeching four-year-old upside down over the pack of red ants, who are snapping and clawing at the victim's upright red hair. "Enough, Guillaume!" one woman scolds Gordon, and whatever it is she says in her snappy Aroostook French seems to work.

Within moments, Gordon is crossing the room to a balding man in a denim barn jacket spotted blackly with rain.

Gordon says, "Hey, man," in a grave way and embraces the guy. Then, pulling away, shakes his head.

The guy says, "He's better off. That was no life, ya know?" Eyes swirling with tears, he speaks in even phrases of his father in some nearby town. In these ways the Settlement can never be and was never intended to be a barred-up place of separatists.

"Your ma got anyone there right now?" Gordon wonders.

"My sister Ginny, but only till Tuesday."

Arriving in the Cook's Kitchen now, a very drenched and arrow-straight Mickey Gammon. A light step, but of course he is noticed by the breakfast crew and cooed over. And the cook herself, Bonny Loo, bullies him into taking a biscuit from a pan. Biscuit burns him but he hangs on to it manfully, nodding thanks.

But he isn't noticed yet by Gordon, who, beyond the archway, still listens to the man in the barn jacket and now suggests, "Let's get a crew together to go over and at least take care of the hay. I'll put it up on the schedule." And then within a moment he has hoisted a diapered just-walking little guy up against one shoulder, his small face pinked from sadness. Points toward another little guy who is leaving the scene on a homemade wooden Trojan-style cow (yes, cow) on wheels. Disappears now through the dozens of tall legs of the breakfast crews and break-fasters coming and going.

Against Gordon's shoulder the child sniffs back nose tears, then wipes his nose across Gordon's shirt, today a plaid of lime and red, almost matching the floor tiles. The child's hair is a thick sponge of copper-colored curls.

One of the card players, a tall straight woman with a white braid, has found Gordon, tugs his sleeve, winks.

Now a wife, also tall: Penny St. Onge. Tucks something in Gordon's shirt pocket, a receipt or maybe a saw logs order, maybe battery level readings or a call on the farmhouse phone.

The old woman and the less old woman vanish into the crowd.

Gordon looks into the face of the child gripped loosely in his giant arm. "My lamb," he says, in a husky way, his throat now less a vortex of desperate words, more a harbor of simple prayer. He reaches to place his hand on the little boy's head.

Maybe the boy, Mickey Gammon, might wonder, as many have, how this father, this husband, this cousin or buddy to all, this giant guy— but indeed, only one guy—could give any one other person enough. How? When spread so wide, so thin, so all about? Not when one friend, one father, one fellow soul is all some of us request of this world. Anything more than that is just a state of drowning.

 Saturday.

Twelve members of the Border Mountain Militia, not including Willie Lancaster (who is "busy," they say), get a tour of the Settlement's short-wave setup. It has an impressive tower structure between two Quonset huts, not on the bald mountain, as was once considered. There is a little studio, its broadcast capabilities as yet nil. "A project that has not yet been top priority," Gordon tells them.

They are also led uphill to see the windmills and then down again for some of the solar stuff. They stand around, some with hands in pockets, for it is a smarting cold day. Snarly, sort of. Bit of wind. No BDU shirts or patches visible, though three of them wear military boots. Army caps.

Down at the old farm place, the rotund ash tree, which had turned early, has leaves flying around on the sand and grass in fingered clumps, yellow edged in mauve. Inside, in the cluttery dining room, the men have a meeting. Nine Settlementers join them, including young Butch Martin, Eddie's oldest, and fifteen-year-old Cory St. Onge. Also Mickey Gammon, who is now both Border Mountain Militia *and* a Settlement person. And, with some embarrassment, has connections with the girlie militia.

They talk about the mail Gordon has been getting from patriots around the country, invitations to attend meetings or just to exchange information. Kentucky. North Carolina. Western Mass. Colorado. Florida. Idaho. Ohio. Oklahoma. Montana. Texas. Rex advises which ones to avoid and which to go for. Rex pushes something across the table to Gordon. It's a patch, olive and black. Then he issues patches to the other Settlement men. He says, "I suggest the group in western Mass. See them first."

Late-afternoon sun, autumnly and solid and cold as a refrigerated peach, roams entirely to the other side of the building. And so this causes a backyard maple and the blue-violet shadows from some old sheds to make a polychrome flush on the dining room walls and on several overly serious faces.

Gordon looks at his patch, front and back, then positions it on the table in front of him so that the mountain lion—or bobcat or lynx, whatever it is, in its dark border of words—is perfectly upright.

Gordon says into Rex's eyes, "I was sort've hoping you guys would go with us."

"Of course," says Rex. And he actually smiles.

Gordon says, "In a convoy, right?"

Rex makes a disgusted face. "Not exactly a convoy."

Gordon says, "Think they'll listen to me?"

Rex is sitting very straight, eyes into Gordon's eyes. "Don't say *democracy* and don't get overexcited. All right?"

Gordon grins. "Okay, captain." Gordon looks over into the faces of Ray Pinette, Paul Lessard, Stuart Congdon, Rick Crosman, Gary Kennard, and Eddie and Butch Martin, who happen to be watching him. He sighs. He looks down again at the patch. "Well," he says cheerily, "this is it."

Meanwhile, Mickey Gammon's own wide, alert, wolfy eyes press upon an old dish hutch, where a heartily and hysterically pink ceramic cherub, which is sort of flying, is definitely pointing at him, Mickey. The cherub's lips smile wicked pleasantly.

♡♡ Secret Agent Jane in love.

He is the new person. He is of the Milishish but beautiful, with a little hair thing in back and nice eyes. I wish he would notice me. If I had new earrings, maybe. And a new outfit from *stores*. Something bright like pink. If I went out on a date with him, I would probably die of happiness with one small kiss. Then a big kiss. But he spends every minute with the sole cars. His name is Mickey but they call him Hey, Mister Sole Man. Last night with these secret glasses I watched him at supper eat a whole pile of FISH and gross spiced stuff, and I could tell he was suffering.

 In the cold blue-wallpapered dining room of the old farm place, Gordon buttons the sleeves of the stiff BDU shirt.

Old Lucienne, one of the Aroostook tantes who live *here* now, in Egypt, stands behind him in the doorway and says something softly in French. And he, in French, replies. Softly.

She *tsks*.

He picks up the olive-green pistol belt from the table and twists the buckle into place, the belt snug around his waist outside the jacketlike shirt.

Lucienne points at the mirror, again *tsk*ing.

He steps up to the mirror, which is small and only shows the collar of the jacket and his face. He can't really admire the full effect, those blossomlike shapes of woodland camo: greens, tan, black, brown.

He hunches a shoulder up to see the patch Lucienne has sewn on the sleeve for him. She had *offered*.

Now she places a hand on the middle of his back and he turns and looks into her face, which is a storm of fine lines all summoning their concern over the scratchiness of this shirt. Her eyes a summery blue. For the moment, she is his buddy, in collusion over this, his transformation. Member of an armed citizens' militia, so-called terrorist.

☆ **In a future time, Claire St. Onge (Gordon's only *legal* wife, although actually now legally an ex) remembers Our Purple Hope.**

The heat was back. Thick like summer. Some call it Indian Summer. Some call it global warming. Whatever, it wasn't October feeling! Bay doors were open wide. Under the high rounded ceiling of the largest

Quonset hut, you could look to your left or right and see the amazing
bright fleet of small electric cars and buggies. Mostly these used replen-
ished special batteries. Only one with collectors. Some of the cars were
not yet equipped, only steel frames. All but two were just buggy-sized,
like ATVs, with big deep-tread ATV tires. Made for pulling small loads.
Made for errands. Some were those we'd been using for a few years, now
in this bay area for repairs. Lightweight with lumpy homemade finishes,
thick paint of your standard fairy-tale red, blue, yellow, rose, or orange.

But that night, the main attraction was the roadworthy, low-slung,
sporty, full-sized, though still windowglassless, Our Purple Hope. The
gate was being opened for a lot of people from around Egypt, Brownfield, even Porter, here to witness the first road test. The brightest light-
bulbs in the whole Settlement were overhead, giving our purple car
reflections like lumpy suns. It felt good to me to have a nice big group
visiting. Events of this size had always been natural to Settlement life,
and it was getting a little bit sickening to be so closed off.

☆ In a future time, Penny remembers back.

Among the townspeople, there was one guy I didn't think looked familiar. Not that I knew everyone from town by name, but I knew their
faces. This guy was a total stranger. Midforties. Square-jawed. Fit. His
brown hair was short and combed with care. His face was shaved. I
couldn't decide if he was a schoolteacher, an insurance salesman–type,
or maybe a churchman. He looked controlled and capable. I offered him
the last of the lemonade. He said, "Yes, thank you." A gentleman. His
accent wasn't local.

☆ Some details Claire remembers.

Outside, the parking lot was packed with cars and trucks. A cheery
gatekeeper crew had been formed. They had set up an ice shack as a
guardhouse by the pole gate near the tar road. But the pole and the mean
signs were tossed into the bushes. Like I say, it was a warm night. A lot
of big male bellies, some torn greasy T-shirts. Those whose fashion statement was *work*. And they each brought along at least a single beer, like
a torch of freedom. There were lots of sleeveless women, many kinds

of arms. And shirtless kids, the pudgy and the ribby. In our Lee Lynn's arms was her baby, Hazel, plump, cherubic, quite naked, scrubbed sweet. At home.

This was the great and grand solar finale. Our Purple Hope ready to set sail at last. This is the sort of thing that attracts mostly men—you know—like moths to light. But every woman of the Settlement who wasn't infirm was here that night in that echoey Quonset hut, laughing to see how many of us had turned up wearing the red sash, not at all planned. Just a synchronized red-sash mood.

May I tell you of the sash? Red wool, the sash. And, in satiny embroidery, suns. Every sash featured a powerful boiling-yellow sun. And vegetation and tiny fairy flies in blues and purples and many greens. The embroidery showed in a wide variety of levels of accomplishment, but all of the sashes were unhesitatingly *red*. We, the sisters, wives of one man. No, the creation of the sashes had not been an agreement, no result of a meeting of yesses, but a spark. One day, one of us made one. Then in a summer, there were many, their meaning remaining a secret among ourselves.

It tickled us all to see how we had each individually thought to wear the sash that night. Even vastly pregnant Vancy wore hers, but over her shoulders, like a priest. And let me remind you, these sashes were *wool*.

Penny.

I saw the stranger turn from facing the center of the room to face the nearest open bay. He watched keenly as Gordon pushed in through the crowd, coming from somewhere. At a glance, I knew Gordon had been drinking, though no bottle was in his hand. Rex York was with him, Rex not drinking, of course, just solemn and interested in the photovoltaic car.

Claire.

There was this great dither when Gordon showed up, people hollering his name, whistling, working their way around others to greet him, and Aurel gripping Gordon's arm and saying something about the *lead wire* and *battery four* and "What you t'ink, t'at iss t'same one somehow sneaked back when my back was turn'—not by Butchie, dere, or Mickey, but somebody acting wa-wa wit'out dere *maman*!" Aurel's eyes crackled with the light of all those overhead watts. The blackness of those eyes! The Indianness of his great-grandparents more evident in him than in Gordon. Like everyone here, I always cared a lot about Aurel, a first cousin of Gordon, even though he brags and fibs, mostly fibs *while* bragging, and I saw that although he was a lively, gifted, snazzy little guy, he was not the showstopper Gordon was, and that night I think I really resented this, that Gordon had stolen Aurel's thunder.

I watched Aurel turn back to work, his khaki shirt always a little loose over his small shoulders, a wetness beaded up and trickling through the hairs of his dark, fussily trimmed pointy beard. And beside him, Mickey. Mickey, who was shirtless that night, way too ribby. His jeans were ragged and splotched black. I remember the moment I realized how those young fingers could literally divine all the perfect connections of that electric and automotive mystery.

Gordon was feeling the fender of the car.

Rex stood between Joel Barrington and Eddie Martin as they all talked quietly. Rex was toned-down militia: dark T-shirt, work pants, army cap. There was something about that relentless light. Though his big sprawling mustache was still dark, I saw that these past months he was getting craggy.

Aurel dropped down in front of the car with a flashlight, eager to show Gordon some "bad news."

And Gordon got down on all fours too, so I couldn't see him as Evan Martin shuffled left or right and someone else moved into the open space.

Then Aurel was up again, barking to the little wide-eyed mob, "We fix our trouble as we go! She going to roll in about twenty minutes. Diss fuckup iss not going to spoil t'iss major plan off e'stacy and delight off dese people! I mean it! And afterrrr"—he really rolled those beautiful *r*'s—"she hass been outside charging up all day, she iss frisky inside, her!" Without even taking a breath, he turned to one of the Vandermast guys, one of Bree's brothers, who had been around all day for this. "What do you t'ink off t'iss nice purple car now, you?"

And I remember this, those last finishing touches: Mickey hot white-gold against the mad purple glow of the car, like a shy apparition. And blond ruddy Joel Barrington leaning close to Butch Martin to confer, and

Beezer with her stocky shape, plump ass in jeans, winking at me as she passed the pliers to Mickey, and soft-looking twelve-year-old Kirky Martin, electrician and electronics man extraordinaire, hands in pockets now, but hovering. And I saw Mickey and Aurel bend over the bank of batteries, and I knew then, as I know now, how it is when chemistries of different bodies combine through rhythm and heat, that when this happens, those five or six human systems will operate in sync, like the miracle of wolves. And tell me, isn't this what we want for our children? Is it so wrong? So outmoded? I looked over at Gordon at that moment and, seeing the back of his head, his rather cowlicky "new" short hair, I knew I loved him more than at any other time. Yes, he had been our savior.

☆ **Penny.**

And then I caught sight of the stranger, who was yakking with some people from town.

☆ **Claire.**

Aurel put a hand on Mickey's bare shoulder and whispered. Then Mickey was grabbing his camo shirt from a pile of shirts on one bench and then easing himself into the windowless cockpit of Our Purple Hope.

Somebody from town was feeling the photovoltaic collectors on the car roof. And Rachel Soucier, who had worked endlessly with her father devising all the elevation charts, stood near with her clipboard. And then I saw big ol' fifteen-year-old Cory leading Jane through the ring of men. She was giggly and antsy and dressed cute, as always. Little plaid smock and black velvet ribbon in her upswept curls. And Aurel was assuring her, "Oh, yess, mademoiselle, t'iss iss a sports car, a Camaro . . . sort of."

And Josée and I smiled at each other; I, for one, feeling that cold-hot up-down sensation I always had, seeing those dark solemn eyes, proud chin, and small shoulders.

And everyone stood around some more while Jane settled into the passenger seat, with Mickey Gammon at the wheel. Buttoning up his militia shirt, he spoke to her, something like two words, some ordinary thing, and Jane (no secret agent glasses tonight) patted her hair.

And Butch Martin threw up a fist and hollered, "To the Revolution!"

And Rex glanced over at Butch with his steeliest look.

Rachel Soucier waved the clipboard, passed it to Mickey, and now Whitney was hollering from nearby, "To the Revolution!"

And the motor kicked on like the innocuous hum of a Frigidaire.

When the car lurched forward, people were screaming, "Hey, Mickey, Mr. Astronaut!" and "Hi, Jane!" and some were toasting the car with beers, and there were whistles, and off into the night the little car whooshed.

☆ Penny.

Some youngsters ran after the car, out there in the night all this laughter and yahoo! and one kazoo buzzing and Michelle St. Onge and Samantha Butler were passing out True Maine Militia flyers. And Aurel was explaining in a series of shouts, "Mister Gammon will take diss purple photovoltaic sweetie up t'at tar road to Lancasters' dere'bouts and help Jane mark t'el'vations wit red on bote charts for now. Juss coming right back. No real travel. No sun, juss stars. And meanwhile, iff t'Lemonade Committee back in force, t'worl'will sing!"

🏚 Meanwhile (present time).

The little car hums along in the night.

🏠 Meanwhile.

A stranger steps up to Gordon, who is standing with Rex and a Vandermast guy. Stranger wears a summery dress shirt, white with narrow pinstripes, jeans, military boots, and introduces himself as "Gary Larch, a patriot."

Rex looks him up and down.

Gordon puts out a hand. "Yessir," says Gordon. "You've come to the right place."

Rex stares at the guy, not so quick to put out his hand, but he eventually does.

Meanwhile, in the Settlement lot.

Rex's daughter, Glory York, steps from her car. She walks oddly. She walks toward the lights and noise. She is accompanied by a friend. Both girls wear short low-cut dresses. Glory's shoes are wooden-heeled clogs. But it is not the clogs or the old ankle injury that gives her that little stumbly sashay

All that dense flashing dark auburn hair swishes around her. Her earrings are long and silvery. In her hand, a stalky late-season clover. She sees her father, who is quietly talking with a stranger, hand on the fender of a Settlement flatbed truck. She avoids her father. No Daddy; no, not Daddy; Daddy just thinks of one thing, one little little little thing and nothing else: *militia*. Old pooperdooper.

What she is kind of swimmingly aiming for is that loud voice, not hard to locate really: Gordon, preaching away to a bunch of visitors, in one of the blindingly bright bay doors, commanding attention as always.

"Electric cars," Glory tells her friend, "are the big thing here . . . besides everything else."

There are a lot of little kids. Fussy. Crying. Fighting. Mothers and fathers and other kids are dragging them off to their beds, *long* overdue.

And there are young guys, some Glory knows from her school days, some older. Some Settlement guys: Butchie Martin. Mmmmm, Butchie Martin. Fit and slim-hipped, cocky in the walk, teasy in the eyes, quiet, dark-haired, one of those really capable ones here. French on both sides. Mmmmmmmmmmmm. He is, yes, giving her the eye now, she thinks. He is looking at her, *definitely*.

Behind her, someone says, "Glory's smashed."

She laughs, whirls around. "Yessss! Jealous?"

And one guy says, "Glory, let me take your car a minute. I'll be right back. I'm going to catch up with those guys and give them a hard time." (Meaning Mickey and Jane).

Glory waves a hand dismissively. "My car is resting."

Gordon doesn't see or hear her coming, so involved in his speechifying about the world being on the brink of total economic collapse, starvation, thirst, chaos, his Atlas-like body almost filling up the open bay. She is just suddenly there, stuffing the long stalky clover into a pocket of his work shirt and hugging his arm. He doesn't notice her breath because of his own beer breath, but he knows she is really *drunk,* which he is not.

She says, "Shara has seen you in the newspaper and she didn't believe you are like a father to me. That I was practically raised here at the Settlement. Tell her it's true, Ghee-yome."

The group of visitors standing near are looking sheepishly at Glory. Gordon is looking at Glory, her face only, forcing his eyes to stay up there away from what he knows is the lowest neckline he's ever seen on her . . . something like a little gold ladybug on a gold chain fine as a trickle of light squirming between her almost entirely exposed breasts.

Glory's friend is nervously laughing.

Glory places her right foot between Gordon's work boots and fools with the button of his shirt. "Shara, you believe me now?"

The friend is wide-eyed, obviously impressed.

"Shara, take a picture of me with the Prophet."

Giggle. "I don't have a camera!" Giggle. Giggle.

Glory gasps. "Shucks! No picture. Nobody will believe it"—she gasps —"without *proof!*"

Gordon says quietly, "Your father needs to take you home." He looks around toward where he last saw Rex.

Taking him by his short beard, she guides his head to face her. "Please, Ghee-yome. Let my friend see your pretty face." She smiles at her friend. "I have never in my life seen such a beautiful man, have you?"

Gordon pries her hands away. He looks at the friend, her eyes with too much makeup and her mouth—something going around in her mouth there. Chewing gum. She does not look drunk. Gordon puts Glory's hands in hers. "Don't let her drive," he says gravely.

But somehow Glory's hands are back, stroking him in the area of his ribs, both sides. She whispers sadly, "Ghee-yome, we love you on the mouth and everything be wifey, everybody be wifey. Ghee-yome is a mighty sheik." And she turns to her friend, gives her friend a little shove toward him, saying happily, "Give Shara a kiss. So she will believe she's been here." But of course, already, Shara is blushingly shrinking away.

And Gordon backs away too, goes to find Rex. But Rex is with the stranger, the patriot, who says he once belonged to the Militia of Montana and knows Randy Trochmann and knew the Freemen well. And he has just given Rex his phone number and explains where he lives, which is right here in town, a rented trailer backside of the Wilson farm place. He explains he has some weapons he'd like to show Rex. Sometime. Whenever there's time. He says he's been working a lot of hours in Lewiston. "Mallory Foods."

Gordon tells Rex, "Your girl is here."

Rex turns and looks toward the lighted bay. But it is plain to see that he doesn't really know what to do about Glory. He looks at Gordon and gives him a thin miserable grimace.

 Mickey explains.

So I'm backing the car into the bay. The little black girl that rode along says, "Thank you for a very nice time." And now everybody's laughing over how the car didn't conk out up the road. Somebody goes by and pushes a jar of lemonade at me, big, like a pail of it. There's also beer everywhere. Hard cider. And sissy cider. Apple pies and pans of apple stuff and sugared-up tomato stuff on the workbenches. Dried zucchini things you'd think were potato chips.

A bunch of us are talking. One guy's suggesting we experiment with what's called a microenergy flywheel. It runs on just a pilot-sized flame of cooking gas. The flywheel has to have no friction. And Samantha comes over, and she has her Indian-style rag around her practically white hair. And a pair of little-little shorts. And a red T-shirt with sleeves ripped off. She looks sticky. Arms, face, neck, and bellybutton. Sweet and sticky. She is not one of them carrying pies. Cory's eyes take all this in. Butch Martin's eyes don't seem to get enough.

I can't believe it, her face getting close to my right eye, right ear. It jumps me. It sucks to act so jumpy in this situation. Everybody's laughing loud, almost drowning out what she's whispering in cold lemon breath, her mouth on my ear, man, I mean like *on* my ear. "Thursday. Seven-thirty A.M. pronto. Out front here by the bays. The True Maine Militia hits the statehouse. Be there." She flicks my hair, the tail.

Laugh. Laugh. Laugh. All of them have forgot flywheels and pilots. It's really not that funny that I have a stupid look on my face.

Samantha is already gone into the elbows and stomachs of the crowd, and all I see is wagging dog tails and small kids' crying faces and some guy's beer gut before my brain remembers where I am. Remembers to think. I am not thinking about the statehouse or how she throws orders, man; no, I'm thinking about how to stop thinking about the little-little shorts before it *shows*.

Late P.M. Marty Lees, once a low-ranking member of the Rapid City SWAT team, now just an operative, is back in his rented mobile home, transferred to this Maine situation, transferred *out* of there, due to complications, due to the fuckups of others and some bad turns.

Now, here he is. Oh, boy. Step one, a success.

Needs to get in that militia. Needs to be helpful. Needs to have that York guy stop staring at him like he is mold on dog shit. Needs to sort out the wacky shit from the real shit and why the Bureau thinks the other one, the Big Puppy, St. Onge, is more useful. Don't matter. They say he's dangerous, he's dangerous. We got time. We got all the time in the world. Like watching an ant farm. Watch those guys lift those big grains of sand. Watch 'em grunt. Blow a little air on 'em.

Next meeting of the Border Mountain Militia is in two weeks. No invitation yet. But there *will* be an invitation. Just need to keep being Mr. Charm and Trust Me. Go with the flow. See what turns up. You have to be like an artist. Thunder and lightning? You paint thunder and lightning. You see bananas and grapes in a bowl? You paint bananas and grapes in a bowl. You see scum? You paint scum. It ain't always pretty.

Statehouse, Augusta, Maine.

In the statehouse Hall of Flags, there is a set of stairs that takes you up to the two legislative chambers, the Senate off to the left, the House to the right. These stairs are marble. Very grand.

At the foot of these stairs are benches, for rest or for waiting. Water fountain. Big nice painting in a gold frame of Joshua Chamberlain, Civil War hero and past governor who has a nice bushy mustache. Self-possessed smile—a quiet smile—not the scary big-teeth smiles of today's politicians. To the right of the painting is the governor's office, a door with a frosted glass window. Paper sign says USE OTHER DOOR, with an arrow pointing to the right.

Old and ornate flags stand in glass cases. Flags with gold tassels, flag-staffs, and ornaments made with care and reverence, the way things were made *before progress*. Some of the flags are grayed and stained, by battle and by time. Yeah, war and time. So many lives and home places shattered or worn away. But the flags remain. Some of the flags are state flags. The rich blue. The moose and his lone tree, the word DIRIGO and radiant star above. The farmer and the sailor lean on their scythe and anchor. The moose, he reclines. The moose, the farmer, the sailor all enjoying great leisure, the lie, the leisure lie . . . this that was a lie then and is still a lie today. For what is life but eternal struggle, eternal vigilance, and breathtaking disappointment?

In the middle of the bright cavernous dome area, a bust of Governor Baxter, long dead, famous for his kinship with dogs and his generosity. And over by the windows, several tables are set up in a horseshoe, black backdrops for posters. Here we have some schoolteachers and their prized science students, science projects, the sixteen best of the year, best in the state, best projects, best students, best schools, top shelf. One schoolteacher is blonde and tense. She stands by the platter of dough-nuts donated by a local business for people to munch on while they admire the noteworthy science projects.

Who are the people who will admire the science projects?

Here comes someone now, a nice lobbyist for Corporate America, for a corporation of magnificent proportions, big insurance company or investment firm, paper company or oil company, incinerator or sludge, or maybe tobacco, maybe nuclear waste "management." Who knows? They are all pink-faced and light on their toes, like stars in a Broadway musical. This one says some nice predictable things about a young girl's wind tunnel. Another young girl's Ping-Pong-ball DNA and molecule diorama. He picks up a doughnut, a chocolate one with crunchy stuff on it. And the blond schoolteacher smiles and smiles at him.

A moment later (same place).

What is that clanking and bonking in the distance? And a big BU-
ROOOOM! Sounds like a big drum. Must be something wonderful,
something to do with our esteemed legislature, not in session but in and
about. Maybe some special performance by another best school, best
student, given to our esteemed governor, who has promised to bring lots
more big business to Maine to "help" small business and "revitalize"
Maine's economy.

All the schoolteachers in the sciency horseshoe smile as another fine
pink lobbyist in his smashing and costly three-piece suit selects a doughnut and compliments the bright-eyed A-plus student who has fashioned
wooden balls that represent atoms moments before and after fission.

What *is* that clanking and bonking and big drum sound? Seems to
be getting louder. Maybe it is trouble with the furnace.

A pair of the corporate lobbyists are now standing near the projects,
talking to each other. Their smiles are wide and white and pre-prescribed.
One of them kind of glances in the direction of the stairs that go down
to the lower hallway and the statehouse tunnel that connects the two
main buildings, the mysterious racket drawing very close now, coming up, up, up the stairs. BUROOM! *Clank bonk* BUROOM! *chunka-
chunka chink chink tweedle zzzzzzzzzz clonk!*

Now a distinctive tromp tromp tromp along with the clanks and
bonks and BUROOOOOM!s. And "Hup!" . . . "Hup!" . . . "Hup!"

Several lobbyists now smile in the direction of the mystery. Their
smiles are expectant and contemplative. But the schoolteachers, sixteen in all, stare unsmiling, their eyes narrowed, foreheads pinched,
lips thin. The sixteen best students are so bright-eyed, ready for whatever hits.

It arrives, a great army, each soldier armed with nothing less than a
placard, a small fluttering graveyard-sized American flag, or a set of
spoons, a cowbell, a kazoo, a flute, or a recorder. There is one fiddle and
one sword, lotsa squirt guns. They are flushed, every one, because
the great halls of democracy are, as usual, fossil-fuelishly overheated.
So much sweaty uneven hair. A few soldiers look kind of grimy,
overdressed or barely dressed, bruised, scratched, muscular or rotund,
mouths with stains; some smell of their breakfasts of smoky meat, butter,

and eggs; some smell like live cattle and sheep; and there's a cheery sweet warm lipstick smell from one single source, a face war-painted with zigzags of crimson Avon. A few tricorne hats are worn, or yarn wigs. And plastic caps with ads on front. Several billed army caps, one bush hat. One Civil War kepi, gray. And what's that over there? A billowing but erect orange plume sticking out of a World War Two U.S. Marine helmet. Lots of BDU shirts of forest camo. A doctor's smock. A purple robe with artificial ermine trim resembling what kings used to wear. Several faces painted like skulls. Others painted camo. "Hup! . . . Hup! . . . Hup!"

A few masks. A gorilla. A lion. One boy about age seven is naked to the waist, his body painted red, his face red, his squirt gun not the cute lime-colored plastic kind; his is made of black plastic, an AK-47. Around his head a leather band and ten chicken feathers. Oddly, one child wears a lovely sundress. She is long-legged, with no war paint, just a beautiful face of African-European-American Indian heritage. She carries a placard that reads THROW OUT THE ALIEN GOVERNMENT.

And that was just the little kids. Big drum (BUROOM!) is carried by a strapping older teen who looks part bull, part biker, horns coming from his head (how does he do that?), leather jacket reads HARLEY DAVIDSON across the back and, of course, the wings. Black T-shirt. Ratty jeans. BUROOOM! Several tall girls walk slowly beside him, pacing their steps with the "Hup!" . . . "Hup!" . . . "Hup!" . . . "Hup!" called out by a small soldier. Small soldier in a yellow raincoat and bush hat, her long dark braid over one shoulder decorated in—yes—dozens of chicken feathers.

Isn't that "Hup" . . . "Hup" . . . "Hup" pace a lot like the graduation march the schoolteachers here would approve of?

A preteen girl with a lovely Nordic-looking face has her thick pale hair knotted up in a pink bandanna. She wears camo pants, military boots, and a black jersey with small cardboard messages pinned all over it, messages the teachers can't quite make out. But the full-sized flag on a long rough stick, which a chubby preteen boy totes proudly, is plain to see. Blue with the Maine state seal—moose, farmer, sailor, tree, star— *but* with something extra, big gold lettering across the top: The TRUE MAINE MILITIA.

Most of the schoolteachers behind the horseshoe feel so disapproving, they could faint. But the blonde one, now snorting with disgust, is
energized.

Such a racket! The cowbells. The spoons. Hollow sticks. Big drum.
Fiddle screeling, poorly played. And now what? Three recorders and a
dozen kazoos doing "Yankee Doodle." Small graveyard-sized American flags quiver in the hands of a long single-file line of small fry at the
rear. No, not quite the rear. More militia hurrying to catch up, churning up the stairway, crossing the great room, and then the whole militia angles to the right and heads for the governor's office.

A sea of placards passes. CORPORATIONS OUT, WE THE
PEOPLE IN!!! and NO MORE FUNNY BUSINESS!!! and NO
MORE GRIDS! ABOLISH CORPORATE PERSONHOOD!!! and
WHOSE BUTT IS AMERICA KICKING NOW???!!!! CORPO-
RATE BUTT!!! YOU BET!!! and PETROLEUM TELLS LIES. and
CORPORATISM IS FASCISM. LOOK IT UP!

"This is disgusting!" proclaims the blonde schoolteacher, her eyes on
fire, her lip curled. None of the other teachers can hear her words. Not
with the racket of the militia storming past.

One really cute, chubby, round-faced blond boy, barely out of diapers, runs up to the teacherly assemblage and passes out fluorescent-
orange copies of *The Recipe for Revolution,* or *Recipe,* which lays out the
steps for dismantling corporate power and putting energy, food growing, water, education, and banking into the control of small communi-
ties only, thus "saving the world!"

Two other chubby three-year-olds, one with distinctive Passama-
quoddy looks and a sleek, almost blue-black bowl-shaped haircut, march
past wearing sandwich signs that read (both front and back) SIEGE!
The teenage boy accompanying them waves his sign, which reads: HAVE
A NICE DAY (AFTER THE REVOLUTION). And then two older figures
with skull faces and tricorne hats trudge past with their placards:
SAVE THE REPUBLIC FROM GOVERNMENT CORRUPTION
AND THE CORPORATE GRIDS' GRIP! and DEATH TO THE
CORPORATE PAPER GODZILLA! LIBERTY TO FLESH AND
BLOOD ONLY!! and *BRING BACK OUR COMMONS.*

The blonde schoolteacher reads a couple of lines of the *Recipe* and
sniffs. "What is this drivel?"

Children hand out copies of the same to the corporate lobbyists, who continue to smile and look immeasurably pleased.

Corporate lobbyists are coming down the marble staircase. Corporate lobbyists are slipping out of the governor's office. Corporate lobbyists swarming everywhere, stepping aside to let the sea of children pass, while the faces of these children remain soldierly and grim, arriving at last at the closed door of the governor's office, not the one that reads USE OTHER DOOR but the correct door.

Now the militia halts in its tracks. The "music" stops. Weapons and flags and flyers rustle. Moccasins and boots and sneakers shuffle. A voice from the militia's center hollers, "Shoulder arms!" and the placards rattle and squirt guns are jerked from holsters. The AK-47 is aimed at the governor's door. Flyers rustle. Placards are now raised high. The highest one reads GET THIS CORPORATE MESS OUT OF OUR GOVERNMENT! And another: ONLY HUMAN HUMANS SHOULD HAVE CONSTITUTIONAL RIGHTS! and yet another: THIS IS NOT ABOUT A FEW STOCKS TO LITTLE WIDOWS, THIS IS ABOUT GLOBAL CORPORATE POWER!!! and THE SOVEREIGN (spelled SOVERN) RIGHTS OF THE PEOPLE HAVE BEEN SHIT ON!!! and WE ARE NICE BUT WE AREN'T PUSHOVERS! and CORPORATE CHARTERS ARE NOT DIVINE CONCEPTION.

Waving on the margins of the group are lots of repeats of WHOSE BUTT IS AMERICA KICKING NOW??? CORPORATE BUTT!! YOU BET!!! (a real favorite of preteen boys).

Now the teen boy with the drum (Harley jacket, horns) leans to one side to whisper something to another teenage guy, one with a small yellow tail of hair and inside-out camo BDU shirt, and this guy whispers to a preteen girl and there's some giggling. And now a whispered phrase ripples through the ranks. Meanwhile, a teen girl wearing a beret and camo BDU shirt unrolls a stiff beige scroll and reads loudly: "We are now here at the People's House! The capitol of the state of Maine!" Her young voice echoes down the long halls, against all the marble, glass, bronze, and gold. "The People's House is where we send the people we elect to conduct the affairs of the state on our behalf! This building belongs to the people of the state of Maine!!!"

"Hear! Hear!" calls the husky voice of a midsized skull-faced teen boy.

"Ahoy, mateys!" shouts another.

The reader continues. "The business here is conducted in *our* name! We not only have a right to be here, we have a *responsibility* to be here!"

The whole militia cheers loudly. A few spoons clank. Kazoos buzz tonelessly. One cowbell clanks merrily. American flags wave so exuberantly they appear as pink blurs. Big militia flag dips with solemn emotion.

The door to the governor's office opens an inch. An eye shows. Eye of a lady in a brown dress. Office-looking lady. Door shuts.

A flash. Another flash. The indefatigable Press, three of them, have just appeared from somewhere.

A lot of people stepping out from doors, peering at the scene.

"Where's the governor?" the teen girl with the scroll calls toward the governor's door.

"In bed with the insurance companies!" another teen girl calls back.

"Naughty! Naughty!" someone scolds. And some real little kids sweetly chorus, "Naughty! Naughty! Naughty!"

Other little kids hiss and boo. "The governor is bad! The governor is bad!"

"The governor does not represent *people*!" a teen girl calls. This teen girl, like many of the others, is wearing a camo shirt and black beret. Three bandannas are knotted on the left bicep, one green, one black and white check, like a raceway winner's flag, and one red. (These represent the Earth, the People, and Revolution.) On the right bicep, a black armband, to express Grief.

Again, the teen girl with the scroll calls, "Where's the governor?" She narrows her eyes on the closed door.

A teen boy in head-to-foot camo and a KICK BUTT sign calls in a deep, almost manly voice, "He won't come out! He's chicken!"

"The governor is scared!" calls out one of the oldest girls.

"Why won't the governor come out and talk with his constituency?!!" cries another girl.

"The governor is a corporate slut!" screams the drum-carrying bull-biker.

"Copwat swut! Copwat swut!" chant the littlest kids.

Older ones in deeper resolve yell "Corporate slut! *Corporate slut!* CORPORATE SLUT!" louder and louder and louder.

More people arrive from stairways and doorways, serious and stern mostly, one or two sort of smiling, eyes sparkling with nervous amusement.

A small militia member passes out copies of the *Recipe* as well as a simple flyer, which reads THE ALIEN GOVERNMENT OF INTERNATIONAL FINANCIERS AND DEBT-BASED ECONOMY IS ILLEGAL. THE PROJECT FOR THE NEW AMERICAN CENTURY IS SATAN!

Some soldiers are waving their water guns. None loaded.

A teen girl with beret, camo shirt, various arm decorations—and cornsilk blonde hair—and crisscrossed cartridge belts of .22 shells (no gun), signs up people for membership, mostly the press. "Sign here and we'll send you stuff," she tells one TV reporter and hands him a blue militia card with his name scribbled on it, under the little American flag and bold lettering: THE TRUE MAINE MILITIA. This recruiting officer has a brick-sized bag of these cards with an elastic around them, all ready to go.

A tall red-haired girl with a deformed face wears the camo shirt and bandanna but no bandoliers, and no beret. Her hair is wild and magnificent. On her shoulders rides a year-old toddler, wearing overalls of a print of red hearts and a rabbit-fur trapper hat. Little face under the big hat is smiling and blinking, little hand points in various directions. Little voice trying sincerely to copy everything that's being said or chanted. "Co-putt! Co-putt! Co-putt!"

And the whole militia screams "Corporate slut!" at the governor's door, until, alas, the clerk of the house (a handsome but harried-looking gentleman, almost a Joshua Chamberlain look-alike) arrives with the capitol security, and one or two plainclothes state cops, to usher the militia *out*. But not before all the science exhibition doughnuts have been stuffed into dozens of hungry militia persons' mouths.

   Shortly.

It is starting to rain from a lavender sky. Some yellow and bronze leaves still resist falling down in the park, where nobody walks enjoying America, enjoying freedom.

Water hits pavement but does not make it clean. The water is from the heavens but no blessings are given, not many wanderers at the moment, just a tattery zigzag of kids and young people dressed weirdly, the true motley crew, heading down the east-facing stairs.

Mickey and CC (whose real name is Christian Crocker) and Margo St. Onge (you wouldn't recognize them in face paint resembling grinning skulls) wearing black robes (resembling judges) and a sign written on now-soggy cardboard (under CC's long arm) which reads NO MORE FASCIST PUBLIC SCHOOLS. NO MORE INDOCTRINATION FOR ROBOTONS!

Another unrecognizable individual with cracking, creaking teenage voice jogs to catch up, gasping, "The People's House, huh? (*gasp gasp*) They threw us *out*!"

Mickey, dressed only as his usual musty, woodsy self, offers one of his rare snorts of laughter and now words, even rarer. "It was an honor."

 A letter is sent to the *Record Sun*.

> To the Editor,
>   There was a time when we saw our capitol as a place of reverence and respect. But no more. Sixteen schoolchildren, presenting their prize-winning projects, half of these children representing the highest science scores in the state, and sixteen teachers, including myself, and several aides, representing sixteen schools, had the unfortunate experience of being at the statehouse this week at the same time as the True Maine Militia.
>   This "militia" is a gang of about forty dirty-mouthed, disrespectful, loud children (some old enough to know better). None were dressed appropriately, considering the place. They marched through the halls with toy guns and pointed these guns at the door of the governor's office. Yes, the governor!
>   This was nothing less than criminal behavior in the making. The literature they were distributing was senseless and antibusiness. While our students looked on helplessly, the "militia" ate all the doughnuts that we had on the tables for people who were interested in viewing the science projects. At this point, I must add that a generous corporation donated those doughnuts. The children of the True Maine Militia might take a lesson from this: the generosity of corporations. If it weren't for corporations, we'd

have no jobs! And no wonderful medicines and, yes, so many other important things we take for granted.

But I am afraid that this gang of ill-behaved unchaperoned children will, no doubt, terrorize many more people before someone puts a stop to it. Such unfortunate behavior makes many of us, who have worked hard to raise and educate <u>civil</u> children, wonder what this world is coming to.

Diane Barteaux
Gardiner, Maine

 A follow-up meeting of the True Maine Militia in the East Parlor, a dictionary and three thesauruses opened on various laps.

"Okay," Samantha says, "*corporate slut* has got to go. No more of that."

Pages flap softly. Margo taps a pen against her knee. "How about corporate suckling?"

The answer is several scrinched faces.

Bree laughs. "I love this."

Kirky asks, "Where exactly are you guys looking, anyways?"

"Right here." Alyson Lessard leans toward him with her tattered thesaurus. He thumbs through his, finally matching her page.

Erin offers, "How about corporate fawner or corporate sycophant or corporate truckler?"

"How about corporate *boot . . . lick . . . er?*" Jane reads, she and Tabitha hunching together over one thesaurus, Tabitha's finger pressed hard to a spot on the page.

Another offering, this by Gabe. "Corporate lady of the night?"

"Corporate harlot," offers Christian Crocker grimly.

Young Sigh St. Onge snorts with appreciation. Mickey smiles thinly, chin up. Mickey is here. Yes, Mickey . . . is . . . here.

"Corporate daughter of joy," adds Christian Crocker.

"Corporate toady," suggests Kendra.

Whitney says gloomily, "Whatever you come up with, it'll make some people mad. Might's well go with corporate slut."

"Right! It's gotta be that *we* like it."

"I like it. *Slut,*" says Carmel softly.

Margo says firmly, "As long as it is true."

Michelle agrees. "Yeah, true."

A lot of nods.

Kirk stands up, closes his thesaurus. "So let's leave it be corporate slut. If we spell it right, isn't that all that matters?"

Jane leans on her chair arm and says in a tone of finality, "Just make sure it's spelled right, and that's that."

A bit later, Mickey tells us.

I'm not really into this, just trying to keep an eye on things and help them feel like a real militia. The next so-called militia thing they're scheming up is—heh-heh! I try to picture Cap'n Rex's militia doing this and I almost crack up out loud. Here it is. A birthday party for a hundred-year-old lady combined with a rally where they say two thousand people will show up—heh-heh, no shit, two thousand—and sing songs with drawings on the song sheets of this big mole thing, which is supposed to be Bigfoot, called the Abominable Hairy Patriot.

They even think they can get a band, some relatives of the Prophet, buncha Frenchmen playing accordions. And everybody will dance—all two thousand—and listen to speeches by the officers about the New World Order and FEMA and centralized banking—which is stuff Rex would definitely be interested in—but also corporate charters and food shortages worldwide, clean-water shortages, CIA drug dealing, and CIA terror on the world, and petroleum price manipulations, and they say petroleum "is everything, even fertilizers for agribiz." And they want to talk about global warming to the two thousand people, and why it is our duty to speak out and *do something*. And when they say *do something,* the older girls sort of hop. Like cheerleaders.

"Because," whimpers Michelle, one of the Prophet's oldest daughters, "the financiers who own our government are taking over the world."

"It's called corporatism," says one very pink chubby little squirt who has to take his thumb out of his mouth to say this word.

Bree, with the hair like red snakes and eyes far apart who is the artist of the mole things, hugs the little guy and that squeezes more out of him. "Mussolini said it. Fascism and corporatism are perfect and the same."

Bree laughs, silentlike, with her head turned toward the others. Everyone thinks the kid is cute. But I am thinking how they all talk just like the Prophet. Probably those over a day old don't suck on bottles. They just talk.

Samantha, who is wearing a desert camo BDU shirt, earrings, olive-drab army pants—the bushy World War One kind for maybe riding a mule—and skinhead boots and her usual hot-babe expression, hollers out, "Op-ed time again!" and raises a fist. With her, everything is a fist.

The small Indian kid they call Dragan squeaks, "Can I do a speech there too? I know Moose-leeny."

The girls are hiding more laughs.

When I reach for my cigs, I realize I've already got one in my mouth.

Late P.M. Marty Lees slouched on the couch of his rented trailer, thinking, Pepsi in hand.

Paid a social call on York this evening at his home. Lives with his mommy. *Tsk*.

Talked "patriot." Talked New World Order. Talked martial law. Talked weapons. Talked the talk. *I* talked. The son of a bitch mostly just stared at me like he was a paid therapist and I was emotionally out of whack. So okay, no Border Mountain Militia invite yet.

I'd like to do something to the son of a bitch's eyes, like make them cry. But not yet. First I want to *help* him. Help him and his buddies get real. Help him with his goals. I just gotta keep being everything he ever wanted in a friend. And showing my incredible capabilities. My possibilities. His possibilities. To show him the difference between a mommy militia and an honorable one.

Down at the old farm place, where the only phone for everyone is, Jane holds the pre-1990s-style receiver to her ear.

She isn't speaking presently, just listening, her brown floofy curly hair in a Settlement-made hair clip of painted beads, beans, and acorns glued onto cardboard. She and Lisa have had countless phone calls such as this, the phone voices miniature, due to wires and plastic, due to the miles. She keeps her face away from the room where others stand. She listens to the voice, miniaturized but also, yes, faltering and worn down. Her mother.

In this moment, Jane is not losing control. No screams and wails. What is it you call it when the blur and belled-out tears won't break free of the little pools, one pool to each eye?

Finally, Jane speaks. "Mum. What about me? Tell them." She has said this feebly, due to her new A-plus understanding of how it is that nothing spoken matters to *the law*.

She listens to the reply. She listens, listens, listens. Finally, the tears swish free. They explore in a zigzaggy way down her impossibly soft cheeks. "Mum. That doesn't matter. I *need* you."

☆ **Penny St. Onge remembers well when the announcement was made.**

Flyers were flying into the mail and onto telephone poles around town and out past the bridge, and even on the way to Portland or Lewiston, those routes to schoolesque field trips.

There were a few quick phone calls.

Nobody asked Gordon or any of us old fogies for permission. We were just advised that this would be a "spectacular event." Quite a few of the elders and some mothers—*most* of the mothers—and some dads were asked to serve on planning committees.

This would be a public meeting of the True Maine Militia, also serving as a one-hundredth-birthday party for our beloved Annie Brody ("Annie B").

Gordon didn't throw a fit this time, though some expected it. He and Rex and the Border Mountain guys were just getting back from visiting a militia in Mass. When Gail and Lorraine showed him the flyer, he just behaved pleasantly. Pleasant and, yes, pale.

So the plan was to have the gate open on *the day* and the unneighborly YOU'LL BE SHOT sign taken down. Instead, there'd be a welcoming crew at the new little guard house (which was actually John Lungren's fishing shack). As prospective rallyers came through, they'd be handed information flyers and song sheets.

A letter-writing committee sent off a plea to Gordon's Aroostook relatives who play in the Band from THE County. Picture an Acadian-rock mix and you've got it. Music to dance by.

The Build-a-Stage Committee was rounded up. The Giant Cake Committee. Crews for the cooks. Five Clean-up Crews. First Aid Crew. Skits and sing-alongs were planned. More True Maine Militia membership cards were manufactured.

And, of course, a big op-ed is mailed off to the *Record Sun*.

Late morning. *Record Sun* reporter Ivy Morelli hurries into the City Room.

There is a note on her desk from Brian Fitch, her editor. Also a flyer, made by an old-fashioned printer and touched up with crayons.

The flyer is the public invitation to the True Maine Militia meeting at the Settlement in Egypt on Saturday, which will be combined with a one-hundredth-birthday celebration for Annie Brody.

Everybody welcome! Bring a dish or salad or bread or dessert. If you aren't much of a cook, bring chips or just bring yourself. There will be music by the Band from THE County, from Eagle Lake and Frenchville, for you to shake a leg by.

In one prominent corner of the flyer there is the Abominable Hairy Patriot (Bigfoot in white winter coat) standing on a mountaintop with a look of Don't-mess-with-me, hands on hips, legs apart. And there is a cartoon version of an old lady who has the same Don't-mess-with-me expression, and a polka-dot dress. And see the personal details about her life written in footnote.

Don't miss this IMPORTANT EVENT if you love old ladies and you love America.

P.S. We will be having an official firing of the official True Maine Militia cannon. So don't miss that!

Let's get ready for the Million Man Woman Kid Dog March!

There are directions to the Settlement, time and date. No rain date. Ivy lays this on her desk and picks up Brian's note.

> *Ivy, yes, we are going with this. Op-ed page and one photo. Bangor's using it too. Everybody is going to be there when those gates come down: local, New England, national. Big media free-for-all. It'll eat those St. Onge people up. Those gun-toting kids are damn cute. One can only imagine the angle on this that will surface. Sheesh.*
> *Just thought you might like the flyer for your mementos.*

Then Brian has drawn the really goofy smiling face that serves as his signature.

S.A. Kashmar finds some really fascinating communications on the Internet.

"Okay, Pretty Boy, I like your style," he declares, then drawling out the name that fills nearly every line of print on the screen. Another agent, Sears, standing behind him, twists open his little shapely bottle of cran-apple juice and says, "Kentucky, aye? Weren't they in the Berkshires last week? These were seventy-seven-year-old white supremacists in Adams. But everything else St. Onge is about is like an afternoon with Mister Rogers." He laughs through his nose.

Kashmar reaches for a printout sheet on his other desk. "I just can't figure him. It's like watching a three-headed billygoat."

"What's this?"

"The satellite one?" He stretches his head to check.

"Yuh."

"That's the place. Study it. We're going to be there when they open that gate. Meanwhile, we've got to get Lees into that militia. These Maine guys need a goal. Something more specific and—uh—more manly than birthday parties for old ladies and cartoon newsletters by little kiddies. And visits to half-dead old white supremacists who just want to talk about sore feet."

"I agree with you one hundred percent."

♡♡ **Secret Agent Jane, almost seven, tells us about her heart-to-heart talk with scarlet-haired fifteen-year-old Bree St. Onge.**

Bree is sometimes my best friend. You would think it would be hard to have a horror-faced person for a best friend, but it's not. I feel sorry for Bree because she will probably not ever get men and she'll never be famous. But if you look at her face a certain way, you can see she looks just like a kitty.

I say, "I still love him. It's worse now."

Bree and I always talk about men. She doesn't mind. But probably inside she minds. She asks me, "What did you two talk about on your starlight ride?"

"Nothing."

"Nothing?"

"Well, we had a flashlight and fixed the chart thing."

"But nothing else?"

I shrug. Bree and I are doing the copy machine for the song things people will sing about scary stuff at Annie B's party. The stuff of the horridable world. She flaps the paper funny before she pushes it in the tray. She says, "Maybe you need to love a guy who talks."

"No, I still love Mickey. I always will."

"You loved him at first sight."

"Yes." I sigh. "But he smokes."

"He'll be sorry someday. It's yukky," Bree says. She herself smokes. Everybody knows it.

"Cigarettes make you have chemotherapy."

"Yes," she says. She presses the button, and the papers start to print. She turns and smiles, her cat face happy. "I have a test for you."

"Oh, no."

"About Mickey," she says, big smile.

I laugh.

"What color are his eyes? *Exactly,* now. Let's see how good your powers of observation are."

"I can't remember."

"Notice next time."

"I notice mostly his clothes." I wrinkle my nose. "He should really fix his clothes better."

"Well, when you get married in a few years, you can fix him the way you like." She kind of laughs funny.

I say, "I will."

"And kissing," she says. "You can kiss for hours."

I get embarrassed just a little.

"Jane and Mickey, sitting in a tree, K.I.S.S.I.N.G."

"Shut up or I'll die."

Bree makes a *smeeerch!* kissing noise with her lips.

"Stop it, Bree! I mean it!"

When we are done with the paper stuff, we both squash our faces on the glass. You do this and push the button and the light slides by your eyes and you get a picture of your face. We also do hands. Once we tried doing a leaf and a flower but they didn't come out. Bree says, "Watch this." She takes off this pretty red sash thing she wears and puts it on the glass. It comes out weird and black. "Well, *that* didn't work." Bree sighs. "But experimenting is fun, isn't it?"

Now we do our faces *shrunk,* which there is a button for. And now some tiny shrunk hands. And now *huge* hands. We laugh and laugh.

Rex afraid.

It is *that* dream again. The one he's had once or twice a month for a couple years now, various variations on the theme where his home is covered with ants. All the exterior of his home—roof, walls, windows—is a carpet of ants, ants the size of squirrels. He keeps his eyes closed and doesn't move because if he moves, the *worst,* the *unspeakable,* will happen.

Click click click click click; he hears the thousands of shell-like feet scurrying all over the clapboards.

Tonight he, in his dream, opens his eyes and sees through a window at least forty of them staring in at him, their heads floating on stick necks but their eyes more human than bug.

He howls, a metal-to-metal sound, climbing his throat and dead tongue, a siren of the night, warning the others. *What* others? He is alone, the only survivor.

Late evening, just before the Big Day.

Hearing voices behind him, Gordon turns on the path between the St. Onge farm place and the Settlement, snaps off his flashlight, waits. He yanks his bandanna from his pocket, works it around in his nose, looks up at the stars through the leaves. It is his cousin-in-law Ray Pinette's voice he hears coming closer, the voice of a big thick-necked man, though Ray is a short guy but, yes, thick-necked, broad-shouldered, bulky. Ray is beaming his flashlight over the rooty path, and there is a young woman trudging along with him, who speaks a few soft words.

When they discover Gordon standing there, Ray complains predictably. "Jesus, you are harder to find than a dollar."

Gordon tries to make out the woman's face in the dark, lit only in outlines by the flashlights pointed at the ground. She is young. A little familiar. Somebody from town.

"She's looking for Mickey," Ray says. "She was parked down by the gate when I was coming in. I could tell she wasn't a TV crew." He chuckles. "So where *is* Mickey?"

The young woman wears a T-shirt with the face of a Persian cat on the chest, sweater under one arm, little shoulder bag there. She is a plump pink-cheeked brown-haired girl no more than twenty-three or twenty-four.

Gordon sees in her face *the look*. Fear. Surrender. *Help me*. He reaches out a hand. She reaches out her hand. Her fingers fold around his thumb. He says, "You're Donnie Locke's wife."

Her reply is a sob, eyes squeezed shut, still gripping his thumb. He takes her into his arms, doing the possible thing, in lieu of all that can never be possible, his desire to erase all suffering.

☆ **From a future time, Glennice St. Onge, devoted churchgoer, remembers.**

Gordon was a pure saint.

🏚 **Rex's dream crescendo.**

The *click click click* of ant feet is almost like crackles of fire. Yes! Like fire. And the smell of it, fire dry, sky weedy-humid. Thousands of stiff feet, marching all over his home, now soft feet, slippered feet, sneaking, whispering past, up and all over his home.

But also, yes, fire, just fire, the ants lost in the incredible past. And now explosions, a thousand explosions inside a thousand more. He hears wailing, the squalls of infants, smells blood and more burning.

He crawls ever so slowly from where he lies, the heavy humidity dripping while he, Rex, feels heavy as ice. Another crisp body, left behind in its entirety, or was it just a hand, just a burger-dried black bone of the leg? All humans here small as children. Tiny cries. Tiny terror. Tiny grief. But replacing themselves. A hundred-hundred more. And why? They are not invincible, he was advised. *Boom!* Another rocket. *Boom!* A collapsing wall.

He is not hurt. He is perfectly perfect, crawling through the doorway into a safer zone of the universe, less humid, dearly dry, and yet a prenatal place large enough for a medium-sized man.

Suddenly he can see his home from a mile away. Why is it so dinky? Is it so small maybe because of distance? But also because Gordon is standing beside it and he is so huge, his head is up there with the sun! And he is waving his arms in goofball fashion, and Rex is trying so so so hard to yell *quit it!!!!!* but Rex can't get out any voice at all, just a miserable little moan, like a wooden ball in his neck. Gordon is now stumbling, falling. His million tons of flesh are falling. Rex screams. He's actually and really sitting up in bed when he is finally awake, heart pounding, his mother Ruth in the hall, "Ricky? You okay?"

👁 FBI operative Marty Lees is up before dawn.

He munches on Cheerios. Cheerios in the bowl. Picture of Cheerios on the box, and there's two boxes of other stuff. Flakes and chocolate puffs. He reads one box, ingredients, daily minimum requirements, bar code, and things you can send away for. Outer-space killers with guns that kill with light. Don't hurt so much. Ain't that cute?

Checks clock. Thinks of the day ahead. The whole St. Onge dog-and-pony show. Birthday party and kiddies' militia. Cute girlies in army boots. Speeches. Singing. A country-rock-folksy band with a buncha Frenchmen. Whatever.

Special Agent Kevin Moore prepares.

This is a different person from Marty Lees, aka Gary Larch. He leans toward the mirror to inspect the bleeding nick on his chin and sees how wide and expressionless his eyes look in this dim light, this bedroom where his new wife, Tara, still sleeps. His baseball cap reads SEA DOGS, the Maine team. He smiles a big smile.

See, I'm a nice guy. I'm one of you. A neighbor—sort of—give or take a hundred miles. Well, you know, Maine is big. But see, I'm just a guy. I talk like you.

Just a young feller with fresh blond honest looks. Probably *A*s in school. Probably wouldn't hurt a fly. Probably loves his new bride. Probably remembers his mother on Mother's Day. Sure! This is all true! There is nothing really to pretend, except his name and his game. Today should be easy. Fun, in fact. Just his eyes. Eyes open. Just instincts. Just charting the course.

Lyn Potter. Yet another agent?

Actually, he's just an operative, no bennies, no recognition, no face, a nonexistent sort of guy, you might say. Just a black line in the text of your dossier.

Wheaties. You eat 'em fast and they don't get soggy. Supposed to be a lotta really good food at the St. Onge thing. Good. Eat their food, then see 'em in court. Good food doesn't make 'em good Americans.

Glory.

Daddy screamed in the night. One of his nightmares. And that got Gram up.

Glory's hangover screamed too. Not a scream of the mouth, just a scream of one's total existence.

But then all was again quiet and she dozed. Now again, a scream. Not his but hers. Yeah, all of her cells ripping free of the 80-proof vodka.

She opens one eye. The clock isn't there. Where is it? On the floor. She can tell by the dimness of the room it is nowhere near time to get up anyway.

♡♡ **Secret Agent Jane.**

Everyone says, "Put on your best dress."

Okay. And now I practice in the mirror the look for my face. Special and sexy. But now I try my secret heart-shapes glasses, which maybe look a little geeky—which I heard Kirky actually say, *Jane's glasses are so geeky*. But they have power. Okay. I think maybe I need to see what's really going on. I can't tell what's really going on. Maybe *nobody* knows what's really going on. Everybody is acting crazy. But with these glasses, I will be able to see what no one else sees. It is important to know people's thoughts.

🏠 **Early Saturday A.M. Settlement parking lot.**

Mickey slows the solar buggy and drops his feet to the dirt, his sneaker toes dragging. Waves the other guys on. He is looking through the frizzy dawn light at a car he does not recognize, at a face he does recognize. Car backseat heaped with stuff, hard to make out what. Looks like a small mountain chain. The face is his mother's.

He snaps off his headlight and kills the motor, the funny weak re-frigerator sound, the source that causes so much here at the Settlement to move, beam, or make toast.

In the silence her soft voice is everything. "Mickey." Her false teeth show. Not a smile.

There are feet running, hopping. He turns on the seat, lifting one leg off the machine as Erika and his sister Elizabeth arrive, huffing and exclaiming.

"See, Mum, he's not dead!" This is Elizabeth.

"I knew he wasn't dead," Britta says simply. He sees she is wearing her old-lady blue sweater but has a girlish barrette in her hair. She has changed her hairdo to be more like Erika's.

"She acted like you were dead," Erika says, smiling.

Britta is looking at the solar buggy.

Erika is pulling at Mickey's sleeve. "Hey, little brother. You're older."

Sounds like a flock of going-south birds, honking back and forth in the sky. But it's coming through the parked cars from the quad of trees.

Erika has wrapped both arms around him. "Not even a little bit dead," she whispers, like a secret in his ear. A choky whisper filled with the sorrow of other losses. He sees, over around her ear and her brown wing of hair, that the honking, hooting flock is his nieces, Donnie's girls, the girl gang.

Still hanging on to him, Erika says, "We can't keep the house. Mr. St. Onge says they'll make us a cottage here. It's been real bad, Mickey."

Micky says, "I'm sorry."

Erika is smiling at him in a funny way. "For what?"

He shrugs.

Britta's eyes rise up to his face again in that sneaking-up-on-you way she has. He believes her if she says she knew he wasn't dead. His mother never lies. But wasn't he dead there for a while, even to himself?

She steals another glance right into his eyes. She has this really mushy look. Like she just found him out, all his worst crimes and fuckups, then erased them totally. Some type of Mother Power. Even a mother like her has it. It's like now he's just all pudgy and little and new. A perfect baby. Clean. It's embarrassing. But an old and tired piece of him likes it.

Before noon on a perfect October day. The True Maine Militia prevails once again.

Three hundred cars and trucks, it is said.

Leona St. Onge and Claire St. Onge are side by side in the doorway to the kitchens. Leona (yes, a wife of Gordon's *and* a cousin to Claire) says with a snort, "You're not surprised, are you?"

Claire answers gravely, "No, I'm not surprised. I only pray that our system for keeping track of the kids works."

Both Leona and Claire wear the red sashes embroidered with flowers and suns. The power of the red sashes, like the warmth of a sisterly embrace. The power of their shared beliefs.

Behind them on a narrow table are several thirty-cup coffeemakers, their red and amber lights glowing. Eddie Martin (married to one of Gordon's cousins) squats there, fiddling with the plug of one of those borrowed from Glennice's church, or it might be the one borrowed from the Mason hall, Crosman Lodge. Eddie is all spiffed up, wearing his jazzy belt of studs and coins and fake jewels. His T-shirt reads WHITE

STAR LINE TITANIC CREW on front and, on the back, MAIDEN VOYAGE HMS TITANIC 1912. And, though you might not notice with his pant legs out over them, new black military boots.

People are everywhere, streaming across the Settlement parking lot, bunched around on the grassy quadrangle and on the porches, still coming up the sloping gravel road. Each minute brings another batch of new faces, and more food, six-packs, or plastic liters of soda. Tables are set up on porches all the way around the horseshoe, out under the trees in the spotty shade and occasionally cascading yellowy leaves, and out in that wide-open sunshine.

Remember Bree, red hair and deformed face? The Vandermasts are her family. They fill up one table: the older brother, married with a big batch of kids and stepkids—all tall, handsomely dressed children, some visiting friends at other tables, relations of their mother's—and Bree's father's girlfriend's people, some of whom visit the Vandermasts' table; and Bree's father sits under a tree with a cup of cider, watching everything. See his raised proud chin and tiredly pleased blue eyes? By the way, where is Bree? Last seen whispering to some of the other officers of the True Maine Militia.

Strangers are taking photos of the sign that now hangs over the door to one of the parlors, a Mark Twain quote: *I never let my schooling interfere with my education.*

Gordon is loud. There is no music yet, but he is dancing the Highland Fling, the cancan, the twist, the Charleston, and a few hold-'em-close waltzes with everybody in sight. And, of course, as Swamp Monster he has devoured a few small screaming tender children. Gordon has only started to drink, so it can't all be blamed on drink. Maybe overtiredness. Gordon, like most of the Settlement people, was up late with preparations, then rose at quarter to four A.M.

Inside a shady porch, a smiling group of retirement-age visitors, men and women, dressed in schoolteacheresque leisure outfits, are comfortably seated and munching. One asks, "What is this green leafy veggie? Tastes like peanuts, only kind of bitter."

"I don't know. But they grow everything here. Things you never heard of."

"Did you try those yet?"

"Yes, they're chocolate biscuits, kind of. You're supposed to put a sauce over them, but I don't see the sauce. Someone took it. It *was* right here."

Suddenly a nearby chair shivers. Easy to see it is a small white flat-faced curly-tailed dog, who is dripping and smells strongly of a body of water that never circulates. He springs to the table, snatches a crispy chicken leg from an unguarded plate, and then, in a side-to-side Charlie Chaplin gait, stepping in platters and saucepans and overturning cups, crosses to the opposite side of the table, lands in the lap of a gasping visitor, hops down onto the floor, among many feet, and away.

"Isn't that something," says one of the retirement-age visitors, gripping his own plate protectively.

 Meanwhile.

Gordon walks among the people now, a little sedately, less playful, the dapply light of the horseshoe of porches and the Quad runs like mice over his face and now flutters onto one sleeve of his new plaid shirt, a plaid of greens with an occasional intersecting red thread, a well-made Settlement-made shirt. And that leafy light stirs in such heavenly sweetness on these people who surround him, older couples, bikers in black, fashion-dressed gangs of youths, quiet groups of working men, possibly patriots, possibly not, so many strangers, but some you would recognize from town, and there are a sprinkling of liberal-looking older women in pairs or trios with their handsome Cleopatra haircuts or boy cuts and perfect teeth. And Gordon overhears that standing nearby is a Unitarian Universalist minister. But these days it's hard to tell who is a minister and who is not. No clerical collars, no big crosses, no Bible in hand.

Gordon introduces himself to a family, a husband and wife, both blond, both pink-cheeked, and their baby and little girl, also blonde and pink-cheeked. The father is missing a front tooth but not afraid to smile and yak. The wife's hair is a punk cut. She is friendly but not yakky. Gordon rests his hand on the little girl's head. As it is so often with kids, her warm skull and soft hair yearn upward against his hand. In his other hand, a beer, a dark and dear Canadian brand brought here by visitors.

Two vans are now backing slowly through the crowd, stopping flush with the high, very new, very temporary plywood stage at the end of the last piazza on the south side of the horseshoe. Now there is the unloading of instruments, fiddle-shaped and guitar-shaped cases, a base fiddle case, and a sax. Three accordions. Some drums. A diaper bag. And a baby.

The vans are splattered with purple and lime-green fleurs de lis, yellow musical notes, and, in big print, THE BAND FROM THE COUNTY.

One musician looks spookily like Aurel Soucier, same glittering intense dark eyes and long nose but such a long bony body, more like that weasel physique of Louis St. Onge (Lou-EE, yes). But *this* guy wears a white smock with blousy sleeves, a red sash, and a French-of-the-past sort of shirt: The *habitant.*

Several men, three women. One woman wears cowgirl boots and a red dress, red lipstick. Heavyset. Her laugh is loud and as lovely and complicated as the liquidy solo of a hermit thrush.

One guy is in his early fifties. Splotchy, almost boyishly soft dark beard. Fit-looking in red T-shirt and jeans. His T-shirt features a picture of three chimps. One chimp holds binoculars to his eyes. The second chimp has his hands cupped around his ears for better hearing. The third chimp is speechifying through a megaphone.

A crowd of teenagers closes in around the vans.

The guy with the Evil Chimps T-shirt screams hoarsely across the nearest long train of piazzas to Raymond Pinette, *"Tout l'mondes, là—ah! ah!—je vais renvoyer! J'ai trop gêné, moi! Je vais tomber mort!"*

Ray Pinette screams back, *"Ah, fermes ta yueule,* Monsieur Show-off!"

A lot of girls make up the teenage swarm. Teen boys too, who try not to seem too interested. They look as if they just happened to be there, just passing through.

Out in the sun, away from the trees, it seems the whole Letourneau family is here from across town, taking up *many many* tables, looking settled and happy and now extremely alert to these new arrivals, all heads turned toward the vans, hearing Acadian patois spoken. And Norman Letourneau, cleft palate and wild dark eyes, party animal in his own right, screams something in his French that even these French can't understand, and now the musician in the red dress and red lipstick calls something to Norman in French, hard to make out because she's also throwing him kisses, and now in English, "Get your dancing shoes on, my dearest!"

More drums are unloaded from the second van.

People are still hiking up the dusty Settlement road. But for a few, no cars are allowed. Gatekeepers are assisting visitors with parking down along the paved Heart's Content Road, and it is reported that these cars now line that narrow road for at least a mile.

The musicians scurry around on stage, setting up a sound system that looks earnest enough to knock anyone over who stands within a hundred yards of it.

A Settlement preteen girl in a long blue peasant dress and bare feet, with hair like cornsilk, longer and silkier than that of Mickey Gammon's dream girl, Samantha Butler, hair almost to her heels, starts an eager jerk of the hips.

"I know this band. They mean business," troll-like Stuart Congdon (the Settlement's head sawyer) tells some visitors with a chuckle. "This whole place is going to be dancing, even those who don't want to. To try 'n' hold still, it would hurt."

📖 History (1819: the past), weavers of Halifax, England.

"We groan, being burdened, waiting to be delivered, we rejoice in hopes of Jubilee."

🏚 Gordon St. Onge: they come to him.

The man who is approaching Gordon now on these long connected piazzas has a thin funeralesque voice, as though remembering a long-gone friend. But his woes concern recent and complex Maine fishing laws. Gordon agrees it is a bad mess.

"Liberty and justice for all, ha-ha," says the man.

Gordon glances into the solemn eyes of three teens next to the shoulder of the sorrowful man. The man goes on. "A lie and a figment."

Gordon replies, "I agree." And his eyes skip a moment to more young guys who are closing in, all in billed caps bearing ads, then to the fifteen or twenty faces of strangers and Egypt neighbors ringed around, and then another half dozen beyond, all staring. Gordon sees a vision of each and every one of those mouths eating a fish from Lange Pond and Spec Pond—this sudden uneasy epiphany: mouths, esophaguses, and bubbling stomachs of a whole planet of shoulder-to-shoulder people—and one last fish, hiding. He sees, yes, *his* children, their hunger, their fingers grasping.

He pushes the thought away. He calls the big quiet dark-eyed man "My brother."

Eventually, he reaches the end of the last piazza, temporarily connected to the high stage, little temporary set of stairs there, going up. So good to see his old friends and distant cousins from Aroostook, THE County. They don't seem at all tired from their six-hour ride. He embraces them all. Now a smooch or three. Some yowls. Then he chats with them, catches up on some things, swept happily along in that cheery hoarse back-of-the-throat Acadian-English mix; then, seeing they have much more setting up to do, tuning, revving up, he turns and sees Rex.

Rex has been standing behind him for how long? There with his thumbs in his belt, feet spread, boots shined, the whole nine yards of military bearing, but no uniform, no cap, just a rust-brown T-shirt and work pants. And no dark cop glasses at the moment. His cold gray-blue eyes have an odd circumspection. As if he wore earphones and was listening to the instructions of a militia dispatcher who is conveying information from militia pilots in choppers or towers, people who have a clear overhead view of the awful, surging, unbraiding mob that is filling up the roads, the Quad, the yards and fields of the St. Onge Settlement.

Gordon raises one eyebrow and gives Rex's shoulder a little hello poke, a shoulder like a rock which, under the brown T-shirt, doesn't give. Rex brings his right hand around and gives Gordon a slip of paper. "I got a call. She was looking for Mickey. His brother's widow, I think. She wasn't doing very well, her and the others there. Upset. I couldn't really make her out much. She wants him to come home and talk or something." He looks down along the length of connected piazzas, open porches, and boardwalks crammed with humanity, the loud drone of voices making him have to talk louder than he likes to. "She was . . . upset. Crying."

Gordon holds the note way out from his face, squints at it. It reads: *Call Erika. Important.* He looks over shoulders and heads and hats into the faces of strangers who are passing by; they are watching him hard from the corners of their eyes. He glances out at the Quad, where there are more and more layers of strangers pressing in, with and without covered dishes, paper bags, and liters of pop. He studies the note again. "This message. It must have been before nine P.M. last night."

"Six-twenty."

"Yuh . . . well. She found us."

Rex nods.

Gordon squint-blinks. Then smiles. "Well." He stuffs the note into a pocket. "She's safe now."

Rex works his lips a bit, like they itch. Then a small snort that means *it figures: one more needy soul.* Maybe even *one more wife. What else is new?*

Gordon asks, "You just the bearer of emergency communiqués? Or are you planning to hang out awhile and maybe . . . meet some nice women?"

Rex flushes. Then a trace of a twinkle skips across the cold eyes. "You mean all these women aren't yours?" Nods toward the crowd, which anyone can plainly see contains over four hundred people, about half of them women.

Vastly, Gordon smiles. He gets real close to Rex, closeness not being Rex's favorite thing, and speaks in a low voice. "Brother, I envy you."

Rex looks away. Rex does not envy Rex. Nor does he envy Gordon. Rex considers both situations deeply flawed.

Gordon and Rex stand there at the screen now and watch more faces coming around from beyond the larger Quonset hut, from the parking lot and road.

Rex says, "I expect you've got a few agents out there."

Gordon tries not to smile at this. "Richard, agents go to meetings of *real* militias. Secret meetings. This is . . . so . . . so wholesome . . . so public."

"Don't matter. You can tell after a while when you got them. They'll try to stir the crowd up . . . agitate . . . or hang out with you and others in charge, win your trust, turn people against you, get you to . . . break a law. It's called neutralizing leadership and entrapment. They do it all."

Gordon squints at this. "When it's in the public debate, you get assent and dissent . . . each side will work real hard to twist the other one's arm for or against. People just naturally make their own trouble."

"You're not making sense. I'm talking about Feds."

"I know what you're talking about."

Rex squints. "You don't have to listen to me if you don't want. Go read your Socialist Commie books for the answers. They know it all."

Gordon grabs a lemon chewy bar off a plate and stuffs it in his mouth.

Claire, her graying black hair worn in a long braid down her back, graceful and rotund as a bubble in her green cotton dress and red sash, passes with a group of women strangers, her voice like a tour guide's, like a professor, her well-projected, sometimes commanding, sometimes breezy voice.

And then.

Out among the tables, under the trees, under the slant of early October sun, reporters scribble away.

"So why are you here today?" a reporter asks a visitor.

"To see what's going on."

"You here to join the militia?"

"Sure."

"Aren't you worried about the reputation of militias?"

"Not really. This ain't like that. This is all of us. Just people. Kids, even."

"Have you heard Gordon St. Onge called the Prophet?"

"Yuh."

"What do you think of that?"

"Pretty weird."

"It doesn't bother you?"

Shrug. "Nobody's perfect."

Strangers stride through the crowd passing out flyers on the U.S. government's role in the massacre of one-third of the East Timor population. Other flyers on Cuba, Iraq, Uganda, Sudan, Chiapas, Guatemala, and Yugoslavia. Colombia. Stealing and plunder. On and on. Bad America, bad.

The Unitarian Universalist minister, accompanied by a friend, chats politics under a tree with a tall thin man in a white shirt and a Maine Greens button.

The band continues to unload and set up.

Gordon speaks in a muffled way.

"Well, I can tell you one thing, Richard." He's munching on his fifth lemon chewy. "There're Commies here. The place is crawling with 'em. Socialists, at least." His teasing eyes hover on the tree-furry crown of the near mountain.

Rex squints. "No doubt."

Gordon draws his face against his upper arm, cleaning his whiskers and mustache on his sleeve. Then, with raised chin, a little smile, eyes on the growing crowd, he says, "Democracy. She's beautiful."

Rex glowers.

 Meanwhile.

Louis St. Onge backs his little yellow seventeen-year-old pickup across the weeds to a high spot behind the Quonsets. He is preparing to unload his cannon, which is about the size of a huge man's thigh but weighs as much as a whole huge man. Its carriage is oak, four small oak wheels, a bore the size of a camera film canister—small for a cannon. But the boom will impress you. It will be heard for miles.

 Bree ignores Gordon.

She steps up onto the piazza where he stands with Rex. She is just passing by, *his* Bree. Intent on something. Her red hair is thick and fresh and savage. Black Settlement-made T-shirt, a full bright skirt that almost reaches her heels, a red sash, and today a necklace, a fleet of little ships and boats, carved from wood. All stained in the grain, sea blue. She doesn't look at Gordon at all.

She is fully and totally and completely mad at him. *Sigh*. Because *he* was mad at *her*. Just this A.M., he had almost sobbed. Red light. Green light. Red light. Green light. Truly. And it is because he, Gordon St. Onge, is all talk, no action. And Bree, genius with oil paints and ink, frisky with words and thoughts, a reader of even more cinderblock-sized books than he is, is *action*. *She* was the one! *She* organized the True Maine Militia. *She* did the op-eds. Gordon St. Onge, crawling like a worm on his belly, while fifteen-year-old Brianna Vandermast St. Onge holds an almost visible torch aloft. So now he supports her. Reluctantly. A drink would help.

And so they pass by, Bree and one of Gordon's little daughters, Angelique. They are carrying cardboard boxes. Mysterious boxes. Something concerning the True Maine Militia, no doubt, that which goes on behind Gordon's back at all hours. You raise kids to be like anarchists and you will be the first power they tear down, especially when someone like Bree comes along to whip them into high gear.

Gordon has spent his whole life wishing for someone like Bree to be close to, to be fused with, soul to soul. Bree, fellow philosopher! Big-picture person! Passionate duty to humankind! Older than her years, a creature like no other! And there she is, walking past him, three feet away, untouchable. Here, but not his. Married by Settlement law but pissed off.

He glances now to the outside wall of the kitchen: three of his other young wives, all with babies, one nursing: Natty with her pale foxy little blade face. Natty with her thin blonde hair parted in the middle, falling carelessly at either side, split sweetly over the back of her neck. The baby nurses at her open shirt, but Natty is staring down the length of the porches. She wears the red sash around her newly restored waist. Is she feeling restless now with the outside world muscling its way in here, all these young men with their verve and unlined faces, and all that danceable music about to begin? She is one of those Gordon feels edgy about. But Bree: *over* the edge. Over and out. He aches to think of it.

Now he looks straight into the eyes of a young man who has just stepped in through the nearest screen door and stands next to a loaded table staring at Gordon. Bald as a stone. A tattooed forehead. Tattoo is of the phoenix, rising not from the ashes but from flames. Though it is noontime and warm, he wears a long heavy coat and corduroy pants of a check print, tight at calf and ankle as pants were almost fifty years ago, and on his feet military boots like Rex's. Hands in pockets.

Gordon doesn't break the stare.

This guy's eyes are so wide, the whites show all around the irises. Not just the head shaved. Eyebrows shaved off. Huge long narrow nose. Spiky short red beard. Mouth a wet thin line. A gold nose ring. Seems he's jiggling one leg.

Gordon glances at Rex, and Rex is—yes—more rigid than Gordon has ever seen him.

Near one of the shop doors, one of Gordon's small sons and two little visitors are having a sword fight, one plastic sword and two big sticks. All three little boys wear a dull-eyed manly concentration. They holler, "Whammo! Whammo! Whammo!"

"*Out! out! out!*" a Settlement woman commands from her sentrylike position in the doorway to the kitchens. The small sword fighters lunge through a group of preteen girls, all dressed in low-necked ankle-length prairie dresses, and a lonely-looking girl who has a motherish grip on her beloved black pet chicken. "Watch it!" one of the girls snarls at the sword fighters.

Meanwhile, Gordon looks back at the bald leg-jiggling stranger, and the guy is looking Gordon up and down slowly with an expression somewhere between madness and well-perfected seductiveness. The eyes come to rest solidly on Gordon's crotch.

Rex makes a sound. Like the sudden blowing and champing and moist snort of a bull.

Gordon steps toward the guy. "Are you hungry, brother? We have plenty of everything. Help yourself."

Brother. If the word were a fine black Caddy, even then, how many could ride in it?

The guy looks at Gordon's hand outstretched to him. The guy pulls from his pocket a stump. No hand. Just a violet-colored stump, made all nice and fatty and smooth by hurried surgeons.

Gordon hesitates by about two beats, then folds both of his hands around the mutilated handless stick. Then he sees that the other hand, now pulled from its pocket, is another stump. "Where're you from?" Gordon asks, loosening his grip and dropping his own hands with a graciousness some people would save for big landowners, selectmen, legislators, movie stars, kings, queens, and high priests.

"Buf," the guy replies, a wetness building on his lips.

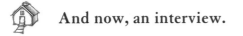 **And then.**

Another leaf lets go. It dips, spins, slows. Down, down. This one a maple leaf, red with a purple center. Lands on a picnic table, among half-eaten gooey rolls and the bone of a lamb.

And now, an interview.

Out by the open bay of the livestock Quonset hut, a reporter finds a woman, wearing an ornately embroidered red sash through the loops of her jeans and carrying a coil of rope, leading a baby goat, a perfect baby goat, brown and white and clean, little hooved tiptoeing dancer's feet. See the most delicate mouth in all creation, gentle inno-cence; see the horizontally pupiled amber eyes, eyes of the Devil, and white tail that shakes like a torn rag in a warm breeze. Baby goat with no name. Fattened on milk, on daisies and clover, on pond water and play.

"Do you live here?" the reporter asks the woman.

"Yes."

"What is your name?"

"Glennice."

"Last name?" Reporter smiles. Reporter is friendly and casual.

"St. Onge."

"Ah." Reporter looks Glennice over quickly and another quick glance at the goat. Reporter smiling. "Taking the goat to show those little chil-dren over there?"

"Yes." Glennice is smiling squintily: sun in her eyes. "You call it a kid."

"Oh, of course."

Glennice smiles. Yes, Glennice, whose teeth are too small for her smile. Nose too small. Glasses too big. Hair too permed. But all of this together radiates an enviable at-home contentment.

"Well, this is quite a day, Glennice. Must be really something for you people who usually have a quiet life here, huh?"

Glennice laughs.

Reporter scribbles these one-word and no-word answers while the next question is asked. "So you know Gordon St. Onge pretty well."

"Yes, I sure do."

"Is he your husband?"

Glennice nods without hesitation.

"What's he like?"

"He is love. He is from God."

Reporter scribbles this, bearing down to get each letter fat and clear and legible. Reporter persists. More questions about Gordon St. Onge, and Glennice's dreamy biblical replies fulfill all reporterly hopes and dreams. And half a notebook.

The sun yearns quickly into its early afternoon position.

When Gordon starts chasing two giggling little boys with a realistic-looking rubber rattlesnake, Rex excuses himself, saying he needs to make a call on the CB in his truck down the road.

Meanwhile, more people arrive. And *more* people. Some in loud bright-eyed groups. Some are loners. Some get tours of farm animals, electric cars, the shops, the windmills, the greenhouses.

In a huddle behind the furniture-making Quonset hut, Eddie Martin (who wears his Titanic T-shirt, a wide belt of coins, and fake jewels and studs and so forth, and beams under a strenuous shave that makes his long jaws look waxy) advises his sons and some other young people who are rotating gate duty and parking assistance and the big job of keeping track of small kids. "Good to spread the crowd out. Keep those windmill tours going. Takes 'em forever to hike that hill."

Aurel agrees. "Den dey doan' suffocate each otherrr as much and mash us." Aurel's searing black eyes study the mountain.

Gordon, who has done some circulating out on the mobbed quadrangle, now returns to the same piazza as before and finds the handless man gone. Shanna St. Onge breathlessly informs him that cars are parked all the way down Heart's Content Road to the Day log yard.

Other teen and preteen girls rush up to him, surround him.

Tall, yellow-haired, fifteen-year-old Whitney, with a crooked funny-faced smile, gives her father's rolled-up plaid left sleeve a little stroking. The din of hundreds of voices seems, at the moment, equal to the engines of jets on a runway. As Whitney's voice gets drowned out, Gordon dips his head down so she can shout into his ear. "Some people were walking on the kids' gardens. Cory yelled at some guys. There was almost a fight."

"Where's Butch and Joel? Where's David? Where's Mickey?"

Whitney shrugs.

Gordon says, "If you see them, tell 'em we got Rusty and Shawn down at the house. Aurel and Eddie got the parking and gate crews rotating. So see if they can rotate with Steven and Joel, and Jaime when he's done helping Glennice . . . see if they can swap off for a small garden crew. They can make some signs. Rope off a little part of that road where the tractor path is." He pushes open the screen and steps out. Whitney follows. And now Samantha Butler sort of hops toward them from the crowd, her newly found olive-drab bush hat pulled on hard over her eyebrows. All that silky blonde hair. Red bandanna around her neck. Black T-shirt. Army pants. Army boots. A kind of far-left far-right fashion mix. A Revolution poster child. Gordon gives Samantha a one-armed bear hug. "I love you," he says, with a choke of tenderness. She is not his child. Nor a wife. She is a smart-ass difficult one, therefore precious.

"I love you too, oh, beloved Prophet." Now she pulls away to fuss with her bush hat, working it back to its cocky angle.

Gordon smiles at each girl. They smile back. Suspiciously sweet.

Now he sees two other girls coming down off a distant piazza, hurrying to reach him. They are gasping when they arrive, eyes on his face, something coordinated here. "Okay, what?" he asks loudly, above the din of the crowd, which is bigger and denser than a few moments ago.

Again, Whitney strokes his sleeve, now one of his ears, *pat pat pat, stroke stroke, hug hug*. "We're worried about our meeting. Like, how're we going to get all these people to sing the songs? We don't have enough song sheets. And now everybody's chickening out on *everything*. Like, we had a great document for everyone to read together, like a chant, but that's out. Like the songs, out of the picture. Nobody wants to do a speech. Bree talked really big like she'd just take over and do this wicked cute speech. But now she's, like, no way. Everybody's such wimps."

"Including you, Whitney!" scolds Michelle.

Gordon looks at Samantha. "What about this thing?" He ruffles Samantha's hat again and hugs her head.

"Not me!" says Samantha. "I'm purely behind the scenes. Secret Service, that's me!" She pulls away, again fixes her hat.

"Soooo," Whitney coos, stroking Gordon's left hand, "we need to scoff up the Prophet. We need him. He's so cute. He wins hearts."

"I'm tired."

"Please?"

"Okay."

All the girls applaud. A couple of them frolic around. Gordon is looking into Whitney's spirited and lovely and way-too-clever green almond-shaped eyes while a couple of the others give his ribs hard hugs.

"I knew you'd do it," says Whitney. "You're just dying to get up there and show off."

He flushes, glances out at the crowded Quad and Quonset hut yards, raises an eyebrow.

Samantha looks at her Rex-like watch.

Margo asks Samantha, "When?"

"Soon. Before everyone leaves."

Gordon says, "Let 'em dance first. Let 'em get tanked up and tired out. Let *me* get tanked—"

"No!" Whitney stands on the toe of one of his boots with one of her boots. "No more of that stuff. We're counting on you to act *grown up*."

"The True Maine Militia," he says, with a wink, "is authoritarian."

"Darn tootin' it is!" Erin shouts, with a pretend scowl.

"Are you proud of us?" Rachel Soucier asks.

"I'm proud."

"Are you really?" presses Carmel, who looks a *lot* like Whitney, although she is younger, less fleshy, more twiggy. And she has a different mother, less jaw, and rounder eyebrows that make even her real scowls look cheery.

Gordon squashes his tired eyes with two thick calloused palms. "I'm goddam fucking proud."

"Proud today, pissy tomorrow," he hears Whitney grumble as they now all hurry away, Whitney's and Carmel's honey-yellow ponytails flashing in and out of pools of sun and shade; and there's Samantha's olive-drab hat and dear Shanna's heavy midnight-black hair in a tail to the backs of her knees, made tame with about six rings of brightly dyed burlap cloth—all their energy making a blur, their arms and shoulders and dresses and pant legs mixing.

 ## Meanwhile, a press conference is taking place on the hillside.

Yellow truck and ramp. Cannon, small; Louis, tall. Wedding ring. Plaid sleeves not long enough. Cannon ramrod in his hand. Softly explaining everything anyone needs to know about black powder, muzzle loaders of every kind, a bit of Civil War history, especially where artillery comes in. The questions come in at Louis from all sides. But he is cool and calm, tapping the outside of one leg with the ramrod. "No. There won't be a projectile. I *have* used a projectile in this, part lead, part wheel weights melted down; you just aim a little high. But what I *really* got this for is for the boom." He laughs to himself, softly. "I use toilet paper for wadding. Makes a mess. And you have to be sure, especially this time of year, that you haven't left anything smoldering in the grass or the woods."

One reporter asks what time the cannon will be fired today. Louis shrugs. "When the True Maine Militia gives the order. I don't know when that is."

 ## The crowd continues to swell.

Once, when Gordon squats down to put his face eye to eye with a small child, a total stranger child with blue amazed eyes wide on Gordon's own, she gives him her stuffed blue rabbit. Floppy ears on the rabbit. Cotton tail. He holds the rabbit while the parents talk about Social Security.

In a while, he moves on to another group. More stories told by small-business owners, more stories of strong-arming by giant chains. Stories of regulations that small biz can't dodge like the big guys can. This from a pizza shop owner, who speaks softly and quaveringly but with certainty, gone hard and wooden across the face: "And we're not even called small business anymore. We are called microbiz. That's like micro organisms. Like being a germ. What happened that we aren't the heart of the community anymore? The words *free trade* are a lie. Even *trade* is a lie. There is no *trade* at all. There's no even-steven. These are evil times, sir."

Gordon says, "My brother, it's time. We have got to band together. We have no representation. We need to turn to our own kind." He starts on about food shortages, the bad news of ruined soils, erosion, water dried up or polluted, peak oil. He insists on small brotherhoods of trade and says, "Our relationship with the soil and forests, the source of our food and water, must be loved like a mother, not sold!" He begins to really boom now. But three elderly ladies interrupt, asking Gordon to autograph their militia song sheets. Which he does. But also he mashes beery kisses on their cheeks.

 ### Gordon illustrates his roar of words.

With a brown, almost empty beer bottle as a pointer, he addresses a huddle of L. L. Bean–dressed fellows (pastel knitted shirts, khaki or olive shorts, sandals, long-visored caps), who to Gordon are, yes, brothers. "You were probably going to say that too, right? Everybody does. Especially wind. Oh my!, too labor intensive. You were going to say that, weren't you?"

One guy confesses, "Maybe." Then laughs brotherishly. The feeling has become solid, rising, pulling.

Gordon smiles, twisted bottom teeth almost grating against his straighter top ones.

"Okay, let's suppose we're dumb enough to—you know—give up our valuable TV-watching time, and let's count in the fact that a lotta guys have been laid off and can't find new jobs half as good as the old ones, and our clocks seem, you know, to be going backward or something. So tell me what's wrong with spending *time*?"

His audience nods or chuckles. Pleasantly, one mentions invertors and lead batteries.

"Man, yes!" Gordon hoots. "I want to figure out this mystery. I mean, we folks here in Egypt are"—he lowers his voice, as if there were hostile listeners in the fields, in the trees, in the sky—"human too. We aren't chimpanzees. We aren't less intelligent than the experts. We just aren't experts." He winks. "Yet."

One guy nods briskly. The others are open-mouthed, caught in *trying* to get in a word.

Gordon cackles. "We aren't lacking humanness. We are only lacking education. All those years we spend in their fucking six-million-dollar-a-year schools, and not one peep about this *emergency* skill!"

Hope.

In and out of clusters of people, moving into the denser shade of the quadrangle trees, there are stories. Now in listening mode, Gordon has left his beer bottle on the edge of the parking lot. He hears these, his brothers, in their distress. Boss betrayals, which lead to government betrayals. Union betrayals. Neighbors calling on hotlines. Neighbors watching to catch you at a crime. "You are our only hope," a red-faced balding man tells Gordon, this man in the company of several other fiftyish guys, caps with ads, solemn slouched shoulders on some. One man is miserably pockmarked, probably since his teen years. These guys are almost certainly not militia. They look too sad. Militia guys aren't sad. Militia guys look paranoid. Yeah, paranoid, the opposite of trusting. The opposite of what a lamb looks like waiting near you, while you scrape that knife across the whet stone.

And militia guys look armed. Usually nothing of a firearm shows, it's just in the eyes. And in the way they walk.

Gordon says, "I'm not your only hope. We do this together."

"But you are the only one who is speaking for us! No one else is doing it. Politicians are assholes."

Gordon frowns. "You say I am speaking for you. Who is it I am speaking *to* about you? Nobody. I speak only *to you*. I say, I am in this sinking boat *with* you."

All the guys in this group look at Gordon's mouth in doubt.

A tall gray-haired man, clean-shaven, with dark-frame glasses, appears from another direction and puts out his hand to Gordon. "Walt Glenn."

"Good to meetcha," Gordon says. "Come to join the militia?"

The man smiles. He fingers around inside his wallet a moment and produces a small blue card for Gordon's inspection. Little flag on the card and the words: *The True Maine Militia*. Card signed by *Bree St. Onge,*

Secretary, and *Samantha Butler, Recruiting Officer*. Gordon hands the card back. Smiles funnyish.

The guy puts a book and a thickness of copied materials into Gordon's hands. "Some good reading there. Good exercise . . . for the adrenal glands." He winks, then speaks in a low, summoning, near-whisper, partly inaudible. "I am honored to meet someone who pays attention." He winks again. Laughs. Turns away.

Now as this tall man moves off into the crowd, Gordon's wife Gail, dressed in a pale blue peasant blouse that shows the full effect of her necklace-of-roses tattoo, shouts into Gordon's ear, "That's the retired physicist Claire was just talking with! Worked for the Navy, once, and NASA. He knows tons of stuff! About the Project for the New American Century. And Russia. And how the dollar is backed by oil. He's great! He's hot shit! There's some others here, kinda like that. A doctor—a gastro-something doctor—a minister, a law professor, all chomping at the bit to be militia!" Her hard, lined face beams. "I thought I was too old for surprises!" She pats his arm, steps away.

Turning, Gordon studies the guy's back, the physicist, who is now having a chat with some liberal-looking women.

Walking straight at Gordon is Rex. He wears his dark glasses now, cold eyes just sparkles of wetness behind the shadowy lenses. And now a dark loose work shirt, although the day has become almost hot. Gordon surmises that this means Rex is now armed.

Rex says disgustedly, "Some party."

Gordon says, "A lotta good people." He presses the book and papers from the physicist under an arm against his own ribs, kind of like Rex's service pistol is right now against *his* ribs, only different. Gordon sighs. "People need to meet like this."

Rex just stares around.

Gordon says, "I appreciate what you're doing, Richard. You didn't have to come here, giving time to something you think is off-the-wall. I'm beholden."

Rex turns and watches more people weaving through the jammed opening between the east side of the shops and porches and the first Quonset hut. "I made some calls. I have some men"—looks at his watch—"who will be here any minute. To keep an eye on things. You can't just go unprotected here. You are a high-profile problem with a militia identity."

Gordon nods.

Rex says, "Anything could happen."

Gordon tries not to smile, but his face betrays him. There it is. His wild-man expression, just as he sees two more old ladies slowly walking toward him, probably working up the nerve to ask, *Are you Gordon St. Onge?* But before they arrive, Rex says, in a gravelly way, "Somebody is going to kill you."

"Don't spook me," Gordon says quietly. Digs into the sand with the toe of his boot. "Don't."

Meanwhile, out in the crowd, officers of the True Maine are recruiting, circulating, passing out little cards, copies of *The Recipe,* and various flyers. Sign-up sheets are loaded. Some of these officers have a small child by the hand. Some of the little ones wear three-corner patriot hats. All small kids accounted for and a great system worked out for the older kids to report in every half hour to mothers stationed in the library.

Gordon shakes the hands of two people, both in their midforties, more or less. They say they have come down from near Greenville. The woman has long dense tight curls of that blank-looking black anyone can tell means *dyed.* Her hand is skinny and cool. Her husband is a big son of a bitch, tall and rotund, with dark glasses, big dark mustache, a little tuft of black under the bottom lip, and huge scabby forearms. Camo T-shirt. Baggy jeans. Red suspenders. He positions himself in front of Rex, dark glasses staring into dark glasses. He says, "Mr. York?"

Rex nods.

Guy says, "We're Greenville Militia."

Rex nods again. Puts out his hand. "How're things up your way?"

"Brewing."

Rex's mouth does something odd, like moving a chaw from one side of his mouth to the other. But really it's just his tongue and one inside wall of his mouth readjusting, the way he often does when he is smitten by irony. He says, "You people came here . . . for *this?*"

"Same reason you're here. And we saw Crowe here with his people, and that common law group from Waterville . . . what's his name? Sandy Coates. And that one from the reservation. He was just lookin' for you. See on the Internet their communications to the governor? They challenge him to declare martial law, round up citizens. They have sworn by the Constitution to defend. No response from the Blaine House yet. The governor's too busy, I'm sure. Too busy for us commoners."

Rex nods.

Gordon stares at Rex.

Rex doesn't give Gordon even a glance.

The Greenville guy says, "Governor is a stupid man."

"He is an *owned* man," says Gordon, and the Greenville couple both look into Gordon's face, eyebrows raised. But Rex keeps on ignoring Gordon.

Greenville woman now asks Rex if there are any preparedness exhibits here to check out.

Rex starts to say no, then says they might be interested in the windmills and electric cars and solar stuff. And the radio setup. Gordon notes that Rex speaks with a look in his eyes not shown in ages. Pride.

 Rex and the Greenville people walk to a high spot (where Rex can point out the road to the windmills).

Joined by two more people from Greenville, Gordon turns away to go yak with some family of Bonny Loo, cousins and such, all of them chuckling about some funny thing that happened at the gate as they were trying to get in, some misunderstanding. They repeat the story three times, the same way, and laugh each time. Eventually, they are on their way toward the porches of food.

An old friend of Gordon's he hasn't seen in what seems a million moons rushes up, waving his True Maine Militia card, a few friends in tow, all gay men of the category Gordon thinks of as flaming.

"Rob," Gordon says, grabbing his old friend's shoulder.

Rob gasps. "I never thought I'd see the day when I'd be joining up with a militia! What has got into me?"

Gordon laughs. "Somebody give you a good sales pitch?"

"I've always been a sucker for blue." He strokes the card with one finger, then slips it into the pocket of his summer knit shirt. He introduces his friends and Gordon says "Good to meetcha" to each, and they talk a bit about water pollution and water privatization. Rob jerks a thumb at one of his friends, a guy whose hair is in a frenzy of yellow spikes, ivory white skin and one dangling earring of eensie elfin figures, a clump of Pans with flutes and lyres.

"He's a conspiracy theorist too," Rob says of the blond. "It was his idea to come."

Gordon winks at the blond, whose name is Neddie. "Every time he calls you a *theorist,* hit him."

Neddie glances at Rob.

Rob gives a shriek of feigned fright. "Don't hit!"

Gordon says, with a grin, "We're all *citizens,* Rob, not conspiracy theorists, for crying out loud. Citizens demand *oversight.* No oversight? Well, then citizens have to form theories in order to make something of the mysteries. To begin their *research.* To compile. The *evidence.* It's like science. The only third choice is brain death." Gordon squints at Neddie. "Neddie is a smart man."

"A True Maine Militia revolutionary," says Neddie himself. He sneers at Rob and smiles at Gordon. The others in their group laugh along.

One says, "I can picture Neddie in a beret with a machine gun."

"Of course!" says Neddie. "Now you've found me out."

They all carry on a few minutes, creating a great tale of Neddie's secret life, Gordon adding some of the wilder details. Then someone leans against Gordon from behind, gathers his arm against her body and calls him "vewwy wuvy man." He sees the deep glossy auburn ripples of Glory York's hair splayed over his arm. She smells too good. The smell that isn't hard alcohol (the alcohol part stinks). "This isn't believable, Pooh." She sighs. "It's because you're famous, isn't it?"

"It's because of all the hard work of the young people here," he tells her.

She frowns, shakes her head. "You know it's only partly that."

Rob gives Gordon a hard hug from the side Glory hasn't gotten herself clamped around. Rob says, "I've got to run. Take care of yourself. Live chastely. And eat plenty of vegetables."

Gordon laughs once, boomingly. "Great advice."

"No fried fats!" Rob scolds, and dances away, the rest of his gang smiling and nodding at Gordon as they depart.

Glory sighs. "Boy bitches aren't pretty like Glory girl." And she pouts. "No kisses for my pretty-pretty ear?"

Gordon disengages himself from her fierce embrace, gives her bare shoulder a little quick pat. "I feel protective toward you. I want you safe."

Hard to read her expression. But what it looks like is that she is deeply touched by these words. Her eyes glide to the left. "My friends are here. But I can't find them now. I'm lost. Wah. Wah." She giggles, sort of like Bree's giggle: a husky but melodious trill.

"Let's walk," he says, and switching the physicist's book and papers to his other arm, leads her by the hand through the crowd. He knows she is not like this unless she drinks. As a little tyke hanging out at the Settlement, she was *almost* as practical as Rex.

She laces her arm around his now, in that old-fashioned way of old-fashioned ladies. He is horribly saddened. A few years of savage partying and close-call driving accidents; will that be it? Or will she be a drinker all her life, long after the party's over? Worse even than his own drinking, which he lapses in and out of, somehow never sinking to depths. Will Glory York lose jobs, disgust everyone, repel all relationships, harm the souls of her children, and die at forty-five with a liver that looks like yellow Jell-O? Her arm against his arm is the same temperature as his own, but skin is soft, barely lived in.

He says, "Annie B is a hundred years old today. Imagine."

Glory laughs. "She's always seemed old to me."

"But ten years ago she was in better shape. She's pretty frail now."

"I haven't seen her lately," she tells him. She still has a white paper in one hand. Gordon can see now that it's one of the True Maine Militia flyers. He touches it with his free fingers.

"Well, Glory. What do you think of the True Maine Militia? Going to join up?"

She gives him a dreamy look. Her eyes too blue. A face much like Rex's except for that mouth . . . Marsha's mouth, he remembers sadly. "Do I need a gun?" she asks. "'Cause I know where I can get about two hundred of them."

He laughs. "All you need is a burning desire to see the human race survive, and— "

"A burning desire," she says, in a wonderfully throaty way, and her eyes fall over the buttons of his shirt.

As they leave the crowded area under the big old trees and start up through an open grassy area of sun, they can see Rex, standing on one

of the brick paths that lead up into the village of hillside cottages. He is
alone, hands behind his back. He is staring up along the tree line across
the fields and gardens toward the northeast.

Reaching Rex now, Gordon lifts Glory's hand from his arm and places
it on Rex's arm. "She was lost," Gordon says. "Now she's found."

Glory uses her other hand to muckle onto Gordon, pulls him by the
shirtfront against her so she is wedged between both men. She laughs
happily.

Some of Gordon's papers slip from his arm. And the book. *Plop!* He
backs away, squatting down to collect them, and hears Rex's low voice.
"Quit it, would ya?"

And Glory to Rex, "Oh, shush, party-pooper Bumpa never know no
fun, only most cute soldier so seeerious Captain Pooh." And she laughs
again, her folded flyer fluttering to the brick path by one of her father's
boots. In front of Gordon, who is squatted there, she bends over so that
her short green dress rises to show off to him her brief, *very* brief, white
panties and, more significantly, the lightly tanned perfect cheeks.

Gordon stands straight, organizing his papers fussily, papers from the
Navy physicist. He glimpses the book, titled *The Grand Chessboard:
American Primacy and Its Geostrategic Imperatives*, reading that someday
might hold his attention.

Now Glory throws her arms around Gordon, buries her face in his
bright flannel shirt, faking little sobs. "Proteck Glory girl! Proteck Glory
girl! Big mighty Proffit famous everywhere, proteck Glory girl . . . from
himself!" She giggles and grabs him roughly between the legs. "Him *want*!"

Rex looks into Gordon's face.

Gordon pushes Glory toward Rex. "Take her home, Richard, and
spank her ass."

Glory laughs. "Bumpa not spank. Bumpa never mean like Profitt.
Mighty Sheik Gordie spank and beat and break heads. Famous mean
guy. Radio talk-show people *saaaaid* so."

Rex's Adam's apple jumps. Rex's hands hang useless. Rex's eyes
unreadable.

Gordon useless and swallowing.

Glory pouts. "My two favorite daddies just have Militia on the brain,
never fun. Everybody thinks you're crazy. Glory just want to rough two
daddies, make 'em play, make 'em lighten up."

Glory's girlfriends soon find her, and after a little more pawing and poking at Gordon, kisses, baby talk, and stroking his beard, she roams off with them, looking for "Selene and Justin."

Gordon says to Rex, "She's going to get in trouble."

Rex says, "She's out of high school. She's on her own."

Gordon looks at him. "Women should *never* be on their own. Not that way." He sighs. "She . . . is . . . drunk."

Rex's lips tighten. "I do not have a big concentration camp like this to hold her in."

Gordon looks pained. "Well, you people in the modern world got goodies like rape crisis centers to fix it all up for you *afterward* . . . and abortion centers . . . and—"

Rex puts up a hand. "She needs her mother. Tell Marsha about this, not me."

Gordon's eyes twinkle. "Blame it on Marsha, eh?"

Rex moves one foot, shifting his weight.

Gordon sighs and fusses with his papers and book some more. "It's worse than martial law, it's worse than corporate tyranny, it's the whole tangled, desolate culture, the whole hellish mess. But I guarantee you one thing. You do not have to worry about me taking advantage of that little girl. That's *one* thing I can guarantee you, my brother."

Bunches of people, seeing Rex and Gordon, work their way up to them.

Gordon is engaged first, while Rex stays out of it, doing his thing, looking unfriendly. But then Rex has company too. It's the man who came around on the night of the solar car unveiling. And he went once to the York residence too, a short weird visit. He gives his name again—"Gary Larch"—and thrusts out his hand. Rex doesn't appear to remember, but he really does, of course. Not that he looks puzzled. He just doesn't give any cheery *Hey, good to see ya*s. He just shakes the guy's hand. With his dark glasses, Rex's eyes are shadows. Gary Larch wears sunglasses too, but his voice is friendly and it's clear he wants to talk. To Rex. That he likes Rex. Has a thing for Rex.

No white shirt this time. This time it's a tiger-stripe BDU shirt with the sleeves ripped off, worn over a black T-shirt. Jeans. His billed cap reads MERTIE'S HARDWARE. A wristwatch like Rex's. He has a thick bottom lip, a kind of malocclusion, and that square clean-shaven jaw. Brown hair. Picture a serial-killer-schoolteacher combo and you've got the effect. The guy is a bit tall, so most people wouldn't notice that he's got a little bald spot back on the crown. He jokes with Rex about the chickens pecking around by the smaller Quonset hut. White Leghorns. Spurs on the heels. Hens with spurs. "Liberated women," he says.

Rex sort of smiles.

The guy points out a woman down there in the crowd with long curly black hair. The Greenville militia woman, just back from the windmills. "Looks like Captain Hook."

Rex nods.

Now the guy talks about Montana. "Lotta agribusiness." He tells Rex how between the banks and the government, "those people out there have gotten screwed royal."

Rex glances over at Gordon's back, Gordon with a small crowd of pretty women. He looks back into this Gary guy's face. He says, "Montana people are well organized. Here it's different."

Gary makes a face. "You could *get* organized. I've seen it happen. Guys just sitting around trying to decide what color patches they want and whining . . . you know . . . the kitchen militias. But then they get a little more focused. Personalities sometimes stall things. You have to have the right group chemistry. I've seen some guys split up 'cause half of them were only into common law while the other half wanted to stress protection. Fine. Everybody's happy. As long as people don't get stalled. That's no good."

Rex studies Gary's face and neck, the crescent of his black T-shirt at the unbuttoned top of his BDU shirt.

The guy tells Rex he was into explosives in Montana. "Guys out there are serious. Not that I knew anyone who had any intentions of *using* explosives, we aren't talking about McVeigh here. These are sane men. Smart men. But being prepared means whatever the enemy has, you have. Except maybe the A-bomb. That's ridiculous." He laughs a kind of Cowardly Lion laugh. A lovable laugh. Infectious.

Rex sort of smiles.

The guy says, "Out there, I was into explosives but I knew, when my father was dying and I was coming back up here, I knew I had to tame down some. Nothing wrong with common law and"—he points up to the mountain—"windmills." He laughs the lovable lion laugh again. "And I got a thing. I can't stand fags' rights. Special rights and all that. I know you guys up here have a lotta bullshit with that. I think it's good to keep people posted on when a bunch of homo-liberals are getting ready to sneak legislation through under the guise of *equal rights*." He makes a face. A little snort of disgust.

Rex says, "You'll be busy."

The guy glances at Gordon, then back at Rex. "Not as busy as you boys are. Holy shit. You're taking on the whole friggin' population."

Rex smiles. "Don't blame me." He laughs. A little. "Kids did this."

"No shit."

Down past the trucks of cider, Glory York has her skirt pulled up to show something on the top of her leg (her hip actually) to her boisterous friends. This Gary guy turns and looks. Perhaps he remembers from the solar car night who Glory is. He looks back around, smiling at the elaborate maze of brick paths. "Nice," he says. "Like the city."

"It's to make it easy for old folks and wheelchairs and baby buggies," Rex says evenly.

The guy's face softens. And his voice, very soft. "The last shall be first and the first shall be last. It'll be God's will."

"That's right," says Rex.

Before the guy roams off to chat with other people, he gives Rex a piece of paper with his phone number on it and his name. Again. In case Rex misplaced it from when he gave it to him *twice* before. Then he pats the opposite side of his own chest and winks. "Keep your powder dry."

Rex says, "Yep. You too."

 And then.

A woman with a short version of a Cleopatra cut, graying, steps up onto one of the porches, followed by two other women, one blonde. The first woman wears something purple, and her eyes look from face to face to face, and she smiles. This is the Unitarian Universalist minister. And see that big burning thing sliding off to the west? That is the tired-out sun.

Meanwhile, a procession moves toward the tiny permanent stage.

It's the one made for skits during warm-weather meals, the one inside the piazza off the kitchens. Two men carry a chair between them, and in this chair rides an old woman with a crisp new tightly curled snow-white perm, a great hooked nose, Indian-dark skin, eyes black behind her linty eyeglass lenses, her legs, long and swinging, dressed in trousers a ghosty shade of blue. She wears a winter sweater with a heavy cable pattern, and she waves limply to people as she is transported past, her smile good-humored and tolerant of all this they do.

Walking along with the swaying chair and its bearers is an army of children, dressed in plastic helmets and feathers, tricorne hats, kepis, and robes, carrying their weapons: sticks, plastic swords, one plastic Uzi. Their faces, solemn. Military escort.

Because Annie B has trouble sitting in chairs for long, a mattress has been arranged on this little stage, with a number of pretty pillows, quilts, and all manner of soft things. The men arrange her there in a semisitting position, and the women give her a patchwork lap quilt for her knees. She waves out to the people at both ends of the big piazza; they cheer and call out, "Happy birthday, Annie B!"

And she nods and smiles.

A young teen voice calls out, "Happy hundred years!"

Annie nods, her head tipped to one side a little tremblingly.

They all sing "Happy Birthday" and bring out the cake, a cake big enough to cover a sheet of plywood. It is bright red and for some reason shaped like a lobster.

There are a couple of small speeches.

There is the presentation of the story box, a box filled with story stones with the oral history of Annie's life recorded in single words and phrases on each stone. Bev and Barbara explain this concept to many puzzled strangers, and there's a demonstration where people who have written on the stones tell their stories: stories about Annie and stories told by Annie to them over the years, stories of a century of ironies and softened sorrows . . . and some stories that are very, very funny.

Out on the quadrangle and in the fields and parking lot, down along the gravel road, word is passed of Annie B's giant red cake and story box, and some say, "Isn't that wonderful."

 Meanwhile, what is Annie B thinking behind those eyes in their satchels of withery skin?

It's cold. They say it's fall. Feels like January. A lot of people want to talk. But everyone whispers. They smile and they hug. That's nice. I like the babies. The world is full of babies. They all look alike. Even those that they tell me are my great ones or great-great-great. They don't walk well. They fall in the most comical ways. While everyone whispers. Everyone racing around, like Wee Willie Winkie.

There's another baby. I like that one. Where am I? Why is Judy here? That's not Judy. Maybe that's her daughter.

Everyone is smiling, holding rocks. Duty. You always got duty. Even in the end, like me. You want to just sleep. But to make them happy, here I am.

 A young man stands smiling on one of the porches.

He is watching them cut the big red cake. His billed cap reads SEA DOGS. He has fresh blond looks. (Yes, right, he is Kevin Moore, a government agent.) A few young women glance his way and wonder about him. It seems *he* is wondering why the cake is shaped like a lobster. He gestures at the two claws, the legs, and, yes, the eyes on sticks and smiles at one of the Settlement women, who laughs, and he seems to hear her words because he nods and laughs too, though it is hard to hear her words due to the commotion of running children, yakking adults, and an electric buggy whining along on the grass, just beyond the screen, giving rides to guests, one of these guests being the Unitarian Universalist minister with the graying Cleopatra haircut and purple shirt. And now a small white flat-faced curl-tailed very homely dog lifts his leg on somebody's shoulder bag left slouched against a tree, a beige semisoft leather shoulder bag, maybe a camera bag. And out between the teeth of the grinning Tyrannosaurus rex (Settlement idea of a jungle gym), a child waves and the sun moves westward another significant notch.

 **And so the cake is eaten.**

Wiped out, actually.

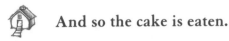 **Meanwhile.**

The musicians test their mikes in earnest. Golden stars of the late-day sun slip up and down the keys and buttons and front plates of the beautiful instruments. Leaves of every color of the soul seesaw softly downward through the cooling air. Around the shoes and boots of the musicians, a few leaves settle. A chicken on the stage pecks at leaves and shadows. Someone helps the chicken off the stage.

 And so.

Before the music begins, Samantha Butler steps up to one of the microphones. She is, for the moment, wearing a black tricorne hat and a frozen smile. Before the crowd is done with applauding and cheering and hooting, Samantha too quickly has begun her announcement. Something about a "speaker" or "speech for her," no one can tell for sure, "after the music is over. So don't leave!" She salutes the crowd, which again cheers and applauds, whistles and shrieks. Samantha steps over wires, between two fiddlers, and disappears down the stage steps to the piazza.

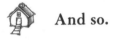 **Jane Meserve stands as still as she can, just a few jiggles.**

She is hearing what the plan is as Bree tells it, the thing Jane will be doing tonight that is "of great importance."

"Are you scared?" Tamya Soucier asks, with big eyes.

Jane laughs. "Why would anybody be afraid of importance?"

 Meanwhile, Mickey Gammon hangs around by one of the Quonset huts.

A bunch of Settlement and town teenagers are there, smoking grass. Mickey is laughing at something someone just said, his eyes pink and a little popped from the stuff, and he notices the air is chilling and he looks straight up into the cloudless sky with its orangey cast of dying October sun and he is glad he is alive.

 Tumult and joy.

As the chilling-down sky behind the near hill darkens, the music becomes the sun and all of life's business. Not much slow dancing, but a lot of dancing that would please the Devil, who is also known to steal souls during sneezes. There are chains of figures, frenzied and giggling through their idea of the bunny hop, and some contra dancing too, lunging in and out of the tight jiggling mass of rock and rollers.

And see there, Gordon St. Onge and the Unitarian Universalist minister (with the graying Cleopatra haircut), doing the jitterbug.

 At long last.

One of the accordion guys—cowboy boots, dress pants, cowboy shirt of a slippery satiny cotton-candy pink, and grimy dark-blue billed cap that reads DAIGLE OIL across the front—speaks a greeting into the mike as the last plucks and wails and drum rolls finally die out around him.

An uproarious applause replies.

"Mercy! Have mercy on us!" he calls out in French-accented English, when he hears hoots of "Encore!" and "More!" from the darkly lighted faces on the packed Quad. "Mercy on us! We arrr going to find some ciderrr, rosin up t' bows, and cool off t'sweat t'at boil us. We willl be back. T' night is still young. It iss not even nine o'clock!"

More wild applause and whistles and happy shouts as the band members exit stage right down the little shaky steps to the piazza into the anonymous near-dark there.

When the last spatters of applause fade, someone in the crowd yells, "Where is the Prophet! Talk to us, Gordon St. Onge!"

A few screams, yips, cheers, and people calling out, "Prophet! Give us the word!" and "Have the Prophet speak!" and "Where is he?"

"He's over there!" calls someone else. "I see him! It's him!"

"Where?" the pink-shirt musician asks, having come back to one of the mikes.

Another musician stands on the little temp stairs at one side of the actual porch stairs, smiling and shrugging.

Pink-shirt musician speaks low into the mike. "Gordon St. Onge. Where are you? Get on up here, you!" He growls the rest: "And talk politics!"

The crowd shrieks and whistles and claps, and various chants begin in different quarters—*Yes! Yes! Yes!* and *Speak truth! Speak truth! Speak truth!* and *Revolution! Revolution! Revolution!*—mixed in with spatterings of applause and happy howls.

Seems Gordon is not out in the crowd. Seems no one has seen him in a while. Where is he?

A long wait. Now oddly quiet. A lot of rustlings and murmurs. A shout. Some laughter. More rustly, mumbly quietness. Thumps and scratches from the tall speakers as the accordion player fondles the mike patiently. "Gordie. Your mother is waiting for you at the concession stand."

Big rocking laughter, cheers, applause, and whistles, and then, when Gordon is seen walking up the stage steps to the mike, the crowd moans happily, with chants of *Truth! Truth! Truth!* and applause, whistles, and cheers like never before.

Gordon stands with his arms across his chest, the Viking-at-ease look, one eyebrow raised, far enough away from them all that most can't see his alcohol-reddened eyes. His dark beard streaked with gray looks green on one side from a nearby glass candle globe. The opposite side of his green plaid shirt looks yellow and pink. Everything is a far-fetched dream this evening.

The accordion player ambles away.

Talk! Talk! Talk! the crowd calls. *Truth!* others scream.

Gordon bows his head over the mike, adjusted for a much shorter man. His voice is soft, soft and sore-hoarse, worn out from the day's thousand and one conversations, and yet the words tumble fast, run on, almost choking. "Are you all trying to say you are tired of losing everything your homes your families your dignity your jobs your independence your life-sustaining skills your hoped-for power to govern as the American people!?"

The crowd now moans in a deep ugly way. And there are hisses and yeses.

"What's the matter?!!" Gordon calls to them. "You don't believe politicians and respectable economists and other experts and so forth when they say everything is going to get better? Maybe you've even heard some of these people saying everything is good *now*! That you are crazy or something because you just think things seem kinda queer. Even the funky weather. It's all just in your silly head, right? Media-approved economists say the economy is glowing! Okay, pal, to hell with the word *economy*. I don't wanna hear how the economy is, I wanna hear how LIFE is, 'cause, pal, I ain't in the ECONOMY, I'm in the Land of Life! That's what you are thinking, right?!!!"

The mob howls. And while Gordon waits it out, there are more spatterings of *Truth! Truth! Truth!* sweet and coaxing. Now, at a motion on his left, Gordon turns and sees Whitney standing beside him. She steps close and pushes something into his hands. She shouts something, but he can't hear it. He assumes she is saying *Put it on!* because it's his camo BDU shirt for Rex's militia, and there is the wide woven green pistol belt with rows of metal-trimmed holes. He hesitates three beats, longer than he hesitated before taking hold of a stranger's handless stump this morning. He looks back around down to the piazza where Rex's face is, shadowy and unreadable. He knows Rex had nothing to do with Whitney bringing this shirt. Mr. Secret Hide-in-the-Shadows York.

He thrusts an arm into the sleeve.

Truth! Truth! Truth! the coaxers coax.

With the shirt on, belt fastened with a twist, olive-green and black mountain lion on the shoulder declaring its place declaring BORDER MOUN-TAIN MILITIA, the crowd goes nuts, shrieks and bellers, mixed with every possible human sound magnified by hundreds. And now, one voice some-where near yells, "Give 'em hell!" another yells. "*Kill 'em! Kill the presi-dent! Kill the governors! Blast 'em all!*"

Gordon waits it out, one hand on the mike, one hand raised to mean *Quiet!* but it has no effect. The noise goes on and on.

But when the crowd has finally had enough of hearing itself and settles down, Gordon speaks softly and reasonably. "Good people. Good Maine people. Good neighbors. You are tired of hearing them tell you that our troubles are caused by welfare mums . . . gay people . . . poor city people . . . foreign people . . . or people who don't work slavishly enough . . . people who complain . . . people who want good pay . . . union people . . . unemployed people . . . disabled people . . . left-wing people . . .

right-wing people . . . people with funny hair and gold rings piercing their eyelids—" Snickers and laughs drown out the next few words.

 On the piazza behind the temporary stage, Whitney and her sisters Michelle and Margo stand arm in arm in darkness lighted only by the weed-scented candles. Whitney is thinking.

In some ways, I always knew I'd see him like this. In my night dreams and in my daydreams there's been this flash of the way he looks to me now, from the back, facing a jillion upturned shadowy faces, and him whispering words of love. No, it is *not* politics, it is *love*. Because my father has always been just twisted up in love and yearning.

 Gordon's voice hops from its whisper, breaks into a run.

"Wondering what all those Washington senators and their ilk are try-ing to hide? Because, man, they are *hiding a lot*. Yes, conspiring. Yes! The controlled media asks, 'What's the matter with people?' *You* are all to blame!" He punches himself in his left bicep. Stomps one boot. "*Bad.*" And then he grabs the mike with both hands and hollers, "Don't you know it's not nice to complain? Or mistrust them! They tell us that it is *unpatriotic* to complain and mistrust; they say *America, love it or leave it;* remember that one, brother? Don't talk back now! It's the New World Order. Big-finance boys want *order*? They want us to shut up! To work! Work, brother, work! Work, sister, work! Little child in school, you gotta work: get As, get honors! Be a more honored child than your neighbor. Work, little child, work! And shut up! Jump through those flaming hoops! Work! Shop! Shop! Shop! CONSUME! And if you can't, join the government's army! Then *die! die! die!* DIIIIIE!" He stops and waits while the crowd makes a truly ugly uni-fied deep growl.

And while this lasts and lasts, Kirky Martin and Jane Meserve ap-pear, lighted by eerie flickering colors, one on either side of Gordon, Jane wearing a black tricorne hat and Kirky bareheaded. They unfurl flags, one the flag of the True Maine Militia, the other the Stars and Stripes. Now the crowd is whistling, yowling, sounds of pride and approval, a whirl of applause, and a few groans.

♡♡   Secret Agent Jane worries.

My hair is a mess. And my sexy outfit doesn't show because Bree and Whitney said I *had* to wear this jacket of the army kind. But hundreds of people are looking at me and I am part of this importance. You would not believe how many people. So: famous, important, *and* horridable looking. *Tsk*.

Being bad.

Gordon spies an open bottle of beer behind the drummer's seat. He dips down and snatches it up. He grips the bottle close to his chest, returns to the mike, looks straight down at the top of it, and says, "We love shopping, right? Fun, right? Lotta choices, right? But tell me—brother, sister, little child—what will shopping mean to you when a loaf of bread is ten dollars, your pay is three dollars a day, and gasoline to get to work and to the store is *eight dollars a gallon,* and your payroll tax comes to half your pay, and there's no more Social Security, just something funny and funky? You are thinking, Oh, Gordie, that won't happen; *they* won't let that happen." He draws something up from his throat, something thick, and spits on the floor of the stage. And while the crowd screams and hoots and applauds, Gordon tips up the beer and works about half the warm contents down his throat, the crowd happily condoning, *Yesssss!* Can he do anything they would not condone?

He growls into the mike, "But you see, these financiers *manipulate* the dollar and the markets. They *make* it happen! But gee, *we're* bad."

Applause. Whistles. Hoots. Agreement.

Now from a nearby folded chair, he snatches a True Maine Militia song sheet and rolls it up. Twists each end to make it look like a huge joint. He pretends to toke it up over the open top of a candle globe and, while the audience roars and whistles and applauds, he pretends to smoke it. He booms into the mike, "EVERYTHING WE ORDINARY PEOPLE DO IS BAD! *Why?*"

He waits.

He asks again, "Why is it everything we do is bad? And even *illegal?*"

"Control, *sir!*" Kirky hollers out in military fashion.

Gordon swings around to Kirky and grins. Then speaks into the mike. "Kirky says it is *control.*"

Maple leaves seesaw between the stage and the dark zone of hundreds of faces.

Gordon plays one-handedly with his dark mustache, sort of grooming, mighty "joint" and beer bottle dangling from the fingers of the other hand. Then he leans toward the mike and makes the big speakers thump and scrape with the effects of his roughened palm. "America is a mean place. Time to move on. We Mainers need to go *home*. We have forgotten *home*."

On the dusky candlelit piazza next to the stage.

The friendly militia guy with sleeves ripped off his BDU shirt over a black T-shirt, a proper businessman's shave, and a fondness for dynamite (yes, he's an agency operative) comes to stand almost shoulder to shoulder with Rex. Much of the Settlement family is bunched around in here, basically women and teen girls keeping an eye on their leader, on the stage.

And, yes, this dynamite guy sure does love to get into Rex's space. Though this time, he doesn't have that Wizard-of-Oz lion laugh and there's no trying to outshout the din of the lusty crowd.

He sees that Rex has his head cocked, sort of, listening for all he's worth to the words and the rustles coming from the gigantic nearby speakers.

Meanwhile, from the stage floor, Gordon smiles at the crowd.

He fussily sets down the bottle and "joint." Snickers and tee-hees float forth. Gordon takes the mike, stand and all, into both hands as if to balance himself. Belching beerily, he asks, "Say, what *is* globalism?"

Answers from near and far are scrambled, overlapped, squeaked and squealed, roared.

Gordon smiles broadly. "Well."

More offerings, some clear, all enthusiastic. Cackles and cheers. Having fun.

Gordon squints at the mike. "Globalism is *one* civilization. Like a net around an orange." Shakes his head. "Civilizations al . . . ways . . . go . . . down. ALWAYS. Like a hornet's nest, it has its season." Closes his eyes. "But the Sumerians and Mayans, Incas and Romans were not in a global net. Frontiers were left between those collapsing civilizations, which had committed suicide by wrecking their soils, cutting every tree."

He is now giving the crowd a sickly smile.

"*No* frontiers left now. Genocide and relocations, sure. But no fresh unspoiled green vistas to trudge or sail to. Sorry." He sighs. He digs into the tightness of his pistol-less pistol belt. He grinds his teeth, softly, privately. "THE PLANET EARTH, OUR ROCK, IS DYING OF SUCCESS!"

Groans answer him. Some light applause shows they are with him. Also some whistles. He likes the groans best. More fitting.

Sorrowfully and deeply, he goes on. "Success. It's the thing modern schools tell us to march toward, isn't it? But, my brother, my sister, the more of that success you have, the better *trained* and the less human you are. You imitate the system, so now you are just a little piece of something . . . something totally without a mind! Pet! Livestock! But you don't even shit in your stall! You are just a knee-jerk lever of the big grid!"

Applause like thunder.

He waits. Then, before it even subsides, he shouts, "Man . . . I . . . want . . . to . . . get . . . back . . . home!" He steps back and wags his head sheepishly as the applause swoops down, crackling and gusting in its returned thunder. A few moos and woofs.

Gordon laughs. A merry moment.

Mickey stands with Butch Martin and another Settlement guy way to one side of the crowd. At the open bay doors of the largest Quonset hut, Mickey is working for Rex, now wearing the service pistol outside his BDU shirt, eyes squinty, watching for the unbelievable. Would somebody *really* try to kill Gordo? Mickey is thinking.

Man, this is a herd. Totally fucking weird. One guy even said he and his dad are from Texas. Willie's here, up on the roof of the Quonset hut for goats. Has a scope trained on the whole thing. He said this is what you get when you let females start militias. And Rex is tense. I can tell, even though he looks just the same as always.

🏠 Meanwhile, on stage, Gordon contemplates.

"The net that is squeezing the orange is a centralized water-food-energy-and-media grid, almost totally. Soon it will be total."

More noises of agreement, overlaid with some partytime sounds.

The Prophet leans back, eyes closed. Praying? Does Gordon pray? With eyes still closed, he bellers, "We want to get OFF! THE! LEASH! Into the arms of THE! MOTHER! the mother of men!, the great turtle Gluskap, the swollen round magnificent green SOURCE of life that is beneath our feet!" His eyes fly open. "Fuck the global grids and their waste and deceptions and sophisticated terror tactics and holy finance . . . so-called civilized. It's immoral madness! We want LIFE! IT'S! RIGHT! HERE!"

He drops to his knees, limber from so much self-inflicted hard labor here in his little Settlement world, which years ago he gathered together out of weakness and fear. "Pretend this is the ground!" he shouts off mike. He pats the stage. He kisses it.

The crowd goes bonkers.

Finally, back on his feet, face reddened and chest huffing a bit, slowly in a whisper, "You guys understand me? Is what I say madness? Or truth?"

Truth! Truth! comes the reply from the living darkness before him.

"The Patriot Movement—those gentlemen believe in preparedness. Better be ready, boys, 'cause no matter which little bit of this monster you are focusing on to bitch about, it's a lot bigger than you can see at any one time . . . or see at all. The government leaders they show on TV? That's *theater*! The real government is secret. Think tanks. Foundations. Corporations. A rogue network. We waste time here talking about government treachery. Dig up the dirt, understand the danger . . . fine. But"—he whispers the rest in an evil voice that almost swallows the mike—"we cannot fix something that is not broken! The system izzz working as designed. It is FLOWERINNNG! Tonight we too, begin a shadow government. We turn our backs on E-VILE. FORGET THEMMMMM!"

A solid wall of sound, almost vitreous, is delivered of the darkness of the Quad, shadows and silhouettes and dreamlike flashes of the many faces, but the sound is a diamond blinding Gordon.

Gordon screams, as if in pain, "FORGET!!!!! THEM!!!!!!"

♡♡ Jane's heart spins.

It's Mum! Out there! It's her! She's there by those two guys with hats! (*Sigh.*) No, it's not actually. It *sort of* looked like her. And the other lady there is *sort of* like Mum too. What's that? That man's face is burned maybe. Scary with no skin. And the man with the neck thing, scarf thing, his nose might be gone. I'm tired of this darkishness, no good lights. I have the Boston germs again maybe and my head hates this *noise*. People screaming, screaming. But it is wicked important to keep the flag up and look mean and soldierish. I peek at Kirky and at his flag too; we are together in this.

 ### Gordon's screaming advice is lost in their screaming participation.

Waiting for a softening in the crowd's voice, he states quietly, "Forget the Constitution. Forget the rat holes of corporatism, state capitals, and D.C." He turns and peers into the temporarily opened side of the nearest piazza, where this event's temporary stage has been attached, the captains of the True Maine Militia huddled there overseeing the spectacle of their creation. He talks to the mike. "Even the great and true *True* Maine Militia got sidetracked a couple weeks ago with corporatism's Augusta branch of E-vile."

Girl voices yell from the piazza their good-natured objections.

"But you had fun, right?" he yells back.

Voices in the affirmative.

"FORGET THEMMMMMM! Forget EVILE!!!!" he screams, holding up a fist. "Shut off the TV! Rescue your kids from the schools! Hurry! Now! Let's build our own cooperatives, local sane *agri-culture*, energy co-ops, trade co-ops, slower, more intelligent travel, neighborly travel, stalwart citizens' militias and more." He is huffing hard now, dripping on neck and nose and down through the beard, sparkles of his passion. Closes his eyes again as if dreaming, head going from side to side. "They want your kids for the armies of corporatism's empire! To murder the planet. You want your kids working with you and your neighbors in *survival*. The public schools are about to be privatized like the prisons. Then *no* oversight! They will be an arm of the army, mark my words, brothers and sisters! *Get your babies,* your beautiful sons and daughters, out of that fucking dangerous place!"

Crowd makes an ugly sound.

Gordon's head is boiling. His fears at last are shared, thus transformed from fear into muscle.

"All those years we spend in their six-million-dollar-a-year schools, and not one peep about these *emergency* skills we need! Where was that and all the other stuff we needed to learn? Real education is like the sun! It's always been there, all these basic principles, but groups of people hoard those principles so they can fleece us . . . so they can bleed our asses and *control* us, the goddam motherfucking fuckers!"

 Gordon is feeling like the twenty-foot-tall guy on the vegetable can.

His heart is hot, blood hot. Lava is cracking his skull, both painful and pleasant. He *loves* these people. *Don't hurt these people* is his prayer. The blackening night above: pure space. Below: them, him, them, him, in tandem.

 Claire watches from the open screen door of another piazza of the horseshoe of shops. From here, Gordon looks so small and wavery, candles around the stage playing tricks. She is thinking.

Once, during a knitting spree back when the world was only young Gordon and young Claire, colt and filly, I made him a pair of hunting mittens with variegated yarn: red, orange, and a wild yellow. With this style, you have a thumb and a separate trigger finger to the right hand (if the wearer is right-handed). But the rest is just mitten, so the other fingers can snug up to each other. He used those mittens for years.

Tonight, his bare hands gesticulate emergency. Like scrambling to get that perfect shot in fast. That perfect buck, perfectly in his sights. Life with Gordon has always been the emergency. There is nothing strange about tonight. As I watch his hands now, thumbs hooking his belt, trying to look casual and intimate, I remember every single time his hands were on me. Some people say, "How on earth can you share your husband with other wives?" But they don't understand. To love Gordon is to share him with everybody. So maybe that makes what he feels for me thinner and what I feel for him somewhat bitter. But beyond all that, I could not expect you to understand.

 Out! In! Out!

The crowd seems bigger now. Not just louder, more voices. Closer. Tighter.

And now more leaves are letting go from the maple and oak boughs overhead, some descending in a pale eerily lighted veil around the Prophet, settling thickest on and around his scuffed work boots, as if by choreography. And the air chills another notch.

But Gordon's face is as polished as a new car. He is swelling his chest, puffing up. He gulps on the first word but recovers—"And never kid ourselves. The system, the great cold steel and paper and oily mother, is *not* too kind or too moral to commit extermination: germ warfare on innocents, guns and bombs on innocents, false flag terror attacks on innocents, sneaky intelligence operations on innocents, plane loads of mean narcotics for innocents. Mono crops and forced debt. Like a mummy or a vampire in a bad movie, it is especially fond of the taste of innocents."

The crowd moves in closer, tighter.

Jane Meserve wiggles her flag a little, dark eyes sultry. And soldierly.

Kirky Martin, with the other flag, stands stiffer, *more* soldierly.

Gordon lifts the mike, stand and all. Beer bottle falls over, rolls away. He steps to the edge of the tall stage, wipes his forearm across his mouth and beard. "Each and every one of you has a wise word, a little something we all need to hear. We need to hear each other. And to listen. Especially me. I need to listen more. Talk less." He hangs his head. There are chuckles.

He rubs the back of his sweaty head hard, causing some hair to stand up in cowlicks. Now he hunches into the mike, speaks in a clear moderate voice, ascending to loud and louder. "We need to prepare. We need to prepare! WE NEED TO PREPARE! The exterminators are moving over the earth—Africa, the Middle East, Panama, Colombia, and on—coming, *coming, coming!* Not for certain *nations* but for certain *types*. Are you useful enough as you are? Or more useful to them *dead* or *incarcerated*? Or maybe something weirder, even. We need to prepare! We need to LIVE!!!!"

Again the crowd makes much noise and then applause, which splatters away to a single person clapping, then stops.

Gordon stands with his head cocked. Then he raises a hand. "Okay. Do that again. Clap your hands."

The applause resumes. Then again splatters away. People turn their heads to smile at each other, enjoying this game.

Gordon says, "Okay. Now let's clap together, all at the same time." And he brings his hands together for one clap and then space, one clap and then space, and all over the Quad and out across the lot and edges of the fields, the people clap, hands in sync—SMACK! . . . SMACK! . . . SMACK! . . . SMACK!—and you feel each SMACK! in your chest, in your jaws. It is as if all the people here are one animal, connected through one heart, a body as big as the Quad, open parking lot, gravel road, and field.

Fifteen minutes of this clapping before some youthful voice screams, "Tyrants *out*! People *in*! Tyrants *out*! People *in*!"

And off to the left another voice. "Kill the fuckers. Gun 'em down!"

But meanwhile, many voices have joined in with "Tyrants *out*!" and then just "*Out,!*" the word *out* paired with the unified single clap, and this takes off: OUT! . . . OUT! . . . OUT! . . . OUT! And the unified big CLAP, overlaid with the unified thunderous word OUT! comes faster and faster and closer together and louder and louder.

Another ten minutes filled with this building crescendo, aching hands, dripping faces, thunder in the bones, human-caused sound salvos, aimed and ready, the sky thick with stars, and—except for the faces in the fore, lighted by flickering green and rose and yellow—this devilish beast like the other beast—the globalized one that now rules—*this* beast too, is faceless.

But now a light sweeps over the crowd. Then light from another direction, painting an even broader light. And then another. And now these lights all come together on Gordon and the two flag bearers. Gordon stops clapping and crosses his arms over his chest, staring down into the closest of these white blazing TV eyes.

For another few minutes, the monster crowd booms on and on— OUT! . . . OUT! . . . OUT! . . . OUT! . . . OUT!—and Gordon just stands there and the flag bearers just stand there and the expensive, not usually patient, white TV light bores upon the stage.

When the crowd's chanting and clapping grows softer, Gordon speaks deeply into the mike, his head cocked, eyes straight into the nearest white glare. "Need a sound bite, huh?"

Chuckles, cheers, mingled hard-to-make-out suggestions shouted from every direction and one low bray: "Kill 'em! Mash 'em! TV scum!"

When the crowd gets sort of quiet, Gordon still stares at the nearest white light. Then he whispers into the mike, "You gonna do one of them nice *big* insurance company ads right after you play my sound bite?"

The crowd shrieks, laughs, and claps, and there is a small start-up chant of *Truth! Truth! Truth!*

Gordon draws an arm back, swinging a leg forward as if to throw a fabulous fast ball, then pitches the imaginary ball to the nearest TV light, and the crowd howls and resumes its clapping and chanting of OUT! OUT! OUT! OUT! OUT! Into this chant, Gordon screams the scream of a ghoul—"DISMANTLE THE GLOBAL BEAST!" and "TAKE OUR HUMANITY BACK!"—and then throws up his fist—"GOD SAVE THE REPUBLIC!" and then shakes his fist, his massive calloused fist—"OF MAINE!"

As if the crowd size had doubled in half a moment, its voice a colossal spasm of agreement, it repeats GOD SAVE THE REPUBLIC OF MAINE! (And see, these six words will become the TV networks' sound bite, the only thing Gordon St. Onge said tonight, along with a stranger's yell of *Kill 'em!* These will run all day tomorrow all across this great big anxious nation.)

One of the distant TV lights goes dark. Either it has gotten all it wants or it has been trampled by the compressed and agitated crowd. Another light draws back slowly, zigzagging, then shrinks away.

And now, as if the Lord God's (or Mother Nature's) fist pounds the nearest mountain down, a reverberating BOOOOM! shakes the night. Six hundred grains of black powder and a wad of toilet paper in one Dixie Gun Works deck cannon, the saintly patience of Gordon's cousin, Louis St. Onge (a gentle man), and real good timing.

Operative Marty Lees still hovering at Rex's elbow in the crowded foody-smelling greenly lit piazza, thinking with disgust (though his face remains gently pleasant).

Maine secede from America? Is this what the big puppy is suggesting so publicly?

And now.

The three-evil-chimps T-shirt fiddler stands at one mike and calls out, "Party's over!" and walks away through the flickering lights.

And so.

Like several hundred snails, the mob slowly and sluggishly moves off into the night.

The Unitarian Universalist minister remembers that day.

I listened to so many that night, overheard a lot of little huddles, and some I plied with questions. And after that night too, I asked people, "What do you think? Do you believe Gordon St. Onge's prognosis for humankind if we don't learn to do things for ourselves?" And "Maybe even secede from the Union?" And "He says stop shopping. Stop depending. Grow up. What of *that*?"

I found that his fullest warnings rarely reached an ear.

He was just a big rumbling television set to them, loud and colorful. They had watched him, true. Inside each American in those days was fear, fear dense enough to fill a bucket, a *generalized* fright. A terror that was real. *Reality* poured through our skins but not through our brains, so it was fear without explanation. Nothing he said could wake our snoozy, hiding brains. That's not what people wanted. They desired a savior, his great long arms, his sky-filled eyes, his empathy, his growls.

 ## Back in the present time: afterthoughts.

Nothing really bad has happened. No big fights. No heart attacks. No serious vandalism. But after the last of the crowd is gone, and after most of the kitchen crew has finished up and gone home to their respective cottages, the dark Quad and parking lots hold a spooky silence that feels more dangerous than all the day's confusion.

Alone, Gordon has settled into a big, intricately carved and stenciled pine rocker. The porch floor creaks underneath, but the chair is too new to creak. He drinks from a bottle of beer. Little glass candleholders encircle him, some gone out, some still dancing.

Out on the Quad, bunched around the ankles of the grinning wooden dinosaur (whose grin nobody can see up there in the dark treetops), several of Rex's militia are still on hand, visible only by the capricious little on-and-off winks and glows of their cigarettes and digital watches. Rex tells them they can leave now if they want. Job done. Security duty complete. But they linger, talking in low secret voices. Among them, only Willie Lancaster's laugh is loud enough to be heard outside their circle. Among them, only Willie has had *real* fun today.

When Gordon hears the screen door slam two porches down and Rex's measured boot steps, he is just finishing the beer.

By the time Rex reaches Gordon's chair, ringed by those nearly exhausted candles, he finds Gordon opening another beer.

Now a big disgusting burp.

Rex can't bear looking into Gordon's droopy bleary eyes. He gazes at the shingled wall instead and says, "Okay. So it's done. What other kind of lunatic things have you got planned?"

Gordon lowers the beer to the floor with his long-armed reach, burps again, and runs a finger under his tight pistol belt. He says in a slurred way, "I told you. This was the conniving of my little girls." He lowers his voice to a whisper more secret than the militia's huddle a few minutes ago under the Tyrannosaurus. "You know this, brother. Women are more dangerous today. They used to be dangerous in little ways.

Now they . . . they're"—big burp—"awful." Shakes his head. "Awful, my brother." He leans forward and holds his face.

Rex stares at the mountain lion on Gordon's sleeve as he says coldly, "The FBI is watching you. They like to know what your vices are so they can twist you up in them and push you over. That wasn't smart, getting them to know you think pot is okay. Even the beer. It's sloppy."

Gordon raises his face. Big drunken squinty-eyed smile. "Right. The FBI." He snickers.

Then he sees something he has never seen before, a look crossing Rex's face. Not the cold eyes, but the mouth. A tightening of the jaw, like maybe Rex wants to hit him.

Gordon says, "I guess you're right, brother."

Rex says evenly, "Self-control is what you have to have if you want to represent the Border Mountain Militia."

Gordon looks up. Nods. He sees another porch candle has bit the dust. Yet another going down.

Rex keeps on. "And when somebody, whether it's an operative or just some bubble brain, is out there yelling *Kill 'em!* you make it clear that that's not in the program, okay? And it's *not* in the program. Not yet. You hearing me?"

"I suppose you're pissed about what I said about the Constitution," Gordon says, with a snort. "And the Republic of Maine. Personally, *that* idea makes me practically horny."

Rex takes in breath. Then silence.

Gordon digs hard into the graying chin of his beard. Closes his eyes. "I can only say what comes to me. I can't preplan. It's the way I am, okay? I am not a machine like you."

Rex stares straight up at the watery unraveling patterns of light on the open beams of the piazza ceiling.

After a lot of silence and a few more bristly words, down to the last working-hard candle, Rex says he's going home to bed.

☆ **Somehow this recipe for Popeye Pie in Bonnie Lucretia St. Onge's handwriting winds up as evidence in the FBI files.**

Get out big old enamel rect. roaster. Line with crust. For extra crowds Sundays use 9 trays. Enuf considering some won't eat it. Use other stuff on tables

for choice. Kitchen crew: chop spinach, break eggs while in the huge colan-
der (that enameled one), steam the spinach. Kettle: add hot spinach, some
butter, baking powder, scrunched bread crusts, and the beaten eggs. Mix this
stuff while crew grates cheeses: Cow, goat, whatever cheeses you have plenty
of. You want a lot of cheese. This is the winner ingredient.

Into the ovens.

Very, very, very popular, even for some who despise a plain green spinach
naked.

Watch your muscles grow!

Back to the present. The clock ticks and the stars move around some.

Lotta band people spending the night here, not ready for bed: kinda
wound.

"It's only two A.M.!" they say, laughing.

They drag out a cooler of classy-looking long-necked beers. And
whoa! Four very pretty bottles of golden black-and-white-label Jack.

Sunday morning.

Mickey is in the Winter Kitchen, that big eating room in the horseshoe building. He eats. Keeps his head down, though not as shy as his
mother, Britta, who lives here now but never eats in these public buildings. Erika is here, a few seats away, with the Locke household's girl
gang. The girl gang has been absorbed into the shrieking, laughing, kazooing confusion of Settlement kids like fresh eggs into cake
batter.

The young guys who are at Mickey's left and across the table are quiet,
just buttering bread, looking into each other's eyes. Something is in the
air. What?

Gordon is not here at breakfast, but his name is. Mickey hears one of
the wives whisper it, a gossipy whisper. Mickey pushes stringy pork
through egg yolk. He looks quick to see that the whispering voice is Lee
Lynn, a wife of Gordon's who is sort of young but has gray witchy hair.
She is telling a group of other wives beyond where Erika sits that Gordon was "very bad" last night. He was "looped" and he "had sex." With
Glory York. Over on the lake. "Some party a bunch of them went to

after the meeting." And "Glory was dancing naked" and "Gordon was dressed, but pissing on himself . . . wore his militia jacket even" and then . . .

From here on, the details are so pornographic, Mickey is not digesting the food, let alone chewing it. He never realized grown women talked this way. Movie women, sure, but not Maine women. He always thought they just talked about fashions and relationships. Or that at least they would use code.

The witchy Lee Lynn further explains. "Gordon's hand was up to the wrist in Glory's vagina. But then he was too drunk to" blah blah blah, "so Glory helped him."

Mickey's stomach is a small cannonball inside. He doesn't look up into the Martin boys' faces, just at the insides of his eyelids, because his eyes are shut. It is not envy this time, it is fear. Because clearly inside his brain he sees Rex's face, and none of Rex's controlled expressions are on it.

 Next day, Monday, in the early A.M.

Long purple shadows and heavy frosty dew. Fat gold sun squeezes up between the mountaintop trees. One of the clean-up crews moves along behind a humming slow-going solar buggy. Cans and paper bags and balled-up tissues and flyers left from the crowds are tossed into the cart. Like the rest of the clean-up crew, Jane Meserve is dressed warm, wearing old sweaters and heavy pants. Jane's old sweater is rust-colored with green fir trees, and it hangs long in a somewhat glamourish way. She pauses from stooping and heaving trash to gaze with longing up into the woods, her chin up, big sultry eyes wet from the chill, nose a little bit red, thinking of her true love, Mickey, for whom she has composed a *long* love letter and needs to deliver it in a secret way as soon as possible.

Also Monday morning at the residence of Richard York, the Agency goes for the throat.

Pulling up now is a late-model truck driven by a stranger. Stranger steps out. Big guy. Big blond guy with a tan and—yuh, he looks like a California type, beachy with a square jaw and fastidiously shaved to imitate eternal youth. But the truck plates say MAINE. He is not Marty Lees aka Gary Larch. He is not the fresh-faced agent with the SEA DOGS cap. He is yet another one. There are plenty.

He looks tired. His pale eyes are reddened. When he meets Ruth York at the door, he will introduce himself as a friend of Rex's. "I need to see Rex." And Ruth will allow him entry, just as that wooden hand-shaped wall plaque inside the glassed-in porch reads ENTER.

This beachy blond stranger shows Rex snapshots.

Rex's eyes dilate, then slip-slide over the first two pictures. He doesn't study them, just the slip and the slide. He doesn't go to the third, fourth, and fifth picture, simply hands them back, eyes into eyes, maybe wondering who the beachy stranger is but maybe not even that; maybe in some way Rex York is falling through a hole in the floor and in the earth into a hot jungly steam of confusion.

Blood brothers.

Noontime, Denise's Diner in East Egypt. Gordon is meeting with a man named Hal Vorhees about a deal on milled lumber. A big deal. Enough to put the Settlement books in the black for a long while. Gordon does not look well. One of those hangovers that lasts several days. Aspirins have no effect. A thousand cute little hot-cold wires electrocute his skull. He knows he will never drink again. Too many regrets, the ones he can remember and the ones he can't. He listens to what the man has to say. He nods. He clears his throat. He finishes his second glass of water. He wears a black wool jacket, Settlement-made. It feels too tight. Thick bags under his eyes. Beet-colored hickies all over his neck. He remembers her baby talk but not her suck-kiss-biting his neck. He pokes at the pancake in his plate. He is facing the door through which customers mosey in, some taking off their billed caps, most leaving them on. The guy, Hal Vorhees, talks. Words. Gestures. Stuff about sealed bids for building a fire station. Stuff about Marty Cain, a name, a familiar name . . . but Gordon is looking up at the door now, seeing just what he knew he'd eventually see: Rex pushing through that door, his Browning semiauto service pistol in one hand.

Gordon grips the table. His head on fire, part hangover, part terror, arms on fire, feet on fire, he begins to rise, not quite out of the booth by the time Rex arrives at the table and traps Gordon there.

Gordon's face has gone from sick gray to the gray of fight-or-flight, his mouth open stupidly. Rex raises the service pistol, flicks off one of the safeties.

Gordon sees this—the hand with the gun and Rex's eyes—all in one huge picture. Rex does something odd with his mouth, like chewing food . . . and he does something odd with his shoulders, like bracing against cold, then tosses the gun into Gordon's plate with the pancakes in it, and the plate breaks in four almost perfect pieces, and the man, Hal Vorhees, is up very very quick, hollering, "Hey!"

Rex looks worse than Gordon, his pale cold-as-ever eyes lost in bagginess. Not tired, more like a person looks after a long cry. No cap. His hair is flat on one side. In addition to the big mustache, a hobo beard has begun to fill in the rest. Chewing gum. Yes, that's what is going on in his mouth. He is chewing gum as if to pulverize it into nonmatter. *Slisk. Slisk. Slisk.* Breathing hard through his nose. The man who never loses control has crossed a line.

People around the diner have gotten mighty quiet. It's as if the place were empty. Maybe it is. Neither Rex nor Gordon look around much.

Gordon is speechless. In this moment, he knows that any word of excuse or apology from his mouth would be flabby and ridiculous.

Rex speaks low. "I am not going to blow the back of your shirt out, you goddam piece of garbage . . . but I am *not . . . your . . . brother.*"

Gordon is visibly anguished.

Rex spits his gum into Gordon's water glass, grabs Gordon's shirt in both hands, and knocks him almost onto the table.

A voice from the kitchen yells, "*Out!*" and "*Outside!*"

And somehow Gordon is pushing ahead of Rex, running, and Rex follows, running, with his head down, breathing thickly through his teeth and nose, leaving the gun on the broken plate. And outside the door, a woman in a Disneyland sweatshirt and jogging pants is in the way, trying to step off the porch, as Rex leaps and has Gordon around the throat from behind and Gordon is trying to shake him and get turned around, and the woman hollers, "Jesus God!" and flattens herself to the board-and-batten outside wall of the diner.

Gordon squirms backward out of Rex's reach, and rams the center of his spine—"Unh!"—into the six-by-six post of the small porch entryway roof. The two men push and shove their way off the porch, among parked cars and trucks, kind of like kids testing each other, checking each other's bulk through the density of shoulder and elbow. Although bulk is not really the question. Gordon is bigger in bulk. But Rex is immense with rage and some weird humid wide-eyed bafflement.

Once they are out into the sandy open lot, Rex drives his fist with perfect eloquence into Gordon's face, seeming to split one eyeball wide, the lid, the brow, made into fissures, and you can almost hear the *gloink* of the blood letting go, and Rex climbs up one side of Gordon now with a baseball-sized rock and smashes up the other side of Gordon's face so fast it's like a hilarious speeded-up old movie, and Gordon drives a fist into Rex's rock-hard middle, but none of his self-defense is anywhere near as mighty as Rex, coming on and on and on in inexhaustible fury.

Gordon is down. Rex goes to kicking yet still hangs on to the slick bloody rock, and Gordon's whole face gleams and streams a surreal paintlike red. Gordon is trying to get up. Once he is actually up on his knees. But Rex comes back again to kick blood from the one remaining unmutilated ear.

More kicking. More rock. More, more, more. Another minute. Another ten minutes. *Another* ten minutes. People shrieking and bellering "Stop it!"

Where are the state police? Where is the sheriff? The game warden? The constable? There's a good crowd of people bunched around, but no one steps in.

Rex hears it in his head, but more real than this parking lot—the explosion. The crumpling dusty *boom!* of the falling wall. Yowls. And *boom! boom! boom!* Rocket City. And he can smell it. But he can't see it. He can only see the singular. The one. The target. But now it is Maine, not Pleiku. Not 1968. No mistake. But there has been . . . a mistake. No. No mistake. The threat walks tall.

The fighting and pummeling are slower. Both men are panting. No cops. The usual wait for law enforcement, Egypt, Maine, not being the hub of anything. Nature prevails. Seems an hour before the first officer's voice is demanding, "Manners! Manners, Mr. York!" By now, Gordon

St. Onge is not recognizable to any who know him. There are the sounds of cop radios and cop feet, the sound of Rex getting handcuffed, though Rex says nothing. There's just his hard raspy gasping for breath.

Gordon can only *imagine* the cold look of Rex's eyes, the squared shoulders and military bearing not in any way diminished by exhaustion or the humiliation of arrest.

Gordon cannot see.

Rex cannot see.

When Rex is pushed into a cruiser, door slammed, somebody asks, "Was the firearm used to threaten anyone's life or threaten bodily injury?"

And someone else asks, "What firearm?"

A woman's voice now: "It was a rock." Her voice is familiar, someone from around town who always wishes Gordon a chipper "Hello!" in the bank or P.O.

Another siren now, drawing near, another staticky radio and voices that ask questions of other voices.

Gordon is still on his knees, hands between his thighs. He is beginning to forget what that nice thought was. The nice voice. Who was it? Worse than the blaze of pain in his shoulders, face, gums, tongue, lips, eyes, cheekbones, ears, temples, skull, collarbone, wrists, hands, stomach, hips, is the feeling that something is wrong with the way the day is going. What?

And now something odd, something in the tissues of his head letting go.

Too white.

The dust of gold.

He just kind of eases his head down, his forehead on the sand, hands still between his thighs.

 Rex.

There is something stupidly comforting about the cement smell of this place and its hollowness. Its dry heat. They are talking to him, instructing, giving him something to wear.

Between times, when he is waiting for another one of them, with more that they want him to do, he thinks about God. He tries to imagine God's voice, if God had a real voice. The voice would be calm and instructive. Do this. Do that. God is never angry. Rex knows this. Unlike, for instance, Doc, who would tell you about an eye for an eye. Yeah, sure, God would feel surprise at times. And fatherly-type anger. But nothing like revenge. And *never* anything like flipping out.

Rex can't imagine life in the coming weeks, years. In a place like this, he can't recognize himself. Richard York no longer exists. He thinks of himself, the way he was before today, not so much as a being, but as a place. And his people. And the way he handled things. He was proud of that. Before today.

They told him Gordon is dead, but he's pretty sure they are making that up to break him. He knows how they work. They want him to bust into tears and tell them his life's story.

His pal, Gordon. His daughter, Glory. All of it.

Gordon. Yeah.

Rex has always liked to think of those moments in early television when spilled milk whooshed up back into the bottle, when a broken dish snapped back into a seamless glossy whole. Hey, and remember when the lady used to smile into her dish . . . and you'd see her face in the dish smiling about how great a job her dish soap did. And in real life too. His mother and father were smiling. They got along. There was a lotta years there where he never knew how nasty life can get. His life then, it was just like on TV . . . yeah, it really was.

♡♡ Secret Agent Jane speaks.

The path is so easy to find. Sometimes woods are okay. You get used to woods after a while. Sort of. I go along in a beautiful sexy way in case somebody in the trees is spying on me. Maybe Mickey. But really probably not. He is with some guys working to make their shortwave radio, which they *love*. They say it will be for "patriot news" when it is finally fixed. Butchie who lives here says soon the only news will be like on horsebacks. This is way weird.

The path gets steepish here and my new moccasins make scruffs, and then acorns roll and there are hard red berries growing in a plant, and once I saw here some white ones with black dots like small eyeballs.

Everybody says don't eat the eyeball ones, they are poison. Ha-ha! Who would eat a thing that looked like an eyeball anyway?

Here is a tiny tree cone. So tiny. So cute. I hold it a minute. Mickey is kind of in the air. Everything feels Mickeyish and wonderful and speedy and leafish and bright.

Now I'm walking in a sunny place of shriveled flowers, but some flowers deep down are still alive and bugs are singing with their legs. This sound is pretty. But also it is sad and autumnish inside you. Most bugs have died in frost. Only these lonely ones now.

The path goes back in the woods and up along a steep part again. A lot of rocks and moss stuff. A lot of up up up in a mountainish way.

Okay, so here is Mickey's tree house right where they said it would be. Looks like a fort. Nobody here because, like I say, Mickey is working on the radio studio. Sometimes he goes with guys and girls (the big women-girls) to bring meat or furniture or wood and they get money or trade. They take trucks when they go. Mickey is so *grown up*.

A very cute ladder. Mickey probably made it himself. He is so good at stuff. Everybody says. Mickey. Mickey. Mickey.

It is very scary sneaking up here, but here I am. I don't have my secret glasses, which was a mistake. But I remembered to bring the letter, which is full of all my love.

Smells cigarettish here. Sleeping bag and blanket and pillow all have got that smell. Two paper bags with some shirts, some socks. All Mickey's.

God. I am going to die touching his stuff; it is really his stuff. And all his magazines in a pile. And a Bible. So much boring word stuff, all Mickey's. Mickey's very own. A cute window with real glass but very small and cute.

Now here is a long thing of cigarette packages, three packages missing. Yes, these are HIS cigarettes. What's this? Under this shirt which is a maroon nice one . . . it's a gun.

Out comes my hand fast. Jeepers. I actually did touch it a little second.

In this other bag is YESSSSS potato chips and YESSSSS cheese curls! And candy. The store kind! And yes, really a Coke. Boxes of Little Debbie pastries. Mickey gets to have this stuff? He is so lucky!!!

I eat just one thing. Fast.

♡♡ **And then, a noise.**

What's that? It's feet on the way here. I'm trapped! Really trapped! Omigod. Yes, it is feet and crunching leaves underneath. The feet are getting on the ladder.

I hold my head together, squeeze my fingers on my face. A head comes inside the door thing. It's HIM. I open my fingers and see HE is looking at me with his gorgeous eyes, and how can I tell if he's mad with a face that never shows expression, which is the face he's got. He crawls over to the middle and he says, "They are looking for you," and he doesn't look at me when he says it and his voice is so soft and sexy I am going to die before I breathe.

"I'm not going to pick up any more trash with them," I say, in a sexy way. "I've done it already for two days."

He is breathing in a way of having walked a lot in a fast way. He looks at me quick and then looks away. He looks down at his stuff.

"I didn't touch anything," I say, pretty quick. But there's the Little Debbie wrapper on top of the bag. "Well, I'll pay you back. I was starved."

"That's okay," he says. He looks at me again, but quick. Now he looks back at his stuff some more, kind of at one spot. Then he looks at his hands.

I have breathed only three times since he came in. His eyes are so gorgeous. He is a gorgeous person. I can't believe this is happening to me. It is even more powerful at this moment than when we were in the sole car, for some reason. It is good to be sexy right now and get him to have me in his heart and stuff, but I can hardly move, hardly breathe. My neck is hard. I swallow and it makes my neck squeak. I am so embarrassed!

He looks really only at his stuff and his hands, and once at my foot, and then he says, "Gordon's dying."

I laugh. "Not really," I say. He can see I'm not stupid. I laugh again.

He blinks a few times, like five times, then looks at his hands. Wiggles his fingers.

I laugh again.

He looks at me kind of meanish. "It's not funny," he says, meanish.

I do just one small laugh and wiggle my foot. He looks at my foot. I wiggle the other foot. He says, "They took him down to Portland 'cause they can do brains. He might need to have a brain operation."

"Brains?"

He pulls his sleeping bag out to the middle and makes himself a seat. He looks over at his stuff. "You been in those bags?"

I say, "No." Then my hard neck swallows again. "Just a little, maybe."

"What did you look at?"

I smile as sexy as I can. "Your pretty gun."

He says, real quiet, "You know anything about guns?" He looks right at me and his eyes are beautiful ice and I am so paralyzed and a little scared that I might have did something.

I shrug and my face has a stupid expression of a mental retard.

He says, "Well, if you don't know about 'em, don't touch 'em. They could be loaded."

I look at the bag, then back at him, and he says, with a little twiggle of a smile, "That one ain't loaded."

Then I do the next stupid thing. I make a big sigh, but it makes my lips vibrate like a small fart. Oh, gawd, I am ruining this. "I love guns," I say.

He looks at me hard, then feels his pockets and gets out his cigarettes. He puts one in his mouth and then he wants a match but can't find one. He gets up on his feet but squattish and then he feels around in his bags and in a little box but no matches.

I say, "I'm freezing. Don't you have a heater?"

"Nope."

I says, "It's nice up here. Pretty and nature-ish."

He looks at me. His cigarette is in his mouth, hanging down but not lit. He looks in a couple more places but no matches in those places.

I say, "I like your sister, Erika. She wants me to do her hair."

"Sister-in-*law*," he says. He picks his cigarette out of his mouth.

"She told me about your little brother."

"Nephew."

"Oh. And who was the man? The one that just died by making exhaust in himself."

He looks at me. "My brother."

"That's awful. Is he ashes now? She said he was ashes."

He looks at me and nods. And says, "Something's weird. Everybody's dying. Or going to jail."

"My mum's in jail."

He nods. He hangs his head in a beautiful way. "Everybody's in jail."
He looks up and he has eyes of tears. He goes looking around all through
his bags some more. He goes faster and faster through the bags. He says
shit a couple of times.

I say, "If we eat here, we won't have to eat with *them*."

He says, "They're having a bird. They think you're gone or something. Gone to the troublemaking schoolteachers' house . . . or fell in a
well. You oughta go down there and make 'em feel better."

"If I had a nice tree house like this, I'd live in it," I say, with a nice smile.

"Well, you can have this one. I'm moving in with Evan and them in
a couple days." He sits down, then scoots backward on his bum till he's
sitting back on the sleeping bag.

"Oh, but this is so pretty."

"Yuh. Pretty. It's all yours."

"Well, thank you."

He hugs his head now so his face doesn't show. His pretty hair, the
little ponytail, sticks up so cute between his fingers. It is the cutest hair.
And pretty. Yellow and brown streaks, like Mum's. In the movies there
would be beautiful love music playing every time they show him. Now
he holds his head forever.

I say, "Tired?"

He doesn't move, except to squeeze down on his head harder.

"Is this 'cause your matches are lost somewheres?"

He doesn't answer me.

I say, "I'll go get you some matches, okay?"

He looks. His face is squeezed and red which makes his eyes look
wicked pale, like white eyes. "There's some here somewhere. I'll look
again in a minute." He stretches his legs out in front of him.

"Mind if I stay awhile?"

He shrugs. "I don't care." He points his thumb at the wall. "But first
go tell them you're okay."

"No way. They just want me to be their slave. It's going to take a
hundred years to get all that trash up."

"Nobody's picking up trash. They're all meeting in the kitchens. Everybody. Even them that went to Madison on that science thing. They're
coming back 'cause of Gordon being in the fight. Some's at the hospital
with him. He'll probably die, or turn out brain-damaged."

"Don't keep saying that. You think I'm stupid."

"Okay. I won't."

I get nice and comfortable. I can breathe pretty good now. I'm getting used to being with the world's most cutest boy. "I can sing. Want me to sing?"

He makes his eyes roll funny.

"I can tell stories good. Want to hear?"

He looks over toward his stuff. "Can you read?"

"Yes. It's easy."

He crawls over to his bags like a cat or dog walking and he shows me a magazine which has big pictures of guns. He finds a page—with a gun, of course—and he says, "What's this say?"

I read all of it easy. It's like school, the real kind.

He pulls the magazine away and looks at the page a minute, thinking and feeling his lip. Then he sticks his cigarette in his lips again and goes over to the pile again on his arms and legs and it's that Bible this time. "Some words are hard," he says, with his cigarette in the middle of his mouth. "Especially in this." He gets on his knees beside me. There's a bookmark made of cloth with a real tassel. He fixes the Bible open on the floor by my leg and one of his hands bumps my arm and my veins turn to blue lightning inside my arm and this is the biggest fattest moment of all time. He says, "What's that word?"

I look close at the word, which begins with *R*. "Well . . ."

"You think it's *Revelation*?"

"Yuh, probably. It looks like probably it is *Relations*."

"*Rev-el-a-tion*. It's got a *V*, see?"

He smells funny, like a million cigarettes. And butter or something. He has a scary smell. My heart is going to kill me with fast beats. After the *R* word, I read a few easy words. But most of these words are very strange, too long or too short. I skip over those. I do just the easy ones. I sneak a look at him and he's holding his head again but with just one hand, and he is kind of rocking just a little, and I can see his face, his eyes staring at the floor 'cause he's listening really good or else thinking about something and he looks sorta sad. I pick the book up and hold it in my lap so I can see better. The words get harder. One begins with a *Z* and there's another *R* one and weirdness.

I shut the book nice and soft and polite-ish. And I say, "I'll just *tell* some Bible stuff, okay? Once a lady had a donkey and a baby and Joseph.

And other animals. Baby was named Jesus. He was the same one who got big later and did all those things, the tree branches and stuff. Anyways, the donkey—I don't know the donkey's name . . . probably Skip—he was always carrying somebody who was too huge. Jesus was a very nice baby. Never cried. Never messed hisself. Everybody in those days wore funny head things. Jesus was very nice to everybody and never did anything stupid and he was completely gorgeous, probably Jewish—but somehow it happened that the bad people who were like cops an' stuff did this thing with nails."

I hate this story so I switch it and Mickey hardly notices. "The only reason Alix wanted summer camp was to ride Kukkaberra, but she falls off. She always loves horses, but they are so big and—*whoosh*—throw some people off them on the road and step on them. And Alix—" I hear a scratchish sound and then smoke all around. Mickey is still staring down but *how did his cigarette get lit?* Somehow he had a match. Smoke shoots out of his teeth and his nose.

I tell him all about how a nice man helps Alix get interested in horses again and she wins a horse show and wears a little hat.

When his cigarette is short, he asks, "Want some chips?"

Of course.

So we eat chips. TOGETHER. Like we are married. And he takes the Coke bottle and gives the cover a twist and it poofs and he says, "You first." And we take turns. Yes, my lips then his lips then my lips then his lips.

"I'm cold," I tell him. I really am. All bumps.

He pulls a shirt from the bag, the maroon one. Takes the gun out first, puts it in something else. "You can borrow this, but I need it back."

I really wear HIS shirt. It's right on my skin. It is so soft and cozy. And has the scary smell.

He says, "I'll walk you back if you want."

I scrinch up my face. "Why don't I stay here with you until you move."

"I don't think so," he says. "They want you back down there." He picks at his socks and looks at me a couple times.

I say, "I've been to Bev and Barbara's house. Have you?"

"No."

"I went in their bedroom. They have got just *one* bed."

"So?"

I say, "Some people like *one* bed."

"Bev and Barbara are lesbians."

"That's the sex thing, isn't it?"

He makes a face like a little smile is about to happen, then looks away. He gets out another cigarette.

"You don't have a real bed here," I point out.

He laughs. He thinks this is so funny. I can actually see his teeth, even though his laugh isn't very loudish.

I say, "You're poor, aren't you?"

He looks at me, *right at me*. "You are too."

"I am not."

He laughs again, teeth and everything. He lights his cigarette. Big smoke pours out of his face.

I ask, "What else is there to do here?"

He says, "I told them if I found you, I'd bring you back."

I laugh. "I'm not going back."

He smokes a minute. Very quiet.

I say, "I brought you a letter from somebody. It's in my pocket, ha-ha."

"Who?"

"A very nice girl. But it's a stupid letter. Maybe I'll get you a better letter next time."

He snorts funny. "The very nice girl is you, right?"

"Maybe."

He smokes and smokes, slow and sexy. The smoke is as pretty as snowish air but you gotta love the stink. Phew! He smokes a lot of this smoke around and then I think he looks very nervous. "Come *on*." He says this pleadishly. "I promised them. They are pretty upset down there. You've got to go back. Play runaway some other time. When things are better."

I laugh.

He gets up on his knees.

I cross my arms to show who's boss. But I'm smiling. "I'm staying here."

He starts walking toward me funnyish on his knees.

I get ahold of one of the wood tree things that goes up the wall. "You can't make me." I laugh very sexy-ish.

His cigarette hops around in his mouth and his eyes are sqwinched in the smoke. He pulls my fingers off the wood. He gets my arm and pulls and I laugh and grab things and things fall over and his magazines slide around and he tries to get me out the door that's made in the floor and down the ladder and we almost fall and the big Coke bottle falls out the door hole and bounces on the ground.

He doesn't yell. He's very quiet but for grunt noises, pushing me and squeezing my arm. He is very strong. Like Gordie. I try to pull away but I can't. He has a wicked grip. I laugh, laugh, laugh. We go along the path and his cigarette has got bent and fire and ashes keep going all over his neck and arm. I fall against him and make my hair push in his face against the cigarette. "Ow, ow! Help!" I squeal, in a *very* sexy way.

He says, "You've got to go back. It ain't me, it's them. They want you."

"Tough!" I giggle and make myself heavy like I'm asleep. But he is so strong, he just drags me. I can't believe this.

He says, with little gasps, "They are trying to figure out what to do about Gordon. Everyone is scared and bawling. Help them out a little. Don't be a brat. Gordon might be already dead."

I laugh.

"It's not funny," he says.

"It izzzzzz. Yooooo are funny."

"It's not funny."

"It izzzzz."

"It's not."

"You are funny. And cute." I laugh like a crazy witch.

He squeezes my arm a little harder and I walk all wobblish. And I fall against him some more and he is like the strongest person I ever felt and it is the best day of my life.

💿 On the doorstep of Marian St. Onge's home in Wiscasset.

They look like two soldiers with chins high, machine-like eyes. Even Aurel Soucier's eyes, that dark fierce gutsy gleam all gone.

The cedar shrubberies on either side of the brick steps seem unusually green. The late-day sun gives their old pickup truck parked in the driveway a white-hot look, although the truck is tan. Leaves spiral down from the tall maples. Marian's voice takes on a soft edge of fear. Something is wrong. She looks into the dark Passamaquoddy eyes of the other, the tall boy, her grandson. "Cory?"

Neither visitor looks too ready to speak. They both just swallow.
Aurel takes off his olive-drab bush hat.

⊙ Gordon St. Onge's long dream.

He dreams that he sees a head, hovering in the stuffy air. No body.
No neck, even. It is just a floating, bulging, burning head. The mouth
suddenly opens, a hole in the fire. There is a stink from the mouth.
And inside the mouth is black and endless.

⊙ Evening. Bonny Loo St. Onge.

There are no chairs in intensive care. When you are visiting your loved
one, you just stand there. And there is no privacy. There is a nurses'
station across the room. The beds of the broken people are positioned
in a crescent with their accompanying dripping bottles and monitor
screens. The little hopping zigzagging spot of light on the screen that is
Gordon's great big heart looks so cheerful, it could almost make you
smile. His heart. Nothing is wrong with that heart, they say. It's the brain
they are watching, the swollen brain inside that mostly shaved head, the
brain behind the face, the face a *thing* that looks like a ripe, purply-black,
tight, eyeless, mouthless rubber bag. Yeh, that's his face.

On the sheet, one to each side, his hands. One bandaged, one good. The
one that is good is closer to where I stand. His thick fingers and short nails
are as familiar as his voice would be if it spoke, but there is no voice.

Standing on the other side of the bed across from me is Bree, in her
usual old jeans and work shirt, tall, tightly laced work boots. She was
working with her brothers at noontime today when Rick Crosman went
to tell her the news. I was with my mother at her house.

We get five minutes for each visit. That's what they give you. Then
you have to leave after your five minutes are up. So many in the family to take up the next available five minutes. I need to make my five
minutes count. But . . . I don't touch him. I don't take his hand. And
Bree doesn't touch him either. It's like we've come to check out some
museum exhibit, some science thing, maybe a fossil, something once preserved in ice. Mostly she and I just look at each other, in stolen glimpses.
I always thought her face was terrible. But now the most deformed and

terrible thing imaginable is lying on that pillow, breathing through broken teeth and tough-looking green tubes, both eyes bandaged, both ears bandaged, no beard, just purple and swollen "skin." Gordon's face, no longer good-looking—though he was never really movie-star material. It had more to do with his personality, the light behind the eyes and at least twenty types of smiles. But now . . . that face . . . it's just garbage.

 Bree St. Onge.

Don't die. Don't die. Don't die.

 Claire St. Onge.

The one small and two large waiting rooms farther down the hall are always filled with us. We fill up seats. We stand along the walls. Then there are people who have come to see Gordon whom we don't know. Only immediate family is allowed to see him. But they hang around anyway, waiting for news.

Immediate family. As you can guess, the St. Onge immediate family has given more than one nurse a bit of a stutter.

There are reporters too. Some identify themselves. We have agreed not to talk with them. But we try to be courteous. None of them act like jerks, so why should we? It's just a kind of war of polite smiles. A war of patience.

When Mary Wright, an old pal of Gordon's, came down the hall, the reporters came to life. "Senator Wright, what brings you here?" She replies, "Same thing you're here for." She smiles. She is a petite person, but her smile is usually panoramic. Now her smile is spare.

Marian, Gordon's mother, does not hang out with us or eat from our baskets of food. I'm not sure where in the hospital she has been going off to, to wait alone. But she has been near. She and I go way back. It hurts to see her handsome face all swollen from constant sobbing. Once Whitney went up to her and hugged her, two lovely tall women, one older, one so young, those pertinacious St. Onge–De Paolo genes. The embrace was a long one, though not a single word was said. I believe there will come a time when Marian embraces *all* her grandchildren, will hold them dear. But not today. She still needs to pretend that her son is an ordinary man.

We always have kids with us. They read to each other, brush one another's hair, play word games, whittle out whistles and animals and little soldiers from basswood in satchels. Some knit or stitch. Some just slump against a parent and look bored. The teenagers whisper a lot. They walk the halls together, restless. They help change diapers or take little kids to the restrooms. "Don't let them sit on the seats," the mothers caution. The reply: "We'll try not to."

Bonny Loo St. Onge speaks.

During the night, Gordon stirs. The doctor tells us he's not paralyzed, that he remembers who he is, where he was born, what year he was born, but not a lot of recent events, but some of that may eventually come back okay. He explains that there is sight in one eye but the other eye needs more surgery and more time—"severed ligaments" and something about the cornea. Trauma. And *blah blah blah*. The doctor smiles, says, "He's tough. Give him a medal."

We cheer. Some of us scream and sing. Cheers and chants go up and down the hall. We are promptly told by a small unsmiling nurse to shut up or leave.

In Augusta, the attorney general sits in his new remodeled office, a few boxes still unpacked.

He stretches his arms over his head, phone receiver between ear and shoulder. He chuckles, drops his arms. "I would say this could be one of those times." He listens, smiling. Then, "Yeah, yeah. That was when I was just a pup. I think you'll find my tastes have changed." He listens. Laughs again. "When?" He listens. "Right. Right." He listens. Laughs. "Yeah, they were the only Democrats in the county. It was lonely for them." He listens and he laughs heartily. Snorts. "Was that one of the figures in their coat of arms?" More hearty laughter.

More listening, shifts in his wheeled office chair, reaches for his pen, writes on a pad. "Yes, uh-huh . . . right." He listens. Writes. He is left-handed. His hand and the pen and pad are twisted as if in a pose of anguish or ardor, waiting for the caller's next words. "I see."

He listens some more, pen raised.

He listens even harder, pen raised.

He listens, pen moving now, down toward the pad. "Arraignment date would be when?" He scribbles.

More listening. "Richard York? With a Y? Well, is Bernie on this? He's our Oxford County guy now." He leans toward keyboard and screen, chair a soundless swiveling, cool leather shoulder-high. He taps into the recesses of the Maine *justice* system. He says, "Oh, of course. That's the reality . . . Yes . . . Yes, I'll see what I can do. You, uh—" He listens and *mmms* as he taps, pokes, taps, jabs, taps. Stops. Eyes sweep the screen. Then lock. "Well, now, it seems as though we don't have to do anything here. Mr. St. Onge *himself* is not filing charges."

He listens. Then, "I have no clue. It's not unlikely. But if *you* people want him out of there, he's going to—"

He listens. He laughs. He listens. "Well, yes. Sure." He looks at his watch. "Okay." He writes REX. He chuckles. He says gravely, "Great nickname. When he's not assaulting his friends, what is he, a German shepherd?"

S. A. Kashmar hangs up the phone, swiveling to scribble up an old, old, old-fashioned pink while-you-were-out memo. His thoughts.

If you want bees to make honey, you have to let them fly around. If you want a large choice of patsies for when you need them, you have to keep them out of jail, keep them out and about. You want all these guys not to trust each other, okay, and you want them to act crazy—but also to be handy as a mop when you need to use their faces and names and bad reputations for what we must accomplish, which I cannot tell you, the public, about, because you, the public, can't handle necessities and complexities. Hell, even some people here in this line of work can't. The numbers of stars in their eyes could light the Superbowl playoffs into infinity.

November

 One of the many calls Lisa Meserve has made from Boston to the Settlement, always scheduled and always answered with the long golden fingers of the child who never gives up.

As always, the dark hair is barretted prettily, gushing in bubble curls from the latest Settlement-made ornament. As always, Jane keeps her face to the wall, away from those who might otherwise see her private expressions. Sometimes she stands. Sometimes she sits, if Gordon's ancient wooden office chair isn't filled with books, maps, letters, or junk. Today she sits. She doesn't wear her powerful pink spy person's glasses. There are just her clear black eyes.

Without any help, she "sees" her mother's eyes, blue "like wonderful jewels." She listens to her mother's voice, which sounds slow. She doesn't know about the drugs called sedatives given out in jail to prevent wailing. She speaks. "Mum, Claire says you are postponed again in the trial thing."

She listens.

Then, "But that's stupid, Mum."

Her mother agrees. As usual. On the workings of the world, both Jane and Lisa have come to unfailing agreement.

"Mum, tell them they are—"

Her mother butts in with a woozy jokey moment.

Jane laughs.

Her mother tells her it'll all work out. She explains this very slowly, almost gravely, due to the wail-preventing sedatives.

Later next year, when Lisa is sentenced to a mandatory life sentence, to be served in a California women's penitentiary, her wooziness comes naturally (drug free) as it does when a person faints while being nailed to a cross or tied to a wheel to be broken and dismembered and buried alive by pharaohs and queens or modern systems working efficiently.

 Jane finds Mickey still living in his tree house. She visits awhile. Mostly painful silence.

He passes the bag of Cajun Tacos to her, and her long fingers squirm happily inside the noisy bag.

He watches her a minute while she isn't looking at him. "So your mother . . ." He jiggles his foot.

"What about her?"

"Jail . . . what's it like? Does she say, how . . . how bad it is?" He jiggles his foot faster.

"Well, she gets to wear a very pretty orange thing." Now she laughs and covers her face. Dark eyes peer out between her long golden fingers, her forehead wrinkled. "Actually, it's hideous . . . orange and hideous."

"What's her cell like, small?"

"I don't know."

He watches his own foot, tries to stop the jiggling. He says in a husky way, "Some people never get out."

Jane's hands drop to her lap on top of the crinkly bag. She frowns. "In Boston, you get fed'ral *trials*. It's in California, the prison, maybe." Jane's eyes flutter, the frown deepening, throat swallowing. "The judge needs a bashed brain. Like under a truck, I hope." Then she gives him a narrow squinty look. "You are very curious about jail."

"Yeah, people I know are there." He does not say *Rex*. Nobody here at the Settlement speaks the name since what happened happened.

Still frowning and yet another hard swallow. "She's probably wearing the awful orange thing."

"He."

"Oh. Maybe he *likes* orange."

"I doubt it."

🌀 Rex in jail.

They come to his cell in a matter-of-fact way and take him to the visiting room. His lawyer is there, smelling like a car interior and fresh air, both alien smells now. The lawyer tells Rex things Rex cannot believe, and boy, this lawyer is unusually wound. Talking fast. Almost a squeak to his voice. Almost a giggle.

Maybe he is as stunned as Rex is by this turn of events. How forgiving, this Guillaume St. Onge. Broken, mutilated, forgiving.

🌀 Ruth York.

He is telling her to please come get him. Everything is dropped. His mother can hear him over the telephone, swallowing, grave as ever.

🌀 Rex free.

In the rain, he waits. He lets the rain wash through his hair and over his face and heavy mustache, down his collar. His mother will arrive driving his truck, so he watches the street down there for the color red. Where the parking lot, court, and jail are it is high, like a battle position. Town of South Paris, Maine. The county seat. Cars passing. People like ants, shortsighted in their routines, breathless with their burdens, blinded by rain. Big sky. Big rainy *white* sky.

Before he sees his truck, his mother's face behind the glass, the rain has turned to a mix of snow that smells like nothing else in this world, each tiny flake designed with care and dainty laborious concentration by the huge hand of God, purely perfect.

☆ Lee Lynn remembers the first day Gordon was home.

He was odd, sweet and odd. The dark universe was uneasy, and the power of this planet to heal was stuttery. We had a lot of rain that week, funny rain, rain mixed with snow, or sleet or freezing rain, then switching back to warm and windy. And there was thunder and flashes of light, which is not what you'd expect in November.

Everyone wanted to be near him. In some ways it was like a celebration, but a most gentle and reverent kind.

We spent a lot of time in the Winter Kitchen and the Cooks' Kitchen, where he sat in that old oak rocker near the stove, surrounded by all the older folks, some half-witted, others clear, and I saw to it that he had many little bitty cups of honeyed sweet-fern tea. And he interrogated the old people as he never had before, wanting to know how this or that thing was done *back then:* farming, logging, sawyering, machinery, sickness remedies, wool carding, and all the stories of record-breaking snows. He seemed to no longer be a species of the *now*. And some words he had lost, so he defined them. Like "the thing you ride in looks to be stuck in the stuff."

We were expecting Réal —you pronounce this Ray-*ahl*— Gordon's third cousin from Aroostook, but Réal's wife, Terry, and teen daughter, Ray-Lynn, showed up too, so there was very special music: parlor music, healing music, fiddle and guitar, and the concertina, which our Ricardo played as if he'd done it all his life. "Cine Cetta," "Waltz of the Wallflowers," "Ashokan Farewell," "She Beg She Mour."

Gordon rocked slowly to and fro with such a look of distance in his eyes, those pale dark-lashed eyes, normally so full of play and green-white fire. And his hair now! Part crewcut, part red scarring from the surgery and wounds, the beard hurrying back, long bristle by long bristle.

Eddie Martin said, "He looks like roadkill."

A child was always near, hugging Gordon's head, a child standing at his chair like a sentry or attendant, eager to please him, whispering and leaning; some small kids sat between his knees and feet. The image of crows standing around carnage crossed my mind. But why? Gordon *always* attracted children.

There was talk about the major repairs necessary on the greenhouses, and pouring the foundation for the new machining Quonset hut, the ground not fully frozen yet, the fierce freeze normal to November nowhere in sight.

The Christmas wreath orders were good that year, neither hurt nor helped by the newsworthiness of the Settlement. CHRISTMAS TREES FOR SALE, CUT YOUR OWN signs posted down by the guardhouse. Meat cutting as usual. This meant you'd have to have people in and out, probably strangers. Gordon seemed disinterested in all this. Quiet. He watched us talk. Decisions were made in his presence, but without much input from him, just a little joke, a nod, and his new quiet smile.

More music. Lots of music. The Aroostook cousins rosined up the bow, prodded the guitar, went at it with leaps and lunges, effervescent (like soda pop) eyes. "Give Me Your Hand" (that one sounded like a little poky donkey and rider in a lighter moment of a *lite* TV Western). Then "Avant de s'en aller," "Westphalia Waltz," "Lovers' Waltz," "Orange Rouge." And "Road to Lisdoonvarna," that one a bit lovely and haunting at first, then a kind of wide-eyedness to it, very nice. But I remember when they finished playing "Metsa Kukkia," swoopy and busy and Old World, he said quietly, "Make that again." He had no expression. His face was like a picture of his face caught between expressions. It was the kind of music that would make you want to stand up and dance, dive about, flinging your partner around, not fast, not like rock and roll but a graceful violence. But he didn't move from his chair. Didn't rock his chair. Just stared into the music. I don't know what he saw.

When the cousins were finished, he said, "Sound that again," in the same dead voice, same stony face.

I said, "Can't you say *please*?"

The cousins laughed.

He said, "Yeah, please."

And again it was played.

 The next day, there was snow, the kind of snow that changes to rain at noon, then to ice, then back to snow, making a cold mush, and so the messages were pretty sparse in the box by the gatehouse. Only four. Among them, this handwritten letter from Ruth York.

> *Dear Gordon,*
> *Thank you for what you did. No one can talk against you, as far as I am concerned.*
> *I always knew you had a specialness, but now I know it best. You know Ricky would never do anything like that on his own,*

especially to you, but that blond young guy Andy who brought the pictures and got him all worked up, like when he has the Vietnam dreams. If I were you, I wouldn't hold on to Andy much longer as a friend. I think you should know that he done that. With friends like that, who needs enemies?

Glory has moved out and broke my heart. We got along so well. We none of us ever fought, not her and her Dad either. But there was something edgy when she left. She was probably in a shock about what Ricky did to you. Like me. I am still in a state. Even when Marsha was living here, Marsha and Ricky never had fights like some do. It was just that other man she had to have. And what did Ricky do about the other man? Nothing. He just let it go. He just kept it all to himself, a silent sufferer.

He has always been like that. He was an easy child. Easier than his brother. And then Glory was always just like him, even when she was a baby. As you know, seeing her so much when she was growing up. I just hope she don't drink no more. She can't handle it. I don't know what's going on now, if she's drinking or not. I don't know. But I wish on a star for us all to be happy.

I am sorry this all happened. You was always family to us, you and Ricky like brothers. It is so spooky to me how he changed that day. Ricky has lost customers. But since you dropped charges, he can keep his guns, which as you know have always meant every-thing to him. I think he is trying very hard now to figure himself out, how he changed like he did, and maybe someday make it up to you. Someday it'll all work out, I guess. I heard you're going to need doctors to work on your face and your teeth. I will pray for you. You were always such a handsome boy. Your parents were handsome people. You had looks, but you have always had personality to boot. Just remember, nobody can take that from you: your personality.

Love, Ruth

Gordon stares at this letter, folded too many times, the creases soft-ened and damp from the damp day. The paper is lavender, cool to touch.

He never knew anything about any Vietnam dreams. Rex never even talked about the *actual* Vietnam.

But he knows Rex hates this Ricky business. But that's mothers for you. And *who* in hell is Andy? Blond? He can't think of any blond Andy guy he'd call a friend. And pictures? Pictures of him and Glory? Oh, boy.

He sighs miserably.

He has almost no memory of that party on the lake after the True Maine Militia event, or of the True Maine Militia event itself, or the next day, and certainly not the next. But those who remember the party on the lake have told him what they thought he needed to know. No one mentioned a camera. No one mentioned the name Andy.

Rex alone.

Militia on hold, he watches TV a lot after work and does little favors for his brother Bob, next door. Now he sits at the table and listens to his mother talk in her soft coaxing way about the Legion. And he eats a cookie, the first in years. Also new is face rubbing. Rubs till his eyelids are pink and his eyebrow hairs turn backward like small quills.

He does not like the way his mother wears so many silver and turquoise rings today, which accentuate her aging hands. He doesn't like anything about anything.

He has even started to sleep too late.

☆ Again from the future, the Unitarian Universalist minister who was at the big Settlement event speaks.

This following of Gordon St. Onge that accelerated over those coming months after his near death was a sign of how bad things had become for those Americans who had normally thought in terms of trust and promotions, rewards for doing one's job better than the other guy, positive thinking, Merry Christmases (shop, shop, shop), faith in progress (that technological wizardry of the high order of humans).

Industrial-era woman. Petroleum man. The age of growth. The age of image overload. The belief that evolution means a species can transcend God.

So now the frightening descent from the thunderous promises of modern education, glossy mags, the six o'clock news team, and screechy sponsors. Now that TV smile was making the La-Z-Boy viewers uneasy.

So yes, from the people who flocked to him, Gordon St. Onge's image was born. I say *image* because who knows what he really was like, other than his close ones?

Was he really so wonderful, truly God's milk? Could his fingertips change you? Surely not! It would not be natural (let alone divine) that it should follow.

Who was Gordon St. Onge? He could have been anything.

The thousands of persons who would adore him would never be embraced by him anymore than I. And I danced with him!

Hear me now. I confess that our dance was nothing like a blessing. It was (this makes me smile) just a jitterbug.

 Mickey alone.

It seems that when he is most hollowed out (chocolate rabbit Mickey) is when he is jammed in with all the St. Onge people on a toasty morning, eating eggs, all their food-smelling mouths breathing at him. "Oh, Mickey, pass the sauce stuff" or "Oh, Mickey, there's no one on the list for Helen's firewood for Thursday. You interested?"

Not depressed. Not like his old school days. *Ha-ha. Mr. Carney, go suck on a pony. Ha-ha. I'm definitely outta there!*

But here in St. Ongeland, he just isn't the real Mickey Gammon. He is ghost Mickey. Mickey Casper-Unfriendly-Ghost Gammon. The rest of them here just seem *too alive*. Too St. Onge-ish. And too many.

Presently, he is sitting on a boulder up in the wide-open sort-of-snowy field; anyone can see him. And the wind is cold and bone-damp and skull-damp today, but here he is, collar open, letting it be cruel. All the big boulder needs is graffiti. A bunch of initials in black paint, maybe pink. Or some obsession maybe. Like Ski-Doo. Or Madonna.

Okay, so he is here on the mighty rock. He is, like, on a hard cloud, only this baby ain't gonna float.

Wishes.

Very quiet for a few moments. The child Jane's eyelids are closed loosely and flutteringly, upon her face the golden stutter of firelight. Eight chubby, thumb-sized Settlement-made candles. One for good luck, seven for the years of her time so far on this mortal coil. Then her midnight-dark eyes go wide and she blows the flames out and the only other person at this party, Gordon St. Onge, claps and whistles.

She sighs and smiles guiltily. "I forgot to wish for the *other* thing. I was all nervous and got mixed up."

Now there is only the sickly and sickening glow of the fluorescent light over Gordon's big desks across the old kitchen.

"You don't need birthday candles to make a wish, dear," he informs her. "It's a free . . . uh . . ."—he closes his eyes, searching—"free *country*."

She laughs and slaps the air between herself and the dim, bluish, gloomily not-very-well-lighted image of his face across the little table, his terribly scarred face, one eye rather St. Bernardish. "You are so funny."

She had specified *only him* and *her* for this party. None of them *up there,* even the Soucier family, with whom she now lives and kind of loves.

And of course, Lisa Meserve, Jane's mum, is not here. It's a bit stomach-trembly to think of, isn't it? The word *mother*. The words *faraway cage.*

Okay, and for tonight she had specified a *pink* cake. And *real* (store-bought) ice cream: Chunky Monkey.

So now a huge (size of a small mattress) piece of cake teeters on the spatula as she guides it to his plate. "Oops!" It flips off the spatula, turns upside down. She laughs, gasping. "I'm"—*gasp gasp*—"very very"—shrill giggles and more gasps—"sorry!" With teary eyes, she laughs on and on as she now guides another huge piece to her dish, which also falls, this time missing the plate and breaking into pieces. "Omigod, this is so bad!" She laughs and wipes her eyes with the top of one hand, plows the wayward cake toward her plate with the other, and wipes both hands on her napkin, her eyes on his scarred, forever-changed face. "This is so bad." She sighs, resigned to the fates that make cake accidents happen.

Now the ice cream. She long-leggedly and gracefully fetches two pint cartons (the round kind) out of the freezer (otherwise empty) and plunks them down, one beside his plate, one beside hers. And two huge spoons. "The rest of the cake," she explains, settling primly back in her seat. "You get half and I get half. Exactly." This is justice.

"Good deal," he says, scooping out all his ice cream in one carton-shaped frozen-hard-as-cast-iron sculpturesque shape on top of his cake.

She proceeds to jab at her pint of ice cream with her big spoon so it gets to be all these little slivers arranged in a pretty way around her cake.

Everything is now ready to go. "Well," Jane says, staring at his face across the two loaded supper-sized plates with their glazed pink and tan piles of wonderful sugary stuff.

He nods.

She nods.

He says, "Happy seven years old, Lady Jane."

"Thank you, old guy," she says, most tenderly.

They both dig in, eyes bearing down on the job at hand.

 Mickey speaks.

At breakfast, I signed up for the use of a vehicle, which you can drive even without a license, as long as you stay on Settlement land. Wound up with a biodiesel farm truck, the one with clutch-ball trouble. One of the dogs jumped up in the seat, one of the black ones. Dogs like rides. I said, "Okay." Me and the dog was instant friends after that. He rode along with his big red open mouth and kept flashing his eyes on me. He watched the road ahead like he was helping me drive. Or maybe he thought we'd get to see a giant walking steak up ahead. Ha-ha.

Well, I take the truck out. Off the land. I just go, okay? It was weird. Something came over me. I didn't give a shit about anybody being pissed. Not them at the Settlement. Not cops. Before I even get to Rex's, I'm passing his brother's place that has the long tar driveway and the cattle pasture fenced up to it and all the brown frizzled weeds not chewed by cows and patches of snow, and there's Rex and the brother up there, both squatted down by the garage with somethin'. Well, I just kept going and got down the road to a turnaround by a field, and the dog looked at me, and as I was backing the truck out to turn, the dog was swinging his tail like he was sayin', *Yes, do it.*

I don't want to meet Rex's brother. I really don't even have anything to say to Rex.

I figured I'd just take this piece'a junk back by Letourneau's and see what they got for this year's Fords for parts and then back to the

Settlement to work on this clutch-ball situation. Tear it all down. Stay out of everybody's way. Maybe Cory will help, if I can find him. He's one'a them that circulates.

But as I was going back by the tar driveway, my hands turned the wheel and up we went, and there I was, braking the truck nice 'n' easy in the dooryard, and Rex and the brother look up at me through the windshield from what they were doing, which was a pump . . . a pond pump . . . a bilge pump.

And Rex stood up and came over to the window, which meant I didn't have to get out and deal with the brother, and the dog was all happy to see Rex, like Rex was what he was looking for, not a big steak. Rex's old jacket was unbuttoned. He was chin up: total soldier. The brother was wicked zipped. You know, zipped to his chin. Neatnik. Well, Rex isn't some slob like me. But he doesn't look like a little boy. The brother, the teacher, he was like some old ladies decided on making him shine. He was shining. His jacket was a funny green and his sweater under that was a pinkish yellow. Even on his fucking day off. A gold sticky star in the middle of his forehead or on the end of his nose would have gone with the rest. He didn't look as Nazi as Mr. Carney but somewhere behind that face was Mr. Carney . . . at least the Mr. Carney gene.

I said, "Sit!" wicked sharp and the dog sat down and Rex said, "Howzit going?" to me. And I shrugged.

And I said, "You busy?" And he said, "It's okay. We need a break." And his eyes were on me funny-like, like he was real glad to see me.

The
End

Please—
Stay tuned.

Author's Note

My old friend Jacquie Giasson Fuller made it possible for Maine Acadian French ("Acadian patois" or as some would say, "North American patois") to be spoken on these pages. She is translator of some, while of some she is their author, their grace. She told me to be sure to say she couldn't have done it without her mother and sister-in-law, Lucienne Merservier Giasson and Lorraine Bissonette Giasson. They all got together and went over the nuts and bolts of this beautiful, mostly oral, language of love, work, and home, no better experts anywhere than they, and I am grateful.

Author's Note #2

In this book, the fictional True Maine Militia shouts out a formal declaration concerning "The People's House" at the closed office door of the governor of Maine. These words are an excerpt from real advice given during the actual Second Maine Militia State House siege in 1996, words of working-class hero Pete Kellman. Yeah, Pete is as real as it gets.

Official and Complete and Final ☺ List of Acknowledgments

The School on Heart's Content Road owes its existence to so many helpful, supportive, and inspiring people that the author feared trying to list them all in this book. Thus, she put all the names in a hat and drew out the following. Those still in the hat will appear in future books. One that didn't get drawn from the hat, who will appear later, is a person who has caused incredible terror in the hearts of most Americans, but has helped Carolyn out so much it brings a lump to her throat. But he's still in the hat. Stay tuned to find out who this frightening person is. Meanwhile, here is a list of the names that were drawn blindly. Huge gratitude goes to:

Bendella Sironen, David White, Bob and Millie and Melinda Monks, Jim Perkins, Bill Kauffman, Robyn Rosser, Rebekka Yonan, David Diamond, Cynthia Riley, Jonah Fertig, Sarah Wilkinson, Ceiba Crow, Dan C., Hillary Lister, Victor Lister, Sara DeRoche, all Jeders of Greene, Maine; Dr. Adele, Dr. Mark, Dr. Maggie, and Dr. Andy (our four family doctors); Yelena and Todd and Stasik, Missy Pinney, Beth

Pinette, Mack Page, Howard Greene, Dennis Twomey, Laura Childs, Pal Tripp, Cecily Diamond, Carol Dove, Michael Vernon, Julian Holmes, Audrey Marra, Peter Holmes (in heaven), Elliott Favier, DDS (in heaven), Cullen, Sarah and Kats, Frank Collins (in heaven), Jerry Webber, Carole Taylor, David Haag, Christina, Mark Hanley, all my family on all sides (Maine, Rhode Island, North Carolina, and heaven), Nick Kingsbury, Morgan MacDuff, Eunice Buck Sargent, Hal and Mark Miller, W. D. Kubiak, Rita Kubiak, Kathy Kubiak, Michael Ruppert, John Sieswerda, Jo Eldridge Morrissey, Brie, Maureen DeKaser, Jenny Pap Hughs Yoxen, Rob Waite, the MacDowell Colony, Elisabeth Schmitz (world's best editor on planet Earth), Sheila Smith, Gwen North Reiss, Patrick Quinlan, Joy Scott, Jonathan Beever (wise man), Tom Whitney, Alison Whitney, Robert Kolker, Sub Steve Kelley, Thomas Naylor, Lt. Col. Robert Bowman, Richard Grossman, Janet Baker, Miss Cathy, Bonnie Jo Campbell, Katie, Nick and Willa, Barbara West, Bruce Buchanan, Michele Cheung, Angelo Roy, Ray Luc Levasseur, Jamila Levi, Ellen LaVallee, Wayne Burns and the Dragon of the West, Evelyn Butler, "cousins" Kelley and Michael, Don Kerr, Colleen Rowley (FBI), Cyndy and Roland, Sandi Hamlin, Cynthia McKinney, Roger Leisner, Edie Clark, Debbie Dearth, Tom Dearth, Abigail Dearth, Balenda Ganem, Guy Gosselin, Wendy Kindred, Isabelle, Ed Gorham, John Muldoon, Daniel Rameau, Ellen Wilbur, Ruth Stone, Molly's gang, all Nelpers, Don Hall, Jane Kenyon (in heaven), Charlene Barton, George Garrett (in heaven), Ken Rosen, Ellen Weeks (postmistress), Rose Metcalf (assistant postmistress), the Causeys, Steve Diamond, Bill Pagum, Barbara and Jerry Korn, Mary Howell Perkins, Dick Perkins, Christine Kukka, past clerk of the House of Reps Joe Mayo (in heaven), Steven and Marie, the American Academy of Arts and Letters, and, as ever, my forever husband Michael "Beek" Chute of Beektown Road.

The rest remain in the bulging hat till next time. Including the mystery man of terror. Guess who?

Keep Going

Character List

The Prophet

Guillaume (Ghee-yome), Gordon or Gordo or Gordie St. Onge, aka the Prophet. Age thirty-nine until September. He is six-foot-four or -five, depending. In the winter, gets a thick waist and an extra neck, but in summer looks like a marble Greek-god type, only tanned. Work, work, work, work, though not without talk, talk, talk, talk, and preach, preach, preach, preach. Darkish hair. Darkish beard with a parenthesis of gray beginning on the chin. Dark brows and lashes with weird pale greenish eyes like some creepy killer bird. Significant French-Italian nose. Add to that a Tourette's sort of flinch to one side of the face, especially the eye. Drink is a problem for him at times, during spells of getting worked up over life's cruelties and injustices. He's often bothered and stirred, moody and broody, loved and hated. He has been accused of loving everyone in the world equally; that his love is too easy, too diluted.

In an earlier time when Gordon was first married to Claire and only Claire, he got some cousins and friends together to start the Settlement on land his mother gave him, land and an old farmhouse where he had grown up. This wasn't just a commune, but a statewide cooperative in furniture, alternative energies, farm produce, and trade. The Settlement is thought to be a school by some who live out in the world. Citizens of the Settlement see it as home.

The Locke/Gammon Family

Michael (Mickey) Gammon. Fifteen years old. Not a big guy, a bit scrawny and shrimpy, with a blond and brownish ponytail so thin and insignificant it twists to one side and up. He does not bathe or change routinely. He stays too busy going and coming back, walking for miles, smoking. His eyes are gray. He has a cold aspect. Not a talker. Much of the time, his jeans and T-shirts are rags.

Donald (Donnie) Locke. In his thirties. Mickey's half brother. Also gray-eyed and not much of a yakker either. A more solid build than Mickey. Married. Father of kids. His hair is a lighter blond than Mickey's, almost white. His mustache is weak in color, pale, pale, pale but quite wonderfully walrussy. Much of the time, he is dressed for "the Chain," his job at a chain store.

Erika Locke. She's in her twenties. She's Donnie's second wife, Mickey's sister-in-law. She's plump. Not stout, not fat, but soft-looking. Round face. Plain hair, cut medium short, medium brown. Soft-spoken. A very ordinary young woman whom you would barely notice in a crowd. Wears T-shirts with pictures and words. Or plain T-shirts or plain tops, shorts or jeans. Mickey enjoys watching her in her T-shirt with the face of a Persian cat.

Britta. In her fifties. Mother to Mickey, Donnie, and Celia. She has had her real teeth pulled. Her false teeth have a noticeable false look. Gray eyes; nondescript brownish hair with some gray. She is a short person, pudgy in some places. Probably her forearms and hands are slim, her ankles too. She is so shy she does not meet your eyes.

Children of the Locke/Gammon household. Britta's youngest is Celia. Isabel is Erika's brother's child. Jola is from down the road. Travis is the baby of another Chain worker. Erika and Donnie's child is Jesse, age two. Jesse is *very* ill. Donnie's girls by another marriage are Audrey and Tegan, plus Elizabeth, his oldest—very active girls.

The York Family

Richard (Rex) York. Captain of the Border Mountain Militia. His age is about fifty. Keeps his thinning hair trimmed and tidy. Wears military boots, usually with pant legs over. His pale eyes have a way of gauging you totally. He is not shy but seems unable to verbalize information unimportant to meetings and maneuvers of the citizens' militia movement of America or the work he does as an electrician. He has a dark mustache, more Mexican than walrus. He doesn't eat desserts. He has an exceedingly fit appearance, possibly due to all the push-ups, deep-knee bends, and sit-ups he has done every day since Vietnam.

Ruth York. Rex's mother, older than he by fifteen years. Her husband (Rex's father), John York, is dead. She now has a boyfriend. She has longish black hair, heart-shaped face, good figure. Wears turquoise "Indian" jewelry and T-shirts with wolves and eagles or western landscapes printed on them. Also oversized chamois shirts. Jeans. And moccasins. She is quiet. Bakes desserts for the American Legion, which she is involved in. And desserts for home. Rex doesn't eat them but his militia does.

Glory York. Almost twenty. Rex's only child. Her mother lives in Massachusetts, divorced from Rex and remarried. Glory is quite freckled, has long thick wow-type hair, dark auburn. She is beautiful in every way. But she flaunts it and has a drinking problem and causes mess and havoc wherever she goes. She is not evil, just young and foolish.

The Lancaster Family

William (Willie) Lancaster. A wild unpredictable thirty-nine-year-old. In some ways he is predictable. Meanwhile, he is a member of Rex York's militia. Willie is gray-eyed and somewhat bucktoothed. Hair, brown. A brown beard, sort of pointed. And an insincere mustache. He's medium height. Has the athletic qualities of a squirrel. His work involves climbing trees with ropes and cleats. He wears the single dog tag of his brother's dead body returned from "the conflict."

Judy Lancaster. Willie's unflappable wife.

Danny Lancaster. Willie and Judy's son.

Ramone Lancaster. A teen daughter. There are three daughters, one unnamed in this novel.

Delores (Dee Dee) Lancaster St. Onge. One of those three daughters of Willie and Judy Lancaster. She is age nineteen but looks eleven. A small, smiley person. She spends a lot of time at the St. Onge Settlement. Her cheery manner has no small effect on the atmosphere of Settlement life. Brown hair, which has natural spurts and cat licks. She is *very* pregnant.

Louis St. Onge (Dee Dee's young husband). Also about age nineteen; Louis (pronounced Lou-EE, as they do up in the St. John Valley of Aroostook, whence he has come) is a cousin to Guillaume (pronounced hard G, Ghee-yome) "Gordon" (nickname) St. Onge. Louis had lived at the Settlement awhile before he married Dee Dee. Now they live in the dooryard of the Lancasters' mobile home complex. The Lou-EE–Dee Dee residence is a weird five stories (each story only sixteen by sixteen feet), painted pink. Lou-EE is built like a tapeworm: no shoulders, just arms, legs, long neck, little head. On top, a big brown mountain hat made of felt. Long black beard protects his significant Adam's apple from view, though the beard is thin, just a scraggly, smoky swirl of a thing. While his father-in-law, Willie, is loud and full-throttle, Lou-EE is like a quaint stage prop but with wonderful eyes, the irises green and golden brown, ringed in black-brown.

Cannonball. A Scottish terrier, huge teeth, broad chest, short legs. She is black, though some Scotties are brindle. She is round and solid, like— yes, a cannonball, cast iron. She likes food and Lou-EE. Willie rescued her from a life tied to a doghouse. Yes, Willie stole her. But she loves Lou-EE. She is not fond of kids. *Hates* other dogs.

Agents

Names sometimes mentioned: sometimes alias, sometimes real. Some of these are Special Agents (S.A.s), others operatives. Agents appear in many scenes, scheming and plotting for "America." There are times when the Settlement is crawling with them.

Jane Meserve (Secret Agent), age six. Yes, only age six but very tall for her age, hushy velvety voice, tells us (very curious people that we are) much about what she observes. Also, she tells her mother (her "Mum") stuff. And unfortunately, she tells stuff to the tape recorder of Settlement neighbors Bernice and son, David. Our Jane is a gorgeous child with a head of dark ringlets, which she generally wears in a queenly, countessy way, high on top with a glamorous spangled squeegee or a flowery one. Jane is a fan of MTV, fast food, and great clothes. Some of these pleasures may have been developed through her mother, Lisa, but Granpa Pete blames it on Great Aunt Bette, long dead, a strong-willed lady who must have seen many personal demands fulfilled. Jane always walks in a graceful royal fashion, unless she's having a tantrum.

Her father, Damon Gorely, is handsome, she is told by her Mum, and talented in rap. He is an African mix person; Lisa—Mum—is a European-mix person. Yes, like most Americans, the Heinz "57 Varieties" types.

Secret Agent Jane's spying career begins after a Settlement person gives her a pair of sunglasses that have pink heart-shaped lenses. Frames are white plastic. Jane's mother, Lisa, says those glasses will give Jane special viewing powers. She suggests that they are real secret agent glasses and that Jane can report to her all she sees. Lisa is in jail, in deep trouble.

Jane's Family

Lisa Meserve. Dental assistant before her arrest. Hair a textured blonde from a product called Light 'n' Streak. Less strong-willed than Jane. Before jail, wore lipstick. Noticeable blue eyes.

Cherish. Like Cannonball, Cherish is a Scottish terrier. Though this is not a common breed, there are, yes, two in this story, completely unrelated. Not *everybody* in America has a golden retriever. Cherish dies when cops leave her in a hot car.

Peter Meserve, known as Pete or Granpa Pete. Owns a gas station. Mild-mannered. Is Lisa Meserve's father, Jane Meserve's grandfather, and an old friend of Gordon St. Onge's. Probably Pete is of average height, balding a bit, graying a bit. Clean shave. Jowls. A bit of a waist. Wears work Dickies or jeans, something like that. No jewelry. Maybe a tattoo, Popeye or a pretty cowgirl. Maybe a tattoo that has gotten blurry.

Some of the St. Onge Wives

Claire St. Onge. About age fifty. Once, she and Gordon were legally married, but then divorced. Now she's back, a wife by Settlement law. Claire is a short woman, short and fat. Graceful and seemingly light on her toes. Both of her parents are Passamaquoddy. She grew up in Princeton, upstate. Many cousins, some who visit from the reservation, some who live at the Settlement. Claire's long black hair, beginning to gray, is often worn up in a bun for that teacherly effect when she has classes at USM (the University of Southern Maine), she being an adjunct history teacher. But often she wears it down and it is comely. While in the Settlement gardens, she wears jeans and long shirts, but much of the time she wears homemade skirts with those frequent displays of embroidery many Settlement women show off in. One of Claire's most striking features are her old-timey spectacles: turn-of-the-century, round steel frames. These give her a severe and grim sepia, quite managerial, aspect.

Bonnie Lucretia (Bonnie Loo) St. Onge. Her legal last name is Sanborn as she was once married to a young man by that name. He died in a tractor-trailer wreck. Bonnie Loo's maiden name is Bean. She is twenty-six. A tall, rugged person, she wears her dark hair streaked orangey blonde from the bottle. She has a child, Gabe, from the trucker husband who died. Two additional youngsters by her present husband (wed by Settlement law), Gordon St. Onge. She wears regular glasses at times, rather bulky ones, but her contacts are her favorites. Her eyes are golden green-brown. Movie-star eyebrows curved exquisitely, one of her best features, but she is raw to look at, sometimes, and snarly of manner. But also curious and smart and witty. Most people at the Settlement think of her as the head cook.

Penny St. Onge. Gordon's first wife to come to him through Settlement law. She is a tall honey-haired woman, late thirties. She is the mother of the oldest St. Onge child, a girl, fifteen-year-old Whitney (Whitney is Penny's legal *last* name by outside law). Penny is a pleasant, easygoing person who enjoys Settlement life. She loves books and quiet evenings alone, but also she's there for the social stuff. She has a lot of overly full daytimes. She enjoys long walks in the fields, often with Gordon. Many people swear that Penny is so classically lovely she is prettier than her daughter who, though a handsome girl, has inherited too many goofy expressions from her father.

Stephanie (Steph) St. Onge. Another of Gordon's wives who joined with him and Settlement life early on. In her early forties, she is a rosy-cheeked brown-haired quiet type. Her daughter, Margo, fathered by Gordon, looks "just like her" and has her mother's wallflower ways.

Gail St. Onge. About age forty-five, mother of Michelle. Gail is another earlier wife of Gordon's and Michelle is fourteen, only a bit younger than Penny's Whitney. The two half-sisters look a lot alike, though Michelle has brown hair, Whitney is more blonde. Both have the somewhat Nordic look of their father (even though none of them are Nordic). Meanwhile Gail, an ex-biker and recovering alcoholic, a semi-recovered smoker, still has a biker style of dress, and her collarbone and entire neck has a ring of roses tattooed there forever. Her voice is husky. Eyes dark and close together. Nose a big puggy. Hard lines in the skin from hard living. Quiet. Reserved. Hair is straight, dark, shoulder-length, and sometimes neglected, sometimes silky and fresh.

Lee Lynn St. Onge. Witchy. Looks witchy. Has witchy ways. Mid-thirties, has a year-old tyke named Hazel, fathered by Gordon. Lee Lynn is busy collecting healing herbs, makes salves and tonics, herbal teas. Very affectionate with everyone. She has wild hair, early gray. She is always braless and wears long flowing dresses, clanking bells (at the throat, for instance), and, around one ankle, a rusty leg iron (looks like the real thing) like a slave. Her high thin voice is cutting to some ears, and her roaring enthusiasm over everything goes against the grain of some of the more curmudgeonly personalities.

Glennice St. Onge. A Christian woman. Late forties or fifty. A wife of Gordon's. She was married before, however, to a man who left her with an envelope of money (his week's pay), their kids, and their home, taking only his beagle puppy and gun. Glennice grew up around tractors and trucks and farming. She's very good with vegetables and machines. She loves the Settlement life and is a wonderful teacher to all the Settlement youngsters. Glennice is a churchgoer and believes in a big biblical God. But she also sees Gordon as a supernatural godlike being, which is a bit of a joke for other Settlement people, who see Gordon as full of the weakness of mortality. Glennice has features too small for her large face. Big glasses. Hair frizzily permed.

Brianna (Bree) Vandermast St. Onge. Gordon's youngest wife. Ever. She is only fifteen. Her hair is thick, ripply orange; orange like a crayon. Honey-color eyes. She has always, and still does, work in the woods with her brothers and father on their logging crew. She is a strong, fit girl, sort of tomboyish. She has zealous revolutionary intentions. Does lyrical writing in bold calligraphy and stunning drawings and paintings. Studies history and current events (not commercial media propaganda) all the time. Has a girlish giggle and romantic hungers. She was born with a deformed face, her honey eyes too far apart, the bridge of her nose stretched wide. She is the founder of the True Maine Militia.

Vancy St. Onge. Also quite young. Pregnant. Not considered pretty, but she is a skilled midwife and natural with elderly and the sick and therefore she is a precious jewel to Settlement life and to Gordon St. Onge. She has a rather square boxy face, square boxy body (even before pregnant). Her hair is flat and rumply brown, never fussed over. She tends to wear big white blouses (even before pregnant). Her eyes are sort of lashless, bottom lip erect, jawline primitive. And yet, yes, absolutely precious.

Leona. One of Claire's cousins, also from the reservation. Leona was one of Gordon's first Settlement wives. Leona has many kids by Gordon, including his oldest son, Cory, who is younger than Whitney by only a few weeks. So Cory is also age fifteen. Katy and Karma are two of the youngest of Leona's kids. Andrea is a bit older. Many in-betweens. Leona has a great tail of black, black hair.

Natasha (Natty) St. Onge. One of Gordon's youngest wives. Age eighteen (almost). She is sharp-featured, blonde. Until arriving at the Settlement, she was a prostitute in Boston, a runaway girl from Ohio. She loves working in the orchards and leatherworking, cobbling, and sugaring. She's a storyteller, always draws a circle around her of listening ears. Has a new baby who has a nice head of dark hair but no thumbs.

Other Relatives of Gordon St. Onge, but Living Elsewhere

Marian DePaolo St. Onge. Actually, her name isn't Marian but Mary Grace but she is into name-changing for status purposes. Her husband (deceased), Guillaume, she called Gary. Guillaume the son is Gordon. She is tall (taller than her husband had been). She has light eyes. Her dark hair has a lot of attractive gray. Her glasses are of an attractive style. She has wonderful posture. Gordon is her only child. Her brothers and uncles are the DePaolo Bros. Construction. They do huge projects around New England such as schools, banks, malls, big box stores, office complexes. They always have a family member or buddy in the state senate.

The Fourth Estate

Ivy Morelli. A native Mainer, Ivy is a reporter and columnist for the *Record Sun,* the big daily. She is twenty-four, petite, with a big raspy *hawhaw* of a laugh. Her eyes are blue in black lashes. Her facial expressions at times would serve her well as a murderess or sorceress in an Elizabethan play (when evil truly reigned and the commons were being emptied). Her hair is bowl style, very black, tinted violet. Wacky wardrobe. Wacky earrings. Drives fast. Is rude to fellow motorists.

Brian Fitch. Ivy's editor. Ordinary-looking guy about forty, editorly pants and shirt and shoes. Twinkling gray eyes. Editorly hair trim.

Other Settlement People

Ray and Suzelle (Gordon's cousin) Pinette. From Aroostook County.

Eddie and Lorraine Martin. Their kids include twenty-year-old Butch, Evan (younger), and Kirk (even younger).